The Land: Swarm

By

Aleron Kong, M.D.

www.LitRPG.com

Books by Aleron Kong

CHAOS SEEDS SERIES

The Land: Founding

The Land: Forging

The Land: Alliances

The Land: Catacombs

The Land: Swarm

The Land: Raiders

The Land: Predators

The Land: Swarm

Chaos Seeds Book 5

Aleron Kong, M.D.

The Land: Swarm
A work of Tamori Publications

This book is dedicated to the people whom have supported me on this year long odyssey. This is only the beginning. Thank you Carrie Ford for always being in my corner. Thank you to my beta readers, Peter Morena, Steve "the sieve" Fleischaker, Ryan Nowell and Brett Davis. Thank you to my gamma readers, Jay Taylor, Dreen Rea, Daniel Le Bailly and Brian Mann. Thank you again to Jay Taylor for helping to grow the community as the moderator for the LitRPG group! Exciting things are on the horizon!

CONTENTS

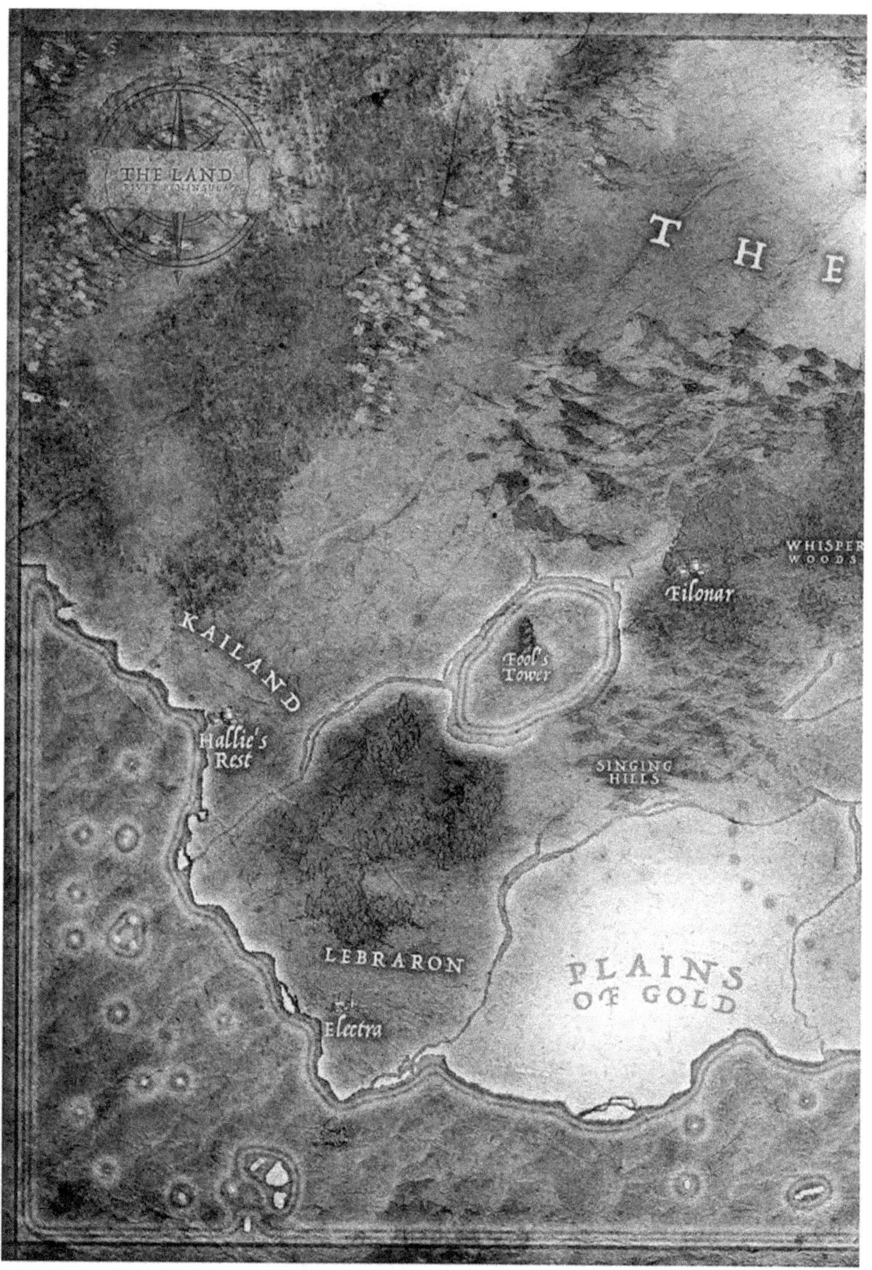
THE LAND
T H E
WHISPER WOODS
Filonar
KAILAND
Fool's Tower
Hallie's Rest
SINGING HILLS
LEBRARON
PLAINS OF GOLD
Electra

WILDS
RIONE
Crucible
Avergoth Swamp
SERRATED MOUNTAINS
FIRETIP MOUNTAINS
Mist Village
YVES
Hearth Tree
Leaf's Crossing
FOREST OF NADRIA
Law
Hungry Reef
Sparrow
Barter Town
THE TWINS

FORWARD

It has been amazing year! We have laughed, we have cried, we have finally worked up the courage to say that we are "in love" with LitRPG! I just wanted to take a second and thank all of you continuing on this journey with me, Richter and Sion. There are many adventures to come. Now, without further adieu!

~ Aleron

Law, the Capital of Yves

A solitary figure stood in the burnt husk of a building. Night was falling. A trio of sailors passed by, unaware of the shadowed figure that stood not more than twenty feet away. The three seafaring men were gamblers who had already lost their coin, having paid more attention to the intentionally distracting prostitutes than their cards. Now, the friends were finding consolation in a bottle. They bemoaned their poor fortune, unaware that the points each of them had invested in Luck kept them alive that night. If they had seen the man in the black cloak, standing silently in the ruin of the warehouse, their next and last sight would have been a visage that had never known pity.

The last rays of sunlight faded away, and the man moved for the first time in an hour. It was time. Guttural words of power spilled from his lips, and unseen black energy surrounded his hands. Five seconds passed while he finished his spell. After the incantation was done, the darkest part of the ruined building began to stir, and a creature of Dark magic became self-aware for the first time, a darkling. This was no summoned creature but was instead a monster born and bred from the terror of murdered men. This fledgling creature may never have fully awoken if left to its own destiny, but the will of the magician could not be denied. It rose from the darkness.

The mage let it feed on the ambient anger and fear that still permeated the charred timbers, but only for a moment. Then he beckoned it with a will stronger than steel. Hating its master and itself, the creature obeyed the command and slinked across the room. Once in front of the man, it bent its head in angry subservience. The darkling began to speak.

For an hour the figure listened to the creature's story. He learned of the slaves that had been kept in the warehouse, and about their rough treatment at the hands of the thieves who held them captive. He listened to the monster's account of a fierce battle that had claimed many lives. The man heard the fear in its voice as it described how the building had caught fire and how it had narrowly escaped destruction by hiding in the dark under a loose flagstone. He heard many things, but only one thing really interested the mage, and that was the person who started the fire.

It took many questions for the simple creature to understand what was needed, but then it formed its ephemeral body into the shape of the arsonist's face. The figure leaned forward and saw the visage of his quarry for the first time. With a wave of his hand, the powerful Dark Paladin destroyed the darkling. The pitiful creature cried out as its young existence was extinguished, but the man barely noticed. All that mattered was that he was one step closer to his prey. The captain of the plague squad left the charred shell of the warehouse and slowly spoke the name of his quarry aloud, as if tasting it.

"Ric-ter."

CHAPTER 1 -- DAY 110 -- KERULT 29, 15368 EBG

Richter kept running through the forest, rage building in his breast as he followed the distinctive trail. Some of the slower members of his party began to fall behind, sweat pouring from their faces. He forced himself up a hill and pushed through a stand of trees, seeing the meadow that extended below on the other side. There, only a hundred yards away, he caught sight of a distinctive, three-pointed crown. The rock giant looked up, its mouth smeared with blood, the body of a slain bear at its feet. When it saw him, it roared both in rage and recognition. Alma, hovering above, screamed back, and the adder raised its body ten feet in the air and hissed. Richter drew his elementum short sword and roared back, "Missed you too, motherfucker! You and I have UNFINISHED BUSINESS!"

Richter used *Analyze* and in an instant knew much more about the monster.

Name: Rock Giant	**Level:** 15	**Disposition:** Hatred
STATS		
Health: 1610	**Mana:** 80	**Stamina:** 2190
ATTRIBUTES		
Strength: 93	**Agility:** 24	**Dexterity:** 31
Constitution: 161	**Endurance:** 219	**Intelligence:** 8
Wisdom: 7	**Charisma:** 4	**Luck:** 9
DESCRIPTION		
There are many different types of giants. Rock giants are solitary monsters, unlike other giants which can have just as complex a		

social structure as average sized humanoids. What rock giants lack in social graces, they more than make up for in ferocity, malevolence, and durability. Their skin acts as a formidable exoskeleton, blocking most damage.

The fucking thing had gotten stronger! Richter ground his teeth in consternation. The giant's heavy tread shook the earth as it ate the distance between them. Richter took the time to send out two thoughts,

Alma, Psi Blast!* *Adder, circle around it!

Then it was in front of him. The giant roared and swung a barrel-sized fist at Richter. The chaos seed spun to the right. One hand swung out to the side, gripping the hilt of his short sword and the other began to contort into a particular configuration. As he finished the spin, his hand shot out, and he shouted, "*Tardi!*"

Even as a blue glow enveloped the giant, slowing its attack and movement speed by 10%, Richter's green short sword raked across the monster's fist. The elementum blade scored cleanly in a line just below the knuckles, and a small spray of black blood covered the ground. In the past, Richter had barely been able to draw a single drop of blood from the twenty-foot tall beast. That had only been because of the magic of his shadow dagger, which had allowed him to ignore a portion of the giant's armor. Not so this time.

The elementum blade gained +10% damage vs Earth creatures, increasing the maximum damage of each strike to 36-41. Richter didn't know exactly what the armor rating of the giant was, but seeing that he could damage it, he didn't fucking care. A bloodthirsty smile broke across his face. The monster reared back with a roar. Just like last time, it seemed shocked that Richter had actually managed to injure it. While Richter watched it hold its injured fist, he realized that his ability to hurt it was most likely why its disposition towards him had worsened from 'enmity' to 'hatred'.

Despite the fact that Richter's blade was enough to harm the giant, the wound was still minor. It paused for barely a second before attacking again. The monster reached its other hand forward, ready to grasp Richter and crush the life out of him. He wasn't alone, though. Alma struck from above.

Swooping down from the sky, she let loose her focused *Psi Blast*. The last time she had attacked the giant with concentrated psychic energy, the monster had barely been fazed. This time, however, her *Psi Blast* was level two. The attack could theoretically stun an opponent for seven seconds, and perhaps for as long as ten seconds when the beam was focused. The giant still had high mental resistance, but it couldn't just ignore the powerful emanations from the diminutive dragonling.

Richter looked on in pleased awe as his cat-sized familiar caused the twenty-foot tall behemoth to collapse. The monster's body struck the ground with an earthshaking thud. Richter had already started running towards the beast's head when he heard Sion call out, "What is that thing? Get away from it!"

Ignoring the sprite's most likely sound advice, Richter shouted back, "It's something that you should be shooting!"

Richter jumped onto the giant's chest and raised his sword high. His arm tensed to drive the elementum blade into the monster's face when its expression cleared, and it affixed him with a baleful gaze. Before Richter could complete his attack, a massive grey fist, three feet across, impacted against his left side. The chaos seed went flying. Almost completely dazed, he thought, this happens way too often.

A sprite arrow imbued with blue force struck the giant in the face, knocking its head back down into the ground. Alma added to the assault with a lightning bolt shot from her small body. The electricity broke across the giant's body, though, and it was unclear if it had a noticeable effect. The rock giant put its arms down to its sides and started to push itself up. A well-placed blue arrow struck the inside of its elbow and knocked it down again. Multiple shouts heralded the arrival of the rest of the war party.

Richter hit the ground and rolled to lessen the force of the impact. The blow and subsequent impact took off seventy-eight health, but his anger at the giant was so great that he surged back to his feet. He had landed more than twenty feet away and from what he could see, he was missing all the fun. Caulder was shouting up at the giant, his steel war door held before him. Terrod stood next to him, sword at the ready. The captain had his wooden shield on one arm, for all the good it would do him against such a monstrosity. Sedrin stood just behind them, thrusting his spear at the giant to keep it off balance. Judging from the telltale purple-black flash Richter saw coming from the monster's chest, Beyan had just finished casting his laughing skull spell, and Jean was firing bolts of dark magic from his wand. Krom was approaching the giant from the right, hammer held ready. Sion was powering up an arrow, the blue of his *Imbue Arrow* skill getting brighter, and Ulinde had just released an arrow that spun of its own accord, showing the archer had used the subskill *Drill Shot*. Richter smiled grimly. It was time to rejoin the party!

Richter reanalyzed the giant and saw that despite the multiple attacks, it still had only lost sixty-three health. He realized that the risk of it grabbing and mauling one of his party was too great for him to allow the fight to continue as a melee.

"This isn't working," he shouted to Sion. "Aim for more vulnerable spots!"

His Companion didn't let up on his rate of fire, but he did shout back, "It is a rock monster! It doesn't have any vulnerable spots!"

Richter realized that his friend was right. The giant's natural armor was just too tough. He had to do something about that. It was time to cast a new spell.

With more than just a touch of trepidation he once again prepared to use Deep Magic. Slamming his sword into the ground, he began moving both arms to start the complicated casting of *Weak Aura Lance*. It was a bold choice to dual cast it, but he put his faith in the increased mental fortitude from his *Psi Bond* with Alma. The spell began with both arms slowly windmilling in opposition to one another.

While Richter cast his spell, Caulder stepped forward with his shield held up, drawing the enemy's attention away from his fellow party member. The giant accepted his challenge. The huge monster kicked the guard as hard as he could. The sergeant caught the blow on his shield. It deflected a large amount of the damage, but couldn't stop the pure kinetic force that had been created by the giant's blow. The heavy metal slab dented and Caulder's shoulder dislocated. The man might have flown back, but the heavy weight of the war door kept him grounded. Instead, Caulder collapsed backward, the shield falling over him like a blanket.

The giant raised its other foot to stomp down on the guard, but Terrod saved his fellow guardsman. He ran forward and placed his body between the giant and Caulder, his longsword thrust upward. The cobalt blade sank between the toes of the giant's foot. The dusky grey sword lacked the power of Richter's elementum short sword but was still able to penetrate the giant's rocky skin. The blade buried into the sensitive webbing of the monster's foot. Still unaccustomed to pain, it reared back, bellowing. The dazed sergeant was spared, and Terrod breathed a sigh of relief that he hadn't been squashed into jelly.

While the monster was off balance, Krom ran up and swung his ebony hammer into the giant's ankle. The large, black sledge impacted the rock monster's grey skin with a heavy *crunch*. The tough exoskeleton fractured and, once more, the giant toppled to the ground with a resounding thud. The dwarven smith shouted in victory. The power of his Ebony Warhammer of Crippling wasn't just its high damage potential. Until the effect wore off, the giant's movement speed would be reduced by 37%. Krom ran back, out of its reach. It was time for the ranged attackers to have some fun.

Sedrin and Terrod were able to pull the still discombobulated Caulder away from the giant. Beyan cast another laughing skull spell which impacted against the monster's side. The effect of the spell was questionable, but the next attack clearly did some damage. Sion finally released the arrow that he had been imbuing for long seconds. The arrow streaked down from the hill he was standing on and struck the giant in the chest. Already lying down, there was no room for it to be rocked back. The force of Sion's strike acted like a hammer pounding the giant into the anvil of the earth. Its natural armor cracked, and it grabbed its chest in pain. It screamed at the injustice of its own newly discovered mortality. The giant's view of the world, and its own place in it, was being rocked by its having finally come up against opponents it couldn't easily dominate.

The ranged fighters and magi kept up their withering fire, incrementally chipping away at the giant's health points. Air mage Jean supported the group in the background, continually recasting *Weak Haste* when he could. At Sion's shouted order, everyone had spread out to encircle the giant, not giving it a concentrated knot of enemies to attack. Despite its natural armor, the fighters served to distract it until Richter's spell was completed.

As Richter had been casting, waves of black energy tinged with gold had been emanating from his body like heat from the desert. The effect had started on his hands and then spread to his arms. A second ripple of energy began to emanate from the center of his chest. The waves from both locations seemed to feed off of one another, creating a turbulence of Spirit Power directly in front of Richter. Several seconds into the casting, a small kernel of black power appeared in the center of the turbulence. It swiftly grew to the size of an orange, then a softball, and finally a basketball. Gold lightning danced across the surface of the sphere. Richter had continued the ten-second casting, each word becoming more difficult to say until it felt like his mouth was full of sand. He had begun to worry that his choice to dual cast the spell had been a mistake. To make matters worse, his mind had begun to play out scenarios of just how horrific the backlash from a failed Deep Magic spell would be.

Ultimately, though, he persevered. Richter could see his friends risking their lives against his dangerous foe. His will firmed, and he pushed through the last seconds of the spell. The ball of gold and black energy rocketed away.

The spherical spell form shot towards the giant, lengthening as it flew. After five yards, it was an oval. After ten yards, it was a cylinder, and after fifteen yards, it was a javelin that flickered between being a light-sucking black and a brilliant, shining gold, millisecond to millisecond. The javelin flew unerringly towards the giant. The accuracy of the spell was governed by Richter's twenty-eight points of Agility, by no means a paltry number. Taking into account the size of the giant, its slowed combat speed, lower Agility, and the scant distance between Richter and his target, the monster had no hope to evade. The flickering javelin struck the rock giant directly in the chest, and the results were spectacular.

As soon as the spell impacted against the monster, the javelin disappeared and the rock giant's skin fractured. Cracks raced through its skin, making pieces no larger than Richter's palm. The pieces began to peel off, like ash being blown away in the wind. Each piece was millimeter thin and broke apart into nothing once free of the giant. The entire process took only seconds, and when it was complete, the rock giant looked exactly the same as before. All fighting ceased as everyone present, including the monster, waited to see if anything else would happen.

There wasn't any outward change, but Richter accessed his combat log and what he saw made him smile.

***Richter** has struck the **Rock Giant** with dual cast **Weak Aura Lance**. All spell-type resistances decreased by 11.8%. Any resistance dropping below 0% will cause a resultant susceptibility to that spell type.*

"It's weaker to magic now!" Richter shouted. "Take it apart!"

Richter wasn't sure if the giant could actually understand him but it hated him with a molten anger. Ignoring everyone else, it started to lumber towards him, if you could call the sprint of a twenty foot tall, raging monster a lumber. Bravely and perhaps foolishly, Richter pulled his short sword out of the ground and prepared to meet it. He shouted his defiance, "Come on, pretty girl! I've got something for you!"

He sent out a mental call and rushed forward. Richter had never felt a battle high like this before. There was no doubt in his heart or mind that he was going to crush his enemy. A cackle of wild abandon escaped his lips as he ran towards his foe. His motions were noticeably faster than the giant's, but its large size still let it cover ground fairly quickly. Sion, Beyan, Jean and Ulinde shot the giant in the back, staggering it somewhat, but it kept running. Terrod and Sedrin immediately began to give chase, but they were too far away, having pulled Caulder to a safe distance. Krom raised his hammer to attack the giant as it ran by but was knocked down by a backhand from the monster. The dwarf hit the ground in a heap and didn't move. Richter sent a quick order to Alma to heal the smith.

The two foes sprinted towards each other, and for a moment, nothing else existed except for their shared hatred. When the giant was only ten yards away, the grey humanoid stumbled suddenly and fell onto its face. In its blind rage and need to harm Richter, the giant had failed to notice the grass-green body of the shale adder shoot forward between its ankles. The twenty-foot snake interwove between the giant's legs and brought it down!

Richter grinned, and his eyes widened manically. He stood before his face-planted foe and raised his short sword high into the air before plunging it down into the back of the giant's head. A foot of clear green metal sunk into his enemy's skull. It screamed in agony, more than half of its total health gone in an instant. Richter hadn't been sure of its physiology, and didn't know if the blow would kill it outright, but he was glad it was still alive. He reached into his bag and whispered with a smile, "Like a spider monkey."

He pulled out the Quicksilver Collar of Submission and swung it around the screaming giant's neck. "You're mine!" Richter shouted in triumph. He reached out with his other hand to grab the free end of the collar. With a mighty pull, he brought the two ends together… or at least he tried to. The damn thing wouldn't fit!

He pulled two more times in desperation, but he just couldn't get the two ends to meet. After the third attempt, it vaguely entered his consciousness that the giant's latest scream of pain had sounded more like a roar of rage. In the next instant, a grotesque and powerful hand reached back and partially encircled the chaos seed's chest.

The giant picked Richter up off of its back and swung him forward, suplexing the chaos seed into the ground, face first. Only luck kept his neck from being snapped. Despite that, he lost consciousness immediately. The next thing he knew, he could hear loud shouts and the sounds of battle. Richter knew he needed to get up, but he couldn't seem to open his eyes. All he could see was his interface blinking furiously with waiting information. One icon was flashing red. With a thudding of his heart, he realized it was the icon that signified Alma. She only had twenty-four health points left!

Richter struggled to open his eyes. When he managed it, the sunlight made his already agonizing headache flare into the worst migraine of his life. Through pure strength of will, he forced himself to ignore the pain and focus on his minimap to find Alma's location. She was only ten feet away. Stumbling forward, he immediately fell prey to a bout of extreme vertigo and collapsed back to the ground. Vomit spilled out of his mouth and over his chest. Richter forced himself back up, crawling as much as stumbling towards his familiar.

He looked at her blearily. It was difficult to focus, but what he saw made his heart clench. His familiar's beautiful body leaked red blood from multiple locations. A large swath of her scales were also missing. One wing was mangled, and her left leg and arm were jutting out in unnatural directions. She raised her head weakly at Richter's approach. All she could communicate psychically though was pain.

Casting a spell wasn't an option. He could barely see straight. Thankfully, there was another option. He stuck his hand in his bag and accessed his inventory. For the first time, it took several attempts to make the 20x20 grid appear. He withdrew several health potions. The first went to Alma.

Richter poured the red potion down her throat, not stopping even as she coughed and sputtered. Each small convulsion spread pain through his familiar's body and, through their shared Psi Bond, Richter experienced his share of it as well. He almost swooned, but he kept going, knowing that if he didn't increase her HPs immediately, he might lose the dragonling. *That* was not an option!

Once she had ingested the health potion, her health immediately began to rise. Satisfied, Richter poured three vials down his throat at once. Taking the potions at the same time wouldn't increase his rate of health regeneration, but it would increase the total amount of health restored. Then he fed another potion to Alma. This time, the dragonling took it eagerly.

Richter sank down on his butt, exhausted even by the faint exertion of feeding Alma. As he sat there, the chaos seed heard cries of pain and the crunch of metal on rock. He knew that this should matter, but his head wound prevented him from grasping exactly why. The magic of the potions continued to do its work, though, and after a few minutes, he could start to think coherently again. Richter still felt extremely confused. Being able to concentrate enough to cast spells was out of the question, but he could at least see what was going on. For the second time in minutes, his heart dropped.

The giant had laid waste to his war party. It stood tall with Richter's short sword still sticking out of its head, the fourth spike for its crown. Krom was back on his feet and was still swinging his hammer, but the dwarf lazed drunkenly, clearly not fully recovered from the giant's backhand. As Richter watched, Krom swung his hammer in a horribly aimed strike and missed the giant completely. His momentum spun him around and he fell to the ground. The dwarf looked around groggily.

Sedrin's spear was sticking out of the giant's side, but the guard was down on the ground. Caulder stood over him with his dented war door held up, but the sergeant bled freely from a scalp wound. The man had a beleaguered expression on his face while he weathered a blow from the giant. The war door rung like a bell.

Terrod was down as well, twenty yards away, moaning and holding his leg. Richter could see a shard of bone extending out of it. Beyan and Jean lay in a crumpled pile nearby. Richter couldn't tell if they were alive or dead. The giant's body looked like a pincushion of arrows, but Ulinde and Sion had been unable to bring it down. They had apparently irritated the monster, though.

While Richter watched, the rock giant untangled the adder from about his legs. Then, using it like a living whip, the monster swung the twenty foot long reptile at the archers. Ulinde dodged out of the way, but Sion was struck by the snake's head. The sprite was knocked off of his feet and flipped end over end before landing in a heap. Richter could barely think straight but he was pretty sure he heard his friend say, "Motherfucker!" in sprite-speak.

Alma screeched and pulled his attention back to her, **I need one more potion, master. Please!**

Richter drunkenly reached into his bag again and produced a red vial. He poured it down Alma's throat while in the background he heard a resounding clang. Again, he knew that he should care more about what was happening, but all he could focus on was Alma. A good deal of the bleeding had stopped, but her scales had not regenerated and her wing remained mangled. Despite that, when she spoke in his mind, the dragonling's voice was cold and determined.

Pick me up and point me at the giant, master. Pick me up now.

Richter did as he was told, his will little better than an automaton's. He picked up the dragonling, who hissed when he jostled her damaged wing. He stood slowly and almost fell but was able to keep his feet. As soon as he was relatively stable, he extended his arms slightly in the direction of the giant. A yellow glow surrounded his familiar's small body, and a second later a bolt of lightning streaked towards the monster. The giant's fist was raised to pound on Caulder's defense again.

Unlike the first time lightning had struck the giant, this time, there was a clear effect. Its body arched and it let out a short roar before falling to the ground. The aura lance had done its job. Alma turned her sinuous neck to look at Richter and thought, **Order the snake to bind its arm, then run over to the body. We have to finish this!**

Richter lumbered forward and sent a mental command as he had been told. The shale adder stirred from where the giant had thrown it against a tree. After a few moments, it started to snake forward. Even though it was injured, it wrapped itself around one of the giant's arms. The animal looped around the giant's limb and then flowed around its neck. Its grip began to tighten. No real damage was done, but it did serve to immobilize that one arm. Richter kept closing the distance between himself and the giant: forty feet, thirty feet, and then twenty. Alma looked at Caulder. The guard looked confused for a moment, but then dropped his shield and shambled towards the giant's head. It had recovered from the stun effect of Alma's lightning bolt and was in the process of reaching its free hand towards the shale adder.

Alma gave one more order, **Throw me towards its head, then grab its arm and keep it from harming me.**

Part of Richter screamed that this was a horrible idea. It would place his familiar in further danger. That voice sounded garbled in his mind, though. The only thing that was clear in his addled consciousness was Alma's voice. He tossed her towards the giant's head and then grabbed the giant's arm. Richter wrapped his legs around the creature's bicep and extended his body along the rocky arm. He encircled the giant's wrist with both arms and arched his back, trying to keep its arm straight. Even with his thirty-three points of Strength, he might not have been up to the task, but the giant had other things to worry about.

His toss of Alma had been enough to get her into position. Her broken wing had almost made her lose consciousness when she landed, but pure spite kept her alive. This thing had dared to harm her master and she would make it pay. She landed just to the left of the giant's head. Wasting no time, she crossed the few remaining inches and latched onto the side of the monster's face. After casting a short spell, she attacked with *Brain Drain.*

She had tried this attack earlier in the battle after Richter had been injured. Not knowing what else she could do to help her helpless master, Alma had latched onto the giant's rocky head. The monster had failed to succumb to the mental attack and had swatted her off like a bothersome fly. Though its blow had been almost absent-minded, the assault had still savaged her small body. While she tried the special attack again, she focused on her anger, rather than her fear, as she drained the giant's life away.

The rock giant strained both arms, trying to reach the dragonling that was killing it. The shale adder tightened its grip further, and Richter screamed unintelligibly as he strained to keep the giant's right arm immobile. Both man and snake were unequal to the task. Despite the efforts of the beast and its master, both of the monster's arms slowly bent towards its face, eager to crush the life from Alma's body.

The giant's left hand was only a foot away from the dragonling when Caulder finally reached his goal. Following Alma's previous mental command, the guard seized the elementum short sword sticking out of the creature's head. A twist and thrust shoved the remaining foot of metal deeper into the giant's brain and stole its remaining health. All strength left the giant's rocky limbs, and both arms fell back. Richter's already damaged head hit the ground, and all he knew was blackness as a rainbow swirl of light encircled his body.

CHAPTER 2 -- DAY 111 -- KUBORN 1, 15368 EBG

Richter woke up naked in his bed chamber. A mist light hovered above his bed, the soft grey light softening the edges of everything in the room. Looking to the side, he could see that Alma lay next to him in the bed. A white bandage encircled her body, binding her wings down and in place, though her arms and legs were free. Her limbs all appeared to have been healed. She slept fitfully next to him, her breathing easy. A peace came over him at seeing her in good health, despite the fact that she apparently needed a bit more healing.

Richter checked his internal clock. It was 2:43 am. He sent out a mental call to Futen. He desperately wanted to know what had happened after he had passed out. His memories after his head had been driven into the ground were fragmented. He was only able to recall bits and pieces of the subsequent battle. Despite his curiosity, Richter didn't see any good coming from running around in the middle of the night looking for answers. Hopefully, the remnant would be able to fill him in. Also, the fact that his war party was still active told him that less than twenty-four hours had passed.

All members of his party appeared as an icon on his minimap, so he felt safe in assuming that the rest of his party had made it back to the village safely. Otherwise, their dot would have disappeared, though he realized he might have just been using game logic. Richter decided to just wait for Futen to receive confirmation. Plus now that he was becoming more awake, he realized that his entire body felt like it had been worked over by a gang of angry carnies. He let out a small groan.

A guard peeked his head into the room, "Lord Richter. You are awake!"

"Yeah, I am," Richter replied softly, wishing the man wouldn't speak so loudly.

"What can I do for you, my lord?" the guard asked at the same level.

Richter winced slightly, "A glass of water would be great, man."

The guard's face turned doubtful, "I am not supposed to you leave you unattended…"

Richter nodded, "And I appreciate that, but I'm awake now. I'm rested and feeling much better. Please grab me the water. I'm parched."

The guard nodded and left. Richter eased his head back down onto his pillow and closed his eyes. In the corner of his vision, there was a flashing notification icon. Not having anything else to do, he mentally clicked on it. The first message set his heart racing.

You have suffered an injury: **Severe Skull Fracture.** *Causes -75% Intelligence, Wisdom, Charisma, and concentration.*

Richter's hand immediately shot up to check his head. Stopping at the last minute from searching his skull vigorously, he started to feel his scalp with light touches. Not feeling any soft spots or deformities, he checked his stats.

Name: Richter	**Level:** 30, 85%	**Age:** 24
Race: Human (Chaos Seed)	**Alignment:** Neutral	**Languages:** Sapient Mortals
Reputation: Lvl 3 "You seem like someone worthy of my attention."		
STATS		
Health: 560	**Mana:** 460	**Stamina:** 350
ATTRIBUTES		
Strength: 25	**Agility:** 28	**Dexterity:** 23
Constitution: 56	**Endurance:** 35	**Intelligence:** 46
Wisdom: 27	**Charisma:** 27	**Luck:** 21
RESISTANCES		

TYPES OF MAGIC		
Air 50%	**Earth** 20%	**Fire** 5%
Life 50%	**Mental** 55%	**Spiritual** 5%
ABILITIES		
Limitless: 100% affinity in any and every skill **Gift of Tongues:** Ability to comprehend almost any sapient languages **Fast Learner:** +30% to speed of skill advancement **Bounty of Life:** +30% growth for the physical manifestation of your Place of Power **Psi Bond:** +20% Mental Resistance Maximum Communication Distance 750 yards		
QUALITIES		
Resolute: +5% Spiritual Resistance, +5% Thought Resistance **Honorable:** +2 Charisma **Implacable:** Awarded *Initiate* rank in Tracking Skill		
MARKS		
Master of the Mist Village	Blood Oath of Vengeance	Forge of Heavens
Dragonkin	Dragon's Cauldron	

He breathed out a sigh of relief when he saw that the debuff had been removed. That sigh turned into a grunt of discomfort because even this small arm movement shot pain through his body. Thank Abrams and Whedon for Sumiko! He couldn't think of any other reason why he wasn't a vegetable. His health potions and healing spells couldn't even heal bone, let alone mend something complicated like a skull fracture. Richter started thinking that he would have to do something nice for the old sprite… like get her a fruit basket… or a gigolo. He started to chuckle to himself, but it made his baseline headache flair. Realizing that he might have just been the recipient of instant karma, he kept going through his prompts. The next one had been auto-minimized as it was from mid-battle. It made him realize that there might be an argument for having some prompts appear in an unobtrusive way while fighting. This one could have saved him a lot of pain.

You are attempting to use an item: ***Quicksilver Collar of Submission,*** *on a creature of the wrong size. This item may only be used on* medium *or* small *creatures. Take it to an Enchanter if you wish for it to be resized.*

Richter grimaced. Well, that explained about the collar not fitting. He had just thought it was too small, but it turned out that certain items were graded for certain beings. From his first lore book, he remembered that humans, elves, and dwarves were considered medium in size. A sprite or goblin would most likely be considered small, though he didn't know what a half-blood like Yoshi would be. He guessed he would put the rock giant in the 'too fucking big' category. In retrospect, Richter realized it had been a dumb risk to stand over a still living behemoth and try to capture it, not once, but three times. As he thought about it, that particular moment felt surreal. He could only remember that it had felt like he was riding a high. In his mind, he had been untouchable, and he could remember believing at a core level that anything he wanted could come true just because he willed it.

Was that the consequence of using Spirit magic, he asked himself. Richter took a long, slow breath. Deep magic was powerful, but it was clearly also dangerous. He resolved to learn more about it and practice it in controlled conditions before relying on it again in battle. Before he got back to going through his prompts, though, he remembered one other thing about using Spirit magic that was even more disturbing. He had loved the way it felt and right now was eager to use it again. Richter didn't feel ready to deal with the implications of that yet, so he went on to the next notification.

Congratulations! You have reached skill level 13 in ***Light Armor****. +26% to defense of all light armor.*

Congratulations! You have reached skill level 2 in ***Beast Bonding****. +2% effectiveness to Tame. +2% attack and defense to bonded creatures.*

Congratulations! You have reached skill level 9 in ***War Leader****. +9% effective distance. +9% attack and defense for all allies.*

You have completed the Quest: **Hunters or Hunted II.**
The dangerous creature your hunters had noted was the same rock giant that you had met previously. The monster had marked you for death for having the audacity to wound it previously. Nonetheless, you and your war party have vanquished it!
+100% experience for your entire war party for vanquishing a mortal enemy of their leader!
Rewards:
37,500 (base 15,000 x 2 x 1.25) experience
Restoration of full hunting grounds for the Mist Village
Village-wide Loyalty +5 (+10 for hunters)
+100 Relationship Points with village hunters

You have trapped the soul of a ***Rock Giant****! Soul level: Luminous.*

Richter paused again and accessed his inventory. Seeing a new, glowing soul stone, he read the description and saw that indeed it contained the soul of the rock giant. Richter smiled and crooked his index finger at the inventory window, waving to the captured creature. "Hey, asshole," he said quietly but with intense satisfaction. The collar may not have worked, but he would take the soul as a consolation prize. More than pleased, he went through the rest of the prompts.

For slaying one ***Rock Giant****, you have been awarded 5 War Points! Total War Points: 271.*

You have been awarded ***10,101*** *experience (base 134,686 x 0.06 x 1.25) from Brain Drain against Level 15 Rock Giant.*

TRING!

You have reached level ***31****! Through hard work you have moved forward along your path. You are awarded the following points to distribute:*

	Per Level	Total
Stat Points	As a Chaos Seed, you gain **6 Stat Points** to distribute to characteristics instead of the usual 4	18
Talent Points	As a Chaos Seed, you receive **15 Talent Points** instead of the usual 10. You receive an additional **5 Talent Points** from your Profession for having a 100% affinity in Enchanting	205
Skill % Points	**+25%** to the skill of your choice	+75%

Crush your enemies, honor your allies, LIVE!

Now that you have progressed more than one level, you must allocate your ***Stat*** *and* ***Skill Percentage*** *points within the next week or they will randomly be assigned for you.*

Your familiar has reached level 28!

Futen had floated into the room while Richter was going through the prompts. With a final smile, Richter dismissed his last notification. Focusing on the remnant, he asked, "How did I get back here?"

"I believe that you were carried back to the village by Smith Krom, my lord."

Richter nodded, "Did all of the members of the war party make it back safely?"

The light at the center of the grey orb pulsed, "There were several injuries, some quite serious. None were fatal, however. Lady Sumiko and her healers fixed the damage."

Richter exhaled a small sigh of relief. His assumption about the war party had been correct. "What about my snake? The shale adder?"

"That is on the floor, Lord Richter," came the monotone reply.

"What?" Richter shouted, sitting up quickly. The movement made his headache flare again, but it didn't stop him from peering over the edge of the bed. Sure enough, after a second he picked out the form of the snake blending in with the grey marble of the floor. It raised its head upon hearing the bed creak and its red tongue flicked out of its mouth before it lay back down again. Richter was seriously creeped out. Every child learned there weren't any monsters under the bed, but *he* had just learned that there *was* a monster under his bed. If he had stepped on the damn thing without knowing it was there, he might have been horribly scarred for years. Not to mention that a shriek of fright would not be in keeping with the badass aesthetic he was trying to cultivate.

Happy that the snake still seemed to be under control, Richter still couldn't resist asking, "And everyone was okay with just leaving this giant predator resting under my bed?"

"When you were brought into the room, one of the villagers actually mentioned that very point, my lord. No one seemed willing to try and lay hands on the snake to stop it from following you, however. I believe it was decided to simply trust in the power you had over the beast."

"Uh huh," Richter said. Not that anyone would have known how long his control would actually last. After what had happened last time, he wasn't even sure if he could risk casting *Tame* again. The Blood magic had seemingly taken away his self-control. He had tirelessly disarmed the assengai queen's traps, not even considering that staying in a monster lair for hours might be a bad idea. He couldn't even say that his decision to charge after the rock giant's trail wasn't influenced by the Blood magic and he had done that hours after he cast the spell. It was true that he probably would have followed the trail either way, but thinking about it now, attacking a twenty-foot tall rock monster head on, after calling it out no less, seemed the height of idiocy.

It was clear that using *Weak Aura Lance* was not completely safe either. Even though the twenty-four hour cooldown hadn't expired yet, he was already itching to use it again. It had felt so… good. Richter shook his head. The Deep Magics were definitely more dangerous than wielding the Basic Elements. It was so frustrating, though. The power of Blood and Spirit magic was incredible. The high level monster lying under his bed, meek as a freshly born puppy, was proof of that. That meant that he would have to cast *Tame* again soon, otherwise the snake would once again become a feral monster. It was also arguable that without *Weak Aura Lance* the war party might not have overcome the rock giant. The sonuvabitch had been tough.

"Gah!" Richter exclaimed, slapping the bed.

Hmmm? What is wrong, master? Alma thought at him sleepily.

Richter immediately felt bad at having awoken his injured familiar. He could see that her health bar was blessedly full, but Sumiko must have had a reason for binding her wings. **It's nothing, my love. Go back to sleep.** he thought to her soothingly.

Rather than following his instruction though, Alma straightened her legs and arms and stood up. She walked over to his face and licked his cheek, **I know that you want to protect me, master, but I am not the simple creature that I was when you summoned me. I am your soul familiar and I am here to help you. Tell me what is wrong.**

Richter was taken aback by her gentle, but firm, tone. He could not argue with what she said. Alma had progressed massively since he had torn a hole in reality to summon her. The gaze she directed towards him was focused and intent. He decided he deserved the rebuke, **You're right, Alma. I'm sorry. I do need to share more with you. What I'm concerned about is how out of control I feel when I use Blood or Spirit magic. Dangerous or not, though, I can't just ignore the power those magics offer. I need to find a way to control myself.**

The dragonling continued to stare at him intently, **I think that I can help with that, master. My race has strong mental defenses. These defenses protect psi dragonlings from dangers without, but also from those within. Our Psi Bond gives you unconscious access to those same protections. With my help, you can begin to consciously use those defenses to control yourself. This will be a journey of discovery for both of us, but I know in my heart that I can help you, master.** The mental tone of her words transmitted feelings of love and support.

Richter smiled at her, **How do we start?**

For the next few hours, Richter and Alma rested in bed and she gently pushed her way through his mind. During their communion, he also began to get flashes of her past life and it was fascinating. She came from a world of dragons. Small and large, intelligent and bestial, dragons of all types were the dominant species of her planet. He wasn't able to get too many details, but what he did see was tantalizing.

The level of understanding between them deepened in the same way that friendship deepened during a night of soulful sharing. She guided him through techniques of mental control that were instinctual to her kind, but instructed him in a way that transcended language. Concepts were offered to him at the speed of thought, and as they swam through each other's memories, they grew to know both each other, and themselves, better. The defensive techniques that Richter learned as they communed were rudimentary, but after hours of training he had earned several prompts.

Know This! The journey to know oneself is a path without an end, but each step brings you closer to your truth. The mental training you have begun has long been honored by mystics and madmen. You have learned a new skill: ***Self Awareness****. +2% mental and emotional control per level.*

Congratulations! You have reached skill levels 2, 3, ..., and 7 in ***Self Awareness****. +14% mental and emotional control.*

They practiced various techniques through the night. Both master and familiar began to enjoy themselves as they launched mental attacks at one another, teaching and learning simultaneously. This continued into the morning and they only stopped when Randolphus came into the room to check on his lord.

"You are awake," the chamberlain said in greeting.

"Nice to see you too, Randy," Richter said with a faint smile.

Randolphus looked down at the adder on the floor and said, "Could we speak in the conference room, my lord? And perhaps your, ahem, pet could stay here?"

Richter nodded and threw back the sheets. He took a set of clothes out of his Bag and while donning them asked, "Do you know where my sword and armor are?"

"Your armor had apparently taken quite a beating, my lord. It is being repaired in the forge. I believe Captain Terrod took your sword there as well."

Richter nodded and finished dressing. They walked out of the room and over to the conference room. The snake started to stir, but Richter mentally ordered it to stay put and it settled back down to the floor. Before leaving, Richter picked Alma up and placed the dragonling in her favorite spot, atop his shoulders.

As they walked, Randolphus asked, "Are you a beast tamer now as well, my lord? It seems that your powers know no bounds."

"Not exactly a tamer," Richter replied. "I do have a skill called Beast Bonding, though."

The chamberlain stopped walking and looked at Richter sharply, "Blood magic?"

Richter paused, interested both in the chamberlain's reaction and his immediate knowledge of the skill. Instead of answering, he asked his own question, "What do you know about it?"

Randolphus's lips twitched in an effort to control his expression. Finally, he said, "I know that such magic is dangerous, my lord. There are countless examples of magician's losing their minds and becoming like beasts themselves. Deep Magic is not to be trifled with."

Richter was initially irritated at being scolded in such a manner, but he controlled himself. It actually seemed quite easy to reign in his emotions. He realized his new skill was already coming to bear. Instead of snapping, he said in a measured voice, "I appreciate your concern, chamberlain. I quite agree with you about the dangers. You must trust me that I am taking steps to deal with this."

Randolphus looked at him for another moment before nodding resignedly. The two men started walking again and didn't speak until they were sitting across from each other at the conference table. The chamberlain stared at his liege and said, "Lord Richter, you were almost killed. Again. I saw you before Lady Sumiko healed you. There was a rock sticking out of the top of your head. When it was removed, I could see that it had left a *dent* in your skull. If anyone other than a Life master had been here, you would have died or been left with permanent brain damage." Randolphus took a deep breath before continuing, "I have the utmost respect for you, my lord. I have the utmost respect for what you have done and sacrificed for your people. I would be remiss however, if I did not say that you are taking too many risks. You do not need to lead every assault, and you do not need to conquer every dungeon. I do what I can to make this village more successful, but you must help me!"

While the man had been talking, Richter could see the stress in his chamberlain. He saw the toll that running the village had taken on his seemingly tireless steward. Randolphus had seen to the daily activities of hundreds of people, of various cultures and various races. Not once had the man complained or wavered. Seeing him lose his cool now though, Richter realized that he had been asking too much.

Richter leaned in and put a hand on Randolphus's shoulder, "I'm sorry. You're right that I need to support you more. You are truly invaluable and I think this village would fall apart without you. I cannot tell you that I will stop taking risks, because I believe the time is soon coming where my strength will be tested. All of our lives may depend on how powerful I will have become when that happens. That means I must sacrifice, gamble and accept the pain that comes from pushing the boundaries of what I am currently capable of. With all that being said though, what can I do to help?"

Silence presided over the table for several moments before Randolphus said, "Well I do have some reports I need to go over with you."

Richter gave a long-suffering sigh, softened by a faint smile at the end and said, "Of course you do. What's the first item on the agenda?"

CHAPTER 3 -- DAY 111 -- KUBORN 1, 15368 EBG

The two men talked for a good hour and a half. Richter also authorized Randolphus to hire two of the workers to serve as dedicated aides. The relief on the chamberlain's face was comical. For a second, Richter felt bad for whomever Randy chose to help out, sure that the man would be a taskmaster, but then he figured it was tough all around.

While they had been speaking, Richter had sent Futen to retrieve Sumiko. The sprite Life master entered the room with her usual flare, "Who said that you could get out of bed? Your brains were hanging half out when you came back! The bones could still be setting together! If you like having a large crack in your skull, I can give you another!" She shook her cane at him threateningly.

Richter raised both hands to placate her, "Thank you, Sumiko. You have saved me again. I truly don't know what I would do without you."

She sniffed at him in disdain, but didn't start haranguing him again. Richter took that as a good sign and continued, "I was told that everyone from the war party is alright. I hope that you can confirm that."

Sumiko rolled her eyes and huffed, "Yes, though many were in almost as bad shape as you were. Those two mages are still resting and being checked over by some of my healers. They both suffered massive internal trauma and will need to be healed in stages. You are lucky you didn't suffer any major brain damage or you would be lying beside them in that pitiful excuse for an infirmary you have me working in. There is no guarantee that even I could repair that type of damage."

Richter felt a chill. Despite his quasi-immortal status, it was both a useful and frightening reminder that there were worse things than death. Living as a vegetable was not his idea of a good time.

Richter thanked her again and also told her that he had picked up on her not-so-subtle hint. Making the healer's hut was a priority.

"What about Alma? Are her wings okay?" This was the other main reason he had wanted to speak with the healer.

Sumiko cast a quick spell and extended her hand towards the dragonling. A nimbus of gold light surrounded both her hand and Alma, and a thin tether of the same light connected them. The healer closed her eyes and lowered her head, concentrating. Soon she opened her eyes and smiled fondly down at the familiar. The spell faded and Sumiko reached out and unbound the bandage. As soon her wings were free, Alma gave a cry of joy and launched into the air, circling above their heads. To Richter's delight, her delicate scales had regenerated as well.

"The vessels and nerves in her wing are small and delicate," Sumiko said, watching the dragonling. "It wasn't anything overly complicated, but as I had never healed a dragonling before, I wanted to make sure that everything was repaired correctly. My diagnostic spell showed that the two wings are working exactly the same." Alma swooped low over the table, twisting in the air. "As you can clearly see," Sumiko said with a small laugh.

Richter thanked her again and stood. He and Randolphus had already finished their work and Richter was starting to feel a bit stir crazy. He felt the need to feel the wind on his face. Telling Randolphus that he needed to check on something, he bid them both goodbye and walked out of the room. Upon crossing the Great Seal, he decided to make a quick stop in the treasury. He gathered several bars of elementum and all of the quicksilver, cobalt, moonstone and high steel he had left there. Each ingot went into his bag. With the bag's weight-reducing properties and his high Strength, Richter barely noticed the increase in load. He left the treasury and walked out into the hallway that led outside. A mental summons to the shale adder was all it took for the monster to slide up alongside him. Alma flew above him, casting shade-filled glances at the large snake. Futen floated along silently just behind his right shoulder. With this kind of posse, Richter realized that all he needed was some theme music. Since there was none to be had, he just imagined the theme song to Green Hornet. Several hundred yards later, the motley band emerged from the tunnel and looked down from the top of the hill that led down to the village.

It was still rather early and the sun had not yet risen. There was a stillness to the village. Faint wisps of smoke rose from one of the longhouse chimneys, but that was the only movement that Richter could see. The feeling was magnified by the barely visible overlay of magical mist. Richter looked out to the boundaries of the village, and the five foot wall that ringed the settlement. Torches were set periodically into the defensive wall. As he took in the view, he was struck by the fact that there was a glaring hole in the defenses of the village. It was just too damn dark out. There was no way that the guards could see more than thirty feet past the wall with only fire light to provide illumination. Maybe they could see a bit further if Quasea and her Dark novices were casting *Darkvision* like they had said they would, but the presence of the torches argued against that. Richter thought about it for a moment, thinking what they really needed were street lights. A smile broke over his face. Actually, maybe they just needed the Mist Village equivalent.

"Futen. If I summon mist lights, can you move them about?"

"I can, Lord Richter," the remnant replied in his deadpan voice.

"That's what I wanted to hear." Richter used his personal mana to summon ten mist lights. The lights were not overly bright, but each light would last a full year before disappearing. It was true that the village mana pool was twice as large as his own, but it only regenerated at about forty mana per hour. His own mana pool replenished much faster. Nearly depleting his magic reserves brought on the typical headache, but he was getting used to it.

"I want you to start making mist lights and posting them around the boundaries of the village," he said. "Each should be twenty feet high and I'm guessing about a hundred feet apart. The point is for the guards to be able to see what is out beyond the wall day and night, so if there are dark spots left when you space the lights out, make the lights lower to the ground or closer together. Make one row that is only ten feet out from the wall, then go out further and make another row. I want to be able to see what is around the village all day long."

"That will require a large amount of mana," the remnant replied. There wasn't any concern in the grey orb's monotone voice, it was just a statement of fact. "Each mist light costs fifty MPs. If I make a large amount of mist lights each day, there will not be any mana left over to summon mist workers or for your own personal use."

Richter nodded, "I already thought of that. Each morning, I want you to use three hundred mana to summon the lights. I'll try and supplement the rest. If the mana pool is full at anytime during the day or night, summon a light so that we aren't wasting potential magic. It will most likely take a long time to do this, but it's important. The mists are only an advantage if we can see and our enemies can't, so night greatly reduces the effectiveness of the enchantment. With the mist lights though, we will be able to see 24/7 and our enemies will still be inhibited."

Futen voiced his assent and floated off to do as ordered. The mist lights trailed behind him. Richter walked down the hill and started moving towards the Forge of Heavens. He was feeling kind of naked without his armor and sword. Also, with the village still asleep, it seemed like the perfect time to practice his smithing.

Richter took a handful of nuts from his bag and munched on them while he walked. The air smelled clean and was heavy with the scent of pine. Dew clung to the grass and the first birds were starting to call out in the forest. The adder glided noiselessly beside him. For fun, Richter started looking for tracks on the ground. The daily crisscrossing of hundreds of people lit up the earth like a Christmas tree. Richter smiled at the evidence of the industriousness of his people.

The forge loomed in front of him and Richter heard a faint clanging. It seemed he was not in fact the only one awake. He ordered the snake to conceal itself and wait outside. It wordlessly communicated that it was hungry. He gave it permission to wander and eat any small rodents it could find. After a second's pause, he also ordered it to never harm any person, domesticated animal or pet it came across within the walls of the village. After thinking for one more second, he amended his order to never do so unless he ordered it.

As Richter walked into the building he saw that the main anvil was unattended, but one of the muscular humans he had seen in the forge before was at a back anvil swinging a hammer. Richter observed for a few minutes before getting closer. The man's sure hammer blows stopped when he saw Richter approach. A quick use of *Analyze* showed the man's name to be Sameen.

"So what are you working on, Sameen?"

The man placed his work back into the furnace and laid his hammer down. "A simple plow blade, Lord Richter. One of the farmers broke hers on a rock."

Richter nodded. He knew the work of a village's forge wasn't only focused around swords and arrows, but also on building and maintaining the mundane tools and implements vital to any medieval society, "But why are you working here before the sun has even risen?"

The man looked slightly abashed, "It is a great honor to be able to work within a Magic Forge, my lord. As long as I perform my other duties well, Smith Krom has given me permission to work at this anvil as long as I do not interfere with the work of the dwarven smiths. So I come early, when no one else is here."

Richter nodded. It sounded like Sameen was paying his dues to earn a place among the smiths. Richter approved. He had always been a big believer in hard work, and besides, he wouldn't interfere with how Krom ran the Forge without a very good reason. Instead, he said something that surprised the human, "Show me how to forge the plow you are making. Explain it step by step, please. I need to better understand the process of smithing."

"I am sure Smith Krom would be a better teacher," Sameen protested.

"I am sure he would agree with you," Richter said wryly. "But you are here and I have asked. Will you refuse me?"

"Of course not, Lord Richter!"

"Then let's get started."

Sameen pulled the red-hot plow blade from the furnace and laid it on the green anvil. He showed Richter the proper way to hold the hammer and how to strike the metal. He also taught Richter the importance of using various hammers at different stages of the work. For beating a lump of metal into a general shape, a large hammer was fine, but smaller tools were needed to sculpt the metal. Most of the work on the plow blade had already been done and soon they plunged it into a barrel of water, eliciting a hiss of steam. Once cooled, they placed it on a nearby table. After that, Sameen walked Richter around the Forge, explaining the purpose of the myriad number of tools, both large and small. The sky was beginning to brighten by the time they finished a full lap of the building.

Richter looked around at the still empty forge and then said with a smile, "Let's make a dagger."

Sameen looked at him in unease, "I am not allowed to make weapons here, my lord."

Richter chuckled thinking at how annoyed Krom was going to be when he showed up, "Meh, I'm sure it will be fine." With that, he went to the back of the building and grabbed a high steel ingot.

Sameen ultimately persuaded Richter to use one of the smaller anvils and also to settle for using only an iron ingot. The chaos seed only agreed because of the look of pure terror on the man's face when he had started walking towards the main anvil that Krom normally used. Handing over the grey iron ingot, Sameen grasped it with a set of tongs and placed it in the cherry red heat of the furnace. After the metal was glowing, the man brought it out of the furnace and placed it on the anvil.

With the first grin Richter had seen on the man, Sameen said, "Just start swinging, my Lord."

Richter grinned back and took his advice.

CHAPTER 4 -- DAY 111 -- KUBORN 1, 15368 EBG

As soon as Richter had started swinging the hammer, eight lights flared in the center of the smaller anvil. Eager to have his shot at learning an enchantment, Richter swung the hammer with vigor. His high Strength made the ingot flatten quickly, but it was only under Sameen's instruction that it began to take shape. After less time than Richter thought would have been necessary, he had made his first blade.

You have made: **Crude Iron Dagger**	**Damage:** 0-3 **Durability:** 7/7 **Item Class:** Common **Quality:** Poor **Weight:** 0.5 kg

Richter held the foot-long piece of metal. It was unbound and unadorned, lacking a cross-guard, and was poorly balanced. Still, he couldn't resist a feeling of pride that he had taken a block of metal and formed it to his will. Sameen suggested that they recast the dagger and try again, but Richter decided to keep this first rough attempt at Smithing. The simple weapon went into his bag. He did agree that they should keep training his skill, though.

Another ingot was obtained and they started the process again. He forged, re-smelted and re-forged six daggers before the other dwarves started to enter the forge. It was almost comical how each one had an emotional struggle written clearly on his face. Not a one of the bastards liked seeing one human working at the anvil, let alone two, but the fact that one of the humans was the Master of this village kept their tongues still behind their frowning beards. Krom was the one exception.

"What in the name of the Banished Ones' pimply left nuts do ye think yer doing?" the dwarf shouted.

Richter paused with his hammer poised above a still glowing length of metal. "Why Krom, I do hope you are not objecting to your lord using his own forge?" he asked sweetly.

"Ay object to ye flailing about on top of that anvil like an epileptic teenage boy on top of his first sweetie! Yer all arms and elbows, just bashing away as hard as ye can. That be no way to treat a lady!"

"And you can tell me how to treat 'a lady' can you?" Richter asked with barely concealed amusement.

Krom scowled for another moment, before a large smile split his salt and pepper beard. "Oh aye!" Then he looked at Sameen and glared, "Do ye na have other work to do?"

The muscular man bobbed his head and said, "Yes, Smith." He moved off into another part of the forge.

"Well you have gotten rid of my teacher," Richter said. "You better be able to take his place. I plan to be a master smith by the end of the day."

"Actually, yer lordship, ay was hoping ye would like to put some of that new enchanting power to good use. Ay can share the enchantments ay already know if ye help me while ay swing me hammer. It will also give us both a chance to learn something new from these damn lights that be dancing in the anvil."

Richter smiled. Using his new Profession was already on his agenda. One thing remained to be done though. He still needed to choose his Specialization. The only thing that held him back was that he didn't know any enchantments yet. If he was going to be helping Krom though, it would seem the time had come.

Before he got to it, he pulled Krom aside. Once they were beyond earshot, there was a quiet moment, then he asked, "Are you okay?"

Krom just stared back for a second before his face relaxed, "It were a tough fight, yer lordship. Ay will na lie and say ay didn't get a knock or two, but at the end of the day, we won. We took that big bastard down and it will na be getting up again." Krom grinned, "Besides, I got to spend a bit o'time with that fine silver-haired sprite lass!"

Richter looked at him uncomprehendingly for a moment before his mouth dropped open in comprehension. "Sumiko?" he asked incredulously.

"Aye," Krom said, his grin widening.

"She's gotta be like a hundred!" he exclaimed.

"Not too old for me to breathe life back into her… as long as ay be breathing in the right place," Krom said with an evil chuckle.

"Gah! I can't hear any more of this," Richter said, putting his hands over his ears. Krom just kept chuckling and walked off. The dwarf said he needed a bit of time to get ready. He ordered one of the other dwarves to stoke the fire in the furnace then walked off. Richter sat on a nearby bench and pulled up his personal interface. He found the icon he was looking for, a sword with a glowing aura that had appeared when he had obtained his Profession.

Richter mentally selected the symbol and once again the multicolored starscape filled his vision. Blue spheres with writing on them floated like planets amidst a nebula. Golden filaments connected all of the spheres. Two of the spheres glowed slightly, backlit against the cosmos. The others were darkened, like lifeless moons. The central sphere had the word "Enchanter" emblazoned on its surface. The second globe was connected to the first by a glowing thread. Across the surface of this second sphere read the words, "Increase Enchantment Strength I."

There was something new in the nebula now. A second red sphere, the same size as the central blue sphere, floated amidst the stars, far to the right of the blue spheres. It had the word "Specialization" carved into its surface. Richter focused on it and suddenly the screen zoomed in so fast that he closed his eyes and dodged back involuntarily. Luckily he didn't actually fall out of his chair. Krom would have teased him mercilessly.

His view had shifted until it looked like he was standing on the red sphere. He had a strange sort of double vision, in that he could see the Forge of Heavens and everyone around him, but he could also see another world. As he looked around, he realized that the prompt had actually seemed to pull him into it this time. He was no longer looking down at the spheres from above, he was now standing on a sphere that had become as large as a planet. A distant part of him realized that he should perhaps be bothered by that fact, but more than anything he was fascinated by what he was seeing. As he focused on his view of the sphere, his perception of the forge faded until it almost disappeared. As the prompt became more real, he was actually able to feel, taste, smell and hear things from this new world.

Richter's feet rested on a desert made of fine red granules the color of rubies. In the distance, dark red storm clouds hovered on the horizon and he could see orange bolts of lightning striking down towards the ground. The sky was a deep pink. The clouds were far into the distance and mountain-sized dunes surrounded him, but he was standing on a relatively flat space. What occupied his immediate attention were the figures standing not more than twenty yards away from him. There were twenty-one figures in all and they were arrayed in a circle around him. Richter could only make out the details of seven of them as the others were shrouded in shadow. What could be casting that shadow was a mystery because there was nothing else around them, but it didn't change the fact that he couldn't make out a single detail of the remaining fourteen. Each figure stood on a short column of black basalt, only two feet off of the ground.

Richter looked at each in turn and was amazed to see that each of the seven figures he could examine had his face. He was about to take a step forward when a prompt filled his vision. A prompt within a prompt, Richter thought to himself with a smile.

Greetings, ***Enchanter****! You have persevered through your Profession for ten personal levels and now have the opportunity to choose your* ***Specialization****. This is not required, but it is the only way to reach the truest heights of power in your Profession. Only one Specialization can be chosen for your Profession and any choice is irrevocable. Choose your Path of Power wisely!*

Richter dismissed the prompt and walked up to a figure on his right. The men that he could see were clustered on one side of the circle. The first one he approached was wearing rings and bracelets that glowed with power. A platinum necklace hung around the man's neck with a swirling black jewel at the end. Richter looked bemusedly at his own face as the man on the pedestal stared off into the distance. Even though he knew the figure couldn't just be a statue, the chaos seed was startled when the man's neck bent and they made eye contact. His surprise deepened when the man spoke with his own voice.

"Hello, Richter."

Not really knowing what to do, Richter responded, "Hello, Richter." His face wrinkled in irritation. This was getting way too meta.

The man on the podium laughed. It was uber-weird hearing his own laugh, but Richter reasoned that this experience was still way better than his trial. Being tortured by Nexus had been whore-reeb-blay, so he just waited for the man to finish. After a final chuckle, the man on the pedestal said, "I know. It's all a bit meta, isn't it?"

Seeing Richter's bemused expression, the man continued, "Well, I feel like this is a bit self-explanatory, but I am who you could become if you choose the path of an Item Specialist. You will be able to make much stronger rings, bracelets and other magical items. My powers are not as straightforward in a fight as a Battle Specialist, but you will be able to affect a wider breadth of enchantments. I, or put another way, you when you become me, could serve your people well to make them strong rings of health or goggles of true sight."

Richter thought about it for a moment then asked the most relevant question, "Are you who I should pick?"

The man on the pedestal cocked his head and looked back at Richter with a, 'Really, dude?' look on his face. It was a particular blend of derision, condemnation and mockery. Seeing it, Richter finally understood why people in his past had always been quick to call him an asshole when they were in a fight. It was absolutely an assholey look.

Rolling his shoulders to let go of his irritation with… himself, Richter asked another question, "If you were me, would you choose you?"

The man on the pedestal looked at him a bit longer but the expression changed to one of grudging respect, "I am not allowed to tell you who to choose. I can't say whether you should go left or right." As he said that last statement, he raised first his left hand, then his right. It seemed like he motioned just a bit with his right hand though. "I wish I could be of more help." The man's neck straightened and he began to look off into the distance again. Repeated questioning didn't get any further response. The man had once again become as still as a statue.

Before Richter could walk away, he received a prompt.

Do you wish to choose the Specialization, ***Item Enchanter****?* *Yes or No?*

Richter backed away and the prompt disappeared. Immediately to the Item Specialist's right were one of the shrouded figures. Richter tried to approach it, but his body locked in place and, try as he might, he physically couldn't take another step.

You lack the prerequisites to know or choose this Specialization. Seek your future elsewhere or wait to improve.

How the hell am I supposed to know how to improve if I don't even know what I'm supposed to be working towards, Richter thought with some irritation. For the thousandth time, he wished there was a wiki of The Land. There was so much he didn't know.

He set his emotions aside and walked over to the next figure in the line. This version of Richter held a radiant sword in one hand and a fiery axe in the other. The figure was outfitted with black, full plate armor that was studded with spikes. As Richter walked up, the man broke his statuesque immobility. He extended a hand and said, "Not too close. My armor gets a wee bit jealous of my personal space."

"What?" Richter asked, confused.

"My armor," the man said again. "If you get within five feet of me, the spikes might attack you. This is all happening in your mind, but it still probably wouldn't be fun for you."

"Good safety tip," Richter said, stopping ten feet away. "I'm guessing you're the Battle Specialist I have heard so much about."

The Battle Specialist gave a haughty laugh, "Well it's nice to know you're not just an incredibly gorgeous face." Definitely too meta, Richter thought. "Yes, if you choose my path, you may one day be able to make the strongest weapon and armor enchantments in The Land. Some of the things I can do are wonderfully horrifying." The man gave a dark chuckle, then kept chuckling for a bit longer. A bit too long in Richter's opinion.

This guy is a little bit off, he thought. It was honestly disturbing to see his own face contort like that. On the other hand, there was no denying that making stronger weapon enchantments had an obvious benefit.

"Is there anything else I should know about your Specialty?" he asked.

The man on the podium gave a coy smile, "I can tell you that I have a few talents that could be... quite useful in battle. Besides, look at my power!" He flipped both his axe and the sword high into the air. The sword fell back down first, the pommel slapping into the man's right hand. The axe fell a second later. The handle almost slipped through his fingers and the man had to reach out to catch it. It left him in an awkward position, and somehow his sword was left pointing horizontally to the right. The man straightened, gave Richter another cocky smile, then resumed his original stance, looking over Richter's head into the distance. Once again, there was no response to further questioning.

Decidedly weird, Richter thought, looking at the Battle Specialist. Are my potential future selves finding a way to cheat the rules here, he wondered. With a faint smirk, he realized that was probably exactly what he *would* do. In the words of Papa Smurf, get'er dun! Both of the Specialists had indicated that he should go to their right, his left. He decided to test his theory. Richter took a step back, dismissed the prompt asking if he wanted to be a Battle Specialist, and walked to the lit figure that was farthest to his left.

This version of Richter held a staff that had a ghostlike, green light writhing up and down it. He also wore a crown and gauntlet that had identical, green lights pulsing within them. Richter hadn't really taken the time to examine the stats of the items on the other Specialists, but he couldn't help himself this time. Unfortunately, all it said was *Magic Staff* and *Magic Crown* respectively. The man on the column turned to look at him and spoke. It was still Richter's voice, but every word was enunciated with a surprisingly regal tone, "Let me help you with that." The man's free hand waved in a spell pattern and he spoke a word of Power. Richter could suddenly easily see each item's stats.

You have found: **Staff of Hyira-kur**	**Damage:** +44-52 **Durability:** 1712/1712 **Item Class:** Legendary **Quality:** Masterwork **Weight:** 6.2 kg **Traits:**

	Item 1 of 3 of the item set: Wraith Mage Hyira-kur. +231% attack vs non-Death creatures. Fires a beam of necrotic energy with a range of 103 yards. **Charges**: 1034/1034.
You have found: **Gauntlet of Hyira-kur**	**Defense:** +79 **Durability:** 1611/1611 **Item Class:** Legendary **Quality:** Masterwork **Weight:** 3.7 kg **Traits:** Item 2 of 3 of the item set: Wraith Mage Hyira-kur. Can siphon health, mana and stamina from enemies upon touch at a rate of 50/sec. **Charges**: 1769/1769
You have found: **Crown of Hyira-kur**	**Defense:** +63 **Durability:** 1835/1835 **Item Class:** Legendary **Quality:** Masterwork **Weight:** 3.7 kg **Traits:** Item 3 of 3 of the item set: Wraith Mage Hyira-kur. +30 to Intelligence and Wisdom. -10 to Charisma. +113% to total defense against Death creatures or Death magic.

Know this! You have found the entire item set: **Wraith Mage Hyira-kur** With this item set, any foes killed by the wearer of this item set have a chance of converting to a spirit, undead or living dead creature. If this occurs, they will be placed directly under your control. Killing one thousand enemies within a mile radius will desecrate that space. From that point on, Death creatures will

regularly arise from this location and guard it against any intruders. They will follow your every command.

Richter blinked in shock. Someone with these items was capable of great evil… but they also could forge an empire. "Where did you find this?"

"Ha," the man on the pedestal scoffed. "Why would I settle for the crap I could find, when I can *make* items like this?" The man laughed at seeing Richter's mouth drop open. He took a small bow and said, "I am a Synergist. I specialize in making item sets. Mine is the highest expression of the Enchanter Profession. Only Synergists can make the strongest enchantments."

"Why would anyone choose anything else?" Richter asked.

"Hahaha," the man chortled. "It's easy to say that when I've got this badass gear right in front of you. The road of a Synergist is not easy, however. You don't want to know how many high level souls it took to make these. You don't want to know about the other… components that I needed." He paused for a second before continuing, "An item set also can't be made of just any common material. This set is named Wraith Mage Hyira-kur because it is made from the bones and essence of a five-thousand year old lich king." The man's face became clouded for a moment, "Tens of thousands died to defeat his armies and vanquish his evil. Even after all of that, you see that his malevolence endures in these objects that I have created."

"How could you make things of such evil?" Richter asked with a tone of recrimination.

The synergist fixed him with a stare and a smile to match, "You know the answer to that. Don't you?"

Silence hung in the air between the two men until Richter looked away and admitted the truth, "For power."

The man nodded, "Of course, the first thing I wanted to do after they were fully formed was to destroy them. In the end… I just didn't have the heart. I could never see them callously cast aside any more than a mother could sacrifice her own child. Synergy is the path to the greatest enchantments, but it is an arduous and time-consuming path. This entire set took ten years to create, and the materials cost as much as a palace. Choose wisely. I wish you luck, but cannot offer you any further guidance."

Right after the man finished speaking, he yawned expansively. He raised his hand to cover his mouth and Richter couldn't help but see that the man's thumb pointed strongly to the left. He made eye contact one more time and Richter could see laughter in his eyes before the figure froze back into immobility, staring into the distance.

Richter smirked and nodded in appreciation. He dismissed the prompt asking if he wanted to be a Synergist. He liked the sound of it, but definitely wanted to know what the other options were first, and he had just been given marching orders. He walked to the next figure.

Rather than standing on a simple column, this figure sat in the lotus position. This wasn't that interesting, but the fact that he was sitting on top of a miniature floating castle and was flanked on either side by humanoid figures made of water and fire respectively was pretty fucking cool.

Just like the rest, the man focused on Richter as soon as he started getting close. He saw the chaos seed admiring his setup and made eye contact. Both arms flexed up in a body builder pose and in the cockiest voice imaginable, he said, "That's right! This is how I roll!"

And just like that, they became besties.

Richter ran up looking at the golems and the castle and said, "This is amazing. Enchanting can do this?"

The guy put his arms down and broke into an easy grin, "It can if you are a Macroenchanter. My Specialty focuses on creating monuments to the fantastic. Everything from simple, elemental golems like these, to great underwater cities or floating citadels so high that you could see the curvature of the world. You need another enchantment to help people breathe if you build that last example, but hey, small price to pay for being awesome. Our works can inspire people for millennia and can bring true majesty to this world of magic."

Richter smiled at hearing the joy in the man's voice. He could definitely see the appeal in devoting his life to making wonders. To actually change the face of the world. Richter knew that this was not his path, though. Maybe one day he could have the inner peace and patience required to slowly build the fantastic, but today he and his people needed something with a faster yield than however long it would take to make an enchanted fortress. The man in front of him read his face. He just smiled and raised his left hand in farewell. Then the macroenchanter's face looked off into the distance and froze into immobility.

Richter dismissed the prompt that appeared as he walked away and moved on to the next pedestal. Strangely there didn't seem to be anything enchanted about this figure. The man was just a perfect copy of Richter, standing barefooted and bare chested, wearing only simple white linen pants. Around his neck was a brown leather cord with a plain circle of white stone at the end. The pendant contrasted against the man's chestnut-colored skin. He smiled as Richter approached and the chaos seed couldn't help but smile back. The man's expression was one of peaceful serenity. He opened his mouth and in a strong, sure tone, he said, "Welcome. What do you think of my Specialty?"

Richter paused for a moment looking over the man again, but couldn't see evidence of what his specialty could be, "Uhhhh…"

The man laughed again. The sound had no derision or ridicule, it was simply an exaltation of life and the man's place in it, "Sorry. I was teasing you. More than anyone, I'm sure that you understand why our sense of humor has been accurately described as 'dickish.' I am what is called an Ambient Specialist. My power is not focused on making a magic ring or enchanted sword, though I can still do that. Instead, a portion of my magic is diverted to affecting the world around me. I cannot fully control what this change is, but the people, things and events around me are… twisted slightly to better suit the needs of my true self."

The man had placed a slight emphasis on 'true'. "What do you mean?" Richter asked.

"I mean that the core of 'what' you are is served by my Specialty. Your conscious mind will sometimes nudge this change, but the true guiding force will be your soul. In exchange for this unconscious change in the environment, you will have a reduction in your total mana. Initially you will experience a 20% reduction, but you can purchase upgrades to increase the amount that is channeled to your Specialty. The greater the amount of mana utilized, the greater the change in your environment."

"Why would I ever want to reduce my own mana pool? What possible benefit could be worth that?" Richter asked, confused.

Rather than answer, the man's face grew speculative. He regarded Richter for a full minute before speaking again, "I cannot know for sure, but I feel that my specific path may not have been offered in The Land before, or at least, not offered in a very, very long time." He paused again before once again adopting an expression of peaceful amusement, "Of course, that seed of chaos in your soul makes you special. Different from almost anyone else in The Land."

Richter's eyes widened, and he began to ask a question, but the Ambient Enchanter just shook his head slightly while maintaining his smile. He cupped one hand and there was a rumble in the red sand under Richter's feet. A stream of crystal clear water shot to the Ambient Enchanter's left and a generous amount splashed into his curled fingers. The spout disappeared and the water already in the air fell down to the ground, leaving a rough line of damp sand pointing to Richter's right. The man drank from his hand, gave a satisfied 'ahhh' and then resumed his original position, completely still and staring off into the distance.

Well I wish he would have answered my question, but that was some impressive, mystical shit, Richter thought with respect. He dismissed the obligatory prompt and followed the surreptitious directions of the enigmatic figure, moving on to the next avatar. This time, he wasn't exactly sure what to make of what he was seeing. The Specialist was as strange as the Ambient Enchanter had been normal.

This version of himself was also wearing only pants, but they were ripped like the hulk's. For the umpteenth time, Richter wondered what type of super spandex Bruce Banner must be wearing 24/7. There was no way the khakis he normally seemed to rock in the movies could have stretched from a size thirty-two to a size sixty-four which was at *least* what the hulk's waistline had to be. If you went back to the 70's show and took the fact that he was always wearing bell bottoms into account, forget about it! Richter acknowledged that it wasn't exactly family friendly to show a set of gamma-irradiated cock and balls flailing around while a green, rage monster killed your loved ones, but hey, at least it would have been realistic.

He came back from his mental meanderings to see the 'man' staring at him. He only loosely used the word, because the figure he was looking at seemed like an amalgam of different monsters. Both hands ended in claws and his arms and legs were insanely muscled. His skin was thickened and covered in thick scales. The mouth was elongated and lined with sharp teeth, the ears were long and rose up like a bat's. Even stranger, there was a barbed tail behind the figure that moved randomly and seemingly of its own volition. The only body part that Richter recognized of himself was the right eye. The left was slitted like a lizard's with a red cornea.

"Are you done staring?" the figure asked in a guttural voice.

Richter's attention snapped to the here and now. His body tensed instinctually, the same reaction any animal with survival instincts would have when confronting a predator. Richter couldn't stop himself. He asked, "Are you me? A me that I might become?"

The figure growled, a deep, low rumbling, "I represent the distinguished Specialty of Flesh Enchanting. Few, if any, Flesh Enchanters exist. It requires not only the Enchanting Profession, but also another skill. You meet the requirements with Beast Bonding, though your skill in that is quite pitiful. Despite your weakness, you have the potential to understand the beasts and monsters of The Land. Through that appreciation, you can start to incorporate their unique powers into your own body."

Richter could see the appeal of having skin like a rock giant or being able to have a venomous bite, but as he looked at this amalgam of creatures in front of him, he felt only revulsion. He wanted power, but he wasn't prepared to become this monstrosity to do it. The growl coming from its chest deepened. He clearly had not done a good job of hiding his disgust because the thing said, "Not all have the strength to sacrifice for power. Be gone!" It swiped one of its claws from right to left, then resumed its immobility.

Richter eagerly rejected this Specialty and moved onto the last lighted figure. Each of the others seemed to have been guiding him here. The man stood tall on his column of rock, lights floating around him. Eight rotated around him in a circle of different colors. Countless more of various colors floated around in shifting patterns, though some seemed to follow a discernible course as they moved. Others flashed in and out of existence at random intervals. The man looked at him steadily, not speaking.

Richter stared back, feeling that he was being tested in some way. The strong visage of the man he was looking at conveyed a no-nonsense gravity. Richter had a feeling that asking pointless questions wouldn't be well received. So instead, he studied the figure, learning what he could before speaking. When he did, it was to make a statement rather than beg for answers, "Those eight represent the Basic Elements." He pointed at another series of lights, "Unless I miss my guess, that deep red light represents Blood Magic and the incandescent one next to it looks like Spirit Magic." The man continued to stare back. His chin lifted slightly to indicate Richter was on the right track. He stayed quiet for another few seconds. Richter realized where he had seen glowing lights like this before, in the heart of the elementum anvils. The green glass distorted the view of the lights slightly, but now that it had occurred to him, the answer was obvious. With a touch of awe, he said, "These lights represent the types of magics you can enchant with… but there are so many."

The man finally spoke, with neither congratulations nor condemnation in his voice, "My Specialty is Essence. Only the Master of a Place of Power who is also an Enchanter can follow my path. My power is to enchant my very soul. Put simply, any spell that an Essence Enchanter knows can be converted into an enchantment."

Richter's eyes bulged. This was the most powerful by far! Maybe he wouldn't get the bonuses of specializing in a certain type of enchantment, but he could make an enchantment for any situation.

The man saw the excitement on his face and held up a hand to forestall him, "As with any path to power, there is a cost. Each lower-level spell you convert will cost you Talent Points. Higher-level spells may require an even steeper price. There are faster and more direct routes to power, but if you have the patience and aptitude, the path of Essence could serve you well. The options are almost… limitless." There was a loud rumble of thunder in the distance. The Specialist showed emotion for the first time. It passed too quickly to be sure, but Richter thought he saw a look of fear flash across the man's face as he looked over his shoulder. It was almost as if he was concerned that he had pressed his luck. When nothing else happened, the man looked at Richter again for a moment, before squaring his shoulders and, like all of the other avatars, once more gazed over Richter's head into eternity.

Do you wish to choose the Specialization, ***Essence****? Yes or No?*

He looked at the prompt. Every other avatar had basically led him here and he couldn't deny that this power suited his Ability perfectly. Richter was acutely aware that he could only make this choice once, however, and he would have to live with it for all the years of his possibly endless life. In spite of his doubts, indecision was not his nature. He selected 'Yes'.

All of the figures vanished except for the Essence Specialist. The man focused on Richter again and beckoned with one hand. Richter stepped forward and the avatar placed one hand on his head and the other on his chest. "For you who has chosen me to be you, a gift." Unseen energy shot down both of the man's hands and, suddenly, Richter *knew*. Then the two merged into one and Richter knew nothing more.

CHAPTER 5 -- DAY 111 -- KUBORN 1, 15368 EBG

Richter blinked. He was back in the Forge with notifications filling his vision. He minimized them for a second and looked around. From the amount of light outside the Forge, it didn't look like much time had passed. He checked his internal clock and saw that it had been more than an hour, though. This more than explained the dry taste in his mouth.

He reached into his bag for a water skin. After taking a drink, he stood and twisted. His back popped with an impressive and satisfying series of cracks. He looked over towards the central anvil and saw Krom hard at work. The dwarf looked up and said, "Did ye like yer little nap, yer lordship?"

Richter rolled his eyes and said, "I was pondering the hidden mysteries of magic. You wouldn't understand, seeing as how it has little to do with banging metal or a woman's bottom."

"Play to yer strengths, ay always say," Krom said with a grin. "Both of those things require a similar skill set. Enough chit chat, though. Are ye ready to try some enchanting?"

"Just one sec," Richter said, wanting to clear away his remaining prompts. Krom affixed him with a doubting gaze. "Really, this time." The dwarf huffed and started pounding on the anvil again while Richter read through the notifications covering his view.

Know This! An unquantifiable entity has gifted you with arcane knowledge.

Congratulations! You have learned the spell: **Create Soul Stone (Common).** Turn minerals into soul stones of various levels. Can create soul stones up to Common level. This is a spell of Light, level 5. Cost: 25 mana. Duration: Instant. Range: 1 foot. Cast Time: 1 second. Cooldown: N/A.

Congratulations! You have learned the spell: **Create Soul Stone (Luminous).** Turn minerals into soul stones of various levels. Can create soul stones up to Luminous level. This is a spell of Light, level 15. Cost: 50 mana. Duration: Instant. Range: 1 foot. Cast Time: 3 seconds. Cooldown: N/A. Requires: Light Magic Level 15.

Richter grinned. The spells must have been the gift that the Essence Specialist had talked about. He was more than grateful. Relying on Gloran to make the stones wasn't something he wanted to keep doing. Heaven forbid something happened to the elf or even that he just decided to move away. It would effectively halt the creation of enchanted weapons in the Mist Village. The second spell was still beyond him, but that just meant he needed to grind his Light magic. Besides, thankfully, there weren't too many higher level enemies out in the mist around the village yet.

Baaa-baba-baba-ba-baaaah!

Congratulations! You have chosen the Specialization: ***Essence.*** *No enchantment is beyond your reach as long as you can learn the spell. Your enchantments are an extension of yourself. Grow your power to grow your Specialty.*

You have unlocked the Profession Quest: **The Essence of Knowledge I**.
Do not let your limitless potential go to waste.
Success Conditions: Learn 5 new enchantments
Rewards: 5 Talent Points
Penalty for failure or refusal of Quest: None
Do you accept? Yes or No

You have earned new Talent Points! By becoming a Specialist, you will now earn additional Talent Points. At 100% affinity, you will now receive an additional 10 Talent Points per level.

Revere your craft, grow your power, LIVE!

You have: ***215 Talent Points****. Do you wish to expend them?*

Hell yeah I do, Richter thought with a smile. He even had more talent points to use than he thought he was going to and the new quest offered a chance to earn even more. He accepted it without hesitation as he brought his Profession window up again. It was time to buy some shit.

The starscape appeared showing the blue spheres. Most of the map was obscured by a thick, grey fog and only an area in the center revealed anything. It showed a large central sphere that said 'Enchanter' on it. Six filaments extended out from this globe and each attached to another sphere. All six balls represented a Talent that could be purchased. He had already bought one, Increase Enchantment Strength I, which increased the potency of any enchantment he created by 5%. It had also revealed more of the nebula. When he had purchased his first talent, that sphere had started to glow and the fog around it had disappeared, revealing three other spheres. Everything looked the same as the last time he had examined it, but now another portion of the map was revealed.

Far to the right, there was another break in the fog. It contained a red sphere. Across its surface he could read "Essence." Unlike the massive network of blue spheres, the central red globe only had four spheres coming off of it. No further filaments extended out into the fog past this first ring of spheres. As he read the description of each Specialist talent, he saw that all four red spheres required a much higher talent point price than any of the blue talents Richter had seen so far. The price was so high, in fact, that he immediately quailed and began worrying that he had made the wrong choice. That only lasted until he read the last sphere, then his smile was ear-to-ear.

Purchase Spell Enchantment I: *Currently, each Basic Element spell costs 1 Talent Point per spell level. Each Deep Magic spell costs 10 Talent Points per spell level. Increase this Talent to reduce this cost. Cost to Upgrade:* ***40 Talent Points****.*

Reduce Mana Cost I: *To translate a spell into an enchantment, a mana cost must be paid. Current conversion cost is 100x spell mana cost. Increase* *this Talent to reduce this cost by 20x. Minimum cost, 20x spell mana cost. Cost to Upgrade:* ***30 Talent Points.***

Unlock Spell School I: *To convert a spell, you must first unlock that spell type. Current Base Cost based on known spells:* ***10 Talent Points per Basic Element. 100 Talent Points per Deep Magic.*** *This one-time cost cannot be reduced. Further costs may be required to unlock certain spells.*
Talent Point Conversion I: *Few Talents for any Profession or Specialty are as expensive as Essence Talents. Binding your Specialty to your soul, however, offers a unique opportunity. Essence Enchanters may sacrifice XP to buy Talent Points. Any reduction in XP will not affect personal level, though the threshold for leveling remains the same. This Talent is not to be used carelessly. Overzealous Essence Enchanters have found their personal level frozen as they feed their Profession and Specialty. Any experience lost will be 250% harder to earn again. Furthermore, once used, this Talent cannot be used again until all expended experience points are gained back. Conversion rate: 10,000 XP per 1 Talent Point. Upgrading this Talent will decrease the penalty to recovering XP to 200%. It will also improve the Conversion rate to 9,000 XP to 1 Talent Point. Cost to Upgrade:* ***25 Talent Points.***

It was now abundantly clear why his alter egos had pointed him in this direction. The ten thousand to one conversion was a bit of a heavy hit and he could see it adding up quickly, but it still meant he had a theoretically limitless supply of talent points. Seeing as how he was basically immortal, he could always slay and capture more monsters, or have Alma drain more high-level beasties to make up for it. At the current moment, increasing his personal level was much less important than increasing his skills and Profession. The only thing that gave him pause were the qualifiers on earning his XP back. It basically meant that he would have to earn three times as much experience to earn his XP back, but Alma's *Brain Drain* ability should help with that. It was clear that he would need to upgrade Talent Point Conversion, but still, it was a game changer.

Richter checked his status page to see exactly how much experience he had managed to accumulate. He whistled appreciatively. He had eight hundred ninety-one thousand seven hundred and fourteen experience points. With that much he could-

Richter was interrupted by Krom loudly clearing his throat. He looked over at the dwarf who widened both eyes and nodded his head quickly as if to say 'Are you coming or what?'

"In a second," Richter said with a bit of irritation. Krom 'harumphed' and went back to work. Richter glared at him. Who was the lord here, anyway? He decided to let it go though, and get back to his starscape.

He had two hundred and fifteen talent points to play with. Before anything else, he purchased the upgrade for Talent Point Conversion I. The Roman numeral on the sphere changed to "II" and the description altered as well. The next level cost fifty talent points. It reduced the earned XP penalty to 150% and also further decreased the conversion to eight thousand experience for each talent point. Hoping he wasn't making a mistake, he bought the next upgrade and his pool of available TPs dropped to one hundred and forty.

The third upgrade cost one hundred points. A very steep cost, but it decreased the penalty to 100% and the conversion to seven thousand to one. He was tempted to leave it be, but as his grandpappy used to say, 'Don't rob Peter, to pay Paul.' He bought it. That meant Richter only had forty talent points left, but he told himself that it didn't matter. Now he had a virtually unlimited supply of talent points, expensive or not. He decided to uncover more of the hidden map that dealt with the blue spheres.

Each of the talents extending from the central "Enchanter" sphere cost five points. He focused on the first Talent he would buy.

Macroenchantment: *Increase this Talent to have your enchantment affect larger items. This is extremely helpful for creating enchanted buildings, ships, engines of war, and other large projects. Cost:* ***5 Talent Points.***

The fog peeled back revealing more of the starscape. Four filaments extended out from Macroenchantment I, and each led to another sphere.

Siege Enchantments: *Gain the ability to enchant siege weapons. You can now create mangonels that fire balls of necrotic energy or scorpions to fire bolts through city walls. Increase this Talent to improve effectiveness of these enchantments. Cost:* ***10 Talent Points.***

Golem Enchantment: *Gain the ability to enchant raw materials for the purpose of making crude golems. These will never equal the power of a Mechanic-created golem, but also take a fraction of the time to create. Increase this Talent to improve the level of your golem as well as other traits. This Talent also allows you to enchant already-constructed Golems. Cost:* ***10 Talent Points.***

Building Enchantment: *Gain the ability to enchant buildings. Create impregnable fortresses or desert homes that generate water. This Talent allows you to make the desolate bountiful and the impossible commonplace. Increase this Talent to build grander projects with stronger effects. Cost:* ***10 Talent Points.***

Ship Enchantment: *Gain the ability to enchant ships. Create vessels that can be sharks of the water… or even of the air. This Talent allows you to add magic to vessels of all types. Increase this Talent to produce stronger effects. Cost:* ***10 Talent Points.***

More filaments extended out from these spheres. Because Richter didn't plan on any large projects yet, he didn't use any further talent points to reveal that particular part of his Profession tree. Instead, he purchased the next enchantment from the inner blue ring.

Increase Number of Charges: *Increase the number of charges on items with finite uses. Will increase number of charges by +10 or by 10%, whichever gives greater yield. Cost:* ***5 Talent Points.***
You have unlocked the talent: ***Increase Number of Charges I****.*
You have: ***30 Talent Points*** *remaining.*

The fog dissipated again. The portion of the star map revealed showed five more spheres. None of them had more filaments leading off from them.

Decrease Required Enchantment Slots: *Each enchantment takes up a specific amount of enchantment slots. Purchasing this Talent will decrease the amount of space each enchantment takes up by 10%. Cost:* ***10 Talent Points.***

Increase Maximum Number of Soul Stones: *Each enchanter can only use a certain number of soul stones per enchantment, based upon their skill* *level. Increase this Talent to add another soul stone to that number. Cost:* ***10 Talent Points.***

Increase Soul Stone Yield: *Increase this Talent to increase the yield of enchantment power from each soul stone. Purchasing this Talent will increase the yield of soul stones by 25%. Cost:* ***10 Talent Points.***

Decrease Charge Cost: *Increase this Talent to decrease the charges expended when an active enchantment is discharged by 20%. Cost:* ***10 Talent Points.***

Increase Natural Recharge: *Increase this Talent to double the natural recharge rate for items you enchant and any items you personally have. Cost:* ***10 Talent Points.***

All five of those talents sounded like they could come in handy. More filaments extended out from each of these spheres. Richter was tempted to purchase each immediately, but decided to just keep unlocking more of his Profession's Talent map. The next he chose was *Deconstruct Items.*

Deconstruct Items: *Gain the ability to deconstruct an enchanted item. Increase this Talent to improve chance for successful deconstruction and to increase chance of obtaining better items after item is destroyed. Cost:* ***10 Talent Points.***

You have unlocked the talent: ***Deconstruct Items I****.*

You have: ***20 Talent Points*** *remaining.*

It revealed only one more sphere.

Resize Items: *This Talent allows you to resize already enchanted items to fit creatures either smaller or larger than the item was originally intended. Resizing carries the risk of a decrease in power of enchantment, durability of enchanted item and/or complete destruction of enchanted object. Increase this Talent to allow for resizing to a greater extent and to decrease risk. This Talent is fueled by soul stones. The first rank of this Talent allows an Enchanter to alter an item by one size rank. Cost:* ***10 Talent Points.***

This sphere had two other filaments extending out from it. Though he was loath to waste ten points on a Talent of limited utility, he wanted to know what else was hidden. It also meant that he might be able to resize the collar of submission. Richter paid the ten points and looked at the two new spheres revealed.

You have unlocked the talent: ***Resize Items I****.*

You have: ***10 Talent Points*** *remaining.*

Spatial Folding: *Can create enchantments that fold space. At the lowest level, you can create Bags of Holding and Expansive Quivers. At higher levels, this Talent can fold space in larger objects and in smaller objects to a greater degree. Cost:* ***30 Talent Points.***

Learn Enchantments: *This Talent provides a small chance of learning enchantments from enchanted items when they are deconstructed. This is by no means a sure thing, but increasing this Talent increases the chances of deciphering the arcane combination of Powers that comprise an enchantment. Cost:* ***100 Talent Points.***

Richter smiled. He finally knew how Bags of Holding were made. He assumed the Expansive Quivers did the same thing, but for arrows. The *Learn Enchantments* Talent showed that there were other options than a Magic Forge to gain enchantments, but it said it was a very small chance. Also, just to learn the first rank of that Talent cost one hundred points! More filaments stemmed from the sphere and he did not even want to think about how much the subsequent Talents might cost. Seeing the high price of the Talent, it further underlined the importance of the Forge of Heavens and its ability to teach enchantments.

Richter could see even more filaments coming off of *Spatial Folding*. Looking at the progression of the other talents he had unlocked, he was fairly certain that those filaments might give more options dealing with making a Bag of Holding. His own bag decreased the weight of what he put in it by 90% after all. That was an amazing attribute and it wasn't explained by the description in *Spatial Folding*. He wasn't willing to spend the points to access either Talent right now, but at least he now knew he had the options.

Going back to the ring of six spheres that surrounded the central "Enchanter" sphere, he purchased another Talent.

Increase Enchantment Potential: *Increase the number of enchantment slots on the object you wish to enchant. Increases enchantment slots by 10%. Cost:* ***5 Talent Points.***

You have unlocked the talent: ***Increase Enchantment Potential I****.*

You have: 5 ***Talent Points*** *remaining.*

Advancing the Talent increased the enchantment slots of whatever he worked on in the future by 10%. It also revealed five new spheres.

Synergy of Items: *Allows for the possibility of item sets. The base items must have something in common for the enchantments to feed off of one another. Increase this Talent to allow for stronger and more extensive sets. Cost:* ***15 Talent Points****.*

False Description: *Allows the enchanter to label an item with a false description even after being identified. Only a specialized spell can see through this. Cost:* ***10 Talent Points.***

Cursed Items: *Allows enchanter to pervert known enchantments to be detrimental to the wearer. Once a cursed item is donned, it cannot be removed without magical intervention. Cost:* ***10 Talent Points.***

Increase Number of Enchantments: *Allows for a second enchantment to be placed on one item. Attempting to create such an item greatly increases the chances of the enchantment failing to take hold in whatever object you are working upon. All enchantable objects are still bound by the same rules of enchantment size and slots. Cost:* ***50 Talent Points.***

Identify Enchantments: *Allows enchanters to identify unknown magical objects. An Enchanter with this Talent can even rival lore masters. Touching an unknown item will give a detailed description of most magical items. This is a passive action. It does not cost anything and the knowledge is absorbed instantaneously. Cost:* ***5 Talent Points.***

Richter looked over the five new spheres and could see the utility of each. He made one purchase without even thinking. The lack of an identify spell had been a pain in his ass since arriving in The Land. He *had* to buy *Identify Enchantments*. At five points, it was almost a gimme.

The next level of the Talent cost ten talent points and was even more impressive. It let him identify stronger magical objects, but more importantly, it allowed him to identify enchanted items from a distance. That meant when facing an opponent, he would be able to know what magical items they could bring to bear. He realized that this might prove to be his most valuable Talent over time.

He bought the Talent, or at least that was what he tried to do. Instead of the sphere lighting up further, he heard a sound like a 'No' buzzer and a prompt appeared that showed he was out of Talent Points. Richter realized it was time to use his conversion talent. Go big or go home, he thought. If the strategy was good enough for drunk sorority girls, it was good enough for him. He spent eight hundred eighty-nine thousand experience points and gained one hundred and twenty-seven talent points! After the transaction, he only had two thousand seven hundred and fourteen experience points left. Richter got back to his shopping spree and bought the talent.

You have unlocked the Talent: ***Identify Enchantments I.***

You have: ***0 Talent Points*** *remaining.*

You have used ***Talent Point Conversion IV.*** *By expending 889,000 experience, you have now gained:* ***127 Talent Points.***

All experience earned will suffer a 0.5x penalty until this experience is repaid.

You have: ***127 Talent Points*** *remaining.*

You have unlocked the Talent: ***Identify Enchantments II.***

You have: ***117 Talent Points*** *remaining.*

Looking at the rest of talents in that section, he realized that he didn't have any specific interest in cursed items or faking the description of items, but he did resolve to be careful about taking things at face value from then on. The *Synergy of Items* Talent was one that he couldn't pass up, though. Of all the avatars he had met in the red desert, the Synergist had appealed to him the most after the Essence Enchanter. He purchased the blue sphere for fifteen points.

You have unlocked the Talent: ***Synergy of Items I.***

You have: ***102 Talent Points*** *remaining.*

One sphere was revealed.

Personalized Enchantments: *Allows enchanters to create enchantments that will only work for a specific person. Advancing this Talent will allow enchanters to create enchantments that only apply to certain groups. Cost:* ***20 Talent Points.***

He decided to leave that Talent alone for the time being, despite the fact that it was intriguing. Could he make enchantments that only worked for dwarves or elves? Could he find a way to make enchantments that only worked for his own villagers? There were definite advantages that he could see, but again, it was a topic for another day. His eyes did linger on the *Increase Number of Enchantments* Talent for a moment. Having multiple enchantments on one item sounded great, but if he was reading it right, the enchantment slots for an item would be split between the two enchantments. Each would only be half as strong as they otherwise could be. Maybe he would purchase the Talent in the future, but the fifty point cost made it easy to pass by now.

The other three spheres also had filaments extending off into the fog. Because none of the Talents were immediately attractive to him, he decided to move on. Richter bought the next Talent from the inner ring.

Increase Enchantment Success: *Increase this Talent to improve the odds of an enchantment taking hold by 20%. Cost:* ***5 Talent Points.***

You have unlocked the Talent: ***Increase Enchantment Success I.***

You have: ***97 Talent Points*** *remaining.*

The sphere lit up and the fog peeled back revealing two more blue globes.

Faster Creation Time: *The creation of magic books, scrolls and skill books is time consuming and laborious. Increase this Talent to increase the speed you finish these tasks by 10%. Cost:* ***10 Talent Points.***

Fortify Health/Mana/Stamina: *Increase this Talent to make Enchantments dealing with increasing health, mana and stamina more effective by 20%. Cost:* ***10 Talent Points.***

Only one filament extended from the first sphere. Richter planned to make magic books sometime soon, so decided to invest the ten points.

You have unlocked the talent: ***Faster Creation Time I.***

You have: ***87 Talent Points*** *remaining.*

The words on the sphere changed to *Faster Creation Time I* and the cost to upgrade increased to twenty talent points. The next sphere revealed said *Soul Bond Object.* The title was self-explanatory and the description matched. It cost fifteen talent points, but Richter didn't hesitate to buy it. One of the largest issues with his rebirth was the loss of items and armor. If he could soul bond his objects to him though, they would be there with him when he was reborn. Besides, there were two more filaments extending off from it.

You have unlocked the talent: ***Soul Bound Object I.***

You have: ***72 Talent Points*** *remaining.*

The fog was pushed back once again, revealing two new spheres.

Break Soul Bond: *Soul bonds can be broken in a number of ways, but almost all of these methods result in destruction of the items. This Talent allows you to sever a soul bond while preserving the object. Success is dependent on strength of the bond and power of the enchanted objects. Cost:* **30 Talent Points.**

More Powerful Soul Stones: *Purchasing this Talent increases the level of soul stone that can be created from a material by +1. Cost:* **40 Talent Points.**

One more filament extended from the Talent dealing with more powerful stones. The sphere connected to it remained shrouded in shadow. Richter wanted to reveal the entire map, but he had to be realistic. So far he had spent fifty-five of his precious Talent Points since converting his XP. He decided the last sphere would remain in shadow for now. *Soul Bond Object II* caught his eye for a moment because it would let him summon soul bound objects to his hand if they were within a certain distance and there were no major obstacles between them. Definitely could be useful but it cost forty talent points, so he didn't buy it.

Richter looked at the two filaments leading away from the Fortify Health/Mana/Stamina talent and decided it was worth ten talent points to know what else might be revealed.

You have unlocked the talent: ***Fortify Health/Mana/Stamina I.***

You have: ***62 Talent Points*** *remaining.*

Fortify Characteristics: *Increase this Talent to make Enchantments dealing with increasing Characteristics more effective by 20%. Cost:* **20 Talent Points.**

Fortify Physical Alterations: *Increase this Talent to make Enchantments dealing with increasing physical alterations (running, jumping, swimming, etc.) more effective by 20%. Cost:* **20 Talent Points.**

One more filament came off of Fortify Characteristics, but Richter held off on purchasing the expensive Talent as there were not even any enchantments captured by the Forge that could make use of it. His gaze went to the first Talent he had ever bought, *Increase Enchantment Strength I.* The Talent increased the potency of all of his enchantments by 5%. It was the sixth Talent of the inner ring, and it had three spheres extending out from it. Each made weapons, armor or item enchantments stronger, respectively.

Increase Weapon Enchantment: *Accessing this Talent will increase the strength of any weapon enchantments by 10%. Talent Cost:* ***10 points.***

Increase Armor Enchantment: *Accessing this Talent will increase the strength of any armor enchantments by 10%. Talent Cost:* ***10 points.***

Increase Item Enchantment: *Accessing this Talent will increase the strength of any accessory enchantments by 10%. Talent Cost:* ***10 points.***

He bought each of them.

You have unlocked the Talent: ***Increase Weapon Enchantment I.***

You have unlocked the Talent: ***Increase Armor Enchantment I.***

You have unlocked the Talent: ***Increase Item Enchantment I.***

You have: ***32 Talent Points*** *remaining.*

Though he was thirty talent points poorer, this branch of his Profession tree was immediately useful, and gave information regarding the sixth, and final, tributary of being an Enchanter. Two spheres extended out from the weapon Talent.

Increase Additional Effect Chance: *Increase this Talent to make the additional effect of an enchantment (ie Burning from Flame Enchantment) 10% more likely to trigger. Cost:* ***20 Talent Points.***

Increase Additional Effect Power: *Increase this Talent to make the additional effect of an enchantment (ie Burning from Flame Enchantment) 10% more powerful. This will increase both the strength of the effect and the likelihood to overcome the target's resistance to the effect. Cost:* ***20 Talent Points.***

A filament led off of each of these spheres into the fog. Again Richter decided to hold off on purchasing talents from the third generation stemming from the central "Enchanter" sphere. He turned his attention back to the second tier.

Only one filament extended out from the armor talent, trailing off to disappear into the mist. He was confused at first as every other filament of a purchased Talent had ended in another sphere. After considering the anomaly for a few moments, he decided it must mean that the Talent the filament connected to must have another requirement that he had not met yet. Richter turned his gaze to the item Talent and the three Talents that had been revealed when he purchased it.

Common Materials: *Increase this Talent to be able to make enchanted items from less rare materials. Cost:* ***20 Talent Points****.*

Material Potential: *Item enchantment potential is determined both by the quality and the material. Increase this Talent to increase the enchantment potential for a given medium allowing for higher enchantment ranks to be reached. Cost:* ***20 Talent Points****.*

Alter Enchantment: *Purchase this Talent to be able to alter existing enchantments. This carries a risk of destroying the enchantment and/or object. Increase this Talent to allow for greater alterations with less risk. Cost:* ***30 Talent Points****.*

More filaments extended out from each of these last three spheres, but Richter's curiosity was finally sated. Though there was still more to know, he could see almost the entire star map laid out before him. Richter felt secure in his choice of Profession. The talents allowed for truly powerful enchantments to be created. Though many of the blue spheres seemed to be calling his name, at that moment he just decided to invest in his Specialty.

Richter had thirty-two talent points left. He had paid a steep price to reveal his Profession map, but he decided you couldn't put a price on information. Richter spent ten points unlocking Earth magic and another six to unlock the enchantment for *Weak Sonic Wail.* The last sixteen TPs, he saved. He closed his Profession page and dealt with another prompt that had appeared.

You have unlocked the enchantment for: ***Weak Sonic Wail***

This enchantment can only applied to one medium: ***Weapons***

You are currently at 0/2700 for the mana cost to learn this enchantment.

You have: ***16 Talent Points*** *remaining.*

Richter immediately allocated five hundred mana from his personal pool. The headache that struck him was horrible, but he had already decided that he needed to not only train his body. He also needed to train his mind and build his capacity to suffer pain. He watched his mana slowly refill and decided to do something impulsive.

Using magic had become a focal point of his fighting style. Something else that his grandpappy had always said was that with women or war, staying power was important. In a prolonged battle, he would need to be able to rally. Knowing it was the right decision, he dumped all eighteen of his free characteristic points into Wisdom, bringing it up to forty-five. Richter smiled as his mana began to refill much faster. He had been thinking about doing this for a while anyway. Not only could he benefit from the increased mana regen, but increasing his Wisdom also gave a bonus to magical resistance and mental fortitude. The eighteen points he invested might just save his mind when he used Deep Magic. Lastly, the 25% went into Enchanting.

He stood up and clapped his hands. Richter made eye contact with Krom and said, "Let's enchant some shit!"

CHAPTER 6 -- DAY 111 -- KUBORN 1, 15368 EBG

"It be about bloody time!" Krom exclaimed. Richter fixed him with a glare until the dwarf added, "Yer lordship."

"That's better," Richter said with a grin. "Like I said, let's enchant some shit."

"It actually do be a good time," Krom said grudgingly, "Ay be about to forge this here axe."

"Good," Richter said. "So what do I do?"

Krom looked at him, confused, "How in the abyssal hells should ay know? Yer the enchanter."

Richter shook his head at the dwarf in consternation, "I've been an enchanter for like two days, man. Help me out here."

"Okay, okay. Do na whine and shimmy like a goblin! Ay will tell you what ay know. When ay enchanted with the elf before, all Gloran did was place his hand on the anvil while ay did the smithing."

Richter figured it was worth a try. Richter placed his hand on the far end of the table-sized anvil. A prompt came up.

Greetings, Master of the Forge of Heavens. You have the ability to aid Smith Krom in enchanting his work through your Core building. For the duration of your time helping him, you will have access to any enchantment either of you know. Do you wish to enchant his work? Yes or No?

Finally, an 'Easy' button, Richter thought. Glad that he had found something that didn't require him to jump through ten hoops first, he selected 'Yes.' As soon as the prompt disappeared, he experienced the strangest sensation of a darkened part of his mind lighting up. In the new corner of himself hovered a blue light and three smaller, white lights. Examining the large one, he found the *Freeze* enchantment that Krom had learned from the Forge. The smaller lights represented the original enchantments Krom had known before coming to the village: *Extra Damage*, *Extra Protection* and *Durability*. He mentally reached out for *Freeze*, but a prompt came up stating that it was not yet time to enchant. Richter smiled and said, "We're good to go. How much longer do you need?"

Krom shrugged, "Probably na more than thirty minutes, yer lordship." He started striking the axe he was working on again. As an experiment, Richter let go of the anvil and found that he was still able to see the enchantments in his mind. That was good because keeping his hand on an anvil when a dwarf was hitting hot metal as hard as he could seemed somehow both dangerous and monotonously boring. To see how long his tether was, Richter even walked around the Forge and found he was still able to maintain the ability to help Krom, but when he got close to leaving the building a prompt warned him that he would lose his connection. This basically meant that he had some time on his hands while Krom finished the axe.

Hopping onto another anvil to train his Smithing skill was an option, but the other dwarves were using them to make things for the village right now. It seemed a bit silly to kick them off just for a bit of skill training. Besides, he could help enchant their projects too and hopefully boost his Enchanting skill faster. He stopped at the other two anvils and accessed the prompt that let him help with enchanting. Each prompt limited him to only the enchantments that particular dwarf knew, but they both knew *Increase Durability,* which still served to let him practice his Profession. Richter resolved to start coming to the Forge when everyone else was asleep. With his Sustenance Belt, he needed a third less food and rest as he would otherwise. That still left the question of what he should do while helping the smiths.

Richter decided to pester Krom and learn some of the technical details of what the smith was doing. Over the next few minutes, he peppered the dwarf with questions. He learned a bit, but more importantly he enjoyed the look of irritation on Krom's face. Even Richter got bored with the game after a while though, so he checked the village mana pool. He saw that there were four hundred and thirty-three points available; the rest probably had been used to summon mist workers. The village had more than enough time to regenerate more before the upkeep was due at midnight, but

Richter still decided to leave the pool alone. He had been dipping heavily into the village's mana during his recent battles, which had reduced village productivity since not as many mist workers could be summoned.

Richter thought for a moment, then asked, "Where is my armor, Krom?"

The dwarf looked up with a slightly annoyed look at being interrupted for the umpteenth time. He put his hammer down though and pulled a chain from under his shirt and over his neck. A steely blue key was on the end, "We put your armor and sword in the chest over there, yer lordship." After he had handed the key over, he started pounding on the axe again.

Richter walked further back into the forge, stopping when he found the chest Krom had been speaking about. It was four feet tall and must have weighed hundreds of pounds. The entire thing was made of welded plates of high steel. Richter looked at the key in his hands and then smiled. He put the chain around his neck and pulled two lock picks out of his bag.

Scanning the chest, he saw none of the tell-tale red glow of traps. Not that he had expected the chest to be rigged, but it had become a habit for him to look for danger after encountering the deadly snares The Land had to offer. Richter went down on one knee and started rooting around in the lock. After only two minutes, the lock clicked open. He sucked his tongue in disapproval and disappointment. The damn thing may as well not even have been locked. There had to be a more secure way to lock up valuables in the forge. Richter had been planning to leave the ingots he had taken from the treasury here, but couldn't if they were this poorly protected. Sighing, he put his hand on the lid to open it, but before he could lift the top, a prompt appeared.

Greetings, Master of the **Forge of Heavens**. *Do you wish to add this chest to the structure of the Forge? This will cost 16 Alteration Points. Currently, there are 97/100 Alteration Points available in your Core building at level one. Yes or No?*

Richter looked at the prompt. He didn't really understand what adding 'to the structure' meant, but maybe it would anchor the chest to the floor. Not really seeing a downside, he chose 'Yes.'

The chest began to glow. Green metal began to flow up from the floor, continuing until it covered the entire chest. At first it looked like a shell, but then the metal seemed to sink into the chest. The white light that was suffusing the chest pulsed one more time. When it faded, he could see that the bottom of the chest had indeed been melded into the floor. More importantly, the entire chest was now the clear green of elementum.

*You have added **Heavy Chest** to the Forge of Heavens. Current Alteration Points available 81/100. Alteration Points will regenerate at 1/day.*

This was something that he hadn't expected. It seemed that he could change the very structure of his Core building. Even more importantly, the damn thing's durability was one hundred thousand. It answered a question that had been in the back of his mind. Krom had mentioned that the forge would produce a weapons rack when he needed it. The dwarf must have been spending the points without knowing it, which accounted for the fact that three of the points had already been spent. Richter shook his head, would the wonders of his Core buildings never cease? He examined his new heavy chest.

It was a seamless block of clear green metal. The glasslike material grew clouded closer to the interior until it was completely opaque, hiding any of the contents. As excited as he had initially been, he couldn't see a way to open it. Hoping it worked, Richter placed his hand on the block and simply willed it to open. Sure enough, a line appeared in the metal and the lid steadily raised until it was standing up at ninety degrees. Inside was Richter's short sword, his armor and three small burlap bags with the tops cinched shut. He smiled as he took his items out, then he spent the next several minutes loading the chest with the quicksilver, cobalt and moonstone. The high steel ingots he left on the floor for one of the smiths to stack with the rest in the back of the Forge.

"What did ye do now?" Krom asked. Belying his words, his tone was one of wonder not annoyance.

"I'm not exactly sure," Richter admitted. "A prompt asked me if I wanted to incorporate the chest into the structure of the Forge. Right before that, I had been thinking that we needed a more secure way to protect items here. Your lock was a complete joke, by the way."

A look of annoyance flashed across the Smith's face, "Did na make the lock to stop a master thief," the dwarf grumbled under his breath. "Can ay get into it, now that it be changed?"

"Good point," Richter said. He willed the chest closed again, and it became a seamless block of elementum.

Krom put his hands on it and pushed up near the top. The lid opened again and the dwarf grinned. The grin widened when he saw that his lord had decided to leave so many ingots of rare metal in the forge. Krom took out one of the small bags and closed the lid again. He called one of the other dwarves over to try and open it, but nothing happened. More than satisfied, the smith clapped Richter on the back saying, "That be a good step up. Ay will admit ay have been worried about storing things of value here."

Richter nodded. He placed his hand on the chest a final time, bringing up an interface. He gave Sion, Randolphus and Terrod access to the chest as well. He let Krom know, seeing as how this was the smith's domain, but the dwarf didn't have any objections. They walked back to the main anvil. The axe was still in the furnace. Krom pulled it out and said, "This be the end. Ye need to be ready, yer lordship."

Richter nodded. He took out several soul stones and prepared to enchant his first item. After another minute, Krom looked at him and nodded. The dwarf reached into the bag he had retrieved from the chest and took out a handful of shining sand. A quick prompt check showed Richter that this was powdered crystal. Krom sprinkled it onto the still glowing red metal.

A notification appeared in Richter's vision.

The following weapon is available for enchantment: **High Steel Axehead**	**Damage:** 16-24 **Durability:** 52/52 **Item Class:** Common **Quality:** Exceptional **Weight:** 2.4 kg

This weapon has 36 enchantment slots (base 15 from weapon quality + 15 from Journeyman rank in Enchanting + 20% for Increase Enchantment Potential I). Available enchantments: Freeze, Increased Damage, Increased Durability. You have seven minutes from the time that this prompt appeared to finish your enchantment.

Richter had already decided to try *Freeze*, but seeing the others made him wonder. He knew that each enchantment had a cost. Since he had seven minutes, he decided to see what happened when he chose *Increased Damage +1*.

Increased Damage +1 enchant cost is ***5n****. This enchantment is static and cannot be increased in rank. In light of its static status, the enchantment is not reliant on charges and will never need to be replenished. Final Yield of this enchantment is +2 Damage (base 1 + 48% for enchanting skill + 5% for Increase Enchantment Strength I + 20% for Increase Weapon Enchant Strength I). Do you wish to power this enchantment? Yes or No?*

Richter chose 'No' and then selected *Freeze*.

The cost of Freeze increases by ***3n****. You have learned up to the 5th rank of this enchantment. Maximizing this enchantment will require 33 enchantment slots. Final Yield from maximizing* **Freeze** *would be 8-9 cold damage (base 5 + 48% for enchanting skill + 5% for Increase Enchantment Strength I + 20% for Increase Weapon Enchant Strength I). 5% chance to unleash the secondary enchantment, Freeze. Do you wish to power this enchantment? Yes or No?*

Hmmm, Richter thought. So even though *Increased Damage* had a larger base cost, *Freeze* ultimately cost more because of the ranks. *Freeze* also had the flaw of relying on enchantment charges. If the weapon was used enough, the magic would be exhausted and it would just become another sword or mace. When that happened, the only choices were to wait days or weeks for the charge to build back up or use soul stones to replenish it. The second option could only be performed by someone with the Enchanting skill. Also, from what he was reading, it wasn't even a sure thing that an enemy would be frozen if the secondary enchantment were triggered. Despite all that though, there was no doubt in Richter's mind that *Freeze* was the stronger choice. He selected 'Yes'.

33 Soul Stone Points *are required to make the maximum enchantment. To finalize, expend the appropriate souls.*

At his journeyman rank in Enchanting, Richter could use two soul stones on one enchantment. *Basic* souls gave a max of six soul points and *common* souls a max of ten. The problem wasn't just that he didn't have an unlimited supply of either, but also that common souls only came from monsters. They were much harder to acquire than the basic souls that could be captured from animals. The two hunters he had kindled Life magic in had shown that they could bring in a small but steady supply of *basic* and *weak* souls, but it wasn't enough to enchant truly powerful items. Should he waste a *common* soul on some random, high steel axe?

Richter could almost hear the seconds ticking by on his seven-minute time limit to finish the enchantment. He quickly checked how many soul stones he had available and ranked them by the soul they contained. Four *poor*, eight *weak*, eleven *basic*, thirty *common*, seven *luminous*, three *brilliant*, three *special* and one *resplendent*. Sighing, he came to two decisions. One, he would just try to level his Profession and not to expend any of his more valuable souls. Two, he was going to expend his remaining talent points.

He bought *Increase Maximum Number of Soul Stones I,* which allowed him to use three stones per enchantment. It unfortunately brought his available talent points down to six. The Talent increased to level two and showed that another twenty points would be required to upgrade it again.

You have purchased the Talent: ***Increase Maximum Number of Soul Stones I****.*

You have: ***6 Talent Points*** *remaining.*

Knowing he didn't have much time left, Richter arrayed three stones on the anvil. The three *basic* souls brought the total number of soul points he could access up to 18. It was enough for him to enchant up to the fifth rank. He didn't see any reason to max out the enchantment and waste valuable monster souls on a random axehead. Richter focused and finished the enchantment. All three stones fell to dust and small swirls of rainbow light flowed into the axe. A faint pressure built in the air around Richter and the axe started to vibrate. Krom's eyes widened in alarm, but the motion subsided quickly. The pressure disappeared and an aura the pure blue of a glacier surrounded the axe blade for just a moment, before disappearing. Looking closely, Richter could still see a faint blue sheen on the metal. The weapon was enchanted!

You have enchanted: ***High Steel Axehead of Freezing****. Damage 16-24. Durability 50/50. Item Class: Uncommon. Quality: Exceptional. Weight: 3.1 kg. Traits: +8 cold damage per attack. 5% chance to cause Freeze for 5 seconds. +10% damage vs. spell barriers.*

Krom raised his eyebrows, "Ay was na expecting something so grand, yer lordship. That be a fine bit o'enchanting."

Richter gave a satisfied nod, "Let's keep going." Krom dunked the axe head to remove any further heat and handed it to one of the other smiths for binding and affixing to a haft, then got back to work.

As his stores of weaker captured souls was limited, Richter started only using one soul stone per enchantment. Futen was sent off to find the hunters and see if they had any more animal souls to contribute and also with a special message for Sion. Luckily, the hunter Life mages had managed to capture another sixty souls. A few of the soul levels were basic, but most were either weak or poor. The level didn't matter so much to the chaos seed as the quantity though. He needed to practice his Profession.

Richter quickly paid the hunters the bonus he had agreed to give them and got back to work. Despite the fact that his enchantments failed twice, in a relatively small amount of time, he finished his quest, Practice Makes Perfect I. He greatly welcomed the five talent points, but seeing the experience penalty he now had to deal with was a bit disconcerting.

You have: ***11 Talent Points*** *remaining.*

The quest gave a base experience boost of one hundred, but with his penalty of experience being 100% harder to obtain, it meant he needed to get twice as much experience as he would otherwise. This decreased the earned experience to fifty. Luckily, his Potion of Clarity still worked and the final experience he earned was sixty-three. He didn't let it distract him long though, especially since finishing the quest had unlocked the next quest in the chain.

You have unlocked the Profession Quest: **Practice Makes Perfect II**
Nothing great was ever achieved without enthusiasm. Practice your new Profession and honor who you are Enchanter.
Success Conditions: Enchant 50 items
Reward: 10 Talent Points
Penalty for failure or refusal of Quest: None
Do you accept? Yes or No

Richter took the quest almost as a personal challenge. He got back to enchanting with a vengeance. At his direction, Krom and one of the other smiths started working on round, metal shields for the guards and each finished project gained +1 or +2 defense depending on what stone he used. The third started churning out daggers for Richter to enchant. The chaos seed teased the smiths, asking if the dwarves could work faster or were they going to come up short? That earned more than a few choice words from the bearded smiths, but they started swinging their hammers with renewed vigor and with smiles in their beards.

The change in production wasn't just to give them something else to work on, but also because Richter had an idea of how to make his guards more effective. During the recent fights with the war party, Richter had noticed that his band had assumed a wedge formation to better play to their strengths. It made him realize that he was missing a possible game-changing strategy: military formations. Now he was no historian, but he *had* seen 300 and thought he got the basic idea. His guards and future soldiers needed to fight as a unit, each man protecting the one beside him. Richter didn't know if he could actually get this to work, but decided to try anyway. Worst case scenario, his guards would have strong shields.

While Richter helped the smiths with enchantments, he kept funneling his MPs into paying the mana cost for his *Weak Sonic Wail* enchantment. The increase to his Wisdom had greatly improved his mana regeneration, to the point that he was regenerating four and a half points every ten seconds, and with his Ring of Flowing Thought, that improved to five point four every ten seconds. It took a little over an hour and ten minutes for him to pay the remaining twenty-two hundred. He was rewarded with a prompt:.

Congratulations! You have learned the enchantment: ***Sonic Damage, Rank I, Level I.***

You have unlocked the enchantment: ***Sonic Damage, Level II.*** *You are currently at 0/270,000 for the mana cost to learn this enchantment.*

That little part of his mind that held his available enchantments lit up further with a small green ball of light. Focusing on the enchantment he found that it added direct sonic damage just as the *Freeze* enchantment did, but it also had a secondary effect called "reverberation". The effect gave a chance to knock something out of an opponent's hand.

The fact that he could level the enchantment was something he didn't expect. The fact that the next level cost one hundred times as much was something he could do without, but he wasn't complaining. Richter did a quick calculation and realized that even with his increased Wisdom, it would take him nearly one hundred and forty hours of uninterrupted mana allocation to unlock the next level of the enchantment. If only he could channel his mana without actively thinking about it, he lamented, looking around at the smithy.

Then he paused. Why couldn't he do that? Using his mana was a mental exercise akin to moving his arm. He didn't think about channeling electroneural energy to stimulate a series of muscles to work together in just the right way to pick up a cup. He just willed it, and the rest happened on a subconscious level. Maybe he just needed to flex a new mental "muscle." Richter closed his eyes focused on his mana pool. He willed it to go into the mana cost and his MPs dropped while the cost was paid. He stopped actively willing it, and the flow stopped. So the question was, how to will his mana to flow without having to consciously will it. It sounded like a bad SAT problem.

Not willing to give up, Richter cleared his mind and thought about it. What he was really trying to do was to make the mana flow not just in the current moment, but also in the future. That was when it came to him. It wasn't the flow of his existing mana pool he needed to direct. It was the flow of his mana regeneration. No sooner did he have that thought than a prompt appeared.

*Currently you are allocating **0%** of your mana regeneration to purchasing Sonic Damage, Level II? Do you wish to increase this? Current mana pool regen rate is 5.4 mana:10 seconds. Yes or No?*

Smiling, Richter chose 'Yes' and willed the percentage to increase to 10%.

*Currently you are allocating **10%** of your mana regeneration to purchasing* **Sonic Damage, Level II**. *Current mana pool regen rate is 4.86 mana:10 seconds.*

Richter decided to try one more thing. A bit of mental flexing later and he got what he needed. He let out a satisfied "ahhh" of satisfaction while he read the prompt.

*Currently you are allocating **10%** of your mana regeneration up to 500 mana points to purchasing* **Sonic Damage, Level II**. *Current mana pool regen rate is 4.85 mana:10 seconds if your mana pool contains between 0-500 mana points. Currently you are allocating 100% of your mana regeneration above 500 mana points to purchasing* **Sonic Damage, Level II**.

His mana wouldn't go to waste again, Richter thought with satisfaction.

After he was done playing with his new capabilities, he was eager to test out his new enchantment. There was something else to be done first though. He had only been able to enchant eleven more objects since he got his new quest. If he was going to make his new project as awesome as he wanted it to be though, he needed the ten talent points finishing it would bring. The problem was the smiths could only make items so quickly. "Can't you go any faster, Krom?" Richter complained.

The dwarf slammed his hammer down on the anvil and affixed Richter with a fierce glare, "Ay'll not go about sacrificing the quality of me work just because ye want to play with yer new Profession. If ye be so eager to enchant things, just enchant the daggers and spears we already done made." Krom turned his attention back to his work, shutting Richter out of his mind.

Richter was going to protest that he couldn't just enchant weapons that had already been made, but then he realized that was no longer true. He knew an enchantment now. Also, since he had advanced to initiate rank in his Enchanting skill, he did indeed have the ability to enchant already completed objects, albeit with a heavy penalty to the enchantment's final effectiveness. He rushed almost gleefully back to the rack of finished spears, arrows, maces and swords. Digging his hand in the canvas sack that held the low level soul gems he was using, he got to work.

Ultimately, Richter had to use almost every one of the basic, weak and poor level soul stones he had. Enchanting already completed items increased the fail rate of his enchantments precipitously, but he still completed the quest. His pool of talent points increased by ten, and his experience got a small bump, again with a penalty. It didn't bother him though because he happily purchased his next talent, Increase Soul Stone Yield I, leaving him with eleven points in reserve. Each soul stone would now give 25% more soul points before disappearing. He also dismissed the prompt that described the next link in the quest chain.

You have unlocked the Profession Quest: **Practice Makes Perfect III**
It seems you are destined to walk the path of the Enchanter. Continue on your journey!
Success Conditions: Enchant 500 items
Reward: 20 Talent Points
Penalty for failure or refusal of Quest: None
Do you accept? Yes or No

Now that he had obtained his new talent, Richter told Krom that soon they needed to make another short sword. This had been his goal all day. He hadn't forgotten the perk from leveling up his Small Blades skill that made dual wielding more manageable. Sion had already come by with what Richter had requested. The sprite also thankfully had the Quicksilver Collar of Submission. Richter had felt a moment of panic when he saw that it wasn't in his bag upon waking, but luckily his bud had come through. Sion walked off saying he had some hunting to do, but that he'd see Richter later. Richter placed both items in his bag. Then he walked over to the chest and removed an ingot of elementum.

Bringing it back to the main anvil, Krom raised one eyebrow when he saw it, "Are ye sure, yer lordship? If we use this ingot, only eight will be left."

The dwarf had a point, but the green metal was a tool to be used, not a treasure to be hidden away. Richter told him he was sure, so Krom took the ingot and called out to the other dwarves that the fire in the furnace needed to be hotter. A dark-colored wood was brought over and fed into the flames. As soon as it started burning, the heat coming out of the furnace increased dramatically. The dwarves stoked the flames for several minutes until Richter's face felt like it was burning, and still they didn't stop. By the time Krom seemed satisfied and placed the ingot in the furnace, Richter was sure he could smell his hair smouldering.

Soon, the metal was glowing red and Krom brought it back out. The clanging of the hammer on metal filled the Forge. Another dwarf continually worked the bellows to keep the fire hot. When Krom had been working with high steel, he had been able to keep it out of the furnace for long minutes, but with the elementum it seemed that Krom had to continually reheat it. He also swung the hammer harder than before, seeming to struggle with shaping the powerful metal.

Clang, clang, cling. Clang, clang, cling. Richter listened to the dwarf shape the metal and marveled at his tireless strength. Sweat poured from Krom's face, his visage a study in concentration. An hour passed, then another. Even Krom's endurance began to flag and the dwarf left the nearly-formed blade in the furnace while he grabbed a green stamina potion. While the smith drank the brew, Richter used *Analyze*, curious as to how far Krom's stamina had dropped.

Name: Krom	**Age:** 47	**Disposition:** Loyal
Level: 9, 2%	**Race:** Mountain Dwarf	
STATS		
Health: 190	**Mana:** 130	**Stamina:** 15/220
ATTRIBUTES		
Strength: 28	**Agility:** 14	**Dexterity:** 13

Constitution: 19	**Endurance:** 22	**Intelligence:** 13
Wisdom: 12	**Charisma:** 10	**Luck:** 10
DESCRIPTION		
Mountain dwarves are a hardy folk that have keen eyesight that gives them excellent night vision. Natural miners, it is said mountain dwarves can "smell" veins of precious metals. Increased resistance to negative physical effects. Mountain Dwarves get three points to distribute per level, and each level gives **+1 to Constitution** and **+1 to Endurance**.		

"Krom! You're only one level shy of your Profession," Richter exclaimed.

"Oh, aye, yer lordship," Krom said with a smile. "Taking out that big beastie put me over the top."

"We need to keep hunting," Richter said seriously. "I need you to get your Profession."

"That thought occurred to me as well, yer lordship," Krom replied with a laugh.

"Tomorrow morning then," Richter said. "Besides, we're only one fight away from finishing our challenge."

"Ay'll be ready, yer lordship," Krom said. Then he reached into the furnace with the tongs and took the elementum out. He placed it on the anvil and started raining blows upon the glowing metal again. Richter walked around the Forge and enchanted the other projects as the opportunity presented itself, using the last of his low level stones. He checked on Krom periodically, but the dwarf kept shaping and heating the green metal with single-minded intensity. Soot covered his body, and muscles stood out like braided cables on his arms. More time passed.

Krom kept at it and it wasn't until about three p.m. when he called Richter over. The smith had made a mirror image of Richter's already-existing short sword. The blade was two feet long and double-edged. The quality was *superb*. The dwarf finished swinging the hammer and was about to speak, but then a green light flared from the heart of the anvil. Krom's ash covered face broke into a wide grin, and he said, "Yer in luck."

A green light shot out of the anvil and enveloped the weapon. It was so bright that Richter had to close his eyes against the glare, but thankfully, it disappeared a few moments later. When he opened his eyes again, the blade looked the same, but Richter saw that the quality was now *exquisite*. Krom laughed and reached into the pouch at his waist to grab some powdered crystal. He was about to sprinkle the crystalline dust onto the blade when Richter told him to stop. The dwarf looked up, confused, but still stepped back. Smiling, Richter opened the bag that Sion had brought to the forge and examined the contents.

You have found: **Concentrated Powdered Crystal**	**Resource Class:** Scarce **Durability:** 5/5 **Weight:** 0.1 kg. **Traits:** This has been the created by grinding down the remnants of a Crystal Guardian's body. The magical properties of this concentrated crystal are significantly more powerful than normal crystal. Any potions or items created may gain extra potency or powers.

Sion had told him that he needed to use half of the contents of the bag, about a handful. The sprite had also warned that there was only enough concentrated crystal to make another ten handfuls. Hoping for something spectacular, he sprinkled the sparkling dust onto the blade.

You have found: **Elementum Short Sword Blade**	**Damage:** 33-37 **Durability:** 162/162 **Item Class:** Scarce **Quality:** Exquisite **Weight:** 1.9 kg **Traits:** +10% damage vs. spell barriers

This weapon has 54 enchantment slots (base 30 for weapon quality + 15 for journeyman Enchanting skill rank + 20% for Increase Enchantment Potential I). Available enchantments: ***Freeze*** *(rank V),* ***Increased Damage +1*** *(static),* ***Increased Durability*** *(rank I), and* ***Sonic Damage*** *(rank I). You have seven minutes from the time that this prompt appeared to finish your enchantment.*

Know This! Your use of concentrated crystal has increased the power of your final enchantment and all additional effects by 237%. Furthermore, using concentrated crystal temporarily boosts all known enchantments to the highest ranked enchantment you know (barring static enchantments). All enchantments now rank V.

Richter's mouth dropped open. He had no idea why the bonus was 237% and not like, 238% or 216%, but he sure as shit wasn't complaining. Even better, every single one of his enchantments was now rank V. That meant he could use his new toy! Richter grinned in excitement. Choosing *Sonic Damage,* he saw that the enchantment cost was 3n just like *Freeze.*

The cost of Sonic Damage increases by ***3n****. You have learned up to the 5th rank of this enchantment. Maximizing this enchantment will require 33 enchantment slots. Final Yield from maximizing Sonic Damage would be 20 sonic damage (base 5 + 48% for enchanting skill + 5% for Increase Enchantment Strength I + 10% for Increase Weapon Enchant Strength I + 237% for Concentrated Powdered Crystal). 17% chance to unleash the secondary enchantment, Disarm.*

Do you wish to power this enchantment? Yes or No?

Richter took out three soul stones that contained *common* souls. Using so many valuable stones made him feel like he was shitting a pine cone, but he knew he needed a powerful weapon. The rock giant had proven that.

All three stones held their maximum capacity of Soul Points, each containing ten. With the 25% increase in soul stone yield, his most recently acquired Talent, it gave him just enough points to max out the sword's enchantment. Wasting no more time, he selected 'Yes' on the prompt and expended the stones. The glowing amber jewels fell to dust and rainbow light poured into the elementum blade. There was a building pressure in the air as the soul power entered the weapon. Then the tightness in the air bled away… and nothing happened.

Not believing what he was seeing, Richter stared at the blade in shock. Had he just fucked his whole thing up? Wasted a precious handful of concentrated crystal, one of his few ingots of elementum and three valuable monster souls just to have a plain and unenchanted sword? "Fuuucckkk!" he shouted.

Everyone in the smithy stared at him in shock. Alma had been sleeping on a nearby weapon's rack, but she shot into the air and screamed a battlecry at hearing her master's frustration. Krom looked at him in shocked concern and said, "What? What happened, yer lordship?"

"The enchantment didn't take. I don't know how this shit works! We wasted all of this time and so many resources!"

Krom looked at him in alarm and concern, and quickly asked, "Ye don't have any more soul stones?"

"Of course, I do," Richter spat. Why was the dwarf asking him stupid questions?

Krom's eyes looked to the left and right while his mouth bunched behind his beard, "Thennnn why na just try again?"

Richter blinked, then blinked again, "I can do that?" When his enchantments had failed before, he had just waited until there was something new for him to enchant.

Everyone in the Forge was just kind of quiet because no one wanted to call their lord a dumbass. One being didn't mind though, *Gyoti! You made me upset for nothing.*

Nobody asked you, Richter thought at his familiar irritably. He quickly pulled out another three glowing, amber jewels out of his bag. Each had that strange electric feel that the soul stones adopted when they contained a soul. The combination was three more common level stones.

Having to use more of his meager soul stone stock was even more painful than the last time. In fact, this time Richter felt like he was shitting an even bigger pine cone… that had the spiky parts pointing down. Nonetheless, he accessed the power in the stones. He held his breath while the stones crumbled to dust. Rainbow swirls of light flowed into the blade just like the last time, and the pressure built in the air again. It felt like when he had gone scuba diving on Earth. The sensation continued to build and Richter could feel the magic starting to swell out of control. His heart beat harder in his chest, *thud-thud thud-thud*, and the chaos seed wondered if he had bitten off more than he could chew. Then, with what Richter could only describe as a *pop*, the soul power overcame the metal's resistance to be enchanted and the weapon glowed green. It was enchanted!

He quickly checked the stats of his new weapon.

You have found: **Elementum Short Sword Blade**	**Damage:** 33-37 **Durability:** 162/162 **Item Class:** Scarce **Quality:** Exquisite **Weight:** 1.9 kg **Traits:** 20 points of sonic damage per attack 17% chance to trigger secondary effect, Disarm. +10% damage vs. spell barriers **Charges:** 350/350.

Krom looked at the weapon's stats at the same time and said, "Fuuuccckkkk!"

CHAPTER 7 -- DAY 111 -- KUBORN 1, 15368 EBG

Richter wasn't done yet though. He still needed to use one of his other talents. Focusing his will, another prompt appeared.

It appears you wish to Soul Bind an item. For a level one soul bond, you must spend soul points equal to the maximum base enchantment potential of the item's quality. This will impose serious penalties on anyone other than yourself who tries to use this item. No one besides you will have access to the item's magical properties at all. If separated from you, you will have a strong sense of which direction it is in. To soul bind **Sonic Elementum Short Sword,** *you must spend thirty Soul Points. Do you wish to do so? Yes or No?*

Richter closed his eyes. He was almost sure that the last two pinecones had mated and left a spiky mutant pinecone baby inside of him that was now slowly crawling its way out. At least this time, he didn't have to use one of his few *luminous* level soul stones. He pulled out a basic stone and two common stones and paid the price. A clear gem appeared next to the sword. Richter picked it up and answered 'Yes' on the resulting prompt. A final prompt appeared.

You have Soul Bound: **Sonic Elementum Short Sword.** *This can only be transferred with an open heart.*

Richter looked at the item's prompt again and saw that it now included the blade's soul bound status. He breathed out, slightly exhausted, even though he hadn't expended any physical energy. The chaos seed stopped and reflected on everything that had gone into making this two-foot blade. It had required a precious metal, the powdered body of a magical monster, smithing skills that had taken decades to hone, enchanting skills and soul stones. Just the soul stones meant that there needed to be someone to create the empty stones, someone else to cast *Soul Trap* and then someone to kill a nearby monster or beast. The special properties of the blade would not have been possible without a magic core to make the Forge of Heavens, not to mention his Profession. He didn't even want to think about the month of torture that he had undergone to earn his title of Enchanter. Richter shook his head. Thinking about how much was needed to make this seemingly innocuous piece of metal, he now fully understood why enchanted items sold for the equivalent of tens or hundreds of thousands of US dollars. He realized that he wasn't looking at just a forge-heated blade. He was looking at a piece of art that had taken many skilled people to create. This blade might truly be worth a noble's ransom.

The other smiths came over to gawk at the heavily enchanted weapon. He understood their fascination, and, for the first time, Richter really saw the beginnings of potential for his Profession. He had to get more talent points. Krom took the blade and doused it in a nearby barrel of water. When he spoke, there was more than just a touch of respect in his voice. "Ay will have this mounted and bound immediately, milord. Ay had no idea ye could do something like this. It just goes to show the power of Elementum."

"I didn't know I could do that either. What do you mean about the elementum, though? The metal didn't make the enchantment any stronger." Richter said. As far as he knew, the metal he used didn't affect enchanting at all.

Krom looked at him like he was a bit crazy, "This here fancy green metal be the only reason the blade did na explode. If ye tried to pump tha much power into a steel blade, we would be digging shards of metal out of our teeth and arses! Ay still did na think this blade could take such magic, but who knows? Maybe the fey metal could take even more. Ay do know one thing, yer lordship. Ye made a one hell of a blade." The smith grinned and clapped his lord on the back.

Richter smiled back, "Haha. Thanks man." He couldn't quite believe it himself. Hearing that certain metals could only hold certain amounts of enchantment energy *after* he had invested several souls worth wasn't the best way to get the news, but it had worked out. The chaos seed knew that he would be a bit more careful in the future though. The pressure and the 'out of control' sensations he had felt when enchanting the blade made more sense now. Immortal or not, the idea of picking shrapnel out of his body did not sound like a good time. He put it out of his mind as something to worry about later. Now that his blade had been created, he realized there was another pressing issue. He still hadn't eaten, "I'm going to get some lunch and check on the members of our war party that are still being held hostage by Sumiko."

Krom chuckled, "Tell the wee lady tha big Krom says hello."

Richter looked at him and chuckled back, "Yeah. I'm not going to be doing that."

Krom just kept making eye contact with a maniacal grin on his face until Richter grew creeped out enough to leave the forge. While leaving, he sent out a mental call to the adder. Alma flew down and rested on his shoulders while he walked, and Futen floated along beside him. Richter had the remnant guide him towards Sumiko's makeshift infirmary. Before long, he stood in front of a large tent. It was made of a patchwork of beige and white swatches of canvas. Sewn on the front was the golden glyph of a circle with an opening at the top, like a cup that was to be filled. Richter's Gift of Tongues ability identified it as part of an old pictographic language. The glyph was an ancient symbol for Life.

A woman came out wearing light tan clothing and carrying a load of dirty rags. She smiled at Richter, giving a warm "Greetings, my lord," before continuing on about her business. Richter smiled back. It pleased him immensely to see his people happily at work. He walked inside the tent and was instantly impressed. Despite Sumiko's complaints about not having a proper place to work, what he saw was a study in efficiency.

The grass was cut low, and a small brazier in the center of the tent made it pleasantly warm, but not oppressively hot. It also filled the air with a pleasantly soothing scent. A row of cots lined one wall, and the other side of the tent had tables laden with bandages, red vials of what looked like healing potions, and numerous dried herbs. Sumiko was standing over a cot and was speaking to a group of villagers dressed in the same tan clothing the woman carrying the rags had been wearing. He couldn't see the patient initially, but when Richter walked closer, he saw a very unhappy Caulder laying while Sumiko described his condition.

"This particular guard decided to attack a monster made of solid rock that was twenty feet tall. Can anyone tell me what is wrong with this patient? Besides the fact that he also has rocks in his head?"

Many of the villagers raised their hands. Sumiko pointed at one and the man spoke up, "He broke his right clavicle and dislocated the same shoulder when the giant kicked the shield he was holding."

"Correct. Now it was a simple matter for me to diagnose that with a spell and mend the bone with another, but what would we do to figure that out and fix it if we could not use magic?"

Again a forest of hands shot up. Sumiko chose a woman, who answered, "Physical inspection followed by manual investigation of the bone. If we found it was broken, we could align the bones and then immobilize that arm to help it heal."

"Anything else?" Sumiko asked.

This time, there was no rush to answer. After a few moments, though, another villager, a teenage girl, raised her hand. When she was called on, she spoke in a hesitant voice, "We could use sirana extract to reduce any swelling and crushed ulin leaf to help the bone mend."

"Good," Sumiko said, clearly pleased. "A tea brewed from krim berries will also serve to preserve the strength of muscles while the bone heals." Her gaze scanned the tan-clad villagers, and when she spoke again, it was with the firm tone of a head mistress, "Remember this. Whether you have healing magic or not, if you are under my command you *will* learn to be a healer. Each of you will inspect the sergeant's arm and clavicle, one at a time. Pay special attention to the musculature of the arm. Though the injury has been healed, you should be able to detect a difference in the elasticity of the muscles when you compare the right to the left."

"Now wait just a minute," Caulder protested. "I did not agree to be poked and prodded by your band of junior leeches!"

Speaking sweetly, Sumiko leaned over the guard and said, "Do we really need to have another talk about the penalties of not being a good patient?" Despite her tone, there was just the slightest bit of ominous emphasis on the word 'talk.'

The sergeant's eyes widened slightly, "Ahhh, no. I don't think that is necessary, Lady Sumiko."

"I am pleased to hear that," she said in the same sweet tone. "I will try to forget that you called my healers 'leeches', Sergeant Caulder."

"Ahhh, thank you, Lady Sumiko. Much obliged," he said, chastened.

Richter observed the scene with no small amount of amusement. He cleared his throat and said, "How is the patient doing?"

Everyone turned to see the lord of the Mist Village standing in the tent. Each of the villagers bowed slightly and placed their hands on their hearts. Sumiko was apparently not as impressed by his august presence and just snorted, "I let the rest of your war party go an hour ago. This one had to have several bones reconstructed though and so I have been watching him a bit longer. I hope you are not here with some foolish request to get him back on duty now!" A bit of heat made it into her voice at the end.

Caulder grasped at the chance to be released from the tent like a drowning man reaching for a life preserver. Already starting to stand, he said, "My lord. I am ready to face any danger that you need. I am your man, and all you need to do is say the word. I am ready to fight by your side." His eyes locked onto Richter's, pleading for all they were worth.

Richter stroked his chin and cocked his head as if pondering a great decision. He slowly said, "You know, I appreciate that Caulder, but I just wouldn't be able to sleep tonight if you came to harm because you left this tent too early." The sergeant quickly opened his mouth to object, but Richter held up a hand, "No, no. Your health is paramount. In fact, Lady Sumiko, I charge you to hold onto this man until he is completely healthy. I mean, you hold onto him if he has so much as an upset tummy. No matter how many days it takes or how many tests you have to do!"

Caulder looked at him in shock and dismay, not believing that his lord would betray him in this most dastardly of ways. Richter looked back and said, "Do you remember when we first met in Leaf's Crossing, sergeant? Do you remember that you tricked me into paying a gold coin to that government worker, Edwin?" Caulder blinked in disbelief that such an event could be coming back to haunt him. Richter plastered a wide grin on his face and winked at the man, "Rest assured, I do, and I'd say we're even."

He turned around and started walking out of the tent. Before he left, he heard Sumiko's whip-like voice ordering her healers to form a line and begin examining Caulder. The man shouted after him, promising that he would pay the gold back. Then he began cursing the first 'heavy-handed troll spawn' that started examining him. As the lord of the Mist Village emerged from the tent and stood in the sunshine, he looked up at the cornflower blue sky with its white, fluffy clouds. Richter let loose an immensely satisfied sigh and couldn't fight the feeling that all was well with the world.

CHAPTER 8 -- DAY 111 -- KUBORN 1, 15368 EBG

Happy to hear that the other members of the war party were either on their feet or about to be, Richter walked with a light-hearted step towards the feast area. Foregoing the high table, he grabbed a wooden plate and heaped some food upon it. Then he sat with his people. Before long, they were all laughing and sharing the details of their lives with him. One man pointed at his daughter and proudly said she was learning to weave. Another woman pointed to her son and told Richter how the boy's Herb Lore skill was increasing as he helped the gardeners each day. In a world where the best most families could hope for was mindless toil and a daily struggle to feed their families, the parents were overjoyed that their children were learning skills that could prepare them for the future.

More and more people came up to his table and told him similar stories. It was revitalizing. All Richter had been worrying about lately was the upcoming battle with the bugbears, the threat of the eaters, and keeping the lands around the village free of monsters and dangerous predators. While he was focusing on the "big" picture, apparently, right under his nose, the miracle that was normal life had continued. His people had been living, laughing and loving each other. It reminded him of what he was fighting for and energized him for the battles to come.

He tried to get face time with as many of his people as he could. He was even able to meet the two scribes that had been hired. They assured him that they would have two higher quality blank books ready within the next few days. Nodding to them, he moved on. Before long, he ran into Gloran. Since obtaining his Profession Richter had been wanting to see the elf enchanter.

"Greetings, my Lord Enchanter," Gloran said with a bow. When he straightened, Richter could see that he was smiling.

"I'm glad I ran into you, Gloran," Richter said smiling back. "I need you to prepare yourself. We need to increase your level. I have already been able to do amazing things as a Professed Enchanter. I won't be able to see to the village's needs by myself, though. We need to equip our people as best we can. We also need to have more to trade. What I'm saying is, I need you to start going out with the hunting squads. I need you to gain experience, and then you are going for your trial."

Gloran paled somewhat, "I have never been much with a blade, my lord."

Richter nodded, "I am not asking you to attack gnolls and goblins. You will be a member of my war party and protected as much as possible. I love that everyone is happy, but we cannot allow this," he said indicating the smiling people around them, "to distract us from the fight that is coming. The mists are not infallible and we need to grow stronger."

Gloran nodded, but still didn't seem convinced.

"The guards will protect you and I will try to bring you out with my group, but I need this to happen." Richter made his voice firm, "Your lord needs this to happen."

Gloran's face lost some of its hesitancy. He placed a fist to his heart and bowed slightly, "Yes, my lord. As you say."

"Good," Richter said. He clapped the man on the back and told him to see Krom later to be outfitted for armor and a crossbow. The enchanter walked off, clearly deep in thought. Richter considered calling after him, but whatever he said would just have been empty words. He didn't like ordering Gloran into harm's way, but he knew he would do it again. The truth was that his people needed to be stronger. Richter knew he couldn't protect every one of them. They needed to learn to protect themselves. If all he had to deal with was a bit of hesitancy, he would count himself lucky, but he didn't think he would be that fortunate. He moved on.

Except for Caulder, each of the other members of the war party found him during lunch and said they were ready to fight. Richter told each to be at the gate at sunrise. He was more than pleased that Beyan had reached level ten.

"So you're ready for a Profession?" Richter asked with a smile.

Beyan nodded happily, "The only reason I have not gone for my trial yet is because of the quest you gave me. As nice as her butt is, I do *not* want to work for that angry, wood elf amazon."

Richter chuckled. He actually thought Tabia was a nice woman. Beyan's dislike most likely came from the fact that Tabia's wife had decked the gnome after he got a little too 'familiar.' As far as Richter was concerned, he wasn't sure if Beyan or Tabia would be a better choice. He actually would love for Beyan to continue his magical studies and become a Professed Mage, but a great first step would be for him to become a Professed Alchemist. At the very least, he would get talent points until he reached level twenty.

Richter said goodbye to the gnome as Sion walked up. "I have something you need to see," the sprite said.

Richter looked around. Most of the people were leaving the feast area now and getting back to work. He nodded to his friend and they started walking towards the meadow north of the village. The two men chatted about this and that as they walked. Richter tried to get Sion to share what he had found, but the sprite just kept saying that he needed to see it for himself. They climbed up the hill to the meadow and Richter took a moment to marvel at how much had changed since he had first come here.

Directly in front of him was a large patch of tilled earth. Herbs of various colors and sizes grew under the careful ministrations of Isabella and her gardeners. Immediately to the west of it was one of Richter's Core buildings, the Dragon's Cauldron. The edifice was a thing of beauty. Created entirely from the incredibly hard substance called 'glass,' the building refracted the sunlight and made rainbows appear on every nearby surface.

The Cauldron was enough to awe any who saw it, but on the northern aspect of the meadow was a true miracle. The snow white leaves of the Quickening shifted gently in the light wind. The celestial tree served to enrich Richter's lands and, perhaps even more importantly, was serving as a cradle for the rebirth of the pixie race. The wonders did not stop there. The far western end of the meadow was dominated by a lake. A waterfall fed it from the cliffs lining the northern side of the glade. Richter, or more specifically Sion, had been able to find a hidden cave behind the waterfall and that had become the location of his new crystal garden. Finally, there was also a small, but precious, clutch of skath eggs he had gained after a life and death battle. The creatures might one day be the key to the village having trained monsters, or even a calvary. Richter smiled. Exciting things were afoot.

"Where are we going?" he asked Sion.

"To the crystal garden. The mist workers have cleared out the crystal that was overgrowing the passage. I went inside this morning. There are some things you need to see."

Richter nodded, "Let's stop at the Cauldron and the lake on the way then."

They walked by the garden, nodding to the workers and Isabella as they passed by. As soon as they entered the Cauldron, Richter saw Tabia hard at work. The beautiful, dark-skinned wood elf stood at a crystal table, slowly adding a purple liquid to a bottle of clear liquid. It was clear that she was focusing hard, so the two Companion's didn't disturb her. When she finished what she was doing, the elf audibly exhaled in relief and placed both vials in holders on the table. Richter decided he might not want to know exactly what she had been mixing.

"Tabia," he said.

She looked over her shoulder in surprise. When she saw who had spoken, she turned quickly, her dreaded hair swinging heavily behind her. She placed her hand on her heart and bowed slightly. "I did not see you, Lord Richter. It is a pleasant surprise."

"Hard at work?" he asked lightly.

"I will be ready with a magnificent potion before the end of the week," she replied with absolute seriousness.

"I'm glad to hear it," he said. "Keep doing whatever you are doing. Right now, I need to use the central cauldron." She nodded and got back to her work.

Richter walked up to the clear cauldron that sat in the middle of the building. He could see glass vessels tracing through the large pot. He could feel the low and slow thrum of the Dragon Cauldron's heart as it pushed glass blood through the building. Looking at his Companion, Richter said, "It's time to feed the beast."

Sion rolled his eyes, but looked on in interest as Richter reached into his Bag of Holding. The first thing the chaos seed took out was the other half of the bag of concentrated crystal. With two fingers, he took the smallest pinch possible and dropped it into the cauldron. A prompt appeared. As always, the building seemed to sense his intent.

It appears you are trying to use the transmutation properties of the ***Dragon's Cauldron****. In order to do this, a functional unit of a substance must be sacrificed. The amount you have provided is insufficient.*

Richter grunted. He had a feeling that wasn't going to work. Trying not to think about the loss, he emptied the bag into the cauldron.

Do you wish for the Dragon's Cauldron to consume ***Enhanced Powdered Crystal*** *for future production via transmutation? The material will be consumed as the Dragon's Cauldron learns its structure. Yes or No?*

Bye bye you sexy thang, Richter thought to his precious enhanced crystal. He chose "Yes," and the pulse of the vessels lining the central cauldron increased in speed. The crystal began to vibrate as the pulse increased and soon it disappeared.

The Dragon's Cauldron has learned to create ***Enhanced, Powdered Crystal.***

Richter repeated the process with ingots of elementum, cobalt, quicksilver and moonstone. He also tried both the blood from the dark aberration and ichor from the crypt mistress in the cauldron, but as they were specific ingredients rather than resources, they were not candidates for transmutation. Richter just kept placing anything that would work in the cauldron. Regular crystal, wood, marbled quartz, even water. Each vibrated until they were consumed by the cauldron.

As each new substance was consumed, Richter found he could access the conversion rate of one material into another. The conversion rate was unfortunately high in almost every case, and there was a clear loss. It took more than two hundred measures of crystal to make one measure of enhanced crystal, but one measure of enhanced crystal only made twelve measures of regular crystal. That was one of the better conversion rates.

It took more than one hundred thousand ingots of iron to make one ingot of cobalt. The conversion of high steel was slightly better at ninety-three thousand seven hundred and eighty-five to one, but was still obviously more than he could swing. On the other hand, one kilo of iron could be obtained from three kilos of wood. Water could buy basically nothing though, most likely because it was so common in his lands. All it showed was a sideways infinity symbol when compared to other resources. Richter wondered if water might be equally traded for gold if his village had been in a desert.

He was about to leave when he had a final thought. Gritting his teeth again against the cost, he dropped a pearl into the cauldron. Surprisingly, the jewel began to vibrate and it disappeared. Richter hadn't really thought it would work, but he supposed it made sense. In the game, jewels had been part of certain spells and definitely were part of certain items that could be crafted. He thought about it for a second and then painfully placed one type of each jewel in the glass bowl. His stomach actually cramped when he saw the gems disappear. When he was done, he added a single copper, silver and gold coin for good measure. Each of them were accepted by the cauldron.

"I know that had to hurt," Sion said, staring at his friend.

"It really did," Richter replied with a haggard expression.

"Are you ready to leave?"

Richter shook his head, "I have one last thing to try before we leave." When he had seen the chest become part of the Forge of Heavens, it had given him an idea. He walked over to a nearby wall and reached into his bag. As always, the space-folding properties of the Bag amazed him. He kept pulling and was able to remove a five foot tall, copper still, even though on the outside the Bag was no more than a foot deep. Hoping this worked, he placed the still on the ground. He almost cheered when a prompt came up.

Greetings, Master of the ***Dragon's Cauldron.*** *Do you wish to add this copper still to the structure of the Cauldron? This will cost 17 Alteration Points. Currently, there are 100/100 Alteration Points available in your Core building at level one. Yes or No?*

Richter selected 'Yes'. Surprisingly, a prompt appeared telling him to take the still outside. He was confused at having a building give him instructions, but did as he was told. Walking outside, he saw a flat floor of glass grow out from the main building. Four short knobs appeared on the ground. He placed the copper still on the knobs, not surprised that it fit perfectly to keep the still in place. As soon as the copper tube was in place, it began to glow. The entire 10x10 foot glass floor began to vibrate as well, so the Companions stepped off of it.

Glass grew up from the floor and covered the still. The light pulsed brighter and brighter until Richter had to shield his eyes. When the light died down, Richter looked to see what had happened and whistled in appreciation. The original still had more than quadrupled in size. A copper pipe ran off from one side and entered a second enclosed copper tube. That ran into a third copper tube that had a spigot attached. Glass had been used to join different pieces that even at first glance could clearly be taken apart for cleaning.

You have added ***Copper Still*** *to the Dragon's Cauldron. Current Alteration Points available 83/100. Alteration Points will regenerate at 1/day.*

"What is this thing?" Sion asked, kicking the still. The large drum rung like a bell.

"You'll see," Richter said gleefully. Then he spoke English for the first time in what seemed like an age. It felt strange for his mouth to be forming the words, but the occasion called for nothing less then a deep southern drawl, "We goings ta have sum fun!"

He walked up to the second drum and inspected it. The Cauldron had even included a doubler. Richter didn't know if the building had read his mind, or it was connected to some cosmic moonshine/alchemy database, but he wasn't complaining. He looked at Futen and gave specific orders to relay to the village cooks. He wanted his mash to start fermenting immediately. Whistling an off-tune little ditty, he grabbed Sion and the two friends walked away.

CHAPTER 9 -- DAY 111 -- KUBORN 1, 15368 EBG

The Companions walked towards the western side of the meadow. Alma flew above them, gliding on air currents with her wings outstretched while the adder slid along in the grass beside them. The huge snake's camouflage was so good that it was practically invisible, despite the fact that Richter knew it was only five feet away. He looked at it as he walked. Soon, he would have to try and tame it again. He just hoped his training with Alma would help him to keep his head this time.

When they were only a hundred yards away from the lake, Richter heard voices. As they got closer, he was able to see two figures standing knee deep in the water. They were laughing and splashing each other. Both were about five-and-a-half feet tall. One was male, and the other female; the similarities in their appearance made it obvious that they were related. More importantly, both were completely nude. Richter was happy to see that their appearances were not *exactly* the same. In fact, there were some extremely interesting differences. The two friends stopped walking at the edge of the lake bank, two feet above the water level.

They were both human, had fair skin and wild mops of brown hair. Their features were refined, and both of them could only be described as beautiful. When Richter analyzed the woman, he could see why.

Name: Deera	**Age:** 19	**Disposition:** Pleased
Level: 7, 38%		**Race:** Human
STATS		
Health: 120	**Mana:** 100	**Stamina:** 130

ATTRIBUTES		
Strength: 10	**Agility:** 10	**Dexterity:** 11
Constitution: 12	**Endurance:** 13	**Intelligence:** 10
Wisdom: 10	**Charisma:** 36	**Luck:** 10
DESCRIPTION		
Humans are one of the shortest-lived, but most prolific breeders in the Land. Humans have a broader affinity for skills than other races. No special bonuses to race. Humans get **4 points** to distribute per level.		

Deera's status was almost a mirror image of the male, Derin. Both had heavily invested in Charisma. In retrospect, he realized he had seen them both before during the night of the welcome feast for the new villagers, but he had met so many people that it had been a blur. He remembered them now. Seeing them both naked and together had an effect that he hadn't truly appreciated before this particular moment.

"Maybe we should come back later," he said to Sion.

Though he had spoken quietly, the two frolicking teenagers heard him. They both turned unabashedly to address their lord. Richter looked at Sion in confusion as to what was happening, but the sprite was just gazing at the woman with a big smile on his face.

"Greetings, my lord," Derin said with a slight bow, "we have been hoping"

"That you would come to see us soon," Deera finished seamlessly. "There is so much we wish to thank you for. Letting us stay"

"In the village, giving us the opportunity to care for these creatures," Derin picked up the conversation again without pause, "and"

"we truly love the raw beauty of our new home," Deera finished with a smile. They had moved closer while they addressed him. Now one of her arms was draped around Derin's neck and her naked body was molded to his side. "We absolutely must find" "a way to thank you properly, my lord. Day or night," Derin said with small enticing smile.

"we are at your disposal," Deera said with an identical smirk. She detached herself from Derin and walked towards Richter, giving him a clear view of her natural possessions. When she was only a foot away, a delicate hand reached up towards him from where she stood in the lake below.

Richter didn't really realize that he was staring until Sion kicked his foot with a snicker. "Uhhh, yes, well… that's a very nice offer." He reached out and helped her out of the water and up onto the bank. Whether by accident or design, as she stepped up, she tripped slightly, and her entire wet body was pressed against his as he caught her. His shirt moistened, and he could feel her erect nipples through the cloth.

"Oh, my lord is so strong," she murmured as she ran her hand along his bicep.

Again, it took Sion coughing loudly for Richter to come back to himself. He knew he was being managed by the small woman, but he also knew he didn't fucking care. Letting her go, he stepped back. Unfortunately, or again maybe not, he didn't realize that Derin had stepped out of the lake while he held Deera and was standing behind him. This time, it was Richter who almost stumbled, and the beautiful man's arms wrapped around him.

"I would never let you fall, my lord" Derin said softly. The man's mouth was too close to Richter's ear.

Sion was openly laughing now, never one to miss an opportunity to revel in Richter's idiocy or discomfort.

Richter, for his part, quickly extricated himself from the man's embrace and, with a gruff cough, asked, "So you are the two villagers Randolphus charged with caring for the skath eggs?"

Derin walked over to Deera, who interlaced her fingers with his, "Yes, my lord. We have always had a"

"High affinity for the skill Beast Taming," Derin continued. "My sister and I-"

"You two *are* brother and sister?" Richter asked, a touch too loudly. They did look insanely similar, as he had first noted, but their level of closeness and affection had made him think that his initial assessment had to be wrong. Their… bits were touching for Christ's sake.

Deera's laugh was the like the light-hearted trill of a songbird. "We are twins, my lord. We share our connection to animals, our appearance and our love for life. In fact,"

"We share anything and everything you might desire," Derin finished. He also made what was, in Richter's estimation, an uncomfortable amount of eye contact while he said it.

Needing to break the odd tension, Richter punched his cackling Companion rather hard in the chest. As Sion's laughter turned into a wheezing effort to catch his breath, Richter asked the twins to show him the eggs. They smiled and started walking along the edge of the lake bank. Sion stood up straight, a triumphant look still on his red face and followed the twins with Richter.

"Did you know?" Richter asked his friend in an urgent whisper.

"Know what?" Sion asked innocently.

"That Billy Bob and Jessie Rae up there were brother and sister. I mean, what's the deal? This is weird, right? Even for The Land?"

Sion chuckled again, "Do not ask me. I think all of you humans are strange. Though, I may have to find some time to spend with Deera sometime soon." Sion's gaze was more than appreciative as he took in her beautiful, sculpted profile.

"You're more than twice her age," Richter said.

Sion's voice got a touch husky, "And there are some things I plan on teaching her."

Shaking his head, Richter left his randy friend to his dastardly plotting. The twins had stopped walking. Deera smiled and beckoned for him to look over the bank of the lake. As he leaned over, sure enough, he saw the clutch of eggs. A small wooden fence had been erected around the site. He examined one of the eggs.

You have found: **River Skath Egg**	**Item Class:** Common **Durability:** 4/4 **Weight:** 0.5 kg. **Health:** 10/10 **Traits:** Will lose 1 HP per day unless properly cared for. Will hatch in a matter of days.

Each egg he looked at, including the bull skath egg, was in perfect health. As he watched, the twins covered their hands in mud and carefully turned each egg.

"How do you know what to do?" Richter asked. When he had tried to care for the eggs, a prompt had told him he didn't have the requisite skills, despite his ability to tame beasts and monsters. There was no way these two could be Blood magi.

Derin smiled up at him, his teeth perfectly straight and gleaming white, not something that was seen too often in The Land, "My sister and I were both born with the same ability, my lord. It is called Empathic Knowledge. The higher our Charisma, the better we can understand the needs and wants of others. It is our ability that guides us in dealing with beasts."

"or man," Deera finished with a small knowing smile as she looked at the sprite. Sion smiled back broadly while waggling his eyebrows.

Resisting the urge to push his friend in the lake to cool off, Richter asked, "So your care for the eggs is completely based on your ability? This 'Empathic Knowledge'?"

"Oh no, my lord," Deera answered. "We have formal training with animals,"

As well," Derin picked up. "Both my sister and I have reached *apprentice* rank in the skill Animal Husbandry and the subskill."

"Exotic Beasts. Our clients at the brothel enjoyed bringing dangerous animals to bed sometimes," Deera finished offhandedly.

Okay, Richter thought, information overload. He opened his mouth to ask one of a dozen questions but then closed it. What he had here was a pair of beautiful, oversexed twins who were apparently former prostitutes, but could also care for, and hopefully train, a set of deadly monsters to fight on his behalf. He decided not to poke this particular hornet's nest of strangeness at this particular moment, and just take it in stride. Instead, he asked, "Can you teach me your skill?"

Both of the twins smiled broadly and invited him down into the lake with them. Ignoring Sion's grin, Richter removed his shoes and rolled up his pant legs as he stepped down into the cool water and smooth mud. Over the next twenty minutes, the twins described what they termed "the link;" a connection to the life force of the animal. As they spoke, Sion also joined them in the water, gently running his hands over the eggs while the twins spoke softly as to what the small, unborn lives inside were feeling.

Richter listened intently, and then just let himself go, reveling in the moment. He didn't try to force himself to feel the link; he just opened his senses. He experienced the gentle tug of the water on his ankles, smelled the sweet, wet earth around him and basked in the gentle sunlight beaming down, all the while gently stroking the egg in his hand. Without warning, he felt it.

Whereas before he had felt only a smooth shell, now he could sense the life of the almost fully-formed creature inside. The baby skath didn't have any clear thoughts, and the experience was nothing like his mental connection with Alma or even the shale adder. This was more of a feeling or emotional bond. Richter could sense that the baby skath wanted warmth and had started to experience a growing hunger. On a deep level, he understood that it was this hunger that would soon force it to break beyond the boundaries of the only world it had ever known. To fill this need, it would punch through the shell of its egg and feel the cool water and warm sun for the first time. While Richter marveled in this sense of connection, a prompt appeared.

Congratulations! You have learned the subskill: ***Exotic Beasts.*** *You can now raise monsters and strange animals. As this is a subskill of Animal Husbandry, you have learned this skill as well.*

Congratulations! You have learned the skill: ***Animal Husbandry.*** *Under your ministrations, you can now raise animals to be stronger and more plentiful in what they yield. It is now within your power to coax the lives of the beasts around you. While the farmer may cultivate grain and vegetables, you will cultivate the creatures of this world.*

Sion looked at him in surprise, "I just learned a new skill! And a subskill!"

Richter looked at his Companion in shock, "Animal Husbandry and Exotic Beasts?"

"Yes," Sion said. "How did you know? Did you look at my status page?"

"No," Richter shook his head. "It's just that I learned the same skills just now. Does this ever happen? Two people learning such specific skills at once."

"It can," Sion replied doubtfully. "What is strange is that I've never had any skill with animals in the past. All of my people have various connections to the forest, and mine dealt with herbs. I was actually forbidden from working with the animals we kept. One of the elders once said that barring actually eating them alive, I could not have made the animals hate me more."

The two Companions looked at each other, trying to figure out what had just happened until Richter posited, "Maybe this is the skill the Quickening increased."

Sion slowly nodded and said, "Maybe," but his tone remained doubtful.

"Congratulations, Lord Richter," Deera said once the Companions were done speaking. She clapped her hands in delight, "We did not think"

"You would grasp the skill so quickly," Derin continued. "Congratulations to you as well, sir sprite. Is there"

"Anything else you need right now?" Deera asked.

"No, thank you," Richter replied.

"Then we will go swimming," the male twin said. "Of course..."

"You are welcome to join us," Deera finished with a small smile.

Not waiting for a response, the twins swam out into the lake and were soon splashing each other and wrestling in the water.

Richter and Sion watched them for another minute or two. "Nothing weird about that," the chaos seed said.

Sion kept his eyes glued on the sexy, naked twins and said, "I like them!" A grin that large should not have fit on the sprite's face.

Richter kept looking as well, "I like them too. Dibs on the girl."

Sion turned his head and looked at him in surprised outrage. Then the sprite just turned back to watching the twins and said, "Meh."

Richter laughed. "Alright, creepy smurf. What did you want to show me?" he asked, reminding his friend of their initial reason for coming to the meadow.

"What? Oh, right, this way."

The two of them walked north along the lake's edge until they reached the waterfall that fell from the cliffs above. Richter took off his shirt and shoes and placed them in his bag. He knew from experience that no matter how wet the outside of the bag became, the contents would remain nice and dry. Sion led the way across the rocks that stuck up out of the water in front of the waterfall. Each was slippery, but they were able to make it safely to the midway point of the falls without falling. Sion then stepped forward into the torrent of water and entered the cave hidden beyond.

Richter followed a moment later and was immediately drenched. He was through in a moment though and stood in the near-darkness of the hidden cavern. He cast *Simple Light*. A glowing white ball appeared above his head and illuminated the area around him. Pieces of harvested crystal sat on the ground where the mist workers had left them after clearing the tunnel to the crystal garden. Richter spent a few minutes loading all of them into his Bag. The villagers were restricted from coming to this part of the meadow, but it still seemed like a good idea not to leave a valuable resource just lying around.

When he was done, Sion led him to the back of the cavern, to the small tunnel that led up to the crystal garden. The walls of the tunnel still had small amounts of crystal attached which tugged at his clothes, but it wasn't a true impediment. The tunnel narrowed and led upward, ending in a hole in the ceiling. Richter soon emerged from the tunnel and pulled himself up into the larger cave system that held the garden.

When he was finally in the upper cavern, he looked around, but couldn't see much. There were mist lights in the far ends of the cavern, but the illumination was only enough for him to make out vague shapes around him. Also, the glow from his *Simple Light* spell only cast a radiance of about five feet, and it wasn't enough to see the cavernous space he was standing in. As Sion climbed up after him, Richter cast *Mist Light* from his personal mana pool. A large ball of grey light appeared before him. He placed his hand on it and pushed it up towards the ceiling where it would stay for the next year. What it showed took his breath away.

He was standing in a forest of crystal. Large and small, the iridescent shards stuck out of the ceiling, walls, and floor. Stone stalactites hung down and were now studded with crystal shards like corn on a cob. The largest crystal he could see was jutting up from the ground and was four feet long and two feet thick.

There was so much. Even though it had made things dangerous for a moment, he in no way doubted he had made the right decision to sacrifice a *special* soul stone to accelerate the garden's growth. He hadn't known at the time that the garden was also going to experience months of growth all at once, but from what he could see, it seemed like that entire growth cycle had occurred as if accelerated by the soul of the demoness he had sacrificed. The garden would probably never experience growth like that again, but, for now, he was swimming in crystal!

"So we need a handful for each enchantment. How many useful doses can we get from this?" he asked.

"Hundreds, probably thousands," Sion said with a smile. "And just to be clear, it is not exactly a 'handful' that determines the appropriate measurement. Your hand is bigger than mine after all. Some crystal is always lost when it's rendered to powder and then purified enough to be usable, but as you can see, there is more than enough raw crystal here to supply the village's needs. There are more crystal patches in the adjoining rooms. Nothing as extensive as this, but it is still a very respectable garden." The sprite's voice got a bit more serious. "This is not what I wanted to show you, however."

Sion led him through the garden. At one point, Richter had to use the pommel of one of his swords to break a shard of crystal that was blocking his path. He put the broken piece in his bag along with the rest that he had collected. As they walked to the far end of the cavern, he cast *Mist Light* again and threw the ball of light towards the ceiling. Soon he could make out something irregular against the far wall. Sion led him unerringly towards the spot. At first, it looked like black crystal set against the grey stone walls, but then he saw that the color was actually a rich red. To be specific, blood red.

Richter cast *Simple Light* again to improve his vision and examined it. His breath sped up as he read.

You have found: **Blood Crystal**	**Resource Class:** Rare **Traits:** Steeped in the blood of Richter, Master of the Mist Village, this crystal has greater properties than a normal crystal. This red mineral is tied to Richter and can make objects and potions specifically tailored to him. The properties linking him to this crystal also mean that it can be used to target him with certain spells or poisons. The damage he would receive would be magnified significantly. This crystal may also be used to augment Blood magic. Further uses of this crystal exist and must be discovered.

Richter looked at Sion who gravely looked back. Then his eyes turned back towards the patch of crystal. The chaos seed realized that he was basically looking at a ready-made voodoo doll that could only be used against him. The patch of crystal was about four feet across. "How much powdered crystal could be made out of this?" he asked softly.

Sion examined the patch, "I won't know until we get it down. Five measures, maybe ten. I cannot say for sure."

"Does anyone else know about this?" Richter asked in the same voice.

"I do not think so," Sion said. "The guards patrol this side of the meadow, and I do not think anyone besides you and I have been inside."

Richter nodded, "Thank you for watching out for me, my friend. Let's harvest it."

The Companions worked in silence. They broke off pieces of crystal with their swords and put the shards in Richter's bag. Sion commented that small red shards were falling to the ground, but Richter had already thought of that. He summoned a mist worker who was able to absorb everything on the ground through its amorphous body. It also helped to break off pieces of crystal. When they were finally done, the worker funneled the tiny, red shards through its body and into Richter's bag. Lastly, it scoured the wall of any red fragments that had been too small for the two men to harvest. When they were done, all that was left was blank stone. In the center of the bare patch was a crater with a small hole in the middle.

"Will it grow back?" Richter asked.

"I cannot say," Sion replied. "If there were some kind of seed that it would grow back from, I would bet that it's down that hole," he said, pointing to the finger's-breadth burrow that disappeared into the stone. "If you truly want to remove any doubt, we could dig into the stone. Or you could use your sonic spell. I doubt whatever crystal seed is down there would survive that."

Richter looked at the small divot and thought about it. He could see substantial gains from using the blood crystal. Personalized items of great power were a powerful enticement. On the other hand, the red crystal could be used to make a powerful item specifically geared to kill him. He thought about it for a few more seconds and ultimately it was the third property that decided him. Right now he was too vulnerable to the effects of Deep Magic. If this crystal could give him the chance to gain greater control or power, then it was worth the risk… for now.

"Futen," Richter said, addressing the glowing orb.

"Yes, my lord," the light in the center of the remnant pulsed slowly.

"Summon a mist worker every day to harvest the crystal in the cavern. Always give them two instructions. To stay at least ten yards away from the focus crystal, and if they ever detect more red crystal, to harvest all they can find, including whatever may fall to the ground and bring it immediately to either Sion or myself."

"It will be done, Lord Richter," came the monotone reply.

"Can you prepare the blood crystal tonight?" Richter asked his Companion. "I don't want it just sitting around and I need to know what the specific capabilities are."

Sion nodded, "It will take all night and might go faster if I had a mist worker."

Richter summoned another two grey workers on the spot and put them both at Sion's disposal.

"Do you want to leave?" Sion asked.

"Not yet. We have more to do," Richter replied.

The two men walked through the maze of caverns. Richter ordered the mist workers to start harvesting crystal and placing it by the waterfall entrance. Alma had flown off when they entered the garden. When he mentally asked where she was, she sent an image of a half-eaten, bloody, rat carcass with guts strewn along the floor. She also sent along a feeling of extreme satisfaction. Richter gagged slightly and broke off the mental contact.

The stone rooms adjoining the main cavern had small patches of crystal, but as they walked further in, the stone grew bare. Despite the explosive growth the garden had undergone, it had not reached too far into the extensive cave system. This actually eased Richter's mind as his first stop was the rune room.

The rune looked exactly the same as the last time he had seen it, a square with concave sides surrounded by a larger triangle. When he focused on it, he again received a prompt asking if he would like to deactivate the enchantment. He still wanted to know if he could retrieve the soul stone that powered the rune, but he didn't have an immediate use for another high level soul stone even if he could. Richter also didn't want to ruin any research opportunities this rune might provide his Scholars in the future. He chose 'No' on the prompt and moved on. His primary reason for wanting to visit the rune chamber was to ensure that the crystal garden hadn't compromised it in any way. Now that he saw it was untouched, he felt better.

He moved on to his next task, making a map. At his request, Sion walked off into the caves. It was time to put the mapping ring to good use. Richter pulled up a translucent mini map in the corner of his vision and watched as blackness was replaced by whatever tunnels the sprite was walking through. Nodding to himself, he started exploring as well with a sense of satisfaction. That mapping ring was worth every copper he'd paid for it.

After about ten minutes, he finally came upon the cavern that held the remains of, and items from, the dark aberration's victims. He had been leaving mist lights strewn about the cavern periodically, but also carried one with him. For the past several minutes, he had been detecting an increasingly foul odor. When he brought light to this cavern, his heart fell, and he knew where the smell was coming from.

Since coming back into the caverns, he had been unconsciously forcing himself not to think about something. He had been able to forget the caves that now held his beautiful, crystal garden had, until recently, been home to a malevolent monster that had resided here for centuries. That coping mechanism failed utterly now that he was confronted with the remains of its victims. The horrors he had personally experienced at the mercy of the dark aberration slithered up from his memory to the forefront of his conscious mind. Richter shuddered involuntarily.

After a few minutes, he was able to collect himself again and forced his mind to look at the scene dispassionately. There were thousands of bones. The clutter was a mix of animal and humanoid remains, some yellowed with age, but others still a relatively pure white. Almost all of the clothing was moldy and tattered, but there were the mutilated remains of a relatively fresh goblin body. He realized it must have been from the group of goblins he had killed, what seemed like so long ago, though it had only been a little over a month. This was the source of the horrid stink he had been smelling.

Coming to this cavern had been the third thing on Richter's agenda and the only thing on his mind was the loot. When he saw layers of dead bodies though, shoved into the large cavern like litter in a hoarder's den, it drove home how the dark aberration had preyed on hapless travelers for countless years. Richter came to a decision. He didn't know who these people were, but he knew they at least deserved a proper burial.

Richter summoned two mist workers from his personal mana, then he addressed the remnant, "Futen. Take some of the mist workers and have them start digging a mass grave for these people. I'll send more when my mana recovers." Richter could have summoned a third worker right then, but he really didn't want to bottom out his mana and risk passing out. "After you get it started, go and get Sumiko. We need her here to bless these bodies so they can't rise again. We don't need a repeat of the bugbear attack."

Richter realized that Sumiko would probably need to order the mist workers around so he told them to follow the orders of any villagers so long as those orders didn't harm anyone else. Then for good measure he added in the third law of robotics and resolved to make these standing orders for any future mist workers summoned.

Futen floated off with the three workers in tow. Richter called after him to gather the previously summoned three as well as to help in digging the grave. Richter squinted his eyes and pinched the bridge of his nose to ward off the mana headache, but it swiftly left as his MPs replenished. With his increased Wisdom, he replenished more than a hundred mana every three minutes or so. In practical terms, that meant he could summon about twenty mist workers an hour. Richter hadn't really counted on an increase in village productivity coming from his decision to invest points in Wisdom, but he saw now that his ability to summon workers quickly could be a real catalyst for village growth.

After resting for a few minutes, Richter summoned another mist worker and ordered it to start pulling the bodies out of the cavern. He singled out the goblin's body first and searched it after his magical servant had retrieved the remains. All he found was a single, ratty pouch, attached to a belt that contained a few copper coins. The mist worker brought the next body out and Richter started searching again.

Every time his mana went above one hundred, Richter summoned another mist worker. He had them start taking the bodies and skeletons to where the other mist workers were digging. Sion joined him before long, the rest of the caverns now mapped. Richter checked his map and saw no other spots of immediate interest. The sprite looked in shock at the ossuary in front of him. Seeing Richter's grim expression, he just nodded at his friend and helped him remove anything valuable from the remains the mist workers were retrieving.

Most of the skeletons possessed nothing of value. In fact, before long, what the mist workers pulled out of the cavern were just jumbles of old bones. Whether because of time or trauma, many of the older bones were fractured and crushed. The bones had been mixed together into a heap and the weight of the bones above had proved enough to break those beneath. Richter just kept up a steady stream of mist workers to help dispose of the remains with as much dignity as he could afford, but even he knew it was basically a fool's errand.

It took several hours to clear out the cavern, but ultimately all of the remains were taken outside. While it remained true that there was little to be found on most of the skeletons, he did find some notable items. Richter took great satisfaction in being able to identify magic items.

You have found:	**Damage:** 3-8 (Max 22-30) **Durability:** 8/67

Cobalt Mace of Mana Stealing	**Item Class:** Uncommon **Quality:** Well Crafted **Weight:** 2.9 kg **Traits:** Mace will steal 13 mana per strike **Charges**: 107/107
You have found: **Summoner's Ring**	**Durability:** 22/116 **Item Class:** Rare **Quality:** Masterwork **Weight:** 0.01 kg **Traits:** Increases level of summoned creatures by +5
You have found: **Glamour Ring**	**Durability:** 5/17 **Item Class:** Uncommon **Quality:** Above Average **Weight:** 0.01 kg **Traits:** Can change your visage to look like someone else for 11 minutes. One use per day.
You have found: **Orcish Flag of Yarosh**	**Durability:** 2/58 **Item Class:** Rare **Quality:** Superb **Weight:** 0.4 g **Traits:** +5460 to Fighting Spirit when leading orcs
You have found: **Sacrificial Bone Knife**	**Damage:** 4-6 (Max 10-16) **Durability:** 41/95 **Item Class:** Unusual **Quality:** Exquisite **Weight:** 0.5 kg **Traits:** This blade was carved from the backbone of an elf child and the pieces were fused with a glue processed from the marrow of his bones. It has taken so many lives that it is has become permeated with Death magic. It is exceptionally suited for killing blows.

	+513% damage when striking a helpless foe.
You have found: **Luminous Soul Stone** x 37	**Durability:** 25/25 **Item Class:** Uncommon **Stone Level:** Luminous **Soul Level:** N/A **Status:** EMPTY **Weight:** 0.4 kg
You have found: **Brilliant Soul Stone** x 17	**Durability:** 30/30 **Item Class:** Unusual **Stone Level:** Brilliant **Soul Level:** N/A **Status:** EMPTY **Weight:** 0.5 kg
You have found: **Special Soul Stone** x 9	**Durability:** 30/30 **Item Class:** Scarce **Stone Level:** Luminous **Soul Level:** N/A **Status:** EMPTY **Weight:** 0.7 kg
You have found: **Resplendent Soul Stone** x 3	**Durability:** 35/35 **Item Class:** Rare **Stone Level:** Brilliant **Soul Level:** N/A **Status:** EMPTY **Weight:** 1.0 kg
You have found: **Scroll Case of Monster Attraction (Luminous)** x 2	**Durability:** 37/102 **Item Class:** Uncommon **Quality:** Well Crafted **Weight:** 0.7 kg **Traits:** This case contains a Scroll of Monster Attraction. Activating this scroll will attract the strongest monster within a one mile radius. This scroll will only affect creatures with a luminous soul level or lower.

You have found: **Bracelet of Smooth Movement**	**Durability:** 23/42 **Item Class:** Uncommon **Quality:** Superb **Weight:** 0.03 kg **Traits:** Removes 29% of movement penalty for going through difficult terrain.

The Ring of Summoning went onto his finger immediately. Right now the strongest being he could summon was the saproling and it was only level five. If he dual cast the spell, it tacked on a couple levels, but this ring would make the creature twice as powerful. His weakest Ring of Health went to Sion, reducing his health by twenty-four but increasing his Companion's by the same amount. He immediately felt slightly less hale, but this new ring was worth the loss. Besides, it was masterwork. No self-respecting A-T-Alien would let bling like this go to waste.

The Glamor Ring was fascinating as well. Richter cast *Mirror* then slipped another health ring off and placing the new ring in its place. With a bit of mental flexing, he activated it. Richter thought about looking like Chris Pratt, hoping to get his Guardians of the Galaxy on, but the ring made him look like a slightly overweight, white human. It apparently had only one setting. Richter placed his hand up to his face and still felt his own features. When he spoke, it was still his own voice. The ring apparently cast only the weakest of illusions, not even changing his clothes, but it could still be useful in the right situation. Richter removed the ring and his visage reverted back to normal. He went back to examining the rest of the items.

The battle flag was interesting. He knew anecdotal stories of weary soldiers rallying around a flag, but in The Land this was apparently a quantifiable effect. He didn't see himself leading orcs into battle any time soon, but it did raise the question of why he couldn't make his own banner. The ratty thing was almost falling apart, so he carefully rolled it up and placed it into his bag.

He placed the Bracelet of Smooth Movement onto his left wrist and stored everything else. In addition to these more powerful objects, Richter also found a number of weak rings of health, stamina and mana. Those he intended to hand out to his war party tomorrow. Sion picked through the bunch first and grabbed what he wanted. There were also many broken weapons, shields and pieces of armor. Those wouldn't have been relevant except that two appeared to be made of a metal he hadn't seen before. Nothing came up when he examined it, so he hoped that Krom could tell him more. There were also the equivalent of several hundred gold coins and jewels of various types and grades, some quite valuable.

Richter summoned another two mist workers to carry away all of the dross. He happily observed that each worker was somewhat larger than before. *Analyze* showed that they were both level six and had a higher health and stamina than their level one counterparts, though their mana remained at zero.

As the workers started hauling the trash away, Richter happily placed his new, empty soul stones in his Bag. The amber jewels were as good as gold to him and he felt all warm and fuzzy as they flowed through his fingers. Looking around, Richter saw that all of the bodies had been taken away so he and Sion decided to leave the caverns. They moved carefully through the crystal garden. Neither wanted to cut or impale themselves on the overlarge shards.

Both men pushed through the waterfall and walked back into the sunlight. The sunshine quickly started drying them and they were in good spirits. As they walked east towards the Cauldron, they just enjoyed the day. Storm clouds hovered above the mountains to the north, heralding showers overnight, but for now the weather was fine. Richter's pleasant mood faded as they neared the large hole the mist workers had dug.

CHAPTER 10 -- DAY 111 -- KUBORN 1, 15368 EBG

The mist workers had already dug a grave that was ten by ten feet and was eight feet deep. The bones had been laid out in rows. Sumiko's tan-clothed healers were taking the time to arrange the bodies where it was possible to do so, but there were still piles of bones. Some pieces were only fragments.

Sumiko's back was to them as they approached. Richter touched her shoulder and his breath caught. The healer's cheeks were tear-streaked and her eyes were red. There was nothing timid in the timbre of her voice though, "Promise me that the thing responsible for all of this death has been utterly destroyed." Her tone was half question, half command. There was no doubt in Richter's mind that if he had said no, she would organize a war party of her own somehow.

"It's dead," he told her. "I can promise you that."

Her shoulders relaxed ever so slightly, but then she started shaking. "These people," her voice caught. "These people suffered agony beyond comprehension. They were tortured and played with. Sometimes they were allowed to heal before whatever did this began to hurt them again. The creature that did this was worse than a demon. It has left a residue on these bones that was pure, unadulterated hate." The healer started sobbing. Surprised that the tough old woman could be so affected, Richter put his arm around her, holding her while she grieved for people she had never met.

Sumiko only allowed herself to vent her emotions for a few minutes. "You were right to call me. Some of these remains are so steeped in powerful emotions, like hate and despair, that if they are not put to rest in the right way you would have more to worry about than some Death mage reviving them. This many tortured souls could have desecrated the land. The evil creatures that would have been birthed or attracted to these remains… it is better not to contemplate."

Richter's eyes widened, "Those remains have been hidden with the dark aberration for centuries, maybe millennia. Why isn't this place already overrun with ghosts?"

"A dark aberration? That is what did this?" the sprite woman shuddered. "From what I know of those foul creatures, they feed on misery. The residual pain coming off of these bones and whatever spirits may still be tied to them must have fed it. As detestable as such a creature would be, its presence kept the evil of these remains in check. Now though, they need to be put to rest. I will do what I can, but we need to align these bones as best we can to truly dispel the evil. I have tried, but," she stopped and almost started crying again. She controlled herself though and said, "but the spell I know to commune with the remains connects me to the unfiltered evil they were steeped in. I have fought undead and monsters for countless years, but this is something different. I simply cannot link my mind to whatever did *that*. Can you help?"

You have been offered a Quest: **Lay to Rest**
The remains of the accumulated victims of the dark aberration are steeped in evil and negative energy.
Success Conditions: Find a way to still these disquieted spirits
Reward: Unknown
Penalty for failure or refusal of Quest: Possible desecration of this land
Do you accept? Yes or No

Well he couldn't let his village get haunted. This wasn't a cheesy '80s horror flick. Why anyone would ever argue with ghosts that told them to leave a house was beyond him. If ghosts had started appearing in his condo back home and told him to get the hell out, well, he'd have gotten the fuck out. Hell, if he left these bones here, he'd be worse than the people in the movies. At least the family in Poltergeist hadn't known that their house was built on an indian burial ground. They'd just been too dumb to leave when the kid started sliding across the floor. He would have to be the biggest dumbass in the world to actually PUT the evil spirits in the ground. Best just to avoid the problem all together.

Despite the clarity that something had to be done, for a moment Richter considered another option. He could just bury the remains far outside of the village. Hell, if he put them in the right place, the undead that rose might even serve as a defense installation against potential enemies. It was just an idle thought, though. Looking at Sumiko's tear-stained face, he reminded himself that these people deserved to be put to rest. Also, he had an idea about how to figure this out. "Futen. Go get Beyan as quickly as possible. When you find him, tell him to hurry."

The remnant floated off and Richter turned to Sumiko, "I trust this won't be a problem."

"Why would I have a problem with your alchemist? I have healed him before," she responded.

Richter and Sion looked at each other before the chaos seed gazed at the village Healer again, "Because he's a Death mage."

Her face stiffened, "A Death mage?" The sprite took a deep breath and released it loudly. "That does not bother me. I love all forms of life… even the lowest forms of it." She locked eyes on Richter, "I am completely fine and relaxed."

Raising both eyebrows, Richter nodded slowly, "I can see *and* feel that."

"Yeah," Sion echoed. "You can cut the relaxation with a knife."

Sumiko said some sharp words to the archer in sprite speak, not appreciating his attempt at humor. Sion suddenly found an urgent reason to be elsewhere. She had spoken so quickly that Richter had to replay the words to understand them, but he pieced together that it had something to do with telling Daniella a story about him and another female sprite named Palya. Before his friend could go too far, Richter asked him to go back to the crystal garden with some of the mist workers and put them to work. The sprite left with fourteen of the grey figures in tow.

Richter had lost count of the workers he had summoned, but there had been almost twenty working on the burial pit. It made him realize that his time might be better spent helping build his village rather than always adventuring around. Using his personal mana pool, he could summon hundreds of mist workers a day. He had been meaning to try his hand at constructing buildings anyway. What kind of man didn't want to swing a hammer from time to time?

Richter joined the healers in trying to figure out how to match up the remains. After about twenty minutes, Beyan came trotting up. Richter sent Futen along with five more mist workers and told him to relieve Sion.

"You sent for me, Lord Richter?" the gnome asked.

Richter nodded and filled him in. He had remembered Beyan saying the first Death spell he had learned allowed him to commune with the dead. The mage had also said that the spell only worked on the recently departed, but Richter was hoping that Beyan had another trick up his sleeve.

Beyan listened with a serious look on his face, not speaking until Richter had finished. He nodded at the end and stepped back. The gnome's left hand wove in a complex configuration and he spoke several words of Power. About a third of the remains started to glow with dark purple energy. Some only faintly, but a few adopted an intense aura. The effect faded several seconds later. Beyan turned to Richter and said, "Lady Sumiko is correct. There is a large amount of residual energy and a good deal of it is malevolent." He looked thoughtful for a moment, "Some of these remains would actually be quite useful to me if you would allow me to take them away."

"What?" came a screech from behind Richter. Sumiko came up from behind the chaos seed and barreled between them, "These people have suffered enough. They deserve to be put to rest!"

Beyan puffed his chest out and his face adopted an annoyed cast, "They are at rest. Whoever these people were has faded countless years ago. All that is left are bones. We could throw them away or I could put them to good-"

"Just like a Death mage," she cut in scathingly. "All you see are components to be used when you look at people."

Beyan's expression relaxed and he gave the Life mage a smarmy expression, "I understand why me using these bones might make you uncomfortable. You are mostly bones yourself. They must look like family."

Sumiko pulled herself up to her full three-and-a-half foot height, "If I wanted a lesson about life and death, I would speak to a full-fledged Death master, not a short, little novice like yourself."

"I am an initiate, woman!" Beyan said indignantly. Looking down at her from his four-foot height, he finished with, "And who are you calling short?"

She slowly looked from his face to his groin then back up. "You," she replied. Raising one hand, her fingers glowed gold for a second, "And to be clear, I called you short *and* little. I am a Life master. I can feel an abundance of life. I can also detect a lack of it… in certain places." Her gaze drifted down for just a moment. Then without another word, she turned and stalked away.

Beyan's face turned beet red and even the shiny bald pate on top of his head turned an angry scarlet. He took a loud, deep breath in, most likely preparing to flay the flesh from Sumiko's bones with scathing comments, but Richter decided the exchange had probably gone far enough. He clapped a hand on Beyan's shoulder and said, "Take a lap man. Don't fight with old ladies. If you win, you're a bully. If you lose, you're a bitch. Just learn not to play."

"But-"

"I know. That was fucked up, what she said. I'm sure you're like a mighty oak with a crazy long branch in the middle of you. That's not the point though, and honestly, even that one compliment just made me crazy uncomfortable. As to your request, I'm siding with her on this. These people deserve to be put to rest. Do whatever you can to help, because soon they are going to be buried. Please."

Clearly still irritated, Beyan still followed Richter's command. He walked over to the jumble of bones and started directing the young healers in regards to the best way to separate the remains. Sumiko immediately gave them other directions. Seeing a resurgence of hostilities coming, Richter ordered two of the mist workers to follow Beyan's instructions and let the sprite govern her own people.

They all worked for the next few hours until most of the skeletons had been reassembled. Some were missing pieces and there were some pieces that did not match any others, but they had done what they could. Besides, there were always extra pieces when you put something together. What was important was that Sumiko could cast a mass spell now that the remains were reassembled. Each skeleton glowed golden for a moment, then the light faded and they looked the same as before. Richter shook his head. As happened so often in life, the conclusion was anticlimactic. He didn't complain, though. After the spell was done, she supervised them all being placed into the ground and the mist workers filled in the hole. The Life mage looked tired, but satisfied.

A prompt filled Richter's vision.

You have completed a Quest: **Lay to Rest** The remains of the dark aberration's victims have been purified and can now be safely buried. **Reward:** 3,125 experience (base 5,000 x 1.25 x 0.5).

For his part, Beyan had found a loophole in Richter's order. The chaos seed has said lay the "people" to rest. The gnome had kept a few animal and monster remains off to the side. Even Sumiko couldn't mount a good argument against that, though she still protested. Richter was concerned about any 'bad vibes', as he called it, coming off of the bones, but Beyan assured him there was no danger. He just wanted the bones for research. The fact that there was a slightly manic look in his eye as he said it was something Richter decided to let go of.

Everyone was somewhat tired when they were done, but both Sumiko and Beyan assured him that the remains were safe now. The sprite healer took one last parting shot at the Death mage, "Have fun with your bones, Beyan. It should be a nice change for you to be able to hold something hard." Before the gnome could respond, she beckoned with two fingers and all of her healers fell in step behind her like Turtle and Drama.

Beyan looked at Richter in offended disbelief, but the chaos seed just shook his head. "Don't try to shout after someone with an entourage. It just makes you look desperate. Let's go grab some dinner."

Sion decided to stay at the Cauldron to prepare the blood crystal. Richter nodded in extreme appreciation, then he banished Tabia and Beyan from the Core building until morning. There was the predictable amount of wailing and gnashing of teeth from the elvish woman, but Richter stayed firm. He couldn't let anyone else find out about the red crystal's unique properties. He told his friend that he would send a mist worker up with some food and he also left three of the grey figures at his friend's disposal.

Richter walked off with Alma circling above and a barely-seen giant snake sliding through the calf-high grass beside them.

CHAPTER 11 -- DAY 111 -- KUBORN 1, 15368 EBG

Richter ate a bit with his people, but his Belt of Sustenance greatly reduced the amount of food and rest he needed. After only a few bites, he was full. He was going to leave, but then he learned the truth that actions can often have unforeseen consequences.

"No! I will speak to him, and I will do it now!"

Richter looked to the side, just in time for him to see Jean grab a woman right before she slapped him. Her face was tear-streaked and her eyes were red. The guard looked back and forth between the woman and his lord, his face a picture of embarrassment and chagrin, "I am sorry, my lord."

The chaos seed analyzed the distraught woman and found out that her name was Loisa. He was confused for a moment, until her remembered Jean mentioning that that was his wife's name. Everything became clear.

"Do not apologize for me," Loisa said to her husband. Her tone was a mix of anger and sorrow. "You were almost killed. And for what? Because your lord needed to kill a giant?" She turned her gaze back to Richter, "Was it worth it? Would it have been worth it if my husband had died?"

Richter just looked at her, at a loss for words. All other conversation had stopped in the feast area. Before he could reply, Jean spoke again, "My lord, I am sorry about this. I will accept any punishment you deem necessary, but please do not hold my wife's words against her. She is motivated by her love for me. I-"

The chaos seed held up a hand, cutting his guardsman off. He stood slowly and faced the couple. The eyes of every villager were trained on the three of them. He chose his next words carefully, "Your husband's life is precious to me, Loisa. Your life is precious to me. The lives of all you," Richter said, addressing the crowd, "are precious to me."

He looked back at Loisa, "I will not be callous with your husband's safety, but he has chosen to stand for something. He decided to fight to protect you and the way of life we are creating here. I repeat, his life is precious to me and I will do what I can to safeguard it, but make no mistake. We are in danger. All of us are in danger. Our enemies are out there and we *have* to get stronger for the sake of the village. For the sake of all of us."

"I don't want to hear about 'all of us,'" Louisa spat. She looked at Jean and her face crumpled, "I only want to keep your name off of that memorial wall." Then she hurried away, weeping. Jean looked at his liege and started to speak again, but Richter stopped him.

"Go take care of her. Don't worry about this," he said. Jean nodded gratefully and ran off after his wife.

Richter stood there, uncertain how to feel. Conversation resumed among the tables of villagers. As he looked around, he felt better when many of his villagers lifted a mug in his direction and when his guards placed their fists over their hearts and nodded respectfully. What Loisa had said was valid. It just didn't reflect the whole story. It was reassuring to know that his people still respected and supported him as a whole.

He saw Terrod walking into the feast area and waved him over. Isabella was with him.

"Good evening, my lord," the captain said.

"Good eve, Lord Richter," the herbalist echoed as she gave him a warm hug.

"I'm guessing you heard that?" Richter asked. They both nodded. "Do you think she was right?"

Terrod looked him squarely in the eye, and then said slowly, "We could have approached the fight with the giant in a better way, my lord." Isabella just stood silently, but then she reached out a hand and squeezed Richter's arm reassuringly. He nodded to her in thanks.

Richter reflected on everything that had just happened for a few more moments, before changing the subject. Both Terrod and Isabella were equally eager to move past the tense moment, "The garden seems to be coming along well," he complemented the elfin woman.

"It is," she replied excitedly, stepping back. "The nalan weeds are budding faster than we could have expected. The forest sage is almost growing faster than we can pick it, and the coral megeny, I am happy to say, is finally sprouting! We were also able to place some seeds for a corinth shrub in the cellar under the Dragon's Cauldron, and I have seen the first tendril of growth. Do you know what that means, milord?"

Richter laughed out loud at the woman's excitement, "I have no idea, but I'm sure it's great. I have a question for you, though. Would you like to be the official herbalist for the Mist Village?"

Isabella's mouth dropped openin an "O" of excitement and she looked quickly back and forth between Terrod and Richter. Then she gave Richter another enormous hug and said, "Yes, yes, yes, yes!" Richter smiled and awaited the prompt saying he had discovered another Job, but nothing appeared. He didn't let her see his disappointment though, and soon she had run off to see the other gardeners and share her good news.

"That was very kind, milord," Terrod said, as he looked at his love, smiling.

"When are you going to make an honest woman out of her?" Richter asked, watching Isabella as well.

Terrod turned towards Richter with a frown, "I assure you that Isabella is an extremely honorable woman, Lord Richter!"

Richter chuckled, which only deepened Terrod's frown until Richter explained, "I *know* Isabella is honorable. I was asking, when are you going to marry her?"

Terrod's face made an "O" to mirror Isabella's previous expression. The captain suddenly grew somewhat shy, "This is obviously something I want with my entire heart. When we lived in Law, it was not feasible under the new king's laws. 'Polluting the bloodline' it was called. If the guards found out, the punishment was... severe." Terrod looked off into the distance for a moment, "I lost good friends in the king's dungeon because of this horrible law."

Richter just stood next to his Companion. There wasn't anything that he could say that would make up for the loss of a loved one. There was no reasoning with someonc else's bigotry. It was madness, pure and simple. Happily, Terrod shook off his melancholy mood and gave Richter a calm smile. "I have considered asking her to bond her life to mine, but there always seems to be so much to do."

"As someone who will most likely never see his birthplace again, take my advice, Terrod. Don't wait for the 'right' time. There are always reasons to wait, but there is not always a tomorrow. Carpe Diem, dude. Seize the day."

Terrod nodded and thanked Richter for his advice. Richter started to walk off, but then the captain said, "Have you had a chance to look at the remains?"

Richter shook his head in confusion, "Remains?"

"Of the spiders and rock giant. We had to use tree trunks to roll the giant's body to the edge of the mist, but once there it was easier. Your familiar summoned enough mist workers to bring the giant back to the village. I had the bodies dragged over to the hunters' cleaning site on the eastern edge of the village."

Cha-ching! Richter literally heard a cash register noise in his head. Who knew what kind of great goodies those remains might have? It might even cheer Beyan up after Sumiko had made him her bitch. Saying goodbye to his captain, he jogged over to the gnome who did indeed perk up when Richter told him what was waiting for them not too far away. The two of them left the feast area.

Beyan was basically skipping by the time they got close to the hunter's cleaning site. As Richter walked, he periodically summoned mist lights and threw them up along the path. Soon his village would be lit up day and night, all year long, he thought happily. When they arrived, none of the hunters were in the area, which was probably best. As Richter looked at the already foul-smelling carcasses of the dead spiders, he knew this was probably going to be super gross.

Raising his eyebrows and pursing his mouth for a moment, he looked at Beyan. The gnome already had a knife out. His head was darting back and forth while he looked at a spider's carcass as if trying to figure out where to start first. Sounding as magnanimous as possible, Richter said, "I suppose I could let you work on the queen if you want. If you find anything good, I might be okay with you using it to make the potion you're using to compete with Tabia."

"Truly?" Beyan asked, excited. "You do not mind?"

"You will have to show me everything you find," Richter said admonishingly. "If the ingredient is super valuable, I might need to keep it myself."

"Of course, of course, my lord! I promise you will not regret this," Beyan said with a bright smile.

Richter pretended to ponder the matter for another minute, but then told the gnome to get to work. Beyan immediately drove his blade into the queen's body and started sawing upward. The dagger made a wet *shlurping* sound. Green jelly immediately poured out over the Death mage's hand and a wretched scent filled the air, like opening a dumpster in July behind a strip club. Richter's face wrinkled in disgust. That was not a memory that he had any desire to relive. He couldn't keep an involuntary "Gawk" from escaping as he watched the alchemist work. When Beyan looked back though, he snapped a strained smile into place and gave the mage a thumbs up. The gnome grinned widely, totally okay with the bit of rotting bug juice that had already landed on his face. Beyan just kept sawing.

Richter turned his back on the gross tableau. He summoned a mist worker and placed it at Beyan's command, and then walked towards the figure that had been occupying his thoughts since he had spoken to Terrod: his old foe, the rock giant. The fading light made it somewhat hard to see, so he cast *Mist Light* again. He was awarded with a clear view of the dead behemoth.

It lay on its back, all twenty feet of it. The top of its chest was a full four feet off of the ground. Richter hopped up onto its stomach and walked towards its head. He was so used to seeing an expression of anger on the monster's face that viewing its lifeless visage was strange. This thing that he had so feared was now dead. A smile of satisfaction grew insidiously on Richter's face without him even knowing it as he looked at his vanquished enemy. Richter drew his elementum short sword from the sheath on his back. The blade made a *shing* as it came free.

Richter hopped down and raised his sword. He had known before he got here what he was going to start with. His blade fell. It took two more strikes before the first spike of the giant's rocky crown fell free. He cut through the other two and then examined what he had found.

You have found: **Spike of Rock Giant Crown**	**Durability:** 211/211 **Item Class:** Unusual **Weight:** 2.3 kg

	Traits: Can create a high-density weapon. This could also be ground down to augment Earth-based potions or used to make a potion of electrical resistance.

Richter put each of the spikes in his bag. Then he started cutting into the giant's face. The eyes did not produce a prompt and neither did the tongue. He had to saw and bash the skull to get to the creature's brain. It started drizzling out while he was working. His sweat mixed with the bits of flesh and blood that were released from beneath the rock giant's exoskeleton. Harvesting useful parts from monsters was definitely not glamorous.

Richter started cutting into the monster's chest. Its natural armor was two to three inches thick and made for slow going. Richter didn't want to ruin it though. He sawed his sword along the side of its ribs, tracing a sleeveless vest pattern. Then he started skinning it. If he didn't have an elementum blade, he didn't think he would have been able to manage this. Even with the wondrous metal, the short sword was not ideal for this kind of work. It was only because of the rock giant's massive size that the weapon was at all feasible. Despite the difficulties though, he was able to remove the rocky chest plate.

You have found: **Rock Giant Exoskeleton**	**Durability:** 648/648 **Item Class:** Unusual **Weight:** 37.1 kg **Traits:** Can create a high-density armor. This could also be ground down to augment Earth-based potions or used to make a potion of electrical resistance.

Richter started on the rest. It took another hour to remove the exoskeleton from its legs and arms. That only left the giant's back to be skinned. Before he ordered mist workers to turn the giant over, though, he started to examine some of the small fragments that had fallen off of the giant's exoskeleton. Even though he had picked up a rock that was smaller than a baseball it weighed as much as a bowling ball. No prompt came up as he examined it, but he had an idea. He cast *Create Soul Stone (Common)* with his left hand. White light bathed the grey-black chunk of rock in his right hand and it began to change. In no time, the rock had been replaced with a multifaceted amber jewel. It had worked!

You have found: **Common Soul Stone**	**Durability:** 20/20 **Item Class:** Common **Stone Level:** Common **Soul Level:** N/A **Status:** EMPTY **Weight:** 0.3 kg

Richter examined the prompt. The loose rubble around him could be turned into common soul stones. The marbled quartz that was spread throughout the hills around the village had been used to make soul stones for the hunters, but it only made stones that could hold basic level souls. Looking around at the many small rocks that had littered the ground, he smiled. There were dozens of rocks here, maybe hundreds. And the pieces of the rock giant made common level stones, a full level stronger than the basic stones the quartz made. Richter collected the rest of the small rocks and put them in his bag. He could always convert them later and if he decided to invest in the Talent that let him make stronger soul stones, he didn't want to waste the materials.

Richter was about to summon several mist workers to roll the giant's carcass over when his eyes fell on a piece of the giant's flesh that had fallen to the ground. Unlike the dark, rocky skin, the meat was a pale pink.

You have found: **Rock Giant Flesh**	**Durability:** 13/13 **Item Class:** Unusual **Weight:** 1.3 kg **Traits:** This tender flesh is found beneath a rock giant's tough exoskeleton. Properly prepared, this flesh can give a strength boost if eaten.

Richter's face wrinkled in disgust. Eat this thing? Could he do that? Richter looked at the massive amount of flesh in front of him and considered the morality of eating a semi-sentient creature. It didn't make him a cannibal exactly, but at the same time how did you draw that line when there were so many intelligent species in the world? Back on Earth, he would have felt bad about eating dolphin. On the other hand, dolphins were not malignant creatures that delighted in the pain and suffering of others. This thing did.

Richter thought about it for long minutes, then thought back to a conversation that he had had with Yoshi months ago. He had been concerned about the sprite judging him for Alma's special *Brain Drain* attack. To feed her more enemies, he would cripple enemies so that she could feed on them one by one with impunity. It meant the creatures suffered longer than otherwise would have been necessary. Yoshi's response was simple and absent of judgement, 'Any opportunity to get stronger should be taken.'

Richter stared at the rock giant's carcass. Yoshi's statement was overly simplistic, but it held a strong truth at the same time. Richter knew that there were some lines that he wasn't willing to cross, but this wasn't one of them. He started cutting into the body.

Large chunks of bloody meat fell to the ground after he cut them free. He sent Futen ahead to the cooks with instructions to preserve the meat. Also, anyone with the Cooking skill should see if they could unlock the properties of the flesh. Ideally, the meat could be turned into travel rations that the strike groups could consume before going into battle.

He kept cutting into the body. After digging into the leg, he uncovered one of the giant's long bones. The durability on the long bones was insanely high to support the heavy mass of its exoskeleton.

You have found: **Rock Giant Long Bones**	**Durability:** 3,792/3,792 **Item Class:** Unusual **Weight:** 37.1 kg **Traits:** The high-density long bones support a rock giant's frame. These bones are too dense to be easily worked into anything useful. It is possible they

	have further uses that may one day be unlocked, however.

Richter was surprised at the lack of organs. The magic that allowed the monster to exist had apparently made them unnecessary, or so Richter thought, until he his blade met something it didn't immediately cut through. It was in the giant's chest, on the left side where a human's heart would be. He cut around the obstruction and found that it was roughly spherical. The short sword wasn't the right tool for the job and ultimately Richter ended up using his hands. His strong hands ripped through the meat surrounding what he had found. After ten minutes of struggle, he was able to shove his arms deep into its chest. His fingers found the bottom of the object and he lifted.

It turned out to be a round rock about the size of a soccer ball. The surface was pitted like a meteorite and it had sharp projections sticking out at odd spots. Strangely, the outside of the stone was mildly reflective in the spots that were not still covered in gobbets of pink flesh or rotting fluid. A prompt appeared.

You have found: **Rock Giant Heart**	**Durability:** 78/78 **Item Class:** Scarce **Weight:** 14.9 kg **Traits:** This metallic sphere is the focus of the magic which powers the rock giant. This metal can be smelted for powerful weapons or armor.

Bong!

Know This! Your Talent: ***Synergy of Items I*** *has allowed you to identify a possible Object Set:* ***Spike of Rock Giant Crown x 3*, *Rock Giant Exoskeleton***, *and* ***Rock Giant Heart***. *This series of objects can be turned into an Item Set, among other options. As of now you do not have the requisite skills to make anything useful from these objects. Take them to other craftsmen to obtain their input.*

Richter looked at the hunk of metal excitedly. Despite his earlier judgement of Beyan for getting covered in gore, he was now standing *inside* of a monster's body, covered in congealed blood and flesh, smiling lovingly while he held a mortal enemy's heart. None of this penetrated his psyche, though, as he was so overcome with thinking of possible uses for the object set. He was so enthralled by his discovery that he didn't see the three hunters that had been watching him for the last few minutes. All three exchanged looks and walked back towards the village proper. They didn't speak, but all of them came to the same conclusion. Their lord was not someone to fuck with.

CHAPTER 12 -- DAY 111 -- KUBORN 1, 15368 EBG

Richter cut up the rest of the body, sending the meat to the cooks and the rest of the thick skin to the Forge. Night had fallen, but with the mist lights overhead, there was more than enough light to work by. Futen had come back while he was working which was the only break that Richter took. He sent the remnant right back into the village to gather Sumiko, Zarr, Quasea, Gloran, Shiovana and Roswan at the Forge of Heavens. He wanted his top casters and craftsmen to look at the item set and see if they could figure out anything useful to do with it. Mist workers carried everything away.

When he was finally done, he walked over to where Beyan was working on one of the assengai drones. "I'm assuming this means you've finished with the cutters and the queen?" Richter asked him.

"That I did," the gore-covered gnome said. "Let me show you." He started showing Richter what he had found by butchering the drones, then he moved on to the cutters and finished with the queen.

You have found: **Assengai Spider Drone Leg** x 292	**Durability:** 19/19 **Item Class:** Common **Weight:** 0.6 kg **Traits:** The hardened tip of this leg can be used to make a strong arrowhead
You have found: **Assengai Spider Drone Web Sac** x 37	**Durability:** 5/5 **Item Class:** Common **Weight:** 0.8 kg **Traits:** The webbing in these sacs has mild analgesic, sterilizing and sedating properties. Each bundle of thread

	produced will decrease the durability of the sac by 1
You have found: **Assengai Spider Cutter Scythe Legs** x 16	**Durability:** 31/31 **Item Class:** Uncommon **Weight:** 2.9 kg **Traits:** The forelegs of assengai cutters can be molded into strong blades
You have found: **Assengai Spider Cutter Poison Sacs** x 8	**Durability:** 12/12 **Item Class:** Uncommon **Weight:** 0.6 kg **Traits:** Assengai cutters spit this caustic poison at enemies. Can make a biologic acid
You have found: **Assengai Spider Queen Axe Legs** x 2	**Durability:** 137/137 **Item Class:** Scarce **Weight:** 4.4 kg **Traits:** The forelegs of an assengai queen, these limbs can be used to make weapons of high durability and damage
You have found: **Assengai Spider Queen Web Sac**	**Durability:** 308/314 **Item Class:** Scarce **Weight:** 4.8 kg **Traits:** The webbing of this sac can create threads of exceptional strength and utility. The gossamer contents of this sac will respond to the will of the person retrieving them from the web sac, producing threads of various magical properties. The level of response is commensurate to the person's Weaving skill. Each bundle of thread produced will decrease the durability by 1.
You have found: **Assengai Spider Queen Egg Sac**	**Durability:** 205/273 **Item Class:** Scarce **Weight:** 15.2 kg

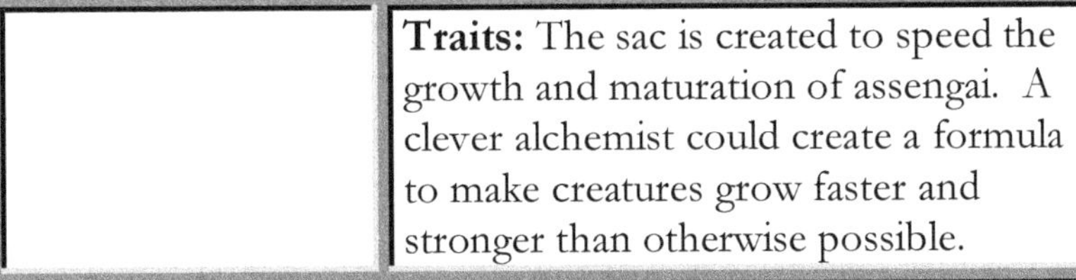

	Traits: The sac is created to speed the growth and maturation of assengai. A clever alchemist could create a formula to make creatures grow faster and stronger than otherwise possible.

"Is that all?" Richter asked sarcastically. The weapons from the cutters and drones were useful, but what had been recovered from the queen was incredible. He would have to review the tablet with all of the villagers on it to see if there was anyone with a high weaving skill. He had no idea what was possible with enchanted clothing in The Land, but he was sure it was potentially spectacular.

He was even more impressed with the egg sac. If he was reading the prompt right, the thing was filled with concentrated growth hormone. He knew just which clutch of skath babies he planned to feed it to. Richter summoned more workers to carry the spider legs to the Forge and the egg and poison sac to the Cauldron. Then he slid the web sacs into his bag. He summoned two more to start dragging the rest of the carcasses to the new pit the hunters were using for disposal.

Helping the gnome, they finished harvesting the last useful goods from the spiders. Richter walked over to a water barrel and cast *Weak Flame*. A gout of orange fire shot into the water and heated it quickly. Both Richter and Beyan used the warm water to clean off the disgusting substances coating them. Once they were relatively clean, Richter put his clothes back on and walked over to the pit. Moving both arms together, he dual cast *Weak Flame*. The orange flame turned an orange-yellow. He kept the flame trained on the remains until his mana was almost depleted. When he stopped the spell, the remains continued to burn. Beyan and Richter walked west into the village proper.

The gnome wanted to go rest after his hours of work, but Richter pulled him along to the Forge of Heavens. The item set was something he couldn't ignore. When he got close, he heard arguing voices.

"The best thing to make be a set of augmented armor, ye ninnies!"

Richter heard Gloran retort, "I still say we can make a golem. Why risk a man's life in armor, when we could create something stronger without him?"

"Can the two of you stop arguing for three seconds?" Sumiko asked in an irritated voice. "I may not have many years left, but I promise that you two will have less if I have to hear you much longer."

"Do na talk like that, ma lovely," Krom said. "I already told ye I could make ye feel decades younger."

Richter heard an incantation and saw a flash of gold right before he was able to look around a weapons rack. He *was* just in time to see a giant gold fist grab Krom and throw the dwarf backwards. The dwarf flew six feet through the air and then skidded until he rolled into one of the smaller anvils. "I will give you worse next time you decide to let your hand wander again, master dwarf!" Sumiko spat at him, shaking her cane.

Richter saw Krom sit up, blinking and looking confused. The light from the furnace cast shadows of red-tinged black that made it difficult to see exactly how badly the dwarf had been hurt. Richter would have been worried, but a second later he saw his smith smile at Sumiko and then blow her a kiss. The sprite woman harrumphed and turned her back on the dwarf. Several feet away Quasea and Shiovana clapped, though it was unclear if they were cheering Sumiko or Krom. Zarr just had one hand covering his eyes and was shaking his head as if embarrassed for his people.

Trying not to laugh, Richter summoned a mist light and carried it in his hand as he walked forward. As good as a clarion call, the new light announced his presence, and everyone bowed slightly, placing their hands on their hearts. Waving the show of respect away, Richter said, "I'm glad to see that you're all having fun. I gather there are some ideas as to what we could do with these items?" The objects collected from the rock giant rested together on the floor of the Forge.

Gloran opened his mouth to speak, but Richter cut him off, "I would like to hear from someone that hasn't already been speaking. Let's hold off on any further inevitable argument for a few minutes, shall we? Just so it's said, I have the ability to enchant an item set, but the pieces apparently have to be made into something useful, first. Now that I know we are all on the same page, what are your ideas?" He looked at Shiovana and nodded at her.

The elfin shipwright shrugged, "I *could* incorporate these pieces into the ship. If I widened the keel, we would be able line the outside with this skin, I suppose, and not tip over, but we would basically be a slowly floating rock. Which is to be expected because this," she kicked the rock giant's skin, "is made of rock."

"Soooo you're saying we *shouldn't* incorporate this into the ship?" Richter asked with a small laugh.

Shiovana closed her eyes and shook her head while slowly mouthing, 'NO.'

"Okay then. Moving on." Richter looked at Quasea who shook her head. Zarr did have an idea.

"I think these items could be used to make a golem," the dwarf said. Gloran raised both arms and looked around in vindication. "I do not know if that fits in with your new profession, but it seems like the obvious option. I do not have the requisite skills to make a golem, however. You would need an Artificer to make a truly powerful one."

Richter looked at Gloran, "Can you make a golem?"

The elf waffled for a bit before responding, "Not exactly, but-"

"Which were my point, yer lordship!" Krom interrupted. "I canna make any fancy items, but I could make a great set of heavy armor and strong weapons from these things and still have plenty of this rocky skin left over. I'll leave the enchanting to yer lordship, but I can handle the rest."

"Any other thoughts or objections?" Richter asked. No one spoke up though Gloran looked regretful about not having a good argument. He turned to Krom, "When can you have it done by?"

Now it was the dwarf's turn to perseverate, "Ah, well ye know, the thing is, yer lordship, time be a fluid thing and-"

"Bah!" Richter said waving his hand back and forth. "We will talk about this again in a week or so. The main point about tonight was to get you all thinking. I won't make a final decision as to what to do with the object set until at least one of you can come to me with a solid plan. Understood?"

A chorus of 'Yes, my lord' echoed around the forge.

"I am going to bed," Sumiko said when no one else spoke. From her tone, it was clear that she would be leaving soon whether Richter liked it or not. Krom started going over the objects again, and everyone else chimed in with ideas. Everyone except Beyan that was.

"Errr, milord?"

"What is it, dude?"

"I would like to have some of the leftover skin, if possible."

Richter just looked at the gnome. Beyan looked around at anything but Richter. The gnome made eye contact for a second and then looked around again.

"You're not instilling me with confidence here, man. What the hell do you want the skin for?"

Beyan took a deep breath and motioned for Richter to follow him. They walked a short distance, and when they were out of earshot, the gnome said, "There was a set of old bones among the rest. A complete set." Richter started to glare at him, "Nonhumanoid, my lord. I swear it," Beyan said quickly. "I didn't even know what they were at first, but I was able to determine that they were from an abyssal siphon."

The gnome looked at Richter excitedly. It was clear to him that Beyan was expecting some reaction to his pronouncement. It was equally clear to Richter that he was getting tired of people using words he didn't know. With infinite patience, he asked, "What is an abyssal siphon?"

Beyan looked at Richter like he was an ignoramus and Richter's fingers involuntarily curled into a fist. Reading the vibe, Beyan fixed his face and said, "A siphon is a creature that can adopt the body parts of other creatures. They can become the most dangerous monsters in a given area. Most other creatures kill them on sight because of this."

"What do you mean 'adopt'?" Richter asked.

"After they have slain something else, they have the ability to incorporate the physical body parts of whatever they kill into their own body. For instance, it could add the stinger from a scorpion, or the claws of a hunting cat, or the nose of a bloodhound."

"If these things are as dangerous as all that, why isn't The Land overrun with them? What could possibly stand against them?" Richter asked.

"As far as I know, they are only found in void planes. They must be summoned to The Land. That's why it is so rare to find the bones of one. My grandfather would have spent almost anything to find something like that. It could make an extremely powerful guardian for any caster."

Richter nodded. He could see why Beyan was excited. It did raise the question, though, "Why didn't you tell me about this when you found the bones? And why did you just look so hesitant to tell me about the siphon?"

Beyan ran his hand over his bald pate before answering, "I did not share that I found the bones at the time because I didn't want that shrew of a Life mage to object. I was hesitant to tell you…" Beyan paused again. "The truth is that I have never used the spell to animate the bones before. It is from one of the spell books that I never learned. In the last fight, though, I reached skill level ten in Death magic. I only need another three levels before I can learn the spell. I am sure that I can master it, though."

Richter frowned, "Is there a possibility that you might not master it?"

Beyan nodded, albeit reluctantly, "There is always a possibility that the magic you try to use might be more powerful than your will. It is one of the main reasons that there are magical colleges. Not just for the spread of knowledge, but also to increase the mental strength of casters." Beyan's face firmed, "I know that I am strong enough to control the spell and what it summons, my lord. I am still at an affinity of 97%. I *will* be a master Death mage!"

Richter looked down at the fierce gnome, "What is the spell?"

"*Create Skeletal Familiar*. It only creates a level five familiar, but whatever bones you use can retain abilities from life. That is why I wanted the skin from the rock giant. If the siphon keeps its ability to incorporate the dead, the giant's skin could make it truly formidable."

Richter thought about it some more, "I have two conditions. One, when you cast this spell, you will do it with me and several others present. If this familiar starts acting savage, I want enough of us around to break it into bits."

Beyan looked pained by the possible outcome, but he nodded. Richter continued, "I need you to give me your books. Just for a short time. I want to see if the scribes can copy them. If they can't, then I'll return them. If you have a level one spell that I can learn to start training in Death magic, I would like to buy it from you."

Beyan's face had grown pensive as soon as Richter mentioned the books. Richter had anticipated that, though, "I know those books are precious to you. I have not forgotten what you have gone through to protect them for decades, but you need to remember something. You are not that same scared refugee anymore. You are a man standing on your own feet and a mage exploring your magic. I will do what I can to protect you while you do so, including helping you to create a powerful guardian, but you need to invest in me and this village." Richter fixed him with a steady gaze, "Either you're really in, or you're not."

Beyan stood quietly for several minutes, lost in thought. Richter did not rush him. From what Beyan had said before, the chaos seed understood that the books were not only valuable, they were also the gnome's only tie to his past and his murdered family. Richter hadn't wanted to push this issue, but every villager would be called on to make sacrifices for the future. Beyan had a treasure trove of spells, and he couldn't just risk those spell books being lost to time. It was way too hard, and definitely too expensive, to find new spells in The Land. Everyone else continued speaking nearby.

Finally, the Death mage said, "Do you promise me that you will not risk the books or do anything irrevocable before you speak with me?" Richter nodded, and Beyan asked further, "And I will get all of the books back when you are done?" Richter nodded again. After a few more seconds, Beyan stuck out his hand. The two men clasped wrists. "I will trust you, my lord. Please do not let anyone else see these."

Richter looked at him, confused, "You have the books with you?"

Beyan smiled and reached down to his belt. He took an overlarge pouch off of his waist. Un-cinching the drawstring, he opened the top of the brown leather wallet. It opened... and opened... and opened! What Richter was seeing didn't seem possible, but the top of the coin purse-sized pouch stretched until the opening was the size of a dinner plate. Suddenly, Richter knew what he was looking at: Beyan had a Pouch of Holding.

Beyan saw Richter's surprise and said, "After my family had to run the first time, we understood the importance of protecting our valuables. As I said, the alchemy shop we ran became prosperous. We spent a small fortune on this pouch, but it was worth every copper. When I told you that I was able to grab a bag with all of our belongings," he hefted the pouch, "now you know what I meant."

The gnome turned his body so the others wouldn't see and started taking items out of the pouch. When the first book was removed, Richter took it and started to read the cover, but after some vigorous head shaking by Beyan, he just put the book into his own Bag of Holding. Book after book came out of the small pouch and went directly into Richter's Bag. Moving like that, they were able to transfer twelve books in no time. Beyan cinched his pouch closed again and retied it to his waist. He looked at Richter again and said, "I am trusting you, Lord Richter. To show you that I am 'in,' as you said, I gift to you the level one spell book in the collection you just received to do with as you will."

Richter smiled and thanked the gnome, "Let's go back to everyone else and tell Krom to leave some of that skin for you." Magic belt or not, after a long day, the chaos seed was looking forward to some sleep.

CHAPTER 13 -- DAY 112 -- KUBORN 2, 15368 EBG

"Lord Richter," came the deadpan but very loud call about a foot in front of his sleeping face.

"What? What's happening?" Richter shot to his feet, his head barely missing the remnant that sped to the side. He grabbed his elementum short sword from the hook it hung on by his bed and unsheathed it, looking around his room for the danger. The guard stationed outside of his door also rushed in, sword drawn.

Not seeing anything, Richter listened intently to check if the sounds of screams or battle could be heard. Not hearing anything besides his own wildly beating heart, he looked at the confused guard and then at the remnant, "What's happening, Futen? Are we being attacked?"

"No, my lord," came the monotone reply. Nothing else was forthcoming.

Not wasting time glaring at the orb, mainly because it never seemed to work, Richter said, as calmly as he could, "Then why did you wake me up? Wait, scratch that question. Why the hell did you wake me up so loudly?"

"You told me that you wished for me to take the initiative and inform you of any relevant information. I was just notified of a village-spawned quest. I assumed you would want to know, my lord."

Richter's heart started beating faster again, "I'm sorry, Futen. You did the right thing. What's happening?" For the village to give him a quest, it must be something vital. The last two had involved him unlocking two of the Basic Elements that comprised his Place of Power.

The light at the center of the grey orb flared, and a prompt appeared in Richter's vision.

You have been offered a Quest: **Know Your Backyard I**.
There are many hidden dangers and treasures within the bounds of your domain. Will you be Master in name alone or will you be the true power of your lands?
Success Conditions: Examine 3 sites that are at least *Interesting* Locations within your domain and determine their importance.
Reward: Unknown
Penalty for failure or refusal of Quest: Increased frequency of future attacks.
Do you accept? Yes or No

Once again, there didn't seem to be a real choice. Richter selected 'Yes' and then looked at Futen. "Where are these 'Notable Locations'? Are these ruins?"

"I do not know, my lord." The grey sphere just hovered there, the light in his center throbbing slowly.

Richter glared at the remnant before he could stop himself, "You don't know? You woke me up to tell me about a quest that deals with three places somewhere within the roughly three hundred square miles that comprise the boundaries of the village lands, and you don't know where I'm supposed to go?" Richter's voice rose in consternation. The guard showed prudence in backing out of the room and leaving his lord to yell at the weirdly glowing ball. Richter didn't even notice as he continued his tirade, "You said you were told about this quest."

"I said I was notified," Futen answered, not in the least bit perturbed by his master's ire.

"What's the difference between being 'told' and 'notified'?" Richter railed, waving his green blade above his head. Alma had been trying to go back to sleep, but now she hissed loudly. It wasn't clear, even to her, if she was pissed at Richter or Futen.

The remnant was quiet for a moment, "I suppose there is not a meaningful difference, my lord."

Richter could literally feel the vein on his forehead throbbing. "You're fucking with me aren't you? Just tell me the truth, once and for all, are you doing this on purpose?"

Futen was quiet for several seconds and then succinctly said, "No."

There was silence.

"No? No what?" Richter shouted. "No, you aren't fucking with me or no you're not doing it on purpose?"

Futen was quiet for almost half a minute before succinctly saying, "Yes."

"Motherfucker!"

The guard on the other side of the door then heard a litany of profanity that he would not have thought possible even moments before. Though the thick door muffled much sound, he was fairly certain his lord was swearing in multiple languages as apparently common-speak alone was not sufficient for the task. The man stood still and simply accepted the experience as a learning opportunity. Several days later, he used his memories of that night to swear at another guard in orcish.

Richter calmed down after several minutes. He even checked his stamina, expecting to find it greatly diminished after his verbal exertions, but the green bar remained full. Taking a series of deep calming breaths, he asked, "Who told you about the quest, Futen?"

"I was notified by the Powers of the village, my lord."

Richter's anger and irritation subsided somewhat in the face of this unexpected pronouncement, "The Powers spoke to you?"

"Not in the way that you mean, Lord Richter. The Powers are no more alive than the Sun or Time itself, which is to say they are completely alive in a way that makes them unable to converse with you or share their thoughts, which would most likely be beyond your comprehension."

Richter blinked. He wasn't sure if he had just been insulted or been given a glimpse of some cosmic truth. He decided probably both, but after his abrupt awakening and the emotional drain of yelling at Futen for a solid five minutes, he was in no mood for existential questions in either case, "So you were notified by the Powers, but they didn't speak to you?"

"No, my lord. I suddenly had the knowledge that there was a danger. I know that this knowledge came from my connection with the Powers. I cannot explain further."

Richter nodded absently, lost in thought. He hadn't really considered the Powers as being alive, but he supposed it was entirely possible that ancient, immortal influences might have a consciousness in some fashion. Apparently, he wouldn't be having a chat with his Life ley line, but it was comforting to know that he might get some advance warning in case of attack.

Richter checked his clock. It was four-twelve in the morning. He hadn't been sleeping for more than three hours, yet surprisingly, he felt completely refreshed. The lord of the Mist Village gave a long-suffering sigh and cinched up his Sustenance Belt. The extra strength he had received from his previous belt had been nice, but for a leader, what he was wearing now was the definitely right choice.

He also changed his mana regeneration. Before going to sleep earlier, he had allocated 100% of his regen to unlocking level two of his sonic damage enchantment. His blue mana bar was still full, but he was happy to see that more than fifty-eight hundred mana points had been earned while he slept.

With that done, Richter pulled up his Traveler's Map, overlaying it across his vision. The three-dimensional picture always made him marvel. It was a study in colors, everything from black-and-white, to greyscale, to rich red and brilliant blues. Everywhere he had personally been was depicted in color, as were the locations Sion had been now that the sprite was wearing the Mapping Ring. Those places either of them had been most recently had the most vivid hues.

The map also showed what had been seen by the Traveler that had made it, but those sections were depicted in greyscale. Experience had shown him that if he traveled over those lands, they would become colored and adjust to reflect the latest information. Rivers would alter course slightly on the map and trees would grow in height. Any areas that had not been explored at all were an impenetrable black.

Much of Richter's lands were still either greyscale or black. On the grey areas, he could see several different areas that could qualify as ruins. Two of the largest were to the south, and one was in the mountains to the north. What he needed was someone to scout those ruins. Someone he could trust to do the job right. A person who could move quickly and with stealth… There really was only one man for the job. A broad smile crossed his face.

Are you ready to do some hunting, my love? Just you and me?

Alma stood on all fours and stretched languorously with her tail extended, **It has been too long, master. It has been entirely too long.**

Richter quickly donned his armor and cloak. The guards on duty each asked if they should follow him, but he left them at their posts. He had a few stops to make before he could leave the village. Once he was out of the catacombs, with Alma on his shoulders, he sent out a mental call to the adder. The snake was nearby and was soon sliding along beside him.

The first thing he did was to go to the Forge of Heavens. He placed a bundle of High Steel Heavy Arrows into his bag and went over to the green chest. At his willed command, the lid rose, and Richter looked inside. A smile crossed his face when he saw that Krom was as good as his word. His new sword lay within. Krom had affixed a thin crossbar hilt to the clear blade. It offered protection for Richter's hands, but also did not weigh the blade down. The smith had apparently also decided to use another small amount of elementum to create a ball at the end of the pommel. Slamming the weighted end of the sword into someone's face would cause major damage. It also balanced the weapon nicely. Richter was pleased. As he held the blade, he felt the slightest amount of vibration. It was time to put the weapon to good use.

The giant's heart and crown pieces were also in the large chest. The skin sat over to the side, drying near the banked furnace. One other item was in the chest.

You have found: **Moonstone Dagger of +3 Damage**	**Damage:** 17-23 **Durability:** 114/114 **Item Class:** Uncommon **Quality:** Superb **Weight:** 0.9 kg **Traits:** +3 Damage per strike

Richter picked the dagger up, appreciating the beautiful simplicity of the dwarf's work. There weren't any fancy enchantments, but the extra damage made for a formidable weapon nonetheless. He was actually missing a good dagger among his armaments. Krom must have recognized the lack and made it for him. Richter happily tied it to his belt.

He closed the chest and moved on. His next stop was the Cauldron. Richter cast *Weak Haste* and ran up the hill to the meadow. The guard posted at the top saluted him. Richter nodded back as he ran past and entered the glass building. Unsurprisingly, despite the early hour, Tabia stood working nearby.

"I need health, mana and stamina potions," he said without preamble

"Greetings, my Lord Richter. I have several prepared," she said with a slight bow.

The cocoa-skinned elf quickly moved over to a cabinet and removed five of each potion. Richter checked them and saw that each had a potion level of *solution* and a strength of *processed.* They all restored 200-300 points over 10-15 seconds. He smiled and turned to leave, but he remembered a question that had occurred to him previously.

"You've reached level fourteen, and you're a journeyman in Alchemy. Why don't you have a Profession?"

Her face grew very still. She looked down and said, "I was planning to tell you this at a later date, but I have not always been a peaceful person, Lord Richter. I have been a mercenary for more than a decade. I was valued for both my sword arm and my Alchemy skill. That is why my level is as high as it is. The truth is that I have never been in a safe place long enough to go for my trial. Because of the new king's laws, I was forced to leave the Kingdom of Yves and bring my wife with me. If this proves to be a safe place for the both of us, I do plan to pursue my Profession soon."

Richter stared at the woman, almost sure that he was not receiving the whole story. He decided to have her take the oath in front of Sumiko as soon as possible. If she was found to be loyal, he would let her keep her secrets. If she wasn't loyal… well, then Beyan might end up being in charge of the Cauldron after all and something would have to be done about her.

The last thing he did before leaving was to have her grab a large, empty barrel. He upended his Bag of Holding and poured out the fragile, assengai eggs he had collected in the spiders' cave. They had properties to slow decay or cure poison. She said that she would preserve them until they could be rendered into a potion. Nodding, Richter took his leave. While he walked, he remembered to load his Ring of Spell Holding. The clear stone on the ring turned green.

The last thing he did was to stop by the area where the quarried stone was brought for the builders to use. He scavenged around and found dozens of small bits of marbled quartz. Each was turned into an amber soul stone of *basic* level and went into his bag. Then, moving like a wraith in the night, he made his way to the village gate, crossed out of his village and went hunting.

CHAPTER 14 -- DAY 112 -- KUBORN 2, 15368 EBG

The first ruin he was going to check was about six miles to the south. He drank a Potion of Clarity and gave one to Alma as well. He considered trying to force feed one to the adder, but seeing as how that would involve him either putting his hand near the mouth of a twenty-foot snake or pouring the solution on the ground in the hopes that the monster would lap it up, he decided, meh, maybe not so much. If he wanted to tame it permanently, it would also happen faster if its level stayed where it was.

With that done, he considered his options. Out alone in the darkened forest, he decided to opt for stealth over speed. Richter pulled the hood of his Cloak of Concealment up and melded into the forest around him. His Stealth skill was only up to initiate rank and moving too quickly would make him visible, so he had to take his time. Luckily that afforded other opportunities.

Like learning the level one spell that Beyan had given him, for instance. He started reading, and the pages turned faster and faster until it slammed shut and fell to dust. As had happened with every other book of magic he had consumed, suddenly, he *knew!*

Congratulations! You have learned the skill: **Death Magic.** *Increasing your skill will allow you to cast more advanced spells.*

> Congratulations! You have learned the spell: **Summon Weak Bile Rats**. Summons a small nest of bile rats. The bites of these creatures can cause nausea. This is a spell of Death, level 1. Cost: 27 mana. Duration: 6 minutes. Range: 3 feet. Cast Time: 2 seconds. Cooldown: 14 minutes.

Once he had learned the spell, he moved out. Richter cast *Nightvision,* and his vision shifted to a spectrum of green and black.

With the moonlight of three moons filtering down, he could see as easily as if it was noon. When he was a short distance from the village, he tested his new Death spell. He removed his new Summoner's Ring and cast the spell one-handed. A disc of purple-black energy appeared on the ground, two feet across. Five rats, each a foot long, rose out of the disc. When they were fully formed, the circle disappeared. The rats were a sickly brown-yellow in color, and they had beady black eyes. The wretched things squeaked and crawled over each other while looking up at him. *Analyze* showed that each was either level one or two.

"Run that way," he commanded. All five rats took off. Richter nodded to himself. At least he knew that the creatures would follow his directions. He started moving forward. After the cool down period had expired, he cast the spell again, this time with his Summoner's Ring on. The disc appeared again, and five rats appeared, but this time they were larger. Each of the rats were now level six or seven. Again he sent them off. Fifteen minutes later, he dual cast the spell. The purple-black disc was larger than before, and this time, thirteen rats stood awaiting his orders, each level six or seven. Richter smiled; his new ring was a massive win. He sent the rats off and kept moving. While the spell wouldn't conquer powerful foes, it felt good to finally be able to cast a spell in each of the eight Basic Elements.

In the dark, his Herb Lore and Tracking skills still filled his world with light. The faint glow from significant plants and the tracks of animals and monsters blazed in his vision. By the time Richter had made his way two miles from the village walls, he had collected more than a dozen herbs. He had also found it was easier to move through the thick sections of the forest than it should have been. Thorns barely pulled at him, and his footing seemed sure somehow. Looking at his new Bracelet of Smooth Movement, he silently thanked whatever poor bastard had left it behind in the cave of the dark aberration.

More important than anything else, though, Alma solo-killed several monsters.

You have been awarded 2,156 (base 57,476 x 0.06 x 1.25 x 0.5) experience from Brain Drain against Level 11 Tree Wyrm.

Richter was surprised when he got the first prompt. He was even more surprised because right before he saw the prompt, there was a swirl of rainbow light that snaked out of the forest and into his bag. The light blinded his night vision-enhanced eyes for a second before he shut them tight. Prior to the soul being captured, he had been moving slowly through the forest with Alma ranging ahead. Richter immediately sent out a mental call to make sure she was okay. In response, he just received a satisfied feeling reminiscent of someone enjoying a great meal. Then she had sent him the image of a three-foot long creature with a mouth like a lamprey. It lay dead on the ground. Richter started to make his way towards her, telling her that he was going to summon a mist worker when he received a massive shock. Mist started coalescing around her, and soon a grey, humanoid figure stood in front of her. It picked up the body of the tree wyrm and started running back towards the village.

What did you do? he asked her.

I summoned a worker and told it to take the wyrm to the hunters. Is that not what you wanted, master? she asked back.

It is, he assured her. **I meant how long have you been able to summon mist workers?**

She flew towards him and landed on his shoulder. A bit of green ichor dripped off of her claws. **What I can do comes from you, master. I think that I may always have been able to do this, but it is only since our bond has increased that new thoughts have been occurring to me. I have always hunted, but this is the first time that I have used Brain Drain on my own or thought to capture souls for you. Now that I have, though, I cannot understand why it did not occur to me before.**

Richter smiled and thought, my little girl is all growns up! He had mostly been increasing *Psi Bond* to improve her self-awareness, but her new initiative was a wonderful and unexpected benefit. The other kills brought him souls as well, giving him two more *basic* souls and one *weak*. He was somewhat concerned about the rainbow swirls giving away his position, but the light moved faster than any predator could follow. He also didn't want to inhibit his familiar's new industriousness.

He continued through the forest and more rainbow swirls of light swept towards him.

You have been awarded 990 (base 26,395 x 0.06 x 1.25 x 0.5) experience from Brain Drain against Level 7 Screechling.

You have been awarded 3,937 (base 104,981 x 0.06 x 1.25 x 0.5) experience from Brain Drain against Level 14 Ash Wolf.

This continued until he got a series of prompts that did not bring a swirl of light with them.

You have been awarded 19,565 (base 521,736 x 0.06 x 1.25 x 0.5) experience from Brain Drain against Level 26 Dire Wasp.

His heart started beating wildly as soon as he saw 'Level 26.' Her hunting was fine, but she had just tangled with a high level beast. The ceiling for her *Brain Drain* to incapacitate her prey was a MAX of level twenty-six. She was completely vulnerable as she psychically fed. The dragonling barely even responded to Richter while she used her special attack, so if her prey was still aware, it could easily kill her!

Alma! Alma are you okay?

I am fine, master, she replied, somehow conveying weariness in her tone.

What are you doing attacking a level twenty-six monster by yourself? You could have been killed. His worry and concern were morphing to the next logical stage. Anger.

She wasn't his soul familiar for nothing, There was more than a bit of bite when she responded, **It attacked me!** Then she sent him a mental replay of what had happened. All of it was from her viewpoint. It started with her looking down as she flew through the trees. A faint buzzing caused her to look up and what she had seen made Richter's mouth drop open.

A pitch-black wasp the size of a cat was barreling down on her, stinger first. She had veered to the side just in time, and the wasp shot by with a cry of anger. It's voice sounded like a high pitched whistle. Alma had immediately cast *Weak Haste.* The wasp had already corrected course and was coming back towards her. What followed was an aerial battle that almost made Richter sick watching it. She had woven in and out of combat with the creature. It was equally if not more agile than the dragonling. It had stayed so close that she couldn't even target it with a *Psi Blast.*

In the end, she had committed herself to an all or nothing maneuver. The dogfight had taken them both high into the air. After raking her claws against the wasp's face, she had dove towards the deck. With a scream of anger, the wasp had gone straight after her. Alma poured all of her speed into the dive, hearing the dire beast screaming right behind her. Richter's own heart thudded in his chest while he relived her experience. His familiar had to have nerves of steel to not look back and check the position of a monster trying to eat her. She didn't though, fully committed to this last chance at victory. Instead, she had flapped even harder to put space between herself and her purser. When she had been only fifty feet from the ground, Alma flipped end over end and unleashed her *Psi Blast.*

The high level creature wasn't completely overcome by the attack, but that wasn't the point. Alma had waited until they were just shy of the ground for a reason. The wasp would have only been disoriented for a few seconds, but that was an eternity in battle. Without even waiting to see the effect her attack would have, Alma had flipped back over immediately. Her wings shot out and she pulled herself out of the dive, barely, her tail brushing the dirt as she gained altitude. The wasp wasn't so lucky. The monster slammed into the ground at over four hundred feet per second. The wasp's body crumpled, and only its high level kept it from dying outright. Still, it only had seconds left to live. Alma gave a hoot of pleasure at seeing her enemy lying broken and dying. Unable to even raise its head, the dire wasp gave a faint mewl of pain as she latched on and stole its last remaining life.

Richter had stopped moving while he processed what the memory she had sent him. While it was true that he could absorb events she sent him much faster than they actually happened, it still took a few moments. Once he was done, the chaos seed checked her stats and was relieved to see that she was whole, though her stamina was low. The chaos seed sent her an expression of love and told her to come to him. She wearily agreed. A few minutes later, she was resting on his shoulder, her tail wrapped around his arm for support.

Richter stroked her scales while she rested and she started to coo. Unable to help himself, he asked, **You couldn't have trapped its soul?** Her only response was to dig a clawed hand into his neck.

"Ah! Ahhhh!" **I'm sorry!** he said, panicked. Was that blood he felt running down his neck?

She gave a disgruntled *huff*, but retracted her claws and relaxed down into his shoulders again.

I still don't like the idea of you fighting such a strong monster alone, he sent to her.

She responded without moving from her comfy perch atop him, **Hush, master. This is my house.**

Smirking slightly, and wondering what it said about him that he liked when women told him what to do, he did as she said. Besides, there was one other prompt that had come with the death of the dire wasp.

Congratulations! Your familiar has reached level 29!

Seeing her level prompt made him realize that he hadn't checked her status page in a while, not since she had killed the assengai queen. The smile on his face grew as he accessed her page. There were points to distribute!

Name: Alma	**Level:** 29, 83%	**Race:** Psi Dragonling
STATS		
Health: 110	**Mana:** 600 *Regen/min: 36*	**Stamina:** 160 *Regen/min:* 6.6
ATTRIBUTES		
Strength: 4	**Agility:** 28	**Dexterity:** 29
Constitution: 11	**Endurance:** 16	**Intelligence:** 60
Wisdom: 60	**Charisma:** 16	**Luck:** 16
SPELL POWER BONUSES		
Air 50%	**Life** 50%	
RESISTANCES		
Air 50%	**Mental** 100%	**Life** 50%
ABILITIES **(Unused Points: 6)**		
Psi Bond – Lvl 5, points to next level: 4 **Psi Blast** – Lvl 2, points to next level: 2 **Brain Drain** – Lvl 6, points to next level: 6 **Psi Channeling** – Lvl 1, points to next level: 1		

Richter was so excited by his discovery that he almost dropped *Stealth*. He caught himself in time, though. He devoted the minimal amount of attention to keep going and devoted the rest to Alma's development. He sent the adder to scout ahead and asked Alma to keep watch overhead.

With six points to spend, he could invest in any one of her abilities. The obvious question was, which one? *Psi Bond* had continually shown itself to be a clutch ability. In addition to her new initiative and increased stats, she was summoning mist workers on her own now. That alone could be a huge boon to the village. *Psi Blast* was a wonderful offensive ability, and it seemed to gain properties as it advanced. *Brain Drain,* on the other hand, had been the secret to his fast increase in levels. It didn't have any extra properties, but it was also the easiest way to increase Alma's level. Richter's eyes fell onto her last ability.

Psi Channeling was the newest addition to her abilities and offered extremely interesting possibilities. One of the biggest problems with his spells was that he had to be almost within striking distance to use most of them. When Alma could swoop past an opponent while unleashing a spell, though, it drastically increased his range. The greatly increased mana cost though, four times the standard spell price, made using the skill prohibitive.

Richter asked Alma if she had an opinion, but she just responded that she trusted her master. Then she licked his face and jumped into the air, mentally laughing. Richter shook his head fondly and watched her. The dragonling was still the size of a cat, albeit a large cat now and not a small one like when he had first summoned her. Despite her small size, though, the level twenty-nine creature was a force to be reckoned with.

That still left the question of what to do with her six ability points. The light coming off of the light wisp was interfering with his *Stealth,* so he had Alma dismiss the spell. Once he was again cloaked in darkness, he examined the bonuses of each area to invest in, but in the back of his mind, he knew that he already had his answer. Even though *Brain Drain* didn't come with a lot of sexy bells and whistles like the other abilities, each new level potentially brought a lot of experience with it. If Alma were able to kill a level fourteen monster, for instance, the upgrade would bring at least another thousand XP. He invested the six points and upgraded her skill. The boost clearly reenergized her because Alma gave a trill as she swooped through the air.

I am going to hunt, master, she thought to Richter happily. *I will stay nearby.*

Richter sent her thoughts of love and encouragement, and warned her not to punch above her weight again. He began a cursory read of the prompt that had appeared, and his mouth dropped open in shock.

You have chosen to increase your familiar's ability: ***Brain Drain*** *to level 7. Successful kills will now give 7% of total experience to both you and your familiar. Drain occurs faster. Stun can occur on enemies level 31 and below. Drain now gives you a greater understanding of Alma's victims. There is a chance to relive the most poignant memory of the target's life.*

He had never thought *Brain Drain* would be more than just an expedient way to gain XP. He had upgraded it because, more than anything else, he needed the experience to buy more Talent points. Now though, it appeared the ability could do so much more. What memory could he have received from Sonirae or the assengai queen? What insights could he gain if Alma were to drain a bugbear captain? For a moment he considered the possible danger of reliving someone else's memories, but he decided the benefits were worth the potential risk. Richter sent another message to Alma telling her happy hunting. He was eager to see if she could trigger the new facet of her ability.

Nothing else of serious note happened for the next few miles. Alma drained several more creatures and then summoned mist workers to carry the remains back to the village. With her high mana regeneration rate, she always had more than enough magic for the summonings. Each kill earned Richter another swirl of rainbow light and several hundred experience. He was especially delighted when she killed a level sixteen carnasid. He had no idea what a carnasid was, but since it gave him almost eight thousand experience, he didn't especially care. Alma told him there was something for him to see though, so she led him back towards the beast.

Alma quickly brought him back to the carcass. He continued to tell Futen to scout around him while remaining invisible. The last thing Richter wanted was a monster up his ass while he was looking at Alma's latest kill. The animal--or monster, Richter thought, realizing he didn't really know how to distinguish between the two if there even was an appreciable difference--was about the size of a large boar. It had spots like a leopard, orange skin and was powerfully muscled. The large fangs in its mouth and its hooked claws left no doubt that it was a hunter. A small black scorch mark marred one side of it and, upon checking, Richter found another, smaller scorch mark on the bottom of one foot where the lightning had exited the body.

I did not think you would need to shock it first, my love, Richter thought to his familiar curiously.

*It was with a larger pack, master. Stunning my prey first also allows me to cast Soul Trap *before draining it,** she answered. He wisely did not mention the dire wasp again.

A larger pack? How large? Which way did they go? His questions came fast, one after the other. Richter suddenly had a vision of being overwhelmed by twenty of these creatures. One of his hands was already on the hilt of his new short sword as he looked around.

Alma sent him a memory of a group of carnasids, seven strong rushing off into the woods. Overlaying the information with what he was seeing, he figured out that the pack had run off more or less to the south. Even more interesting to him was the fact that there were three small carnasids running with the adults. A slow smile grew on his face. If those oversexed twins could train skaths, why not angry little piggies? Besides, the pack was roughly going in the same direction as the ruins he was heading towards.

He sent Alma ahead to find the pack and summoned a mist worker to take the carnasid's body back to the village. His people would be eating good today. Then his mind started flirting with the idea of how to invent barbeque sauce, or at the very least figure out a local equivalent of KFC's seven secret spices. A dry sliding noise brought him back to the present moment, the shale adder slithering through the grass near him. Richter sent it a mental message to follow him, and he moved south as quickly as he could.

Richter checked his clock and saw that he still had at least an hour before dawn. He wouldn't have time to scout other ruins before dawn, but if everything went well, he would be able to be home not long after daybreak. Before too long, Alma sent him a mental picture of the carnasids resting together in a pack. She had flown above the pack unseen and was now perched in a tree looking down at them. The animals were sheltering together for warmth and security, but it just made them easy pickings for the chaos seed and his reptile band.

Richter sent the adder forward--towards the pack--and he followed, stealthed, making sure that both of them stayed downwind. When he was only twenty feet from the slumbering creatures, he stopped behind a tree and quietly summoned two mist workers. Then he ordered Alma to *Psi Blast* the entire group, holding his freeze short sword at the ready.

Alma sent back a happy assent and launched silently into the air. She flew off a few yards and then tipped into a steep dive. Timing it perfectly, she fired the narrowed beam of her psychic attack, catching all members of the pack at once. The animals fell to the ground en masse, only a twitching leg here and there showing that they weren't dead.

Richter and the adder rushed forward while Alma immediately latched onto the head of the largest carnasid and began draining it. Richter ordered the two mist workers forward to grab the young and then started culling the herd. He cast *Soul Trap* on the animal that Alma was attacking and plunged his blade into its breast. Frost-rimmed the edges of the wound as it slid inside, causing massive internal damage. The animal died almost instantly, and a ribbon of light swirled around the chaos seed before disappearing into his bag.

The adder had wrapped its length around one of the carnasids and had latched its fangs into the neck of another. Blood flowed freely from the puncture wounds. The mist workers grabbed the three carnasid piglets and were holding their limp bodies aloft. Richter made a quick assessment and knew that he didn't have time to kill the monsters one at a time. He also didn't want to waste the experience, though. His lips tightened against what he was about to do, but he didn't hesitate to draw his second blade and then lay into the still forms of the pack. At most, he had another three to four seconds before the animals roused. Then they would either attack together or scatter to the wind. Neither option worked for him, so he systematically cut their hamstrings.

One blade stabbed down and then another. Richter repeated the process with the remaining two. He had just finished when the animals came out of their psychic shock and started braying in pain and anger. They all tried to get to their feet, but each and every one fell back down as they found one of their legs did not work. Richter carefully approached each again and stabbed them in another leg to ensure they couldn't escape.

Though they were just animals, hearing their cries of pain pulled on his heart. He had no love of needless suffering, but he also wasn't willing to waste the experience they could give him and Alma. He had done something very similar when he had first encountered the eaters, removing their legs and letting Alma feed on them one by one. He hadn't had a moment's hesitation. Alma finished with the animal she was draining and hopped into the air towards one of the injured ones. The hapless predator snapped at her, but she easily maneuvered over the bite and then clamped onto its body at the base of the neck. The carnasid's body began to spasm. Richter cast *Soul Trap* and quickly ended its life. As Alma moved onto the next, he repeated the pattern, reminding himself that the ends justified the means.

Was the life of these animals any different from the life of the eaters? Did the minute of pain they had to suffer before the end really make any difference? Hearing them cry out in pain evoked sympathy in him, but did that kind of sentimentality really belong here in The Land? Was he actually just a hypocrite for even considering these questions, when he had executed helpless men for the sake of expedience and butchered retreating bugbears in the name of vengeance?

Richter rammed his sword into the fourth carnasid he had crippled. A rainbow of light rose into the air, and Alma shot into the air with a savage cry. She flew up ten feet and then locked eyes on the two carnasids the adder had immobilized. Both were close to death, one from asphyxiation and other from blood loss. The creature the adder was biting had struggled to get free. It had failed to escape the snake's powerful bite, but as it struggled, it tore a large hole in its own neck. By the time Alma cast *Soul Trap,* it was barely moving and was nothing more than a light mental snack for the dragonling.

As he pondered his own morality, Richter looked at the snake he had enslaved that was now killing in his name. He looked at the faceless grey automatons holding the young carnasids he hoped to train into obedient killers. He looked at Alma, his familiar, who killed with wanton abandon, and possibly even with brutal joy.

He looked at what he had wrought, and a faint smile worked its way onto his face. He realized that he had been asking the wrong questions earlier. It was not a question of if he would kill in a given situation, or even if he would risk the suffering of innocents to further his own ends. The question was 'Would he go as far as was required to secure his kingdom in The Land?'

Richter drew back his sword to thrust into another helpless creature and answered himself, 'Of course he would. After all, blood had always been the mortar for the foundations of an empire.'

CHAPTER 15 -- DAY 112 -- KUBORN 2, 15368 EBG

They finished with the carnasids and, between Richter and Alma, another four mist workers were summoned. The workers carried the bodies of the pack back to the village. Before he sent back the two holding the carnasid piglets, Richter penned a short note to Randolphus, instructing him to get the twins to come check on the young animals. He gave the letter to a worker with instructions to pass it along to the gate guard.

Going after the animals had forced Richter to detour from his initial objective of the ruin, but not too far. He stealthed again and started moving east. Less than ten minutes later, they were within range of the ruins. Nothing so far had given Richter any indication that there was an enemy encampment close by. He had approached as quietly as possible and didn't think anyone could have noticed him. Still, he decided not to be cocky.

Maintaining *Stealth,* Richter stalked forward towards the location of the ruins on his map. He sent Futen ahead to scout and pushed through the trees to get his first view of the ruins. Before arriving, he had zoomed in on his map and examined what the Traveler that had made it had seen. On the map, there was a compound about the size of a soccer field. Twelve buildings dotted the area. From what he could see, it looked like this had once been a small village. Richter tried to zoom inside one of the buildings, but apparently, the Traveler had not explored inside them because all he saw on the map was blackness.

Richter had never gotten a good answer as to how long ago it had been since the unknown Traveler had made this map. As he had walked through the forest and saw rivers deviate slightly and trees that were much larger than depicted, it had become clear that--at the very least--hundreds of years had passed. This village was no exception.

Not one freestanding building stood where the map had depicted them. All he saw where the buildings should have been was a nest of bracken and the decaying forms of fallen trees. Other trees even grew amidst the compound. If he hadn't had a map to follow, Richter could have passed by this area without a second thought. It was just another patch of forest.

Futen came back and spoke quietly while still invisible, "I was not able to detect any hostile creatures, my lord."

Richter sent a mental query to Alma who confirmed that she couldn't sense any monsters or dangerous animals in the immediate vicinity. He looked out over the area the ruins were supposed to be in and drew his swords with a sigh. It was time to get to work.

The good news was that between his Strength of thirty-three and the power of his elementum blades he was able to cut through the undergrowth without too much difficulty. The problem was that the bushes and thorns were springy new growth and gave before his blows, so the process was still time-consuming. Part of him wanted to cast *Flame* to burn through the undergrowth faster, but he resisted the temptation. In an ideal world, it would burn off the leaves and make his work go faster. If the fire got away from him, though, he had no way of stopping it. He wouldn't risk a forest fire endangering his people just for the sake of expedience.

It took more than an hour, and the sky was starting to lighten, but he was able to clear a path to the closest 'building.' Things went a great deal faster after he started summoning mist workers. Embarrassingly, it was Alma who came up with that particular brilliant idea. He was cursing at a particularly stubborn snarl of thorny vines when a worker just reached past him and pulled it taught. With the tension provided, it was easy to cut through. Richter looked up at his familiar, who was lazily circling above him. She sent a mental chuckle to him through their *Psi Bond* and then let loose a trumpeting toot to praise her own superior intelligence. Richter mentally called her a brat in mock irritation, but she just flew off, still laughing and praising her own magnificence. The worker continued to pull at the thicket.

Richter took a step back and summoned several more workers. While they worked, he reflected on why he hadn't come up with the idea himself. In retrospect, summoning help was an obvious idea, but he had fallen into the same trap that he always did.

He tried to do everything himself. Richter had been raised to be strong and independent. It was a trait that had served him well back on Earth and, if he was being honest, had served him well since coming to The Land. He realized that he couldn't keep thinking like that, though. He couldn't just be an army of one. Even coming out here on his own this morning had been a mixture of wanting a bit of freedom and honestly thinking it would be easier just to explore by himself. Richter resolved to do better.

Between the chaos seed and the dragonling, they soon had twenty mist workers pulling the trees and bracken away. The workers couldn't form their limbs into blades nearly as strong or as sharp as Richter's blades, but they made up for that with numbers and single-minded devotion to their tasks. When Richter saw that he wouldn't be back to the village before everyone started waking up, he wrote another note and gave it to a mist worker. He detailed where he was, what he was doing and that he would be back soon. Richter could already see the look of disapproval on Randolphus's face, but hey, sometimes a man just needed a nighttime walk through a monster infested forest to explore long-forgotten ruins. The chamberlain would understand that, right?

Richter chuckled to himself and thought, yeah right, and if toads had wings maybe they wouldn't bump their asses when they jumped. Then he thought, damn Tia Carrere was hot. Richter looked out at the now relatively clear space and was somewhat disappointed. He still didn't really see anything that would indicate the ruins that had once been here. Not knowing what else to do, and not ready to give up yet, he ordered the workers to start digging. He himself sat on a nearby rock and took a bit of trail mix out of his Bag. Munching on the local equivalent of a cherry and some nuts, he summoned a few more mist workers and set them to help out. After that, he took out one of his short swords and started going through sword forms.

The next time he saw Yoshi, he intended to ask for instruction in the half sprite's dual wielding style. He knew that if he neglected what Yoshi had already taught him, though, then the chances of learning more were next to zero. When he thought of the sword adept, cuddly and easygoing were not the words that came to mind.

As he practiced, he continued to get periodic notifications about Alma using *Brain Drain.* Each time they were accompanied by a ribbon of light. The kills were all simple animals, yielding only weak or poor souls. Alma continued to summon mist workers as needed but had them bring the kills back to where Richter was training. He, in turn, put them to work with the other workers to start digging.

Another hour-and-a-half passed, and Richter was getting to the point of giving up, but then he heard a loud crash. One of the teams of diggers had collapsed into an underground space. The other three teams kept digging without pause. Richter called out and stopped the other groups and then ran over to the collapse. A hole about twenty feet across had been exposed. The northern aspect of the collapse had created a rocky slope down the newly-exposed floor, ending ten feet below where he was standing.

Excited, Richter half-walked, half-slid down the slope. Alma flew down to land upon his shoulders, and he sent out two mental calls. One, for the adder to stay above and two, for Futen to become visible and to join him. Two of the mist workers had landed safely and were even now still digging into this new floor. Another was leaking mist from a large rent in its side. A quick use of *Analyze* showed that its health was down to 10% and was dropping another percent every few seconds. Of the other two, there was no sign. Richter assumed they must have been destroyed by the collapse and dissipated.

The morning had advanced enough that seeing what was around him was no problem. He dismissed the injured mist worker and ordered the other two to stop digging; then he looked around. Richter was standing in a cellar made from square blocks. The stone was almost completely covered by dirt, but a falling stone had scraped a wall, and he could see grey stone underneath. Other than a large hole in one wall, he didn't see anything else.

Richter cast *Simple Light* and looked around further, but still didn't see anything. He was preparing to go back up and when he got closer to the hole in the wall.

You have found: ***Mature dungeon.***

Everything stopped for Richter. He had never gotten a confirmation that the age scale used for dungeons was the same as it had been in the game, but mature dungeons had meant they had been around for anywhere between one hundred and one thousand years. It didn't necessarily mean that what you found inside was going to be more dangerous than any other dungeon, but it was enough of an indication that Richter seriously considered getting the fuck out of Dodge.

He backed up and looked around, expanding his senses, but didn't detect anything dangerous. Richter looked at his familiar to see if she had anything to add, but the dragonling just looked back at him, waiting for his decision. He came to a decision. Whatever had been down that hole might be long gone by now, but even if there was still a danger, it would be best to do some scouting. This could very well be the reason that the village had given him a quest.

Another point was that his quest counter for Know Your Backyard I was still at a disappointing 0/3. As of right now, all he knew was that he had found a big hole in the ground. If he didn't explore further, the last several hours would have been a waste. No, he had to figure out what had happened here or at least what type of threat it might pose now. If he was going to go exploring, though, he was going to put his best foot forward.

He called the adder down to join him and sent Futen to scout ahead invisibly. Richter looked at his Ring of Spell Storage and decided that *Weak Sonic Wail* might not be the best spell to place there. He was here for reconnaissance more than anything else. He didn't need or want, to get into a knockdown fight. He actually needed a way to avoid one. Thinking about the possible tight spaced underground he made his decision. Richter dismissed the previously stored spell and the gem on the ring reverted back to a clear crystal. Then he started the cast of *Weak Rending Talons*. Rather than manifest the spell, however, he channeled it into his ring. The inert stone set into the band started to glow with a soft green radiance again, showing that the spell had been captured.

While he waited for Futen to return, Richter examined the hole that was the entrance to the dungeon. When he had first seen it, he had guessed that part of the falling ceiling had struck the wall. On closer examination, he saw that he was wrong. The stones around the hole were pushed outward toward him. Looking even closer he got a chill. Claw marks could be seen on the side of the stone that faced the tunnel beyond. What monster had been able to leave claw marks on solid stone? Richter had no idea, but he was starting to get an idea of what had happened to the people that had once lived above.

As soon as he had that thought, a quest prompt appeared.

You have been offered a Quest: **Proper Rest I**
The people who lived above fell victim to an unknown attacker. Though this incident most likely occurred long ago, these people deserve better than to just be forgotten.
Success Conditions: Find some evidence of their fate.
Optional Condition: Put their remains to rest.
Reward: Unknown
Penalty for failure or refusal of Quest: Unknown
Do you accept? Yes or No

The quest seemed in line with what he was already doing and, besides, fighting the good fight and laying people to rest was kinda his jam these days. Richter selected 'Yes' and the prompt disappeared.

Richter started to seriously second-guess his decision to enter the dungeon on his own. The claw marks were basically a big, flashing 'Keep Out' sign. The only thing that would have tipped off his danger sense more would have been a sexually-repressed librarian chick saying, 'Jinkies.' Yeah, it was time to go. He sent a mental call to the remnant to return.

Minutes passed, but still there was no sign of Futen. Richter sent out another mental call, but still nothing. Alma landed on his shoulders and snaked her head around to look at him.

Something is wrong, master. The irritating light should have been back by now.

I think you're right, my love. Richter's lips firmed, **We cannot leave him down there, though. Even if he is an irritating light.**

Sighing deeply, Richter looked into the dark hole.

"Fuck."

CHAPTER 16 -- DAY 112 -- KUBORN 2, 15368 EBG

"Now see. This is exactly why you don't go adventuring on your own," Richter said to himself. He started a dual casting. If something had happened to Futen, then speed was now more important than stealth. It also occurred to him that his *Stealth* skill was most likely not going to be effective in the dungeon. The remnant could turn fully invisible. Compared to that, his own camouflage abilities were paltry. Yup, he thought, it was time for a show of force. He cast *Summon Weak Saproling.*

A green disc appeared in the air. It was six feet in diameter and even before the saproling emerged Richter heard a hunting cat's roar. The forest creature dove through the green disc. Each time he used this spell, the minor forest elemental took a different form. This time, it was in the shape of a mountain lion, four feet high at the shoulder. It had six legs, and, instead of fur, it was covered in countless small, green leaves. The lion looked at Richter, and he saw that its eyes were actually red agates striped in white. It let loose another snarl and stood at the ready. Richter used *Analyze* to get a better grip on its capabilities.

Name: Barrow Beast	**Level:** 12	**Disposition:** Friendly
STATS		
Health: 260	**Mana:** 250	**Stamina:** 270
ATTRIBUTES		
Strength: 16	**Agility:** 28	**Dexterity:** 17
Constitution: 26	**Endurance:** 27	**Intelligence:** 25
Wisdom: 17	**Charisma:** 8	**Luck:** 11

DESCRIPTION
A low-level forest elemental, a saproling can take many forms. They are often summoned by Novice Earth mages for a variety of tasks. Though helpful for mundane tasks, they can also attack with deadly force when needed.

A smile ghosted across his face. His Summoner's Ring had worked. The creature was five levels higher than any creature he had been able to conjure before, and, more importantly, its stats matched. The elevated Agility and Dexterity meant it would be hard to hit, but its Intelligence also spoke to the possibility that it could be a caster. Richter was about to tell it to go into the tunnel when he thought about his mental connection to the shale adder. His *Psi Bond* had been synergistic with his Beast Bonding skill, allowing him to psychically communicate in a limited way with the snake. Who was to say that he couldn't do the same thing here?

Richter searched that part of his mind that Alma occupied and saw her thought pattern shining like a noonday sun in summer. In the same section, he was able to detect the adder's mind. It appeared like an easily-seen, but distant star. Unfortunately, he didn't see anything else to indicate a connection to the saproling. Undaunted, he reached his mind out to the forest creature, willing a joining to occur. Nothing happened.

He stared at the forest elemental, straining to use an ability that he had never consciously utilized in the past. After a minute, Richter exhaled in frustration. He might as well be trying to move rocks with his mind. At the sound of his irritation, the saproling turned to look at him. Their eyes met, and he felt a connection. Another distant star appeared in that part of his mind. It was slightly fainter than the light representing his connection with the shale adder, but it was there.

Know This! Your mental fortitude has brought your ***Psi Bond*** *ability to new heights. Eye contact offers the chance to connect with other creatures in a limited way. The extent of the connection will vary based on the mental abilities of yourself and the recipient. Never forget that doors can swing both ways.*

Ominous much? Richter waited for a moment, but nothing bad happened. The saproling continued to look at him with its agate eyes. Feeling like he had wasted enough time, he tried a few sample commands: move left, move right, lay down. The saproling followed each of his instructions as soon as he finished thinking them. Nodding to himself, he sent a picture of Futen with his mind. The construct didn't give any indication that it understood, but he figured that it couldn't hurt. Richter cast *Far Light* and shot a ball of light down the hole.

The light sped forward for fifty feet and affixed itself to a wall. Richter cast *Far Light* several more times, but at an angle, affixing the balls to the walls of the tunnel. Then he cast *Simple Light* and climbed into the hole. He gave a psychic order to the saproling and adder, sending them ahead of him. Alma wanted to scout too, but he kept her on his shoulders. There was no knowing what was ahead of them. Richter hadn't come across anything that could have detected Futen before. Though he didn't want to sacrifice either the saproling or the snake unnecessarily, if something bad was going to happen, he wanted it to happen to them, not him or Alma.

Richter waited until his commanded creatures were twenty feet ahead, then he climbed into the hole himself. The tunnel beyond was a mix of stone walls and earthen floor. The air was stale, and he caught the faint scent of rot and damp, but it wasn't overpowering. He drew his frost sword from his back sheath and left his other hand free for casting.

Richter reasoned that Futen couldn't have been too far away if he was just stuck somehow. Originally, the remnant had only been able to travel one hundred yards away from him if they weren't at the village. That distance had more than doubled in the time since he had become Master of the village, but Futen still couldn't travel too far on his own. Of course, that might not matter if something else had captured him, but Richter would cross that bridge if and when he came to it.

He reached his first light and saw that the tunnel curved to the right. Richter cast *Far Light* several more times. This segment of the tunnel only went straight for about another twenty feet. Richter sent his summoned creature ahead with the snake again and followed afterward. The impromptu party followed that pattern for the next five minutes. Richter grew concerned after they had traveled more than three hundred yards from the entrance to the dungeon. Something had happened to Futen.

A few minutes later, the tunnel leveled out, and they reached a large cavern. Unlike the natural and irregular stone of the tunnel, this room was clearly man-made. For the first time since entering the dungeon, Richter didn't need to cast *Far Light* to see. Two large braziers hung from the ceiling and inside of each burned bright, blue flames. In their light, Richter had no difficulty seeing the figure that was holding Futen.

It was a humanoid dressed in black armor. It stood six feet tall, and a large axe hung from its back. Its helmet was held in one hand, making it easy to see that whatever it was, it was no longer alive. The face was gaunt and wizened. Moldy holes pockmarked the head in places, and on its scalp, yellowed bone even peeked through in places. That didn't stop it from standing upright, though. A well-defined burn stretched across its face in the shape of a handprint. What captured Richter's attention though was that in its other hand, it held Futen.

A nimbus of purple, black light surrounded the remnant. A writhing tether of the same color extended from the grey sphere and led to the undead thing's open mouth. Pulses of light flowed regularly from Futen towards the figure. In just a few seconds it took to take this all in, Richter could see that Futen's light was dimming with each pulse of light. The fucking thing was feeding on him.

"Let him go, motherfucker!" Richter shouted as he used *Analyze*.

Name: Decaemur Knight	**Level:** 37	**Disposition:** Angry
	STATS	
Health: 387/510	**Mana:** 283/360	**Stamina:** 251/480
	ATTRIBUTES	
Strength: 31 (46)	**Agility:** 16 (31)	**Dexterity:** 15 (32)
Constitution: 51	**Endurance:** 48	**Intelligence:** 36
Wisdom: 21	**Charisma:** 12	**Luck:** 12

DESCRIPTION
A Decaemur Knight is a dangerous enemy. They are often employed by stronger undead to lead weaker units. Decaemur knights can utilize both magical and martial skills, though they normally specialize in melee combat. A true knight leads a retinue and decaemur knights take this to the extreme, often enslaving fallen victims to serve them even after death. Wounds caused by these knights have a high likelihood of becoming necrotic.

Richter didn't understand what the parentheses meant, but as he watched, the knight's Strength, Agility, and Dexterity rose by one. The damn thing was getting stronger. Feeding off of Futen must be restoring it somehow. A few seconds after Richter shouted at it, the knight turned its head and glared at him. The tether broke, but Futen remained trapped in the purple-black nimbus of Death magic. The undead's eyes glowed with an inner light, and it spoke in a powerful and scathing voice.

"YOU DARE INTERRUPT MY MEAL? I HAVE BEEN GUARDING THIS PORTAL FOR CENTURIES, LOWERING MYSELF TO FEED UPON THE VERMIN AND WEAK SOULS THAT PASS THROUGH THIS CAVERN. NOW YOU WOULD **DARE TO STOP MY FEEDING?** I WILL CONSUME THIS THING, AND THEN I WILL TEAR YOUR SOUL FROM YOUR PATHETIC BODY!"

Richter glared back at it, "Or maybe I'll just kill you, then skull fuck you. Then leave a note here that I skull fucked a decaemur knight. That's another option. What do you think?"

The undead monster blinked in complete surprise and even in death looked completely shocked. It could never have conceived of a human coming into its lair and talking shit. Well, Richter thought, I'm an American. We give zero fux about anything. With that profound mission statement ringing in his mind, he sent a mental command, **Attack!**

The saproling let loose a screeching roar and bounded towards the knight. The snake started slithering faster than Richter would have thought possible towards his enemy as well. Alma launched into the air and cast *Weak Haste* on herself before launching herself forward.

The three-pronged attack shook the undead fighter out of its stupor. It let go of Futen, who unfortunately still stayed immobilized in the field of necrotic light, and immediately began weaving one hand in an incantation while it shouted guttural words of magic. With its other hand, it placed its helmet on and then freed the axe from its back. Before any of the attackers had crossed even half the distance of the long hall, the knight finished his casting. A ball of purple-black light shot forward ten feet and hovered for a moment before exploding and shooting in multiple directions. None of the light struck Richter's three helpers. Instead, it struck the walls, ceiling, and floor before disappearing. Maybe that's all that will happen, Richter thought with false hope. Of course, that was when the whole frakking room started shaking.

A low, moaning wail filled the chamber. Ethereal creatures started floating into the room from where the purple light had struck. Five, then ten, and finally fourteen ghostlike figures phased into being. To make matters worse, the light had awakened more than just specters. In three different places, bony hands shot up from the floor, displacing the flagstones. Skeletons rose from the ground, and not the simple collections of bones Richter had fought in the past. These bones were thicker than they should have been for human remains and sharp projections rose from their flexor joints. Bony thorns stuck out of their elbows and knees and capped each finger. When balls of purple light started glowing in their eye sockets, Richter thought, Enough already! You're badass. We get it.

The snake and saproling continued on to attack the knight despite the massive amount of reinforcements it had summoned. Alma showed much more wisdom. She slowed down and started casting as many buffs as she could, namely: *Weak Life Armor* and *Weak Life Aura.* A golden nimbus surrounded the dragonling as she swooped in to attack the specters. The small but nimble creature dived towards a knot of ghosts and unleashed a new spell, *Weak Banish Undead.* One of the ghosts winked out of existence. Alma trumpeted her success and flew off to attack the next one.

Richter didn't even notice the effectiveness of the spell. His sole focus was on casting his Spirit spell. Since ordering the attack, he had been casting *Weak Aura Lance.* The spell had a long cast time of ten seconds, but Richter had a feeling that the decaemur knight was no ordinary enemy. The fact that the knight had summoned almost a full score of minions further underscored that truth.

Waves of black and gold power rose off of him as he dual cast the spell. The energy focused in front of him, beginning as a small sphere. As he continued to cast, the sphere grew larger. When he was only a few seconds into the incantation, Richter realized that this casting was much easier than when he had used the spell against the rock giant. When he had tried it last time, Richter had felt buffeted by various emotions and concerns. The spell had resisted him. This time, it was much easier, the movement and words flowing with greater alacrity. He could only think that it was thanks to Alma's mental training. Richter focused on his objective and kept chanting.

The saproling was fighting the decaemur knight. The two were battling fiercely. The knight swung his axe with two hands at the forest creature. The saproling responded to the attack instantly. As soon as the weapon moved towards it, the forest creature stopped its forward movement and changed direction on a dime, springing to the side. The motion seemed almost impossible, but its powerful six legs let it dodge the attack. Fangs out, it swiped at the knight, its thorn claws screeching across the knight's armor, but failing to do any serious damage. The knight swung again, and this time, the saproling ducked under the blow. The fight continued.

While this was going on, the adder struck at the specters weaving around it. The snake struck faster than the eye could follow. With its mouth agape, it impacted an ethereal being and passed right through it. Before the snake could even withdraw, the specter counterattacked. Though the snake didn't seem to be able to harm the ghosts, the spirits had no such limitation. Its bony hand struck the snake's back making a small gouge in the tamed animal's scaled skin. Red blood leaked down from the wound, and the edges of the cut began to blacken. The snake drew back, but before the animal could do anything, ten more ghosts descended. The adder started writhing on the ground as ghostly claws started taking its life away in a hell of a thousand cuts.

Alma was doing her best to help, but the banishing spell had a cooldown of five minutes and so couldn't be cast again until that elapsed. Luckily, she found out that her very body was now a weapon. Some of the ghosts had immediately converged on her, flying through the air to attack. When their hands came into contact with her glowing body, though, they wailed and pulled back, unable to tolerate the Life magic surrounding her. Smiling a draconian smile, she dive bombed through the bodies of the ghosts attacking the adder, while simultaneously casting *Weak Slow Heal* on the snake.

Just before Richter finished his spell, the lion saproling showed the importance of summoning higher level creatures. The three skeletons had fully emerged from the ground, and they were converging on the forest elemental. The decaemur knight had managed to score a blow against the outnumbered saproling, but it wasn't enough to hinder the creature. With a powerful jump of all six legs, the lion leapt twenty feet away and then whipped its head around to look at the knight. A yowling roar shook the hall, and a green glow enveloped the saproling's body. Green vines shot up in a five-foot radius with the knight in the center. They wrapped around the legs of two of the skeletons and the undead summoner, temporarily rooting them in place.

With a final shouted word of Power, Richter finished his spell. The basketball-sized sphere shot forward. It was black as a moonless midnight one minute and then a ball of molten gold the next. The sphere lengthened into a javelin that struck the knight in its chest. Immobilized as it was, the knight had no chance to evade. Just as with the rock giant, its skin broke into countless pieces which floated up and dissipated. Afterwards, the knight looked the same, but Richter could see the vines holding it climbed a bit further up the undead fighter's legs. The saproling dove in again and hit the remaining free skeleton with a flying leap. The two went down in a rolling pile, several yards away from the knight and the other two skeletons.

Now that his casting was done, Richter wanted to know more what he was facing. He used *Analyze* on the knight's summoned creatures.

Name: Decaemur Ghost	**Level:** 6	**Disposition:** Angry
STATS		
Health: 130	**Mana:** 40	**Stamina:** 110

ATTRIBUTES		
Strength: 12	**Agility:** 12	**Dexterity:** 14
Constitution: 13	**Endurance:** 11	**Intelligence:** 4
Wisdom: 5	**Charisma:** 2	**Luck:** 10
DESCRIPTION		
A Decaemur Ghost is a low-level specter. Its ability to deal damage is minor, but when it strikes, wounds often become necrotic. The ethereal nature of this being lets it ignore mundane physical damage.		

Name: Decaemur Skeleton	**Level:** 12	**Disposition:** Angry
STATS		
Health: 220	**Mana:** 10	**Stamina:** 280
ATTRIBUTES		
Strength: 17	**Agility:** 16	**Dexterity:** 16
Constitution: 22	**Endurance:** 28	**Intelligence:** 1
Wisdom: 1	**Charisma:** 4	**Luck:** 10
DESCRIPTION		
A Decaemur Skeleton is the infantry soldier. They have bones of greater density than normal skeletons and are equipped with natural weapons in the form of bony knobs.		

Neither the skeletons nor the ghosts posed any real danger to Richter individually, but the knight was a potentially serious threat. The three bound enemies were already pulling themselves free from vines. Looking around, he quickly assessed the situation. The saproling had pulled one of the skeleton's arms free and was now savaging the other. The leaves that covered it had turned black in large swaths, but that only appeared to enrage the forest elemental.

Alma was flying through the ghosts, causing small amounts of continual damage. The snake, though, was looking the worse for wear. It bled from countless cuts. Richter decided to aid his tamed animal. Running forward, he cast *Weak Life Aura* on the snake and also cast *Weak Slow Heal.* The adder had just been lying in a defensive coil, but Richter ordered it to attack again. Obedient to its master, the snake raised its head and shot its head towards a ghost. Unlike the last time, the ghost reared back from the adder's attack. With a hiss of animalistic vengeance, the snake laid into any ghost it could find.

Richter turned his attention to the knight. The skeletons were still bound fairly tightly, but the knight was almost free. "Where you going, bitch?" Richter called out. The knight looked at him, the flames in its purple eyes dancing in anger. Richter cast *Grease.*

All three bound figures fell. Not giving them a chance to recover, Richter released his stored spell, *Weak Rending Talons.* A swirling maelstrom of claws sprung into being and started damaging the prone undead. Not done, Richter cast one more spell. He shouted, "IGNO!" and a gout of orange flame shot from his hand. The grease caught fire and a ten-by-ten foot area caught flame, burning all within. The knight had been able to ignore the talon spell, but as with all undead, it reacted badly to fire. A strained yell came from the undead summoner.

Leaving them for the moment, Richter drew both swords and threw himself at the ghosts. As with the first time he had tried dual wielding two blades, he felt off balance and unsure. The emotional flood from using Spirit Magic wasn't helping, but his new Self-Awareness skill kept the worst of it at bay. Richter rushed forward, concerned that his blades would not have an effect on the non-corporeal spirits, but oh boy, was he wrong!

The sonic blade cut into the first ghost and not only did damage, but it also left a rent in its ethereal body. He followed up with another overhand chop with his ice-enchanted blade. The result was just as spectacular as the first blow. Another ghost struck him from behind, but between the weakness of the attack and the quality of his armor he was able to shrug it off with only a point or two of health being lost. Richter spun into the sword form *Samara Seed Falling,* both blades held out, one hundred and eighty degrees to each other. One blade finished the ghost he had been attacking while the other cut two more decaemur spirits that had the misfortune of being inside of his attack radius. Alma finished off one of those with

Weak Life Bolt, and the third drifted off. Master and familiar shared a triumphant look.

I think I can finish this off, my love. Let's not waste the souls though!

I will take care of it, master, she thought gleefully.

Richter laid into any spirit he could reach, and Alma flew above casting *Soul Trap* again and again. The adder continued to help with its Life magic enhanced body. Once she had cast the spell on all the ghosts, Alma flew over to the almost dismantled skeleton the saproling had been fighting and cast *Soul Trap* again. With things well in hand, she attached herself to the skeleton and used *Brain Drain,* quickly stealing its remaining HPs. Everything was going great until the knight shouted, "ENOUGH OF THIS!"

Richter looked over towards the grease fire and saw that the knight had managed to roll free. The flames had been great at damaging the undead, but they had also weakened the magical roots that had held the knight in place. Despite the fact that it was still burning and coated with grease, the undead summoner stood tall. It wove its fingers into a particular configuration and purple light coalesced around its arms. Not sure what to expect, Richter finished the ghost he was fighting and raised both swords. Again, neither he nor the nonhuman members of his party were the target's of the knight's spell.

Instead, the purple light on its arms shot out in tethers to the remaining summoned dead. The ropes of Death magic looked just like the one it had connected to Futen, and it drew the remaining energy from the skeletons and the ghosts into itself. Multiple swirls of rainbow light wove through the air and into Richter's bag, but he barely noticed. All he could focus on was the knight as it restored itself to its full glory.

The damn thing had grown six inches! Richter used *Analyze* again and saw that all of its stats had risen to full power. Also, its health, mana, and stamina were completely restored. Even the flames had gone out. It walked wide around the still-burning grease fire and started towards Richter. The saproling and adder took up positions on either side of him, and Alma floated above, staring coldly at the knight. Richter downed several potions, then brought both swords up, waiting for the thing's next move.

The knight stopped forty feet away, both hands holding its large axe. Futen still hovered in the prison of Death magic, but

Richter was relieved that the remnant's inner light hadn't gotten any fainter. The undead spoke.

"WHEN FIRST YOU INVADED THIS PLACE I MISJUDGED YOU. LONG HAVE I DWELT IN THIS HALL, CHARGED TO GUARD THE PORTAL. I CONFESS I WAS DRUNK ON THE CONSUMED ENERGY OF THIS FLYING STONE. AS ONE WARRIOR TO ANOTHER, I WOULD OFFER YOU TERMS. IF YOU HELP ME TO DEPART THIS PLACE NOW, I WILL RETURN YOUR CAPTURED COMRADE. I ASK ONLY THAT YOU HELP ME TO DESTROY A RUNE THAT HAS BOUND ME TO THIS DUNGEON. FURTHERMORE, ONCE I AM FREED I WILL TRAVEL FAR FROM THIS FOREST, NEVER TO CROSS PATHS WITH YOU AGAIN. FOR YOUR HELP, I WILL ALSO TELL YOU A SECRET OF THIS PLACE. IF YOU CHOOSE TO NOT DEPART, THEN I OFFER YOU THE HONOR OF SINGLE COMBAT. IF YOU CHOOSE TO ACCEPT, I WILL SUMMON A MINION TO TELL YOU THE SECRET IN THE EVENT OF MY DESTRUCTION. WHAT SAY YOU?" The knight's voice boomed in the hall. Despite the room being large, the sound still echoed slightly painfully in Richter's ears.

You have been offered Discordant Quests:
Quest #1: **Freedom for the Fallen.** The decaemur knight has been forcibly bound to guard this room and an unknown portal for centuries. **Success Conditions:** Free the decaemur knight **Rewards:** Futen's safe return A secret of this place.
Quest #2: **Honorable Combat for the Honorable Dead** The decaemur knight offers to fight you one-on-one, without any minions. The offer is made that if you win, you will still learn the secret from one of its minions. The knight has been trapped here for so long that even the possibility of an honorable death seems tempting to it. **Success Conditions:** Win in single combat **Rewards:**

Futen's safe return A secret of this place
Know This! Both quests cannot be accepted. Choosing one will lead to the refusal of the other. What is your choice?

Richter stared at the knight in surprise. When the undead had drained the life force from the other Death creatures, he had expected the hall to turn into rock'em sock'em robots and had just secretly been praying to be the blue one. Evidently, he had proven himself, though, and the knight was willing to bow out.

He told Alma what the quest said and asked what she thought he should do.

You are an honorable man, master. I have full confidence that you could destroy this foe. On the other hand, I say that we should just stall for time until our mana regenerates, and our spell cooldowns elapse.

Richter smiled broadly at her, feeling a peculiar mix of pride and excitement, like seeing the gangly neighborhood girl you grew up with stretching in yoga pants for the first time. She smiled back and continued, **Besides, I don't think your saproling is looking too good.**

He looked at the forest cat and saw that she was right. The leaves that served as its skin were beginning to fall off exposing the wicker lattice underneath. A green disc appeared and the saproling entered it without even a farewell snarl. The time on the spell had elapsed, and the elemental had returned to wherever it called home.

"WHAT SAY YOU?" The knight boomed again.

"Just a second," Richter said in admonishment. He sheathed one of his swords and looked at the adder. The snake had small, black marks all over its body. It wasn't at death's door, but it was really looking the worse for wear. Richter extended his hand and cast *Weak Slow Heal.*

"WHAT ARE YOU DOING? GIVE ME YOUR ANSWER?"

"My pet is injured! You say you're an honorable knight, but you are willing to let an innocent animal suffer because you're impatient? If you want to go mano a mano, head-to-head, your pikachu to my squirtle, then you have to wait a goddamn minute. I know you want an answer, but I'm absolutely distraught over my pet suffering. Really! This snake is like part of my family. You've been down here for centuries; you can wait another minute or two."

The knight glared at him, purple light flaring in its eyes. Richter wondered if he had overplayed his hand. He tightened his grip on his short sword preparing to defend himself, but the knight gave a curt nod. The undead began to pace, muttering to itself. Could the undead mutter?

Richter healed the snake three more times and the knight's agitation grew each time that golden light flared. Finally, the undead had had enough and shouted while hefting its axe, "CHOOSE NOW!"

Richter looked up with a smile. He could never be sure if he was under the influence of Spirit magic or not, but he said, "Well if you're going to be a dick about it, I'll give you my answer." He pointed at Futen, "The fact is, you fucked with my boy. Soooo, I think all of us will just need to fuck you up."

"YOU HAVE NO HONOR!" the knight accused.

"Says the guy that eats people," Richter retorted. "Let's do this!"

You have refused both Quests.

Richter cast *Weak Life Aura* on the snake and sent it forward. Alma cast *Weak Life Bolt* at the knight, who ducked under the attack and began a casting of its own. A circle of purple light appeared on the floor as the knight began its spell. Alma started casting buffs on everyone while Richter re-summoned the saproling. He looked at the knight behind its spell barrier and thought; you might think you're safe jabroni, but just wait. I've got some Forge of Heavens weapons coming for your ass!

The green disc appeared again, and the mountain lion reemerged. All damage it had sustained before was gone. The cat bared its teeth and leapt forward to attack the knight. Richter started casting buffs on himself: *Haste, Weak Life Armor, Barkskin,* then he downed another two mana potions. As ready as he would ever be, he drew both swords and ran forward to attack the barrier and reach the knight beneath.

The undead warrior had not been idle, though, and as Richter ran towards it, the knight finished its own spell. A purple-black disc popped into existence, and a rank scent filled the air. Three skeletons in chainmail tromped through the disc before it winked out of existence. They were a full foot taller than the previous skeletons and all held weapons. The knight sent them forward with a wave of its hand. "YOU SHALL NOW MEET DEATH AT THE HANDS OF MY SKELETAL WARRIORS! I WILL FEAST ON YOUR, WHAT!?"

One of the skeletal warriors the knight had been crowing about glowed golden for a moment, then disappeared. Alma trumpeted her triumph. Richter grinned and threw one of his short swords at another warrior. The blade sunk into its chest, popping rusty chainmail links with ease. With his other hand, he cast *Weak Banish Undead.* A golden glow surrounded the warrior. The skeleton resisted the spell for a moment, but Richter's mastery of Life gave the casting a 50% bump in power. The gold light sunk into the Death creature and it faded away.

The last skeleton swung its sword at Richter's head. The chaos seed committed himself to the sword form *Reaping Wheat.* Dropping to one knee, he swung his blade horizontally through the skeleton's knee. The green metal of his elementum blade cut through the hardened bone with ease. Richter stood quickly, and as he did, he grabbed the blade that was sticking out of the skeleton's chest. It came free easily. The undead warrior hit the ground, and Richter swiped down with his sword, separating the head from the body. The rest of the skeleton lost cohesion.

The decaemur knight looked at Richter, eyes widened in shock. It clearly had not expected its minions to be dispatched so quickly. Richter held up one blade and walked up to the spell barrier, "Don't worry, sweetheart. We'll be together soon." Then he swung his sword.

The barrier didn't last long. Richter's Forge of Heavens Mark gave his attacks +10% damage versus spell barriers. Coupled with the +10% damage against spell barriers that weapons made in the Forge gained, each strike took nearly eighty points away from the shield. Within a minute it collapsed, and the final battle was joined.

The purple-black shield dropped and the saproling dove forward. The knight swung a heavy blow from left to right at the elemental. The lion had been able to avoid the previous attacks, but this time, the knight was back to full strength. The black axe head struck the saproling in one of its middle paws, and the force of the blow knocked it to one side. The axe had cut deep, rendering that paw useless. With five to spare, however, the summoned creature wasn't out of the fight.

Alma fired a lightning bolt at the knight. Its decreased resistances made it susceptible to various magics. Originally the undead creature had 0% resistance to Air magic, but now that had dropped below zero, it was vulnerable to her attack. The stun effect took over, and it toppled forward. Richter wasted no time capitalizing on its weakness. He rushed forward and stabbed his sonic sword into the crook of the knight's neck. The sword slid down into its chest, doing massive damage.

The stun effect did not last long. The low-level Air magic did not have the power to completely overcome the knight, weakened resistance or no. The decaemur fighter stood, showing no concern for the weapon sticking out of its neck and blocked Richter's next attack with its black-armored forearm. The elementum blade bit into the armor, but not enough to cause the knight meaningful harm. It pushed the blade away and grabbed Richter by the throat.

The chaos seed's strength was not inconsiderable, but it could not match the undead knight's fully restored power. The saproling yowled from the side, preparing to dive at the decaemur. Rather than wait for the attack, the knight dropped its axe and wove its hand in an arcane pattern. The saproling sprung, but a beam of necrotic energy shot from the undead's gauntlet. It struck the saproling in the chest when it was only a foot away. The cat crumpled to the ground, black energy eating its body. The shale adder wove around the knight's midsection, squeezing as hard as it could, but the undead just ignored it. Richter stabbed his remaining sword through the undead's torso, but it did not have living organs, so the hit did not register as critical. The knight squeezed harder, and Richter began to see stars.

Alma had not wasted the distraction. She descended from behind the knight and latched onto the back of the knight's head. Though it had ignored a blade that was still sticking out of its body, the psychic attack could not be so easily shrugged off. It reached up with its free hand while continuing to strangle Richter with the other. The chaos seed wasn't going to let Alma be mauled, though. He reached out with both hands up and grabbed the knight's free hand.

It struggled against him and squeezed his neck harder, but Richter didn't let go.

He started to hear his heart throb in his ears and his vision darkened, but he knew he just had to hold on until his dragonling could kill this fucking thing. He let go with one hand to slam a fist down on the sword sticking out of its neck before frantically grabbing the knight's arm again. Even letting go for a moment had allowed the knight to move its arm a few inches closer to Alma. He could only hope that he had hastened its end. The throbbing in his head spoke of impending unconsciousness, though, so he doubted it. Everything went black.

The next thing he knew, he had been thrown into the air. The saproling had recovered from the Death magic attack and had just enough strength left to rush at the knight. This time, it just aimed at running through the undead's legs. The knight might be much stronger than the cat, but it couldn't ignore physics. The elemental had been able to pick up enough speed that it knocked the knight off its feet. Richter was thrown free in the confusion. Looking up, he saw the knight on all fours, Alma still attached to its back. He knew he couldn't wait.

A strangled cry came from Richter's throat as he scrambled to his feet. He dove at the knight, arms outstretched. His hands grabbed the blade sticking out of its chest and pulled it free. Richter took a risk and cast *Soul Trap*. A quick use of Analyze showed that the creature only had a few dozen life left. The knight looked up at him a snarl on its wizened face. In a variation of the sword form *The Drunken Barber*, Richter swung his sword and decapitated his enemy.

A ribbon of rainbow light swirled around Richter and then disappeared into his bag. The undead knight had been laid to its final rest.

CHAPTER 17 -- DAY 112 -- KUBORN 2, 15368 EBG

With the knight's death, the purple light holding Futen in place winked out. The remnant dropped like a stone. He made a solid clack as he impacted the ground. Richter rushed over to the remnant. Alma flew into the air with a cry of triumph, while the adder and saproling simply waited for further instructions.

Richter picked up the remnant and held Futen close to his face. The white light at the stone's heart continued to pulse regularly, though it was dimmer than normal. "Futen. Futen! Can you hear me?"

The light started to pulse a bit stronger, "I can hear you, my lord. You are breathing on me." The remnant's tone was as deadpan as ever. Richter couldn't ignore that the voice was somewhat querulous, though and that there might have been just a touch of relief in it as well.

Richter laughed. He definitely was relieved. As frustrating as the remnant was, the little floating night light had become dear to him. "Can you fly?" he asked.

"I will need to absorb mana from the village pool, my lord. I was unable to access any mana while I was being held in the decaemur's spell. With enough magic, I will heal enough to be able to travel. I will need to return to the Great Seal to heal completely."

"Do what you need to do," Richter said.

The white light at Futen's core started pulsing faster, and Richter monitored the village mana. Two hundred and seventeen points were consumed in short order, and the remnant floated into the air.

"I am feeling much improved, my lord." Futen's voice was indeed stronger.

"Good," Richter said nodding. "Then I need your help. The knight kept going on and on about a secret he had and a portal he was guarding. Search the room and see what you can find."

"As you wish, my lord." Futen floated off.

Richter checked the adder and saw that it was still bleeding in places. Richter cast *Weak Slow Heal,* and the wounds closed. The snake hissed in relief and coiled upon itself, exhausted. He could admit that the fight had tired him out as well. His stamina was full now, but he still felt a bit mentally drained. The effects of casting the Spirit spell were nowhere near as overwhelming as the previous time, but he could still feel that his emotions were in flux. Controlling them was also taking a toll. Richter was actually surprised that he had so much more control after only a bit of training, but he supposed it was the same as fighting naked or in leather armor. Leather armor didn't offer much defense to a sword strike, but it was still worlds better than getting struck wearing only one's skin.

Putting such thoughts aside, he focused on the notifications he had earned.

You have trapped the soul of a ***Decaemur Ghost****! Soul level: Common.* ***x 9***

You have trapped the soul of a ***Decaemur Skeleton****! Soul level: Common.*

You have trapped the soul of a ***Decaemur Knight****! Soul level: Luminous.*

You have been awarded 4,064 (base 92,887 x 0.07 x 1.25 x 0.5) experience from Brain Drain against Level 13 Decaemur Skeleton.

You have been awarded 65,805 (base 1,504,103 x 0.07 x 1.25 x 0.5) experience from Brain Drain against Level 37 Decaemur Knight.

Richter broke off reading to give a "Woot!" He was well on his way to restoring the XP he had spent. The knight had been a serious opponent, and if this guy was only the gatekeeper then wherever that portal it had been talking about led might be an XP gold mine. He got back to his prompts.

Your familiar has reached level 30!

Your familiar has reached level 31!

Congratulations! You have reached skill level 11 in **Small Blades***. +2% attack speed. +2% bonus to damage.*

Congratulations! You have reached skill levels 2 and 3 in **Dual Wield***. Base accuracy penalty in primary hand reduced to 23% and in offhand by 48%. Attack speed increased by +3%.*

Congratulations! You have reached subskill level 10 in **Grace in Combat***. Dodge increased by 19% while wearing all Light Armor.*

Congratulations! You have reached skill level 8 in **Life Magic***. New spells are now available.*

Congratulations! You have reached skill level 3 in **Beast Bonding***. +1% effectiveness to Tame. +1% attack and defense of bonded creatures.*

Congratulations! You have reached skill level 8 in **Self-Awareness***. +2% mental and emotional control.*

You have received 625 (base 1,000 x 1.25 x 0.5) bonus experience for reaching level 10 in the subskill: **Grace in Combat***.*

Congratulations! You have advanced from Novice to Initiate in: **Grace in Combat.** *Your understanding of how to move in Light armor has increased. +5% movement speed if wearing all Light Armor. This effect is cumulative with successive ranks.*

All of those prompts were good news, but what really caught Richter's attention was the last one. Its border was clear, but it pulsed with white light.

Congratulations! You have captured a memory from a **Decaemur Knight***. This memory can only be accessed for the next twenty-four hours before dissolution into the ether. Experiencing this memory will be instantaneous in regards to your timeline. Do you wish to access this memory? Yes or No?*

Richter smiled. He could only imagine what the memory held. If it was something important, could it perhaps be the secret the knight had been referencing? Either way, Richter felt better after reading the prompt. One of the things he had been worried about was getting caught in a memory for a long period of time. It wouldn't be so good if he was immobilized for a long period of time. He would never live it down if The Land's equivalent of a Dragon Warrior blue slime slowly beat him to death while he just stood there drooling.

Richter selected 'Yes' and his vision went black.

He panicked for a second, but a green light flared. Not the dark green that he normally associated with Earth magic. This was more of a brighter neon and, for lack of a better word, ethereal light. Richter realized that he was kneeling with his head slightly bent, as if in prayer. His position didn't inhibit his view of the chamber in any way, though a moment later he wished it had. The green light was coming from two braziers suspended from the ceiling. The dancing, lime-colored flames flickered in-and-out of existence. Observing the strange fire was the last thing on Richter's mind, though. All he could focus on was the upright, X-shaped stands that screaming people were attached to.

Men, women, and children were being devoured by some type of… demon animal. Most of the bound figures were human, but there were also several elves and even a few sprites. The beasts were built like rottweilers, but their skin had been removed, showing the bones beneath. The same neon green energy that illuminated the hall showed through rents in their exposed flesh. There were only five of them, but they were systematically mauling the dozens of people tied to the sacrificial stands.

Several men and women were already sagging dead, their entrails on the ground, mixed with blood and fresh excrement. The monsters methodically tore into the victims one at a time, savaging limbs and genitals to prolong the pain. The beasts seemed particularly pleased when they struck an artery. He saw one animal strike a child's leg and a jet of scarlet shot into the air before subsiding. A moment later, another stream of blood washed over the boy's tormentor, in time with the child's panicked heart. The undead beast clamped its mouth onto the gusher and drank deeply. The child screamed in pain and fear. Before the boy died, though, the monster loosened its bite. The blood loss slowed considerably, letting the small child suffer for a bit longer before death.

A stream of the same green energy came off of each of the dogs and extended back behind Richter's field of vision. The ribbons of light grew darker and thicker as they were fueled by the pain and death. The man whose eyes Richter was seeing through took all of this in but focused mostly on the bloodied body of a screaming, human girl. One of the demon dogs was taking its time tearing off small pieces of her leg and swallowing each bloody chunk whole. In his mind, Richter heard the knight think in tones of shame and love; I am sorry Krista. I am *sorry* Krista. It will be over soon. Please let it be over soon.

Richter felt, or rather the knight felt, a bony hand on the back of his neck. A voice like a dry whisper echoed in his ears, seemingly coming from all directions at once. "You have done well, Jorgen. I accept your sacrifice. As promised, I shall now give you power, and life through the ages."

The figure crossed into his view and Richter saw where the ribbons of light were going. They ended in the chest of a gaunt figure. Its chest was bare, and its skin was desiccated and grey. It wore an open robe of dull red silk and simple, black pants. Thin white hair fell down from its head, but Richter could not see its face, for it was looking at the people screaming for help and an end to their pain.

It raised one hand and started an incantation, still facing away. After a few moments, green fire enveloped its hand, but it showed no discomfort. It spoke in the same whispering voice, making Richter feel as if a spider was slowly walking across his mind, "Say the words."

Jorgen began to speak. Even though Richter could remember that this was its memory, he felt sickened as he relived the man's betrayal, "I forsake life and offer the lives of my loved ones and the blood of my blood. I forsake life and offer the lives of my loved ones and the blood of my blood. I forsake life and offer the lives of my loved ones and the blood of my blood."

It showed no emotion as it turned to look at the knight. Through the soon-to-be-damned man's eyes, Richter could finally see the figure's face. Stark and sunken cheeks framed a cruel, male gaze. Its features were fine like an elf's, and its eyes glowed with the same ubiquitous green light that was spread throughout the chamber, "Thrice heard and witnessed." With that pronouncement, it plunged its hand onto the knight's face. Richter felt a searing agony as the fire marred Jorgen's face and an even worse pain as energy from the magical flame reached inside and perverted the man's immortal soul.

Jorgen/Richter screamed, his vocalized pain mixing with the wails of the sacrificial victims. Unperturbed by the suffering around him, the figure spoke again, "You will serve me by guarding the entrance to my realm. The suffering of these victims will continue until The Land crumbles. Their spirits shall remain bound to this plane, and their perpetual agony at being kept from their rest will power your life and my magic. You will be bound through eternity, damned to remain here at the site of your betrayal of light and life. Your only company shall be those who you slay in my name."

The flames disfiguring Jorgen's face went out. The newly born decaemur knight fell to the ground and wept. Richter's disgust deepened as he realized that the man was grieving not for the people still suffering not thirty feet away, and not even for his daughter whose legs were now only stumps. He grieved for his own future, moaning on the floor with eyes that could no longer weep.

The red robed mage lifted Jorgen's chin. The man flinched, but the mage's grip on his chin firmed. Once they were gazing into one another eyes again, the caster spoke, "You will reside in this place unti…" The fires in its eyes intensified and its gaze deepened. Richter started to feel panic. It felt like the undead lord was looking through Jorgen and seeing him. Confirming his worst fears, it said, "Who are you, Agent of Chaos?" Richter felt it reaching even deeper into Jorgen's mind in an effort to pierce his own. The chaos seed knew instinctively that this was not a foe he could resist, at least not in this type of contest. He felt its will brush up against the edges of his mind, and Richter could sense its hunger to learn his secrets. With a furious exertion of will, he broke the memory link.

Panting, and with sweat running down his face, Richter looked about frantically. He was back in his own time. There were no sacrificial victims, no blood-drinking hounds and, most importantly, no neon green fire or undead master. His legs gave out, and he slumped to the floor in relief. Alma flew over and sat on his lap in concern, mentally asking her master what was wrong. Richter just pulled the dragonling close and held her. He thanked god that he had escaped whatever that thing had been and also that his small love hadn't had to live through what he had just experienced.

CHAPTER 18 -- DAY 112 -- KUBORN 2, 15368 EBG

Quest Update: **Know Your Backyard I**. You have found a Notable Location. This dungeon was the site of a massacre and horrible sacrifice. The knight guarding the entrance to this dungeon was duped into sacrificing his family only to be turned into a slave. You have discovered the importance of 1 of 3 locations.

Quest Update: **Proper Rest I.** The people who lived above this dungeon were sacrificed by one of their own. It was a horrible tragedy and an unforgivable betrayal. You have 24 hours to fulfill the optional requirement and put their remains to rest.

You have been offered a Quest: **Who is the Master?**
You have bonded with your Place of Power but have just been shown that you are not the only authority within the boundaries of your domain. You have narrowly missed being discovered by an undead lord, but can you trust that its power will not one day threaten you and your people? Will you explore this undead realm?
Success Conditions: Find the portal the decaemur knight spoke of and remove this danger
Reward: Unknown
Penalty for failure or refusal of Quest: Unknown
Do you accept? Yes or No

Richter checked his internal clock. Only seconds had passed since he had accepted the memory and that time could be attributed to what he had done since coming 'back.' Alma continued to ask him what had happened. All he could think about though was the pure evil of the mind that had almost touched his. The quest prompt hung in his vision until he perfunctorily selected 'Yes.'

After a few minutes, he calmed down enough and related the story. The dragonling didn't interrupt while he mentally shared the information, at a much faster rate than mere words could have accomplished. He made sure not to share any actual images with his familiar. As soon as he was done with the tale, she let her feelings be known.

Fool! You could have been killed or possessed. You cannot dive into psychic spaces without any defenses in place!

Richter, still somewhat traumatized, didn't try and defend himself. He just asked, **What do you mean defenses?**

She mentally blasted him with a few more invectives, then rubbed her face against his, trying to console him even while she herself was wracked with anger and worry. When she spoke again, though, her tone was patient, **I am sorry that I yelled, master. I was scared for you, and I must accept that this is partly my fault.** She put a heavy emphasis on 'partly.' **You should have told me that our connection was awakening new capabilities in you. I did not know that you had progressed to the point of making mental links. That is a versatile skill, but it is dangerous as well. If I had known, I would have given you training to protect yourself.**

Like when you taught me my Self-Awareness? he asked.

That skill is about inner control. In my homeland, however, there were many creatures that possessed psychic powers. My kind use psychic abilities on an instinctual level, but since my intellect has increased, I can see that my race has instinctual defense mechanisms to protect ourselves from creatures that would use those abilities against us. Her mental tone grew determined, **We will work together each day to train your mind in defense. I WILL NOT lose you, master!**

Richter was both touched by her obvious love for him and taken aback by her ferocity. **I have my 45% mental resistance and I know you have 100%. What else can we do?**

The mental connection to Alma grew staticky. Somehow he knew that meant she was frustrated. She looked up at him thinking of a way to explain herself. Until that moment, Richter had never known how incredibly cute and humorous it could be to see a pondering expression on a dragonling's face. He made sure to keep that thought buried, though. He wasn't in the mood to have her fire lightning in his face. After a few more moments, she apparently came up with an analogy.

Your Small Blades skill is increasing, right, master? He sent her a mental assent, *Sprite Yoshi does not rely only on his Blade skill level in battle, but also in his training and technique, correct?* He sent another assent. *The same is true for your mental defenses. Your increased mental resistance will protect you somewhat from straightforward mental attacks, but even with my 100% resistance, I must still be wary of subtle mental manipulations.*

So, you're saying that my defenses are like a castle, but I have been leaving the gate open? Richter thought to her, feeling good about gaining her point.

Alma looked at him quizzically and then with a long-suffering tone, thought back, *Sure, master. If it helps you to think about it that way. I will help make your 'castle' stronger and teach you to keep your drawbridge up.*

Richter looked down at the impudent little dragonling. "I think my analogy was fine," he muttered under his breath. He also thought it must be an odd quirk of the universe that women were always telling him to keep their 'drawbridges' up. That thought must have leaked through the bond because Alma blew a jet of air into his face. Then she set about teaching him as best she could.

It wasn't easy for her to translate eons of genetic instinct into a set of relatable instructions, but just like when she taught him the skill of Self-Awareness, their mental bond allowed for a steep learning curve. Richter had expected them to start this when safely back in the village, but she said that since they were waiting for Futen to search anyway, there was no reason to wait. He didn't receive any prompts showing a new skill this time. Instead, she guided him in techniques to create his own mental safeguards. Her analogy had been accurate, and the experience was vaguely reminiscent of learning Yoshi's sword forms. It taught him to use what he already had, making him much more effective.

The two of them got lost in their mental communion. Neither even noticed when the saproling returned to its home plane. Despite her initially dismissive tone, Alma stayed with the idea that Richter's mind was a castle. She showed him how to shore up the defenses, raise the walls and even started teaching him to imagine defensive thought forms as guards patrolling the walls. It wasn't until Futen floated up and told them that he had found something that they stopped the training. Alma informed Richter that his mind was already more secure, but was nowhere near being acceptably defended. She promised him more training again soon.

Alma flew up into the air, and Richter stood. He checked his clock and was shocked to see that almost an hour had gone by. He penned another quick note and summoned a mist worker to run it back to the village. Thinking a bit more, he summoned three more to escort the first. The workers had almost no offensive capabilities, but he ordered the extra ones to sacrifice themselves if necessary to increase the chances that the first might make it back to the village safely. He could only imagine Terrod swearing up a storm at his irresponsible lord running off on his own.

As the mist workers left the dungeon, Richter walked over to the body of the decaemur knight. He had been so preoccupied with his prompts that he hadn't searched the body yet. The first thing he did was to remove his blade from its body. He wiped the bits of rotted matter off with a rag from his bag and then dropped the soiled cloth in distaste. The short sword went back into his back sheath, and he examined the knight.

You have found: **Decaemur Steel Barbut Helm**	**Defense:** +8 **Durability:** 58/62 **Item Class:** Uncommon **Quality:** Superb **Armor Type:** Medium Armor **Weight:** 2.3 kg **Traits:** Must be undead to safely wear +1% Strength of Death spells
You have found: **Decaemur Steel Breastplate**	**Defense:** +10 **Durability:** 82/91 **Item Class:** Uncommon **Quality:** Exceptional **Armor Type:** Medium Armor **Weight:** 8.8 kg **Traits:** Must be undead to safely wear

	+1% Strength of Death spells
You have found: **Decaemur Steel Bracers**	**Defense:** +7 **Durability:** 58/62 **Item Class:** Uncommon **Quality:** Well Crafted **Armor Type:** Medium Armor **Weight:** 3.7 kg **Traits:** Must be undead to safely wear +1% Strength of Death spells
You have found: **Decaemur Steel Gauntlets**	**Defense:** +7 **Durability:** 34/40 **Item Class:** Uncommon **Quality:** Exceptional **Armor Type:** Medium Armor **Weight:** 2.3 kg **Traits:** Must be undead to safely wear +1% Strength of Death spells
You have found: **Decaemur Steel Greaves**	**Defense:** +8 **Durability:** 54/59 **Item Class:** Uncommon **Quality:** Exceptional **Armor Type:** Medium Armor **Weight:** 4.2 kg **Traits:** Must be undead to safely wear +1% Strength of Death spells
You have found: **Decaemur Steel Boots**	**Defense:** +7 **Durability:** 32/32 **Item Class:** Uncommon **Quality:** Well Crafted **Armor Type:** Medium Armor **Weight:** 3.5 kg **Traits:** Must be undead to safely wear +1% Strength of Death spells

Congratulations! You have obtained an entire set of matched armor: **Decaemur Knight's Armor**. Defense given by each piece increased by 25%. Special Bonus: Controlled Death creatures will be one level higher.

You have found: **Balanced War Axe**	**Damage:** 17-21 **Durability:** 72/83 **Item Class:** Common **Quality:** Exceptional **Weight:** 4.1 kg **Traits:** +10% to Accuracy

Curious about the restriction on the armor, Richter took off one of his gauntlets and slipped one the black decaemur ones on. Immediately he gained a poisoned icon, and his health started dropping. Focusing on the icon told him that he would lose five health per second and that upon death would become an undead in the service of whatever being had created the armor. Shivering involuntarily, he quickly removed the armored glove. The icon disappeared, and his health stopped falling. He cast *Weak Slow Heal*, restoring the few points he had lost.

The knight didn't have any other items of note, so Richter just shoved all of the items into his bag. He didn't know what good the decaemur armor could do, but he thought he'd show it to Krom to see if the dwarf had any ideas. At the very least, he could sacrifice the armor to the Forge and, hopefully, gain an enchantment. Richter summoned a mist worker to take the body back to the village. Beyan or Tabia might also find something useful. Futen waited silently nearby. Once Richter was done, the remnant led him several hundred yards to the back of the hall. The shale adder slid silently behind them.

Futen stopped in front of a blank wall. The light inside of the remnant flared, and a circular ward appeared, hugging the wall. Richter's eyes widened slightly, daunted by what he saw. Previous wards he had seen had one, or perhaps two, circles on the periphery. The number of circles was proportional to their complexity. This ward had four circles, each filled with tiny symbols. He looked at Futen, "Can you even disarm this?"

"I studied the pattern before coming to notify you, my lord. That is why my search took so long. I am fairly confident that I have figured out how to disarm it." Saying nothing else, Futen's light flared again, and the circles on the ward began to spin. They twisted back and forth like tumblers. It took several minutes, but finally the ward flared and rose into the air before dissipating.

"Good job," Richter said, relieved. He hadn't really liked hearing Futen say 'fairly confident.' It had worked out, though. The chaos seed leaned forward and started examining the apparently blank wall. It didn't take him too long to find a finger-width indentation between two of the stones. His Pierce the Veil skill once again showed its worth and a faint blue glow appeared. Richter smiled.

That particular shade of azul indicated that he had found a hidden compartment. He scanned all around the indentation to make sure that no telltale red glow appeared, but thankfully it didn't look like there were any traps. He took his gauntlet off and slipped a finger inside, feeling for the release mechanism. Richter's finger went in about three inches, curling to the side, but he couldn't get it in any further.

He felt around for another second and was able to detect a small hole at the end of the indentation. It was too small for him to worm his finger any deeper though. Richter pulled his finger out and frowned. He hadn't seen any other secret caches and the fact that it glowed blue meant it wasn't just an irregularity in the stone. The indentation curled so he couldn't use one of his lock picks. He took a step back and tried to reason it out.

There had to be a way in. The release was most likely at the end of the small hole. The real question was how the undead knight had managed to release the catch when it was too small for fingers… He chuckled to himself. The answer was obvious.

He drew his white dagger and walked back over to the mist worker holding the body. Richter checked both hands, and, sure enough, one of the knight's fingers was denuded of flesh, showing only bone. Richter braced the finger against the edge of his blade like he was getting ready to cut into an apple. He pressed down, wincing slightly at the sound of cracking bone, but was able to cut the finger free.

Richter walked back over to the indentation and inserted the skeletal finger. He snaked it around until he felt it align with the small hole. Another slight push sunk the finger another half-inch. The wall began to vibrate. Richter stepped back with a smug grin and looked at the knight's severed appendage. He chuckled to himself, a skeleton key.

A portion of the wall swung open. The edge of the door was crenelated to follow the line of the stone blocks the hallway was built of. Behind the wall was another chamber made of the same stone blocks. The light from the two hanging braziers in the main chamber was not enough to fully see, so Richter summoned a mist light. The grey-white light filled the room.

Two pedestals sat in the center of the circular room, one white, the other black. They were each five feet tall and triangular. Both pillars had runes carved into their faces, the white much smaller than the black. Against the far wall was a sturdy wooden door with a ring. Nothing else was in the chamber.

Walking up to them he saw that--just as with the large rune he had seen with the dark aberration--there were many little details, but at the core of each were two larger symbols. One of the symbols comprising both runes was the ancient sigil for Death. Richter recognized it from his Lore book. The other symbol on the black pillar was a slight variation on the dark aberration rune for containment. The last sigil he didn't recognize, but it looked like the opposite of the containment rune. With a flash of insight, Richter realized that the two runes must work in conjunction. The containment rune kept the knight from escaping. The other rune though, must have been there to keep the knight from getting too close to either pedestal and deactivating them. The perfect trap.

Richter walked up to the white column and after pausing for just a moment placed his hand upon it.

Welcome, Master of the Mist Village. You have accessed the ***Rune of Death Repulsion****. It serves to keep a specific being of Death magic outside of the range of the spell. You have conquered the antechamber of this dungeon and can now access its functions. Do you wish to deactivate the runic magic? Yes or No?*

Richter thought about it. He hadn't worked up the nerve to deactivate the Rune of Dark Holding in the aberration cave yet, but if he understood this correctly, the rune on the white column was only meant to keep the knight out of this antechamber. Since the knight was now dead, truly dead, what was the worst that could happen? Promising himself for the umpteenth time that he would stop tempting fate with stupid questions like that, Richter decided to see what would happen when he deactivated the rune. First though, he decided to make a rubbing in case the rune was destroyed.

He took a piece of paper and some charcoal from his bag. Placing the paper over the rune, he started rubbing the charcoal vigorously over the top. Richter could feel a tingle of power coming through the thin sheet. He had wondered how paper was made in The Land for a while. The sheet was nowhere near as thin or easy to write on as what he could have bought at any Walmart, but it was still better than what he would have thought a medieval society could produce. Richter shrugged, imagining the answer must have something to do with magic. Seeing as how he had two scribes in the village, he should be able to have the answer easily enough.

Richter finished making a copy of the first rune and inspected it. Except for one area, he had been able to capture all of the little details. He carefully placed the etching back into the same position and ran over the part that was lacking. A minute later, the rubbing was complete. Satisfied, he carefully put the paper into his bag. Checking his inventory, he saw that the paper had taken up a single square of the 20x20 grid. Richter was sure that it would stay safe there. To be completely safe, he took another thin piece of parchment and made a second rubbing of the white rune; then he repeated the process with the rune on the black column. When he was done, and the parchment was resting safely in his inventory, he placed his hand back on the white rune.

Richter selected 'Yes' to deactivate the rune and it started vibrating under his hand. He snatched his palm away from the column and watched as the center of the rune changed. First it grew transparent, and then ghostly in appearance. A soul stone floated out from the rune and hovered in the air a foot from the column's surface. Richter looked at it, surprised, but then the rune returned to normal, and the stone dropped. It was because of his high Dexterity that was he able to catch it before it hit the ground.

Know This! The soul contained within this stone has been expended. To reactivate this rune, you will need another luminous level soul.

You have found: **Luminous Soul Stone**	**Durability:** 25/25 **Item Class:** Uncommon **Stone Level:** Luminous **Soul Level:** N/A **Status:** EMPTY **Weight:** 0.4 kg

Richter smiled. The soul stones were retrievable. True, it seemed the souls contained within were lost, but empty soul stones were still valuable. Wasting no time, he deactivated the other rune. This time, two stones fell out, one *luminous* and one *common.* Two-fer! Richter quickly pocketed the empty soul repositories. He immediately started thinking of the much larger rune in the dark aberration cave. There was probably an even stronger stone waiting for him back at the village.

Each rune looked the same as before, but they no longer gave the tingle that they had when they were active. Richter looked around but didn't see anything else except for the wooden door. He walked up and examined it, but found nothing notable, not even a lock. Confirming with Futen that there were no magical traps, he pulled the door open. What he saw took his breath away.

It was an archway of black crystal.

Upright in the archway was what looked like a pool of oil. Richter ran forward, not even taking the time to scan the room and laid his hand on the arch.

You have found: ***Novice Portal.***

This was a smaller version of the portal that had brought him to The Land. It matched in almost every detail. It also matched the image in his mind of what a portal should look like, at least according to the knowledge he had gained from the Tefonim queen. It was a major 'Duh!' moment for Richter. He could have examined his last memory of Earth and compared it to what he had learned from the queen at any time, but it didn't click until he was confronted with an actual portal.

Coming back to himself, Richter took stock of his surroundings. There was nothing else in the room. Alma had already examined their new surroundings and told him there was no danger. Her mental tone made it clear that she disapproved of his lack of awareness. Richter waved her disapproval away and continued examining the portal.

He knew that many materials went into the creation of a portal, not least of which were several POUNDS of gold. From the knowledge he had gained, he knew that they ultimately all combined to make the impossibly-hard, black crystal of a portal's frame. Unfortunately, he also knew that he couldn't salvage parts from this portal to make his own. The process was irreversible. As he continued to explore the black arch and compare it to his own knowledge, he discovered there *were* options on what could be done with the remains of a destroyed portal. Very interesting options…

"My lord. Do you wish to cross through the portal?" queried Futen's deadpan voice. The question interrupted his musings.

Richter thought about it, "Are we sure that we'll be able to get back?"

Futen floated closer to the gate, "The activation and destination keys are present on this side, my lord, otherwise the portal would not be able to activate. It also means the activation key must be present on the far side. There is no guarantee that the destination key is present on the other side, my lord. If it is not, then you could be stranded."

Richter nodded. What Futen said was consistent with what he understood about the portals. Each portal had a specific activation key that only worked with that one portal. It enabled the possibility of incoming and outgoing travel. To travel from the portal you were at to another location required a second key though, the destination key. For a novice portal like the one in front of him, it could only travel to one place and so only had one destination key, though Richter knew it was possible to make copies of the same key.

"How do you know so much about gates, Futen?"

"My memory is still fragmented, my lord, but I believe my knowledge stems from the fact that there is a portal in the village."

Richter's mind split in half. A portion wanted to say 'What the deuce?' and the other part wanted to go with 'Say whhaaaat?'.

He settled for spluttering for a few seconds, then saying, "Where the fuck is the portal?"

Futen pulsed silently in the air for a moment before replying, "The doorway to the catacombs, my lord. You have been through it."

"That's a portal?" Richter asked loudly. "But it doesn't look all weird and shimmery, and the doorway isn't made of black crystal."

"I believe the portal we are looking at and the type that you are describing are one and the same, Lord Richter. Such gateways deal with traveling down a ley line from one physical location to another. The portal that leads away from the Great Seal is an example of traveling to various levels within the same ley line. I have told you before that the Great Seal is the physical representation of the nexus of ley lines that creates your Place of Power. The nexus permeates every level of the catacombs. To access a door in the catacombs, you need simply to physically go through it, my lord. Then you can instantly reach that point again."

Richter got a confused look on his face, "I felt a slight tingle when I crossed through the doorway leading down to the first level of the catacombs, but I still had to walk up and down stairs for more than a mile. I had to carry the bodies of those dead kobolds up while they bled and dripped… other stuff all over me. Why didn't I instantly appear back in the room of the Great Seal when I left level one of the catacombs?"

"Did you try to teleport back up to the Great Seal, my lord, or did you simply start walking back up the stairs?"

Richter ground his teeth and closed his eyes. "I simply walked back up," he admitted.

Futen just floated there, the light at his center slowly throbbing. To Richter it looked like the damn remnant was blinking at him and letting the silence communicate a simple message, 'That happened because you're a dumbass, dude.'

Richter wanted to yell at Futen for not giving him information before now, but he just decided to take the 'L' on this one. The truth was he could have asked. Richter let the matter drop. The question remained, what was he to do with the portal in front of them.

The adventurer in him wanted to go through the portal and vanquish the bad guy. The smart part of him knew that this was probably beyond his capabilities without help. He needed to move forward in force, but until he was ready, he really didn't like the idea of leaving a portal to the netherworld or wherever the fuck this thing led unguarded in his lands. Luckily, his knowledge gave him options in that regard. He placed three fingers of his left hand at the top of the archway, then turned them counterclockwise while projecting his desire.

Greetings Master of the Mist Village. Available keys: ***Activation*** *and* ***Dark Ley Line Destination****. Do you wish to access the keys of this portal? Yes or No?*

Richter went through the interface and deactivated the activation key.

The activation key is now separated from this portal. To use this portal again, the activation key must be replaced.

A circular space appeared in the uppermost point of the black crystal arch. Out of this hollow floated a small, circular object. Richter reached up and grasped it. The pool of inky blackness disappeared, leaving only an empty arch of black crystal.

You have found: **Rune of Kirimuratq**	**Durability:** 90,000/90,000 **Item Class:** Rare **Weight:** 3.6 kg

The disk was cream-colored and was the size of a child's palm. For its small size, it was remarkably heavy. One side of the disc was blank, but the other had four grooves that started as parallel lines, and halfway across the disc became a snarled mess. The circular space in the arch disappeared leaving only smooth, black crystal again.

Richter kept looking at the disc. Kirimuratq. He ran the word through his mind, but his Gift of Tongues ability couldn't translate the word. He supposed that it might be because it was written in a language his ability couldn't translate. When he had met Xuetrix, the imp had spoken in some type of 'higher' language, and he hadn't been able to understand it. Something about the word tugged at his mind though so he just kept thinking about it.

"Ki-ri-mu-rat-ka," he said slowly. His brow furrowed. "Ki-ri-mu-ra-tic." Richter blinked and then said in a questioning tone, "Kiri-mura?" Neither 'kiri' nor 'mura' meant anything, but the words sounded remarkably like 'kirin' and 'murat'. Richter wasn't sure what language he was accessing through his ability, but those words meant 'home' and 'vapor,' respectively. He blinked a few more times then a slow smile crept across his face. A village was kind of like a home and what was mist if not vapor? Was he holding the 'the mist village' rune? He wasn't sure what the 'tq' meant at the end of the word, but the rest of it made sense. Richter felt a thrill of accomplishment at having answered this riddle.

Richter called Futen over and asked the remnant to confirm his guess. The orb's monotone voice didn't seem as excited about his discovery as it should have in Richter's opinion, "Yes, my lord."

He put the rune into his bag and accessed his inventory. Finding what he wanted, he pulled out the Rune of Chuthriom. He had found this disc attached to the armor of a long dead adventurer in a dungeon. At the time, he hadn't been able to figure out anything more than that it allowed him to use a portal. Now he tried to phonetically break it down, though. It was a bit like trying to guess what the answer was on Wheel of Fortune when you didn't know the clue, what language the answer would be in, or even what alphabet was being used.

After a few minutes, Richter got a couple possible matches: the goat's hairy tongue, foot cloud pin, and cross muddy tree, to name a few. None of it made much sense except for one that he hoped he was wrong about. The words 'chutit', 'hern' and 'iobm' could be translated as Valley of the Forgotten Apostates. He *really* hoped he was wrong about that one.

Richter put the rune back into his bag. He could deal with that later. He hadn't even found the corresponding portal yet. Richter looked around the small room he was in. There was nothing else of interest, except, of course, for the light blue outline on the wall.

He rushed over to the left side of the room and the blue color deepened, leaving no doubt that a secret panel was present. The hidden compartment was three by three feet, a perfect square.

Richter searched for traps or a complex locking mechanism but didn't see anything. Carefully, he placed his hand on one side and pushed. The small compartment swung open on a swivel, revealing what was hidden inside.

Bones. Piles of bones. The wall had been hollowed out and used as a storage locker for what looked like the remains of dozens of people. Most of the bones had been thrown in like so much rubbish, but on top of the pile was a large, purple pillow. It shown like velvet in the mist light and had tassels of golden thread falling from each corner. A full set of bones were stacked carefully atop the pillow in perfect symmetry, the skull taking center stage. They were the bones of a child.

Richter's sighed deeply, remembering a screaming girl undergoing unimaginable torment. "Hello, Krista. I promise to give you whatever peace that I can."

CHAPTER 19 -- DAY 112 -- KUBORN 2, 15368 EBG

Richter gathered all of the bones, placing them inside his bag. From Jorgen's memory, he knew exactly how many people had been sacrificed. He counted the skulls as he worked and found them all to be present. The final tally came to one hundred and seven. Seeing exactly how much space the bones of more than one hundred people took up was horrifying. Even more, than that, he was shocked by how much the bones began to weigh. If not for the weight-reducing properties of his Bag of Holding, he would not have been strong enough to carry it all. When he was done, his bag was one hundred and twenty-four kilograms heavier, which meant he was carrying more than twenty-seven hundred pounds of remains!

Richter kept reaching into the cubby, pulling out skulls, ribs, and long bones, and trying to keep the horror of what he was doing from reaching him. When he had cleared out the remains from the dark aberration's cave, the bones were just what was left from victims in a forgotten past. Not so here. He actively resisted trying to think of the people he had seen being tortured. The bones of the children were the worst part. He remembered seeing their young faces reddened from screaming. After only a few minutes, he started silently praying for it to stop. It took more than thirty minutes for him to finish.

Richter walked back into the chamber with the runes and looked at the two pillars again. He was tempted to summon more mist workers and have them hammer at the columns bases until they broke free so he could bring them back to the village. Two things stopped him, though. One, that it seemed… inelegant somehow, and two, it kinda seemed like a bad idea to hit complicated magical runes with chisels and just hope for the best. He walked on.

Alma flew up and settled onto his shoulders as he crossed back into the main hall. The ceiling braziers still burned with a blue flame. The adder slid up beside him. It was time to leave this place of death.

Morning was well underway when he made it out of the collapsed basement. Bird song surrounded him, and the dew had been burned off of the grass beneath his feet. Richter winced when he was confronted with how many hours had passed since leaving the village. He dual cast *Weak Haste* on himself and then took off at a jog.

He was able to make good time. No large predators reared up to block his path and before long his village was in sight. The secondary trench had been dug around the village, nearly ten miles long and shaped like a broad "U," where each tip ended against the cliff faces that rose to the north of the village. The trench was at least ten feet deep and ten feet across. The distance was too great to patrol, so the displaced earth had been gathered to make a series of earthwork towers spaced every few hundred yards. Mist workers continued to make the ditch deeper and wider every day.

Only three sections across the secondary trench had been left alone. Each was about ten feet wide. Wide enough to cross easily, but not wide enough for an army to surge across en masse. One of the sections was to the west; another was to the southwest, and the third was directly south of the village. It was to the southern bridge that Richter headed now.

Each section was manned by a five-man squad, and two earthwork towers were clustered behind the passages with a crossbowman on top. The squad leader saluted Richter as the chaos seed approached, clapping a fist to his chainmail shirt, directly over his heart.

"Greetings, my lord."

Richter used *Analyze* in what had become almost an instinctive maneuver, and he said, "Hello, Delino. Is all well?"

"Quite well, my lord. Captain Terrod left word with each squad to communicate that he is looking for you." After giving that message, Delino gestured with his head, and one of the other guards jogged off towards the village.

Richter chuckled wryly, "I bet he is. How mad did he look that I wasn't in the village, this morning?"

A smirk threatened to break Delino's forcefully stoic visage, "I am sure that I could not say, my lord."

Richter laughed aloud and clapped the guard on the shoulder, "Of course you can't." His levity was cut short when he saw the other guards clutch their weapons tightly. Richter looked behind him and saw that the shale adder had caught up and had begun sliding across the narrow path.

The chaos seed quickly held up both hands and said, "It's with me. That's my snake!" Still, he saw no reason to upset his villager's unduly. A quick mental order ensured that the snake would hunt around the periphery of the village, but not wander too far. The adder reversed direction and activated its camouflage. In less than a minute, it was hidden even from Richter's view. He stared at the creature. He would have to try and tame it again soon. Seeing what a danger it could be, though, he knew that if he failed to master it, then he would have to destroy it.

Richter let go of such dark thoughts and started walking back towards the village. To either side of him were patches of tilled earth and he was happy to see that the crops were thriving, but it was no great surprise. Three factors were working to make a bountiful harvest almost a guarantee. Richter's Life ability, Bounty of Life, increased crop growth by 30%. Isabella's new spell, *Virol's Blessing*, increased the yield of the plants by 5% every time it was cast. It had a cooldown of one day, but the effects were cumulative and could ultimately increase a plant's final growth by 100%. Last, but not least, there was the presence of the Quickening. As the tree had reached level two, all resources in his domain yielded 25% more than they otherwise would have produced. Richter wasn't sure if this included growing food, but on his village interface, food was listed under resources, so it might. Whether the Quickening affected the crops or not, the reality was that some of the plants were already massive. Crops had been destroyed during the bugbear attack, but from what Richter could see, that loss had been made up.

As usual, his villagers were pleased to see him. Each and every one of them greeted their lord with a smile and a hail. He smiled back and waved while Futen and Alma flew along behind him. The mist worker carrying the knight's body brought up the rear.

"Futen, go find Sumiko. She is probably in the healer's tent. Ask her to come to the northern meadow. Tell her there are tortured souls to lay to rest."

"Yes, my lord," Futen replied before floating off. Richter kept walking.

The gate guards greeted him as well, communicating Terrod's desire to speak with him. He nodded with a slight amount of irritation and kept walking. He knew it was a bit cocky for him to have left on his own, but jeez! He *was* the lord of these lands, wasn't he? Terrod was just being a bit of a mother hen.

"Went on a little walk, did you?" a melodic, yet masculine voice called out.

Richter looked to the side and saw Sion walking up with a broad smile on his face. He raised his hand and gave the sprite a high five. The Companions fell in lock step together. "I didn't plan to leave for so long, but things happened."

Sion looked back at the mist worker carrying the nude undead knight and said, "No shit."

Richter just shrugged. He filled his Companion in on what had happened during the morning. Sion reacted with shock about hearing of the ritual sacrifices. His mouth dropped open at hearing that an undead lord could still be laired up somewhere nearby, "My mother works so hard to ensure that evil cannot gain a foothold in the forest, and you are telling me that Death magic sacrifices are taking place?"

"I don't know if it's still taking place, but they did, and apparently it has allowed evil to endure. That leads me to the next thing you, and probably the Hearth Mother, need to know. I found a Dark magic portal. I'm not sure where it goes, but I am almost sure that it leads to somewhere in my lands. We are going to need to explore it, and remove whatever threat we might find."

Sion's face adopted a grim expression, "Just say the word."

"I knew I could count on you," Richter said, clapping his friend on the back.

Sion nodded, "Always. Now will you tell me why we are going up to the meadow?" A smile broke out across his face, "Unless you are trying to hide from Terrod."

Richter stopped walking, "No, I'm not fucking hiding from Terrod. Terrod works for me. Just what has he been saying?"

Sion held up both hands, "Whoa, whoa, whoa. Why are you getting all worked up? He just wants you to be safe."

"Hmpf, maybe he can hold my cock while I piss then." Richter started walking again.

"Might not be a bad idea," Sion called after him, "but when he has to keep looking to find it, things might get awkward."

"I wouldn't start talking shit, Sion," Richter responded without even looking back. "Daniella told me some stuff about you."

Sion stared after his friend, not sure what he should say. "What stuff?" Richter just gave a sardonic smile and kept walking. The sprite started jogging after Richter, "What stuff did she tell you, man?"

CHAPTER 20 -- DAY 112 -- KUBORN 2, 15368 EBG

They reached the top of the hill and as per usual, Isabella and the other gardeners were hard at work. She waved to Richter with a brilliant smile when she saw him. Her love was next to her. Terrod's expression was decidedly less sunny.

"Greetings, my lord," Terrod said curtly.

Richter let loose an expansive sigh, "Go ahead. Speak freely. Let the haranguing begin."

Terrod didn't hesitate, "It is my job to keep you safe, Lord Richter. It is my job to ensure that you remain alive so that you can lead us. That job is made much harder if you keep running out into the wilds by yourself. The monsters that we are seeing on a daily basis are all dangerous. You are powerful, my lord, but you are not all powerful. If you had run into that pack of skaths on your own, they would have eaten you. Torn you limb from bloody limb! You are also not the only one at risk. Only these mists protect us from hostile forces. Where would we be if you… did not make it back?"

Richter didn't interrupt Terrod while the man was speaking. The captain clearly had some things to get off of his chest. Initially, the chaos seed was just planning on enduring a lecture. Afterwards, he would apologize, and they could all move on. When Terrod almost slipped up and revealed the truth about his resurrections, though, he understood that this was no small matter for his Companion.

Terrod was not a man with loose lips. The captain had operated an underground railroad in Yves for years. To put it another way, the former innkeeper wasn't the kind of man to let secrets slip. In this current moment, he was apparently so upset that he had almost revealed Richter's most precious secret.

The lord of the Mist Village looked at Terrod and, as calmly as he could, said, "Come with me. You too Sion, this is a Companion type of talk."

Richter led the way with his two Companions, away from the garden and towards the freshly turned graveyard. He started summoning more mist workers as he walked. When they arrived in front of the monument to the fallen villagers, Richter set the workers to digging. Their grey hands formed into shovel heads and they set to their appointed task.

He looked out over the area he was standing in and took in the almost grass-covered mound that contained the remains of the villagers that had died in the bugbear attack. He then looked at the denuded earth that marked where he had buried the remains from the dark aberration caverns just the day before. Now he was about to dig another hole. When you included the dead goblins he had buried upon first claiming the Mist Village, he was averaging almost one mass grave a month. Richter shook his head. Did that mean that his actions were leading to all of this death? Or was he acting like a scalpel, cutting away diseased sections of The Land? If that were true, then the process might not be pretty, but it left the patient healthier. Or was he instead living up to his name? Was this simply the natural result of a being a chaos seed?

"What did you want to say?" Sion asked gently. He recognized the pensive look on his friend's face and so brought him back to the current moment.

Richter nodded his appreciation to the sprite. He looked at his other Companion, "Terrod, I want you to know that I hear you. I appreciate all that you do on my behalf and the way that you are training our guards." The captain nodded, but Richter wasn't done, "You need to understand something, though. While your job is to protect this village and to protect me, my job is to prepare for the future. My job," Richter pointed to the mound that contained the bodies of his villagers, "is to make sure that *that* does not happen again. I cannot do that by playing it safe." His expression softened, "Also, with only a few exceptions, no one in this village is stronger or faster than me. If you train an absolute badass who can be my personal guard, all well and good. Until that time, though, I'll knock down who I can and run from the rest. I will not allow good men and women to be killed facing opponents that are beyond them. Our enemies are coming, Terrod. I have to be stronger. Do you understand?"

Terrod's face showed that he didn't like what he was hearing, but he nodded.

Richter was thankful that he had gotten through to the captain. There was one more thing to say, though. His face hardened, and he clearly enunciated his next works, "Despite any of that, though, you must NEVER share the secret of my resurrection with the other villagers."

His captain nodded again, "As you will, my lord. I apologize for my near-indiscretion."

Richter held Terrod's gaze, "Like I said, I think you have a good point. We are in this together. The Universe has made us Companions. Honor me and I will be with you to the death. Train the men hard and then I will start taking them with me. Until then, I will not have them be fodder for monsters that are too strong for them. Can you do that, my friend?"

Terrod smiled faintly and clapped his fist to his chest, "I will redouble my efforts!"

"I know you will," Richter said, smiling back. They clasped wrists, each glad to have been heard by the other. The two men fell silent.

"You guys going to make out or should we get back to work?" Sion asked.

Richter smiled at his friend, thankful to him for dispelling the small amount of residual tension. "I'd give you a kiss, but my legs are too stiff to bend down."

"My lord, you should never admit you'd be more comfortable with your legs in the air," Terrod quipped. Richter and Sion looked at the former innkeeper in surprise; then a broad smile broke out over Sion's face that basically said, 'You should have never started this, man.' And with that, Terrod became a true shit talking Companion.

Richter chuckled as he listened to Sion congratulate Terrod. Both of them started verbally going toe-to-toe without any signs of stopping. He looked around to see if Sumiko had come up to the meadow yet, but there was no sign of her or Futen. Knowing they had a bit of time, Richter decided to lead his Companions to the Quickening. Something inside of him wanted to bring all of his

Companions into one place, despite the fact that Elora was still cocooned.

The three of them walked along while Alma flew in circles around them, leaving the mist workers to dig. Richter left Futen to direct them. As they neared the celestial tree, two figures phased into view. They were the guardians Hisako had left behind to ensure the celestial tree's safety. What had hidden the sprites wasn't exactly the same as invisibility. After they appeared, his mind knew that he should have seen them before. It was almost like *Stealth*, but he admitted that the sprites Concealment ability was superior, albeit limited in that it only worked in the forest. No matter how it worked, it was always amazing to see someone appear out of nowhere and he was happy that the sprites were his allies. The now visible warriors greeted him.

"Hail, Lord Richter," one said.

"Well met, brother," said the other to Sion.

"Is all well with the Quickening?" Richter asked.

The two sprite warriors exchanged glances, "All is well, but the light coming from the cocoon has intensified. It also shudders from time to time as well."

The other sprite opened his mouth for a moment, but didn't say anything. Richter looked at him meaningfully and nodded. The sprite took the prompting, "I am the only one that has detected this, but I believe that I hear a voice. It is very small, but I know that it is calling to me. The voice does not speak aloud, it communicates to my heart. It started yesterday after I had gazed upon the cocoon."

Richter considered what he had just been told, "What does the voice say?"

The sprite looked at him, somewhat embarrassed, but still said, "There are no actual words, Lord Richter. Despite that, I know two things. One, that I will not be alone for much longer. Two, it talks about a sprite woman. I have cared for this woman for some time. The voice urges me to tell her about my feelings. It says that she is part of my destiny."

The other sprite snorted when his fellow stopped speaking. Richter looked at him, "So I take it you haven't heard any voices?"

"No, Lord Richter," the sprite responded with a laugh. The other warrior looked at him in irritation.

"Who do you think was talking?" Richter asked the first sprite.

The sprite who had heard the voice looked Richter in the eye and said definitively, "It is one of the pixies. She is telling me that she will be here soon."

Richter smiled, "Well that's good news. Let's go check on them." The five men walked under the canopy of the Quickening. While the outward appearance of the tree was that of a gigantic willow with huge velvet-white leaves, the underside of those leaves was something else entirely. Richter looked up, enjoying seeing the light reflected off of the silvery bottoms of the foliage. Mist lights had been summoned in the past and they still hung there, promising illumination for the next year.

They all continued on until they were standing right next to the trunk. Eight silver roots extended up from the ground, each five feet in diameter. They interwove into an octuple helix, leaving gaps so the hollow interior could be seen. When Richter looked inside, he saw the cocoon of spun silver that housed Elora and the first pixies that would be born into the Land for countless years. Just as the sprite guardian had said, the light coming from Elora's cocoon had intensified. Only the other day, Richter had observed the cocoon and he had seen filaments of gold, yellow, blue and black light seeping through the threads in places. Now, the four colors shone through like a spotlight.

"I hear it," Sion suddenly exclaimed.

Richter looked at his friend. The sprite's eyes were widened in shock and he had the expression of someone listening intently for something that was barely audible. "What do you hear?" he asked.

"Shhhh!" Sion said, waving one hand for silence. He cocked his head to the side, then he blinked and looked down. The sprite laid one hand flat on his chest. He looked at Richter and said, "I hear it here." Sion looked at the other sprite who had heard a voice too. The sprite nodded back with a slightly relieved expression, likely pleased that he wasn't going crazy.

"What do you hear?" Richter asked for the second time.

"He was right. I am not hearing actual words, Richter. It is more like a feeling." Sion closed his eyes, listening intently. When he opened them again, he smiled, "They will be born tonight."

Richter smiled broadly in response, "Is there any way that we can tell your mother? I know she would want to be here for this."

Sion shook his head in response, "Not in time to be here."

One of the sprite guards spoke up, "Are you sure that the birth will be tonight, Sion?" Richter's Companion nodded. "Then I can notify the Hearth Mother."

The sprite took a pouch off of his belt and reached inside. He pulled out what looked to be an acorn without a top. The sprite brought it to his lips and spoke softly to it then he dropped it to the ground. Before it struck, it started spinning quickly and when it struck the ground it burrowed in like a drill bit. In a moment, it was gone.

Richter watched the seed disappear and realized it was the only means of long distance communication he had seen since coming to The Land. It drove home just how isolated and alone he was in the forest. He was so busy each day that he didn't think about it much, but the truth was he knew nothing of what was happening in the world around him. The current state of affairs in Yves, whether Count Stonuk was still plotting against him, or if his friends in the kingdom were faring well. The truth was, he didn't even know anything about this Jupiter-sized world except for the small bit of geography that was the River Peninsula. Richter knew he couldn't ignore the world around him forever, but he also knew that it was not something he could resolve today.

"The messenger seed will find the Hearth Mother and notify her of the birth," the sprite said.

"That's an awesome trick!" Richter exclaimed. "How can I get one of those?"

The warrior smiled, "They grow from a specific tree, Lord Richter. I am sure the Hearth Mother would be able to trade you for something of equal value."

Richter shook his head. "What happened to you guys? When I first came to The Land, you were all touchy-feely and didn't care about money at all." He missed those simpler times. Still, being able to communicate over long distances would be worth investing in. "How long until she gets the message?"

Sion answered, "Messenger seeds can cover many miles in an hour. She will be notified soon."

Richter nodded. He bade the sprite warriors to continue protecting the tree. The two walked away and, before they had moved twenty feet, they disappeared. He led his Companions back towards the gravesite. Sumiko was waiting, and behind her was her entire troupe of healers.

"Really? Again?" she asked waspishly. "What did you do and where did you find more remains? How many are there? More importantly, what is that *thing* you have the worker holding?" She was pointing at the decaemur knight's body.

Richter sighed and resigned himself to relating the whole story again. He started talking, making sure he stayed well out of her cane's striking distance. Her expression softened as she heard about how he had found the bones and became sorrowful as he told her about the torture these people had endured. Her face became like granite though when she heard about the undead lord, "I am coming with you when you go to cleanse that nest of evil."

The chaos seed looked skeptically at the older woman. Sumiko was indeed a Life master, but she was also… old. The sprite woman snorted when she saw his disbelief, "Do not worry about me, *young* lord. If the two of us went into a den of Death creatures, and only one walked out, I guarantee that it would be I."

Richter decided not to push the issue. There was no way in hell that he was going to take a geriatric into a fight though, so he changed the subject. He started unloading the bones of the sacrificial victims and laying them down. Sumiko looked at him and said, "You do realize that we are running out of room for mass graves, correct?"

"That thought did occur to me," he said. "Now are you going to help or not?"

She glared at him for another few moments, but then set her healers into action. They began to categorize the bones and tried to match the skeletons. Sumiko cast a spell and confirmed that the spirits were indeed still tied to the remains. Just like last time, she told him that in order to set the souls free, she would need to align the skeletons first. The mage was about to say something else when she focused on something behind him. A nasty expression came across her face and she walked away. Richter sighed and before he even turned around said, "Hey Beyan."

Richter saw the Death mage was inspecting the decaemur knight's body. "This is amazing! Can I have it?" Beyan asked excitedly.

Sion and Richter shared a look. It was the sprite who spoke up, "I feel like I already know the answer to this, but I have to ask anyway. This is not a sexual thing, right?"

Beyan glared at the sprite, "No."

"Then why do you want it?" Richter asked He shared a faint smile with his best friend over the fact that they had been thinking the same thing. The two gave a no-look fist bump.

Beyan kept glaring at Sion for a moment before answering, "I am not strong enough to make a minion of this level, my lord. This body would afford me a special opportunity. It is still mostly intact and has already turned into a creature of Death. I think I could reanimate it with one of my spells, *Claim Weak Death Servant*."

"This thing wasn't exactly weak, man. Believe me," Richter said.

Beyan shook his head, "You do not understand. This is not just an empty body and those aren't simple remains. I do not know how it was done, but even though the body is empty, the spirit is still bound to this plane." He looked at the blank expressions on both Companions faces and let out a long-suffering sigh. When he spoke again, he did so slowly. Insultingly slowly as far as Richter was concerned. "The body is still magically active. I can make use of it."

"Isn't that what you always do?" Richter asked a bit irritated. "I've seen you make zombies before."

"It is not the same thing," the gnome explained. "After death, a soul normally lingers for a short while. That is what allows me to summon it back with my spell, *Weak Commune with the Undead*. When I make the zombies, however, I am forcing a completely different creature, a spirit of Death magic into the body."

"What happens to the person's soul?" Richter asked.

Beyan shrugged, "That is more of a philosophical question, my lord. There are ways to directly damage someone's soul, but I imagine that it goes wherever souls normally go after the body ceases to live."

"So why are you so excited about finding this body?" Sion asked

"Because it is special. As you said, I can turn almost any dead body into a zombie. My *Summon Weak Zombie* spell summons a Death creature to inhabit the body. The creature would only have a base level of three, however. 10% of the dead body's experience is added to determine the zombie's level, but it is still fated a weak servant. The spell is also a summoning for all intent and purposes, and the Death creature will leave after a time. My zombies only last one hour."

Richter raised his eyebrows impressed. His saprolings only lasted five minutes, "That still sounds like a pretty great duration for a summoning spell."

Beyan nodded, "Yes. My zombie spell will last longer than a similar summoning in a different school of magic, but you must keep in mind that I require a dead body to be present. Even when a body is present, the power of my zombie is dependent on the type of body present. Reanimating a squirrel, for instance, would not be of much use in a fight."

Sion spoke up, "I still do not understand why this body is different."

"I know," Beyan said, "I will explain that right now. Any dead body is still a vessel of Life magic. It will feed the living, then rot and become fertile ground for new life. A dead body is simply part of life's cycle. One of the few lessons I learned from my grandfather was that when a Death spirit entered a dead body, the body is altered on a fundamental level to accommodate a creature of Death. This is what leads to the loss of level. Despite the body being changed, however, the corpse is still inherently a vessel of Life. That is why the Death spirits I summon to create my zombies cannot stay in the body forever. *This*," he said, patting the knight's head, not at all creeped out at all by the sloughing skin and wide open mouth, Richter noticed, "has been turned into a vessel of *Death*."

Richter thought for a second and thought that he understood why Beyan was so excited, "So that means-"

"It means," Beyan interrupted, sounding completely giddy, "that I can still summon a weak spirit to reanimate the body, and the level will most likely be preserved."

Sion nodded, "I think I follow, but what use is a servant, no matter how powerful, if it only lasts an hour?"

"That is the best part," Beyan said, grinning, "I will not just be summoning a zombie this time. I have another spell, *Claim Weak Death Servant*, that lets me try to gain control of a Death creature indefinitely. It would not work on a dead body, even right after death, because there is no spirit inhabiting it and, as I said, dead bodies are still fundamentally vessels of Life. My spell would also not have worked against this creature while it was animate. The incantation only works against creatures level seven or below. That is what makes this so perfect. I would be casting the spell on a level three Death spirit, in a high level body. Nothing could go wrong!"

Beyan had been getting close to convincing Richter that this might be a good idea, but his last statement set off alarm bells. It was like hearing, 'You'll double your money, it's a sure thing.' or even worse, 'Don't worry. I'm *sure* I took my pill!' Richter had more questions, but Sion beat him to the punch.

"What about the large holes in it?" Sion asked. He turned to Richter and pointed at the gashes left by the chaos seed's short swords, "Those are your handiwork, I'm guessing?"

Richter shrugged, "Play stupid games and you win stupid prizes. This asshole wanted to play games." He looked at Beyan, "Sion makes a good point, though," he said to Beyan. "I just killed it. Isn't the body too damaged for you to use?"

Beyan smiled and spoke quick words of magic. The words of the Death spell grated consonants together in a way that made Richter's spine shiver. After only two seconds though, the gnome finished contorting his fingers and his hand glowed purple. At the same time, purple-black energy surrounded both gashes in the knight's skin and the holes began to close.

Richter's hand shot up to his sword hilt, concerned that Beyan might have just reanimated a dangerous enemy. Thankfully, the undead creature remained lifeless in the mist worker's arms. His heart beating wildly, Richter turned his ire on Beyan, "Shit, man! Do not start casting Death magic when we are talking about reanimating a deadly monster. What the fuck is wrong with you?"

Beyan bobbed his head and apologized, but the grin that remained etched on his face showed he really didn't mean it. Richter still wasn't sure about relinquishing the body into the too-eager Death mage's care, "What if you can't control it? I don't want a high level undead running amok in the village."

"I can," Beyan promised. "Though the body is strong, the spirit is weak. I will easily be able to dominate such a weak creature. We can turn an enemy into a loyal servant. Forever!"

What Beyan was saying was starting to make sense to Richter. Even though the gnome's happy-go-lucky attitude didn't fill him with confidence, he had just finished giving Terrod a speech about how chances needed to be taken. Before Richter could respond however, someone else spoke up… loudly.

Sumiko had been silently watching the exchange. She had almost used her magic to teach the Death mage a lesson when he cast his odious spell near her, but she knew Richter frowned on her completely reasonable hatred of Death magic. When she heard the loathsome little mageling selling lies to her new lord, dressed up as pretty truths though, she had to speak up, "Enough! This is wrong and should not be allowed to happen. That *thing*," she said, pointing at the knight's body, "is a perversion of nature. It must be destroyed!"

"Who are you to say what is right?" Beyan spat. "My magic is one of the Basic Elements, just as yours is."

Sumiko ignored the Death mage and addressed Richter instead, "Do you intend to put these souls to rest or do you intend to profit from their deaths? I heard your story about what this knight has done, but would you really consign him to further torment as the slave to a Death mage? Will you not even consider that his spirit should be allowed to pass on with the rest of his people?"

Beyan opened his mouth to protest, but Richter wasn't in the mood to let this argument spiral out of control. Besides, Sumiko had a good point. She had also reminded him that he had a quest to fulfill, giving the villagers proper rest. If Jorgen was considered a villager, like Sumiko insinuated, Richter wasn't willing to risk failing the quest just to give his necromancer a new toy, no matter how useful. "She has a point, Beyan. I'm not willing to ignore the fact that you say a soul is still attached to the body. What happens to that soul if you fill the body with the weak Death spirit you're talking about?"

"As I said before, if you are asking me what happens to us after we die, no one knows for sure, my lord. I am sure even our vaunted Life master would admit to that." Richter looked at Sumiko, who didn't look happy, but didn't interrupt. Seeing that she wouldn't challenge that particular point, Beyan continued, "I believe I have a compromise. I can help to determine what these people would want. Why should we so callously discuss their fate? I can cast the very first spell I was ever taught, *Weak Commune with Dead.* That way the spirits themselves can tell if they want their betrayer to move on with them." The gnome smiled in satisfaction, plainly confident that the aggrieved souls of the sacrificial victims would reject the idea of the knight's soul finding peace.

It wasn't a horrible idea, Richter thought, but he did have one question, "You told me that only worked right after death."

"That is because the soul normally leaves the remains, my lord. It should be possible to speak with them in this case."

Richter looked at Sumiko, "Do you have any objections? Besides your normal and obvious hate for Death magic?"

The sprite woman spit. She actually spit! She didn't raise arguments against the course of action though, "Do you as you will, but do not complain when fooling with Death magic goes wrong. We have assembled several skeletons now. I am going to start laying these poor creatures to rest." She turned away and with a flick of her hand, dismissed Richter, Beyan and the whole affair.

Just happy that he wasn't going to have to mediate another dispute, Richter gestured to Beyan and said, "Let's begin."

CHAPTER 21 -- DAY 112 -- KUBORN 2, 15368 EBG

Beyan smiled, feeling that victory was only a few short spells away. He walked over to the pile of remains and was about to begin when Richter told him to stop. The chaos seed walked over and found one particular child-sized set of remains that he had set aside, Krista's.

"This was his daughter. If anyone would speak on the knight's behalf it would be her. She is who I want you to cast your spell on."

Beyan frowned slightly. Richter assumed it was because the mage felt the deck was being stacked against him, but he did as he was asked, "The spirit will be somewhat weak because we are in full sunlight," he warned, "but the binding to the bones should keep it in this plane long enough to speak. I cannot promise that the spirit will choose to speak, however."

Richter nodded his understanding and Beyan started chanting. Purple-black light gathered around both of the gnome's hands as he spoke the grating language of Death magic. The bones began to vibrate and then a sickly green light began to emanate from them. A few seconds later, a spirit of the same color rose into the air. The body was that of a six-year-old child. Krista wore the same night gown Richter had seen in his vision, it was torn open and ghostly entrails hung past her knees from a horrific wound in her stomach. Her legs ended in bloody stumps beneath. The ghost stared forward, unconcerned with the injuries she had sustained in life. The apparition was much less solid than the ghosts the knight had summoned. Whether that was because the knight had used a different spell or because the spirit was weaker in direct sunlight like Beyan had warned, Richter had no idea.

"You can speak with her now," Beyan said.

Richter walked up to the spirit, who continued to stare straight ahead. "Hello, Krista." The ghost showed no response. "Krista, we are going to release your souls to the ether. Everyone that was tortured will finally have peace. First, I have to ask you a question, though. Do you want your father released with you?"

The ethereal girl finally looked at Richter. When she spoke, her voice echoed oddly like she was speaking down a long tube, "My father… Yessss, yesss. My father should be here." A strange expression that Richter couldn't read crossed the ghost's face. It was there and gone in a moment, then she kept speaking, "Please summon my father's spirit, good lord. I would like to see him. It has been so long." She had a tone of longing in her voice. It was almost a hunger.

Richter had heard enough. He turned to Beyan and said, "Summon the knight's spirit. I know that you might lose your chance to claim the knight's body if the spirit leaves the body, but if his daughter can forgive him then we will reunite them."

The gnome nodded in resignation, "Yes, my lord. I think this is a waste, but I understand." Beyan cast *Weak Commune with Dead* again, this time on the knight's remains. Another spirit appeared. Jorgen appeared as he was in life, without the undead mage's handprint on his face. He was dressed in simple pants and a tunic. Bare feet stuck out from the bottom of his pants. This second apparition was just as insubstantial as the first. The ghost was not as calm as Krista's had been. As soon as he materialized, his eyes darted around, before settling on his daughter.

Jorgen's shade went down on one knee and held his arms out, "Krrriiisssttaaa," the spirit wailed. In that one word were centuries of pain, loss and sorrow. In that moment, he was not an undead killer, he was simply a father reaching for his daughter, begging for forgiveness. Krista's shade floated forward until she was in Jorgen's embrace. He wrapped his ghostly arms around her and wailed, the sound echoing distantly, just as Krista's had. Jorgen bent his head forward and buried his face in his daughter's neck. No tears could fall from his ghostly eyes, but he continued his low moan of sadness.

Krista's face remained impassive as she was being held, something that was not lost on Richter. He was about to say something to Beyan, but then the small ghost's form solidified somewhat. Her body burst into bright green flames, the same color as the fires Richter had seen in Jorgen's memory. At the same time, her small hands elongated and adopted wicked spectral claws. Jorgen began to howl, this time in agony, as her ghostly fire burned him. He attempted to let go, but she drove her talons into his back, locking them together into her fiery embrace.

"My fatheeer," Krista said gleefully. "I have learned so much. I want to show you. To thank you. For all the long years, I, and the other villagers, continued to be tortured and torn apart." The flames around her intensified and Jorgen's wails of pain increased proportionally. "That pain taught me, fatheeeer!" Her voice was stronger and sounded not unlike a gale whistling through mountain peaks. "I want to share what I learned. We aaall do!"

Krista released one hand from her father's back and spat magical words in a rapid string. Her hand contorted and with a last, shouted, "Sugidettt!" ethereal green light shot towards the bones of the other sacrificial victims. The light bathed all of the bones, and spirits began to rise. Only ten seconds had passed since Jorgen had foolishly embraced his daughter. Richter would have left the man to their judgement, but the newly arisen spirits did not seem to only be interested in punishing Jorgen. A horrible moan that that stole the heat from Ricther's bones came from their collective spectral throats, then more than one hundred spirits attacked everyone present!

Alma rose in the air with a scream of defiance and cast *Weak Life Bolt* at one of the specters. Having learned from the last battle, she then quickly cast Weak Life *Aura* on herself before continuing her attack. The ghost she had attacked flew towards her while the others attacked whatever being was closest to them. That happened to be the mist workers. The scant seconds that it took for the grey figures to be ripped apart let everyone else begin to counterattack.

Richter analyzed the spirits to know what he was facing.

Name: Tortured Spirit	**Level:** 14	**Disposition:** Hatred
STATS		
Health: 220	**Mana:** 30	**Stamina:** 110
ATTRIBUTES		

Strength: 16	**Agility:** 18	**Dexterity:** 16
Constitution: 22	**Endurance:** 11	**Intelligence:** 3
Wisdom: 4	**Charisma:** 1	**Luck:** 6
DESCRIPTION		
The spirits of these simple villagers were betrayed in a manner most foul. Their torment did not end with their deaths, however, as a powerful Death mage bound their spirits to their remains. They continued to be tortured on an ethereal plain and their suffering fed the magics and life force of the evil necromancer. The once pure spirits have been corrupted and twisted with foul magic until little remains of their original selves. Their only motivation is to share their torment with the living.		

Richter checked a few more spirits quickly and found that their levels ranged between eleven and fifteen. The one notable exception was Krista. The small ghost child was a whopping nineteen. Richter scanned the information again and his eyes locked onto 'bound their spirits to their remains.' "Destroy the bones!" he shouted.

Everyone else was already in action. A few villagers had come to see why a new hole was being dug. They all ran away screaming at the sight of over a hundred screaming spirits. Richter didn't begrudge them that. He was just glad that he wouldn't have to deal with trying to save them as the fight commenced.

"Make the war party," Sion shouted. He was firing an imbued arrow at the mass of spirits attacking the mist workers. The blast would damage the workers as well, but large rents had already been created in their grey bodies. The specters' claws were mercilessly raking across their bodies, and wherever they were struck, mist flowed out to dissipate into the air.

Richter nodded and selected Sion, Terrod and Beyan. No one else from his main war party was within his sphere of influence. He would have added others, but at the last minute he remembered the challenge he had to complete, *Leave No Man Behind I*. He had already been through four of the five war party battles required to fulfill the challenge, but if he added anyone new to the war party, he would fail. Besides, other than Sumiko, there weren't too many others at the grave site. With that thought, he whipped his head to check on the healer, while he cast buffs on himself. A smile broke across his face when he saw her. She was doing fine.

Sumiko had immediately ordered her young healers to retreat to the path that led down to the village. Far enough to be away from the battle, but close enough to help anyone wounded in it. After that, she proved the validity of her earlier boast. Her opening salvo was so impressive that Richter no longer had any doubt that she should accompany him to attack the undead lord.

An unbroken string of arcane words spilled from her lips as her arms moved in tandem. Even watching for a moment, Richter could see that she was dual casting. Five seconds after she started her incantation, she finished by slapping her hands together. A ball of golden light shot from her fingers towards the spirits. It did not impact against any of them, but instead stopped in midair. A second later, the spirits started being pulled into the ball of light. They struggled against it, but their bodies stretched like water going down the drain. More and more spirits were pulled into the ball, and as each disappeared, the light grew more dim. More than twenty spirits were consumed by the luminous ball before the light died completely. The ball winked out of existence. Sumiko was already working on her next spell.

Terrod had started running towards the spirits, sword drawn, but Richter ordered him to protect Sumiko. The captain hurried over to do as he was told. Sion continued to fire imbued arrows, but he had now attracted the attention of several spirits. The sprite fired into the collection of bones, but it had no effect. Richter didn't know if his theory was wrong or if the whole skeleton needed to be destroyed, but the moaning wail of the specters continued. It mixed with the haunting sounds of Jorgen's odd screams and his daughter's sadistic laughter. As he took in the whole scene, Richter decided that this was some major league creepy shit!

Surprisingly, Beyan was somewhat useless in the battle. The Death mage's low level spells focused on summoning and direct attacks. Because his attacks utilized Death magic though, they would only make the spirits stronger. "Richter!" the gnome shouted in frustration as his lord ran into the fray.

Richter saw the helpless look on Beyan's face and he just shouted, "Do what you can!" Then he ran towards Sion. Only an abnormally high Dexterity was keeping his Companion alive as he narrowly dodged the ghosts' attacks. Sion couldn't take the time to fire another imbued arrow, beleaguered as he was by five spirits. His thorn-like rapier would also be of no help. The ethereal nature of the ghosts would have made them immune to such attacks. "This way!" Richter shouted. Past the sprite, he saw Sumiko let loose her next spell. Whirling blades of golden energy cut down another ten spirits.

Sion ran directly towards him. Before he had even reached the sprite, Richter swung both swords. His friend dove under the strike and then Richter was in the middle of the spirits. The time he had taken to cast *Weak Life Armor* and *Weak Life Aura* served him well. The ghosts shied away from him. They were too strong to be greatly damaged or fully repulsed by the spells, but it still let Richter use his blades to devastating effect.

The accuracy penalty of wielding two blades made Richter feel off balance again, but being in a swarm of ghosts meant that he didn't need to be precise. His sonic short sword swung through a spirit. When the blade passed through it, Richter felt a resistance similar to pushing through thick spider webs. The ghost wailed in pain. Richter swung his short sword of freezing through another, earning a second ghastly cry of agony. He stood in the center of the group moving both swords as quickly as he could, putting on a better show than the Benihana World Series of Ginsu, and anyone who doubted that was thrilling hadn't watched ESPN 8 at three in the morning.

One spirit attempted to flee his attack, but Alma appeared, her body still glowing gold and she dove through the spirit, claws extended. It fell back towards Richter with a cry and he plunged both swords upward into its body. The ghost faded to nonexistence.

The moments of respite had allowed Sion to knock another arrow and imbue it. The magical attack flashed forward and struck a spirit. Immediately afterwards, two more blue streaks struck the same ghost and it dissipated into the true death. Richter's heart cheered even as he continued to lay into every spirit he could reach. The sprites guarding the Quickening had joined the fight!

Despite the efforts of Richter and the sprites, the real show stopper was Sumiko. Terrod had engaged several spirits with his enchanted blade to give the Life master the chance to cast her spells.

He bled from several places, but still was able to aggro most of the spirits. A few had flown past the captain to attack Sumiko directly, but they were foiled by the bright golden sphere of protective magic she had erected. The spirits moaned and wailed in frustration, but she didn't even waste time gloating at them. Instead, she finished a third spell. A golden disc appeared above her head, parallel to the ground. A raucous cry filled the air as more than twenty large birds flew through the portal and into the meadow.

The birds looked similar to hawks, but each had a wingspan of three to four feet. Their feathers were pure white, but when they opened their mouths gold light welled up, like seeing magma at the bottom of the trench. Some of the birds attacked the spirits that were near the Life master, but the rest flew after the spirits that had left the immediate combat area. The Life creatures worked in tandem, flocking around one spirit at a time. Their mastery of the air was obvious as they evaded every counterattack. In turn, wherever the bird's talons or beaks struck the ghosts, ethereal rents appeared in spirits' bodies until they faded away, leaving only a pile of dust behind.

The battle was almost done when Richter heard a scream of rage. His head turned to the right and he saw Krista advancing on Beyan. There was no sign of Jorgen's spirit. The gnome quickly wove his hands and a cylinder of purple-black light sprung up around him. The spirit girl shoved both hands forward, talons out. The shield began buckling immediately. Beyan cried out and placed his hand forward, feeding more mana into the shield, but her clawed fingers kept creeping closer. Richter started running.

The booms from imbued arrows continued to echo against the other spirits, but Richter's attention remained on the Death mage. Beyan fell to one knee and a line of blood traced out of his nose. There was a silent explosion and the cylinder collapsed. Richter felt a faint splash of energy wash over him. Beyan dropped to the ground bonelessly, overcome by the spell feedback. Krista loomed over the Death mage, hand raised to slash out his throat. Only Richter's thrown blade saved the gnome's life.

Krista screamed in rage as his weapon passed through her insubstantial body. The magic of the blade harmed her and she turned her ire on the chaos seed. The ghost flew towards Richter, both stumps of her legs trailing slightly behind the rest of her ethereal body, her claws outstretched. He shouted back at her and kept running. One hand wove into a spell form. A brief one-second cast was all he had time for, then they were toe-to-toe. So to speak.

Krista swiped at him, but his Life magic-enhanced chest plate stopped the blow. He swung his short sword in the form *The Lady's Fan Opens*. The defensive move forced the ghost back and Richter flowed into the next, *Forest Wind*. His blade swung across at shoulder height, the tip swiping through the young girl's spirit.

Richter's free hand contorted into the specific configuration of another spell. Red light surrounded his hand and flames shot forward. The fire bathed Krista's form, doing further damage. The ghost shrieked and flew directly up into the air and over Richter's head. He tracked her as best he could, but lost sight when she flew in front of the sun. The chaos seed squinted trying to see her, but then was hit directly in the chest by the quick ghost. He fell back, his Fire spell ending, but he managed to keep hold of his sword. Richter raised it defensively from his prone position, vainly hoping to ward off the dangerous spirit. He needn't have worried. Before Krista could strike again, Alma launched an attack of her own.

The dragonling clawed at the spirit's face. While normally this attack would do nothing, the magic from her Life spell still made her body a living weapon. Krista cursed and swiped at Alma, driving the familiar back, but the damage was done. Richter had been able to recover. He rose and smoothly extended his sword up and out, executing a near flawless *Crane's Neck*. His sonic short sword penetrated the spirit's body and, with a final wail, the ghost fell to dust.

Richter looked around, panting, and saw that all of the spirits had been dispatched. Even Sumiko's summoned birds were flying back. Her cadre of young healers were right behind them. Richter nodded in approval. He wasn't sure how proficient they were at Life magic, but they were well-trained. The group had followed Sumiko's orders without hesitation and now that the danger had passed were rushing back to help however they could. The ones in the front of the pack were even running.

He moved over to Beyan's motionless body and cast *Weak Slow Heal*. The gnome didn't wake up or show any change. Richter bent down and was about to pry one of the mage's eyes open when he felt a hard poke in his back.

"Move out of the way! I hope you now see what happens when you play with dead things."

Richter looked back to see Sumiko's furious expression behind him. He decided it might be a good idea to get out of the way. The older sprite cast a spell and Beyan's body glowed gold. After a moment, she harrumphed and said, "He is merely stunned. That does not change the fact that this should never have happened. You were lucky that I was here. How could you make such a stupid mistake? What were you thinking bringing such horrible creatures into the village? Your people could have been killed!"

"I was only trying to help," Richter said quietly. It wasn't a protest because he knew she was right. "I brought these bones here so that you could lay their spirits to rest. I was trying to do something good. There is no question that I am responsible for this, but outside of that, how can you help me to avoid making a 'stupid' mistake like this in the future?"

Sumiko glared at him, but then said, "You are right, Lord Richter. I should have tested the remains myself as soon as I saw them. I knew that they were anchors for the spirits, but I did not know they were also conduits the spirits could use to re-enter this plane. I won't make that mistake again," she gazed at him intently, "and neither will you."

The Life mage placed one hand on Richter's head and another on his heart. Energy flowed into him and he *knew*!

> Congratulations! You have learned the spell: **Weak Detect Hostile Intent**. Casting this spell will reveal if any creatures within ten yards have an active, deadly intent towards you. This is a spell of Life, level 8. Cost: 38 mana. Duration: 1 minute. Range: 15 feet. Cast Time: 2 seconds. Cooldown: N/A.

Though it had happened several times before, the sudden explosion of knowledge still filled Richter with awe. He wasted no time casting the spell. His fingers contorted into a specific configuration, golden light suffusing them. He finished the spell and looked around. Everything looked the same except for the bones, which now had a sinister, red glow.

"The bones are still glowing," he exclaimed. He rushed over to pick up his thrown sword and then rushed towards the remains with a blade in each hand.

"Stop!" Sumiko commanded. Her voice was like a whip. Richter briefly wondered if she was related to Mama somehow. "You can break those bones to pieces and it would most likely work to destroy their bond to this plane, or you can just let me put them to rest as I intended."

"Those things tried to kill us," Richter protested.

"Yes, because they were corrupted by evil, torment and," her face twisted, "eldritch magic."

Richter looked at her in confusion.

Sumiko looked back sternly. Her gaze shifted to Beyan's unconscious form and then back to Richter. She leaned in and spoke softly as if not wanting to be overheard. "Death magic has a high likelihood of corrupting the user, in my experience, but, I admit, it is not inherently evil. Life and death need each other. Eldritch magic is something else entirely. It is not one of the Basic Elements. It is a parasitical magic that only manifests by corrupting something else. The green flames that the girl spirit controlled were clearly born of this foul energy. Be careful and do not let the gnome stray from his element. Death magi may be foolish and selfish, but they are nothing compared to a practitioner of the eldritch."

Richter's face became more and more concerned as she spoke. The neon green color of the magic she had just seen was the same as the magic used by the undead mage. Richter had felt reservations about attacking a Death mage in his own lair, before this conversation. According to Sumiko, though, he would be attacking a user of an even more dangerous magic.

Sumiko continued, "Let me return to my work. I will separate the souls bound to the bones from all concerns of this plane, including the wrong that has been done to them. They will have at least a chance to find peace. This story can still end well." She started to turn away, but then looked him in the face again, her expression fierce, "You were an absolute gyoti to bring them here without properly assessing the danger. Let me be absolutely clear on that point. Your foolishness stemmed from a good sentiment, however. Look to your friend, the Death mageling. He is waking. The ghostly manifestations of the spirits will not be able to coalesce again before I am done cleansing the bones. Believe me, the danger has passed for now."

Richter looked at her, his nerves still frayed from the battle. He took a deep breath though, and tried to let the tension go. "Sumiko. I don't know what I would do without you. Thank you for winning us this battle, and even more, thank you for your wise counsel."

Sumiko harrumphed, "That is the first smart thing you have said all day. As for what you would do without me? You would most likely die horribly. Everyone would sicken and the smell of this place would be enough to kill an ogre. I won't even get started on…"

The Life mage kept up a running monologue as she walked away. Richter smiled, knowing that if she was happy enough to scold him like that, then everything was okay between the two of them. He did as she suggested and walked over to Beyan. The gnome had propped himself up on his elbows and was blearily looking around. Richter reached down and extended his arm. After a few seconds, the Death mage oriented on his hand and reached out with his own. Richter pulled him up.

"Are you alright?" he asked.

Beyan blinked a few more times, "I will be fine. I am merely dizzy." Beyan seemed to remember something all of a sudden. He whipped his head around, then grabbed it with a groan. After a few moments, he reopened his eyes and looked around more slowly. When his eyes fell upon the knight's body, he grinned and jumped free of Richter's supporting arm. Of course, he immediately fell down again, groaning anew.

Shaking his head, Richter helped him up again. "What the hell is wrong with you, man?"

Beyan looked at him with a smile, his eyes showing both pain and joy, "It worked."

"Whaaat worked?" Richter asked slowly.

Beyan's face grew slightly pensive, "Remember, my lord. I was only following your orders."

"What orders?" Richter asked with a touch of warning in his voice.

"You told me 'Do what you can'. I did not have any spells that could fight the spirits. All I could do was remove one spirit and hopefully create a fighter to distract the rest. So I…"

"You claimed the decaemur knight," Richter finished resignedly.

"I claimed the decaemur knight," Beyan echoed excitedly. "Stand up!"

Richter looked at the gnome, prepared to ask who the small man thought he was talking to, but then the naked knight's body stood. It had fallen in a heap when the mist worker holding it had been ripped apart. It just stood there, staring off into space. The awareness that had been in its eyes before was gone.

"Are you in control of it?" Richter asked. "What happened to Jorgen's spirit?"

"I am in absolute control, Lord Richter," Beyan said confidently. "And Jorgen's spirit is gone." The second statement was said with a bit less confidence.

"You're sure?" Richter asked.

Beyan looked at him, pursed his lips slightly, then said, "Yes."

Richter had had enough, "Alright, that's it. Command this thing to take orders from me, then you, then Sion, then Terrod and Randolphus, in that order. Do it now and be clear that this order can never be revoked."

"But, my lord…"

"Now," Richter said. There was steel in his gaze as he spoke. The stress of the ghostly attack, the guilt over once again having brought danger into his village and the frustration of feeling circumvented by Beyan threatened to spill over. It might have been his imagination, but it almost felt like the new walls in his mind that had appeared when he had gained his Self-Awareness skill were being assaulted. "I am the lord of these lands. I value you Beyan, but I will not allow you to take liberties with the safety of your fellow villagers. I will not allow for this undead thing to harm anyone if you are nowhere to be found. I have fought it once, I will not be surprised by an attack from it again. I will see it hacked to pieces and burnt now before the sun has moved another inch across the sky first." His voice never rose in volume, but his grip tightened on his swords and the point of his freeze blade rose slightly, "Now do as I command."

Beyan's face took on a slightly shocked look, but by the end of Richter's speech he was simply listening quietly. It was clear to the gnome that he was hearing the lord of the Mist Village, not the often humorous man that walked about in his skin. No one else spoke, until Beyan stepped forward and offered his hand. Richter looked at him for a long moment, but then drove the blade of one his swords into the ground. He reached forward and the two men clasped wrists.

"It will be as you command, my lord," Beyan said. "You are the lord of these lands and I am happy to have given you my allegiance."

Richter nodded, "Thank you, Beyan. I value your service."

Not wasting any more time, Beyan beckoned the knight closer. He stated simply that Richter was the undead's true master and to follow his instructions before anyone else's. After that Richter asked the undead to indicate its master and it pointed to the chaos seed. Beyan then gave the others authority over the undead knight as he had been instructed. Finally he stated that the orders given could never be changed, unless Richter commanded it.

"Thank you," Richter said placing his hand on the gnome's shoulder. "Believe me when I tell you I plan for all of us to grow in strength." Beyan nodded. "If that thing is going to fight for us, it should be properly outfitted." So saying, he removed the knight's armor from his bag, except for one gauntlet to be sacrificed to the forge. He didn't give it a weapon though. No reason for it to be armed if it didn't have to be.

Any irritation or bad feelings Beyan might have had about Richter laying down the law seemed to disappear when he saw that his lord was going to trick out his new ride. Richter told him to have Krom fix any damage in the armor, then left the gnome to it. Richter had prompts to read.

CHAPTER 22 -- DAY 112 -- KUBORN 2, 15368 EBG

You have trapped the soul of a ***Tortured Spirit****! Soul level: Common.* ***x 5****.*

Congratulations! You have reached skill level 4 in ***Dual Wield****. Base accuracy penalty in primary hand reduced to 22% and in offhand to 47%. Attack speed increased by 4%.*

Congratulations! You have reached skill level 10 in ***War Leader****. +10% effective distance. +10% attack and defense for all allies within sphere of influence.*

You have received 1,250 (base 2,000 x 1.25 x 0.5) bonus experience for reaching level 10 in the skill: ***War Leader****.*

Congratulations! You have advanced from Novice to Initiate in: ***War Leader****. Maximum party size increased to 10. You may now have two other war leaders create their own war parties under your command. These war leaders must be of a lesser skill rank than you. Your sphere of influence is increased from 50 to 100 yards. New Badges are available for purchase. New skilled positions are available. Field advancements are now possible for heroic efforts. +200 to Fighting Spirit. You can now access the real-time numbers for the health, mana, and stamina of everyone in your war party.*

Congratulations! Your war party survived an attack from a numerically superior force. For facing and defeating a force ten times larger than your own, your party has been awarded the Promotion: ***Overwhelming Odds I****. +10 to Fighting Spirit.*

Congratulations! Your war party survived an attack from a numerically superior force. For facing and defeating a force twenty times larger than your own, your party has been awarded the Promotion: ***Overwhelming Odds II****. +20 to Fighting Spirit.*

Fighting Spirit for your war party has increased from ***+280*** *(100 Champion (Richter) + 100 Champion (Terrod) + 80 Captain of the Guard while fighting inside of the domain of Mist Village) to* ***+510****.*

Woot! He had progressed to the next rank in War Leader. If he was reading these prompts correctly, it looked like he had just become exponentially more badass. Despite his elation, the last prompt gave him pause.

Richter looked at Sion, "Hey, bud. Are you feeling any more... violent?... than before?"

Sion looked up with a concerned expression. "I thought I was imagining things." He slowly opened and closed his fists. "I have been wanting to destroy something. To bash something in. It started… as soon as I looked at your ugly face." Sion gave an evil chuckle and turned away, shaking his head at his friend's stupidity.

"Fucking Toy Story reject," Richter muttered. He didn't let his friend's oh-so-not-funny comments bother him. It was good news that the increase in Fighting Spirit didn't make everyone in his war party a homicidal madman. Still, he didn't quite understand the significance of it. He remembered that the Morale of the Village could affect it. He also remembered seeing mention of it being decreased when Yoshi had killed an enemy champion. Richter still needed more info.

He focused upon the icon for his war party, a gauntleted fist, where it hovered along the corner of his vision. A translucent window appeared to cover his visual field. After scanning it for a moment, he found a button in the form of a capital "FS". Choosing it brought him the information he sought.

A number line appeared in the window, looking much the same as the slider he had seen before for Loyalty, Morale and Health on his city screen. This had different names and values, however. A quick count showed a total of eleven ranks for Fighting Spirit, or FS. There were five positives, one neutral and five negative ranks. The progression was: *Broken Spirit, Panicked, Frightened, Unnerved, Disheartened, Neutral, Aggressive, Violent, Ruthless, Savage and Blood Lust*. His war party had been fighting at the first positive rank, '*Aggressive*'.

That had apparently given +10% to damage. Each higher rank in FS increased the damage and also made it less likely for his troops to run away or be susceptible to fear. There was no mention of whether this damage was limited only to melee, magical or ranged, so he would just have to wait and see, but Richter kept his fingers crossed that the bonus was universal. He still wasn't exactly sure what it meant to be a Champion, but he let that particular bone go unchewed. There were more awesome prompts to read!

You have completed your first Challenge: ***Leave No Man Behind I****! You survived a total of five battles with common soul enemies or higher without losing a single party member.*

Reward: ***250 War Points****.*

Total War Points: ***521****.*

You have unlocked a Challenge: ***Leave No Man Behind II****! Survive a total of ten battles with common soul enemies or higher without losing a single party member. Fail Condition(s): Adding new party member. Death of a party member. Reward: 500 War Points.*

Know This! War Points are awarded based upon the soul level of slain enemies. For slaying one hundred and seven ***Tortured Spirits,*** *you have been awarded four hundred and twenty-eight War Points!*

Total War Points: ***949****.*

Double Woot! He had hundreds of war points to spend. His fingers tingled as he mentally accessed the badges that were now available. Daddy was going to do some shoppin!

Badge	Cost	Description (applies to entire party)
Melee Attack I	25	+5% to melee attacks
Melee Defense I	25	+5% to melee defense

Ranged Attack I	25	+5% to ranged attacks
Ranged Defense I	25	+5% to ranged defense
Magical Attack I	25	+3% to magical attacks *Must specify spell school upon acquisition. May only choose spell school used during battle leading a War Party.
Magical Attack II (Life)	50	+6% to magical attacks *Must specify spell school upon acquisition. May only choose spell school used during battle leading a War Party.
Magical Defense I	25	+2% to magical defense *Must specify spell school upon acquisition. May only choose spell school used during battle leading a War Party.
Skilled Positions	100 to unlock each	Available Positions: **Tank I**: +10% more likely to aggro, +5% defense **Scout I**: +10% to Stealth, can "assign" enemies, will appear as red glow to party members *Scout position works outside Sphere of Influence **Healer I**: +10% to healing spells, first aid and other healing efforts
Lead by Example I	150	As war leader, you may adopt the benefits of a skilled position in addition to whomever you assigned. *Purchasing this badge will only apply to skilled positions unlocked at the initiate rank of the War Leader skill

Movement Speed I	100	+10% Movement Speed *Must specify terrain type upon acquisition. May only choose terrain type that the War party has traveled on.
Favored Enemy I	250	+10% Attack and Defense when fighting a favored enemy *Must specify enemy acquisition. May only choose enemies which have been fought while leading a War Party. Only one favored enemy per War Party formation.
Trainer I	250	+5% experience earned for War Party members
Power Level I	125	10% of the experience earned by the entire war party can be channeled to a specific member *Experience recipient must be within sphere of influence
Sphere of Influence I	250	Increase range of sphere of influence by 100%

Is there such a thing as a triple woot, Richter asked himself. His gaze immediately went to the skilled positions. In recent battles, one of the biggest problems was that his weaker members had been swarmed with the same frequency as those with greater defense. They had been able to ameliorate that with tactics and rudimentary battle formations, but it still left his casters vulnerable. With no hesitation, he purchased *Tank I*. He knew a certain Sergeant of the Guard that would benefit from this.

Almost as if by magic, Richter saw Futen floating back up and behind him ran Caulder and dozens of guards. He called out to Terrod to go meet them. The captain rushed forward to assure the guards that the threat was indeed over. Caulder just nodded with sweat running down his face, clearly still ready to fight if it was required. Plenty of the guards looked ready to fall over though after having run in their armor for a few miles. One even vomited when he stopped running. Frowning, Richter made a mental note to tell Caulder to increase the calisthenics the guards were undergoing each day. If their stamina was that weak, they would be butchered in a standup fight against the bugbears. Seeing that his mana had refilled, he summoned four mist workers and sent them to help Sumiko. He also allocated his mana regen to start paying the cost to unlock the next level of the sonic enchantment once his pool reached five hundred points again. Then he turned his attention back to the badges.

The interface had changed slightly. The other skilled positions still cost one hundred each. A new badge had appeared now for *Tank II*. The cost to upgrade the position was only fifty points. Richter was surprised at first that it was so low, but then supposed it made sense that unlocking the position would cost more than merely improving it. Level two increased aggro and defense to 20% and 10% respectively, but it also did something else. Whoever took the position of tank now had a ten-yard sphere of influence that increased the defense of any allies in it by 5%.

He paid the fifty war points with a smile and the interface changed again, now showing *Tank III*. Almost everything was greyed out on the new badge, though, and the only thing that Richter could see was a small message saying that he could not upgrade to Tank III until he increased his war leader rank. Richter turned his attention to the other positions. After seeing how useful the second level of tank was, he wasted no time purchasing the other two skill positions as well, as well as the upgrades. Each greyed out at level three. His smile deepened when he saw that *Scout II* came with a wonderful boost. Not only did the stealth bonus increase to 20%, but the assign target function came with a weak version of Analyze. Each assigned enemy would show its level to the whole party. Richter could see how, strategically, this information could be clutch. It would let them take out weak outlier units before battle and let them take out high level enemies quickly once battle was joined. Healer II increased healing by 20% and decreased the mana cost of healing spells by 5%.

He was fairly certain of who would fill each position, Sion would scout, Caulder would tank, and if Sumiko did indeed come with them to raid through the Dark portal, she would obviously be the healer. Otherwise, Krom would fill the role.

So far he had spent four hundred fifty war points, leaving him another four hundred ninety-nine to play with. He looked over the available badges again, trying to decide what the best option was. Increasing attack and defense was always a good idea, but it seemed like an immediate satisfaction rather than a long term yield. What his eyes were drawn to was *Power Level I.*

Every day, Roswan and dozens of others were working to build the village into something amazing. Richter still believed that the key to the village's future success was to build his people into something amazing as well. He could envision a society of Professionals and Specialists. The Morale and Loyalty of the village was already high enough that he was fairly certain everyone would choose to stay after their one year contract was up. That just left leveling them.

Unfortunately, the fastest way to level someone was also the most dangerous: combat. He needed to get his people to level ten, so they had the chance to get a noncombat Profession, especially those that already had a journeyman rank in an appropriate skill. Luckily, the mere fact that they had become journeymen meant that they had also gotten twenty thousand experience points from reaching skill level forty. Seeing as how it only took forty-five thousand XP to advance to character level ten, any journeyman should already be most of the way there; he just needed to get them across the finish line. This new badge could make that a lot easier by letting him channel a portion of the war party's experience to a noncombatant. He purchased *Power Level I.*

One hundred twenty-five points were deducted from his war points pool, and the opportunity to buy *Power Level II* appeared. This next Badge cost two hundred fifty war points but increased the experience allocation to 20%. He could also now divide the allocated experience to more than one person. Perhaps most interesting, *Power Level II* allowed the recipients of the allocated experience to be further away from the fighting and still get experience. Specifically, twice the distance defined by his sphere of influence. Obviously, the problem with taking noncombatants into combat was that they could, in fact, be drawn into combat. Allowing them to hang further back could greatly increase their safety. He purchased the badge. *Power Level III* appeared and unlike the skilled positions, this badge was not greyed out. It did cost five hundred war points though.

After his shopping spree, he only had one hundred twenty-four points left. That also, unfortunately, made *Sphere of Influence I* too expensive, which would have been an indirect way to increase the distance the noncombatants could have been from the action. He decided to look at what else was available.

The other Badges could all be useful, but the two that were truly tempting were the ones that increased movement speed and increased earned experience. *Trainer I* cost too much though. He decided to increase his movement speed. Richter focused on *Movement Speed I*.

Several options appeared: forest and underground. Once again, it seemed that he could only choose from terrains his war party had been exposed to. The grasslands of Yves were not an option, for instance. Richter purchased the first forest upgrade. Now one hundred war points poorer; he only had twenty-four points left. The next level of the forest upgrade cost two hundred points, so he decided to save the rest. Richter was more than happy with his group now being able to move 10% faster through the forest.

After seeing how useful the war points could be, he resolved to earn more ASAP. The best way to do that was to kill as many dangerous creatures as he could. Richter recalled his guilt over killing the saber bear but quickly shut it out of his mind. He needed to get stronger, and he needed to make his lands safe. Everything else was secondary.

He wanted to test the new upgrades out now, but they wouldn't go into effect until he had reformed his war party. That was something he couldn't do until tomorrow. Richter looked over and saw that most of the skeletons had been reassembled. It was time to plan for the night. He sent a mental call to Futen. The remnant floated over.

"Yes, my lord?"

"Go tell the cooks that tonight is a special occasion. The tables should be brought up and arranged in front of the Quickening. There will be a wonderful surprise. I want every man, woman, and child here until it happens. Tonight we will laugh, sing, eat and rejoice."

"It shall be as you command, my lord," Futen said as he floated away. Richter looked around. Despite the possible tragedy that could have occurred with the ghost attack, everything had worked out. He had no illusions as to why it had worked out; they had been lucky to have a master of Life magic present at the time of the attack. Still, a win was a win. Everything looked like it was well in hand. Terrod had been the only one to be injured, and even those were minor and easily healed. Sumiko was already blessing the bones, and it looked like she was more than half done. Sion was collecting 'something' from the ashen remains of each of the ghosts, and Beyan was putting the armor on the knight, badly. Richter chuckled slightly.

"Beyan, stop. I didn't mean for you to try to put the armor on right now. How is Krom supposed to fix the armor if you put it on the knight?" The gnome looked at Richter sheepishly. The Death mage had managed to affix a piece of the greaves to the knight's arm. Richter waved him over. After seeing Beyan's excitement over claiming the decaemur knight, he'd had a thought, "With you grinding to improve your Death magic, will you really have time to do the alchemy quest? Even if you win, are you still prepared to do what is required to run the Cauldron?"

Beyan took a deep breath and sighed, "I have thought of that, Lord Richter. I agree that I cannot devote myself to both."

"So does that mean you are withdrawing from the quest?" Richter asked.

An evil smirk worked its way onto the gnome's face, "I thought that maybe I would let Tabia keep working and announce my withdrawal right before the deadline. After all, she is there almost constantly. I even saw her wife yell at her for being gone too much. It would be a shame to ruin that."

Richter laughed, "That's kinda fucked up man, but also kinda funny. Your quest is your quest, I suppose, and I won't interfere. BUT! It may take years to level your Death magic to journeyman level. I need your Alchemy skill now. More specifically, I need you to be a Professed Alchemist now. Once you are, I don't care if you spend Talent points in Alchemy or hoard them until you become a Professed Mage, but I don't want you to waste levels of potential points. What this all means is that you will work in the Cauldron and you will work under Tabia. I don't want to hear any bitching and moaning. You can have your fun now, but I need you to do your best to work under her. For the good of the village."

Beyan looked like he was going to argue, but Richter went further to say, "I could also always tell Tabia that you don't plan on competing. Or better yet, I could tell her wife, Mimi, that you are planning to toy with her. How's your eye feel?"

The gnome blanched and winced involuntarily. Beyan took a deep breath and let out a long-suffering sigh, "As you say, my lord. I will work under her direction."

"Great," Richter said with a smile. "Does that mean you're ready to go for your trial?"

Beyan thought about it and said, "I suppose I am. Right after-"

The Death mage never finished his statement. A black disc appeared in the meadow to the startled oaths of everyone present. Before anyone could run, a giant black hand reached out and grabbed Beyan. It pulled him back through the disc, and it disappeared.

"What the fuck!" Richter shouted. "Did you see that?"

Sion nodded, "The same thing that happened to you."

"THAT'S what happened to me?" Richter shouted.

Sion nodded, "Pretty much."

"And that didn't worry you assholes? That was a giant fucking hand! Incidentally, I'm pretty sure that hand is attached to a sadistic giant. Soooo, thanks for all the concern guys."

Sion *pfff*'d, "You made it back okay. Quit complaining."

Richter's nostrils flared. He was about to let loose on the sprite, but his Companion was already walking away. Everyone else wisely avoided eye contact. Richter looked around, incensed, and then shouted into the air, "You can't just take people like that, Nexus! I need him here. You couldn't have waited?"

Another black disk appeared. This one was right in front of Richter's face and was only a foot across. A human-sized, black hand shot out. Despite the fact that it was smaller, Richter still felt a thrill of fear, wondering if the otherworldly being was going to punish him for his insolence. The hand stopped just shy of touching him, though, and after a moment's pause, it turned to show him its backside… then it flipped him off.

The hand disappeared back into the black disc to the sound of mocking laughter, and Richter was left fuming and looking into thin air.

CHAPTER 23 -- DAY 112 -- KUBORN 2, 15368 EBG

Happily, the decaemur knight remained calm after Beyan was taken to his trial. Richter had stared at it for a moment with a hand on his sword hilt, but it just stood there. Not knowing what else to do, he ordered it to just sit down on the ground. For some reason, it made him feel better to do that. Sumiko called out that she was finished. The mist workers had dug the grave large enough to accommodate all of the remains. Richter helped to lay the skeletons in one by one. The process went quickly with so many mist workers and people available to help. Soon only a patch of bare earth marked the grave and the site of the ghostly battle.

Everyone walked away. Richter even sent Terrod to escort the decaemur knight to the forge. The undead carried its own armor. He told the captain that until Beyan returned, he could use the knight as he saw fit. The mist workers were sent along with Futen with instructions to divide them between helping the cooks set up for the feast and for Roswan to use as he saw fit. Sion had said that he had to get back to the Dragon's Cauldron and for Richter to meet him when he was done. The chaos seed had thanked the sprite guards who had already gone back to guard the Quickening. After a few minutes, Richter was left alone. He just stood there for a moment, keeping vigil over the new grave. After a few minutes, he realized that the quest icon in the corner of his vision was blinking.

> You have completed a Quest: **Proper Rest I.**
> The slain people of Jorgen's village were horribly corrupted by countless years of torture. It twisted them into malevolent spirits. By the strength of your arm, they have been defeated. Through the ministrations of your Life master, they have finally been put to rest which fulfills the optional success condition of this quest.

Reward: 10,625 experience (base 17,000).
Reward for fulling Optional Condition: A call for aid.

Richter furrowed his brow. A call for aid? Aid from whom?

No sooner than had the thought crossed his mind, a pale, translucent figure appeared over the graves. His body immediately tensed, and he unsheathed his swords. He couldn't believe this shit was starting up again. He cast *Weak Detect Hostile Intent*, hoping it would reveal any other spirits that he couldn't see yet. Richter had already crossed half the distance to the ghost, running on a new grave, when he stopped. Surprisingly, the ghostly figure wasn't glowing red. He kept his swords up and at the ready, but took a moment to examine the ghost.

It was Krista. Unlike before however, the girl's body was whole. She stood upon the graves, both legs intact. She wore her slip, and there was no evidence of the damage the monsters had done. Her face was also peaceful, though touched with sorrow. Her fingers were no longer claws; they were only the small hands of a child. What made him feel better overall though was her color. Gone was the neon green of eldritch magic; instead her clothes and body were the pristine white of fresh snow.

Krista's spirit stood unmoving and looked at him. She made no move to defend herself from his impending attack. Hoping he wouldn't regret it, he sheathed both swords. They both stood there silently. After a few moments, Krista started walking forward. When she was within a few feet of him, she stopped and raised one hand. Her fingers moved into an easy roll. It was not a spell form, to Richter, it looked more like the sleight of hand illusionists on Earth would use. Magic or not, she was suddenly holding a white coin.

The dead girl looked at Richter's hand intently. He raised it, palm out. She placed the ghostly coin in it and let go. When she broke contact, the coin gained substance, real and tangible in his plane. Krista then stared right into his eyes. They made a psychic connection. Richter started to panic, but she did not approach his mental defenses. Instead, she communicated her yearning to cross over to her next destination, but he could also feel her residual anger at the abuse she had endured. Sumiko had said she would make it possible for the spirits to be free from the concerns of this world, but they had decided to stay. It was with a bit of shock that Richter realized that Krista was telling him that she, and the other spirits of the victims, were keeping themselves in limbo to offer their aid. Her message conveyed, Krista took a step back and waved goodbye before disappearing completely. He examined the coin.

You have found: **Krista's Summoning Coin**	**Damage:** 17-21 **Durability:** 1/1 **Item Class:** Rare **Weight:** 0.0 kg **Traits:** This coin is made of Krista's essence. Using this will allow you to call for her aid one time. This is a one time use item, and it will disappear within one month. This item cannot be damaged by mundane means.

You have received a Quest: **Proper Rest II**
The spirits of the sacrificial victims have decided to put off their well deserved rest to seek revenge against the eldritch magic user who tortured them. You have one month to use her aid, then the spirits will move on. Help them to destroy the creature which tormented them for so long.
Fail Condition: Wait for more than one month to call upon Krista and the other spirits
Reward: Aid in your battle with the undead lord
Penalty for failure or refusal of Quest: Unknown
By accepting Krista's coin, you have accepted the quest.

Richter put the coin in his bag. He looked around just to be sure no more ghosts were going to pop up, but thankfully everything stayed quiet and copasetic. It was a relief. He'd had enough ghosts for the moment. He turned away from the grave and started walking back towards the Cauldron. Sion had told him to come by before he left.

Richter started jogging. The sun was high in the sky, and large, fluffy clouds drifted overhead. A barely audible buzz of insects surrounded him, and tufts of grass seed drifted up with each step. The thigh-high lawn made him sneeze. A thought occurred to the master of the mist village that made him stop. He looked critically at the lawn and then extended his hand and summoned four mist workers. The level six workers listened to him and soon they had scythes at the end of the arms and were cutting the grass down to a more manageable level. He made sure to specify that they only cut grass. The last thing he needed was his summoned creatures chopping at the Quickening. Suddenly he'd find himself in a war with the sprites that would probably end with Hisako smacking him in the back of the head and calling him "gyoti."

Richter watched them work for a few moments and then kept moving. The blades the workers could manifest were relatively dull, but they were still getting the job done. He made a mental note to have Krom forge some scythe blades or maybe even some of the twisted blades so he could try to make an old school rotary mower. A faint smile graced his face as he wondered if the one thing he would be remembered for millennia from now was 'discovering' a good way to keep a manicured lawn. Yup, he was a regular Tesla.

Richter crossed the final distance to the Cauldron and walked inside. Tabia was working at one of the stations, monitoring a series of bubbling, glass beakers. The high elf was shaking her head slightly as she stared at the color of a particular liquid. Sion was standing at the central cauldron. Richter watched while the blue liquid in the cauldron rose into the air and filled a set of vials the sprite was holding. Richter cleared his throat, and Sion waved him over.

"Perfect timing. While you were out bringing an army of ghosts back to the village, I was doing something useful," Richter rolled his eyes, and Sion smirked. "Specifically, I was working on a few potions. This last batch just finished brewing. Admittedly, I have had a few failures over the past few days. At my apprentice alchemy rank, I normally only have a 50% chance of successfully making a *solution* level potion, but this final attempt came out well. Of course, the fact that being in a Core building makes potions 10% more likely to be successfully prepared didn't hurt." Sion beamed with pride, "I am happy to tell you that not only is this a *solution*, it's also *fortified* strength. There may have been many people who thought that you should have made something different with the Magic Core, but they were wrong. The copy ability is amazing. Here are your potions."

You have found: **Mana Potion** x 30	**Potion Class:** Uncommon **Potion Level:** Solution **Potion Strength:** Fortified **Durability:** 5/5 **Weight:** 0.01 kg **Traits:** Will restore **196** mana points over **17** seconds

Richter's eyes widened. One hundred and ninety-six mana? And there were thirty of them? When Sion had initially been talking about potion strength and potion level he had gotten confused again, but seeing the prompt made it easy to remember. Potion level affected the duration of the potion and potion strength determined exactly how powerful the effect was. "Sion, this is awesome!"

The sprite closed his eyes and gave a self-satisfied head nod. "My alchemy skill is not as high as Beyan's or Tabia's, but at level thirty-four, I still get a 51% bump to potions I make. At my apprentice rank in alchemy, it is more likely for me to make an enhanced strength potion rather than a fortified strength potion, but" Sion smirked again, "I got lucky. I was able to make three draughts of the initial potion at once and I used the central cauldron to make nine more doses of each."

"You're the man!" Richter said, giving his friend a high-five.

Sion took the accolade as his due, "This one really did come out well. It took me more than an hour to make the initial potions, but it paid off."

"How are we doing for ingredients?" Richter asked.

"With the gathering that I regularly do and with the amazing yield in the herb shed and Isabella's garden, we are doing okay."

"You're great, man!" Richter looked at his friend and came to a decision, "I wasn't sure what I was going to do with this, but I want you to have it." He reached into his Bag of Holding and pulled out the Bottle of Royal Jelly from the aswani queen. Abbas, the trader, had sold it to him for a whopping two hundred and eighty-two gold. Put another way, the honey colored substance in the jar had cost him more than twenty-eight thousand bucks. Considering the fact that it added +2 to the Strength Characteristic, though, it was worth it. Sion was his best friend and closest ally. If he could increase his Companion's fighting potential, it was worth any price. That was why he was so surprised when Sion refused the gift.

"You should not give that to me," Sion said. "It would be a waste."

Richter looked at his friend, confused, "What are you talking about? Is this part of your people's hippie dippie 'I don't need possessions' bullshit? You're my best friend. You're worth it."

"That's not what I mean," Sion said with an edge in his voice.

"Then what do you mean?" Richter asked. His arm was still out, offering the jelly.

Sion looked at him with irritation, "If you must know, it would be a waste because of my size."

Richter just shook his head slightly and looked at Sion with an irritated expression of his own, "I'm really getting tired of people giving me half-answers. I am NEW here! Just tell me what's going on, Sion."

The sprite huffed. He looked over to the side and said through gritted teeth, "I am under four feet tall. That means that *technically,* I am a 'small' creature. My Strength stat is only 70-80% of my baseline Strength characteristic. There are exceptions for certain races, of course, but I would probably only gain one point of Strength if I used that."

Richter furrowed his brow. He doubled checked his friend's status page and saw that Sion's Strength characteristic was eighteen, "Does that mean that your Strength would be twenty-two or twenty-three if your size was normal?" Sion looked at him sharply, "Errrr, I mean, *my* size?"

Sion looked away again, "No," he said sullenly. "My Strength is mostly from my armor. Characteristics added by items and armor are not affected by the size modifier. They are added directly to my stats."

"Well that's not so bad then," Richter said with false cheer.

"No?" Sion asked looking at him sharply. "How many characteristic altering items have you found since coming to The Land? How many of them are created to work for someone of my size? Even these bracelets you gave me are so big that I have to wear them like arm bracers. I couldn't wear that belt you gave to Caulder unless I used one hand to keep it up the whole time."

"There is no shame in needing to use a hand to keep it up," Richter said lightly. The look Sion gave him made it clear that the sprite wasn't in a joking mood. "Okay then, my friend. I can see this is a sensitive topic. Let me say that no matter how tall you are, I wouldn't have anyone else watch my back. You and me, til death." Richter reached out his hand.

Sion looked at him, then ruefully smiled. He clasped wrists with his friend.

"Is there anything else I should know about your… stature?" Richter asked delicately.

"Small creatures also get a bonus to Agility and Dexterity and my dodge is increased overall."

Richter nodded. Knowing that there was an inherent alteration of characteristics due to certain sizes, it further explained why the rock giant's Strength had been so high. He would have to keep that in mind. He brought the conversation back to the potions, "Well these are totally awesome, man. Thank you so much. If you don't have anything else to do, can you try to make some health and stamina potions too? Tabia seems…" a feminine curse came from the back of the building, "busy. So now that Beyan is gone, you're all I have. Tomorrow we are going to get that shiverleaf frond."

"I'm on it," Sion said. "You should know that I was also able to gather a large amount of ectoplasm from the remains of the tortured spirits. With a bit of experimentation, I might be able to make a spiritual poison out of it."

That was music to Richter's ears. "See what you can do. If you get a good recipe, we will get Tabia to make it, so it's as strong as possible. Also, get Fudave up here and talk to Randolphus and see if any of the other villagers have the Alchemy skill. I want a stockpile of useful potions."

"That is a good idea. I saw Fudave helping out with the farmers and herb gathering near the outer moat. I was meaning to discuss bringing him up to the lab. "

Shaking his head in self-recrimination at not utilizing his people to their full capabilities, Richter reached out to the central cauldron to give Fudave user permissions. "I've added him," Richter said. "You can give anyone else permission that might be helpful."

"I will take care of it. Before you leave, you might want to put this away in your bag as well." Sion untied several pouches from his waist and handed them over. He told Richter that three held the rest of the concentrated crystal. The last two he didn't speak about, just looking at Richter meaningfully.

Richter opened one of the pouches and saw red crystalline granules. They were filled with powdered blood crystal. A prompt told him that there were nine measures of the stuff. He looked at Sion with appreciation and nodded. Sion just gave another smile. The two friends high-fived again and Richter walked off. He had another stop to make before he left the meadow.

Where are you, my love? Richter sent out.

Hunting, she sent back happily.

He wished her luck, but it set him to thinking. If she was outside of the village walls, then she would be too far away to capture the souls of anything she killed. *Soul Trap* would only work if an empty soul stone was within a certain distance. Richter was all for her keeping down any dangerous wildlife, and he was reasonably sure that she could take down most anything that she came across. He also knew that she was smart enough to avoid any large packs of dangerous animals or opponents she couldn't handle on her own. Seeing as how he hadn't come up against any flying monsters yet, Alma should be able to evade anything out there. No, he wasn't really worried for her, but he also didn't want the souls to go to waste. Luckily, he thought he had a simple fix. He sent out a mental call to Futen and let his familiar have her fun.

Richter walked to the lake on the western side of the meadow. Between the waterfalls and flowering lake plants, it was a beautiful sight. He appreciated it for a moment, and it reminded him that he hadn't just relaxed for a long while. After the stress and sweat of the fight, he decided there was no time like the present.

He removed his armor, one piece at a time, and placed it inside of his bag. Then his sweaty clothes came off, and he let them drop into a pile. All he was left wearing was jewelry and his dagger tied to his thigh. He summoned a mist worker and gave it instructions to carry his dirty garments to the section of the river where the washer men and women cleaned clothes.

As the worker walked away, he looked after it and reflected on how summoning the grey helpers had become commonplace since he had invested heavily in Wisdom. Before, he had always summoned the workers from the village mana pool and usually had left that task to Futen. He had seriously underestimated just how important the magical constructs were, and with his new summoning ring, they were stronger and more versatile than ever. If he had his way, the mist village was about to experience a boom in productivity akin to the industrial revolution. He turned back to the lake; those thoughts were for later.

Richter reached into his bag and took out his Fish Ring. It allowed him to breathe underwater for up to three minutes. One of his rings of health took its place in the spatial folds of the bag, which he then dropped on the embankment. As the bag fell, he also discarded his worry over battles, deaths, stress, responsibilities, and the innumerable enemies that were out there waiting for him. If only for a few minutes, he was pushing the Pause button. Right now, he needed to relax and become one with the land and water that comprised his dominion. The only other thing he did was to cast *Weak Haste* and to load his Ring of Spell Storage. Richter took a deep breath and, with a running jump, dove into the lake. His body slid under the surface that reflected the sky and surrounding cliffs like a mirror. In a few moments, the ripples from his entry faded away, and there was no evidence of his passing. All was still.

That only lasted until Richter came back up with a loud curse, "Holy fuck, that's cold!"

CHAPTER 24 -- DAY 112 -- KUBORN 2, 15368 EBG

Despite his initial outburst, Richter's body quickly acclimated to the cold water. He swam out into the lake, his form strong from countless childhood afternoons spent at the "Y" and his body strong from leveling. His fluid and sure freestyle strokes took him away from the shore quickly, and he aimed towards the center of the lake. He didn't swim the entire way, but the lakebed dropped quickly. When he judged that he was far enough out to have a good dive, he tread water and raised one hand above the water, casting *Simple Light*. It was no easy feat twisting his fingers into the right configuration while he kept himself afloat. It occurred to him that this might actually be good training to increase his concentration. After a simple word of Power, a golden ball appeared in the air beside his head. Richter dove.

He kicked down from the surface, aiming for the bottom. The light stayed behind his head, illuminating the water in front of him. Richter maintained a strong breaststroke, and soon the ambient light from the surface faded. He kept swimming. Fish swam away from him, startled by his presence in their domain. Pressure built in his chest. His air was running out. Steeling himself to trust the Fish Ring, he took a breath.

Richter hadn't known what to expect, but the wait was anticlimactic. The ring grew cooler on his skin, but that was the only strange thing that happened. His breath came as easily as if he was standing on land and the pressure in his chest disappeared. He kept swimming. After another final stroke, his hand hit the muck on the bottom of the lake. He held onto the bottom for a moment and then looked up. The surface of the lake looked like a large, shimmering portal to another world. The sun shone in the middle, a diffuse golden disc.

He stayed there, encapsulated against the world. Hundreds of feet of water stretched above him and countless liters surrounded him. Richter enjoyed a moment of being perfectly alone. All sounds were muted, and he just floated. A small smile crossed his face. For a few brief seconds, he simply was.

A fish swam by his face, breaking his meditation. As he turned his head to follow it, he noticed that there was a faint light off to his left. Several breast strokes later, he was in front of the glow and discovered it was his Herb Lore skill coming into play. Several of the plants along the lake bed were glowing to indicate they were useful in some way.

You have found: **Toadmore Ochre**	**Herb Class:** Common **Weight:** 0.2 kg **Uses:** *Novice:* This common plant has bulbs that will act as a lubricant *Initiate:* You have a feeling that it could also replenish your stamina if properly prepared. *Apprentice:* The roots of this can make a pleasing dye.

More herbs began to glow as Richter swam along the lake bottom. He collected a few of each, but then he saw an herb that glowed brighter than the rest. His chest was getting tight again, the magic from the fish ring nearly expended, but the strong orange light drew him on. A few short strokes later and it waved lazily in front of him, moved by faint currents.

You have found: **Stillwater Lantern**	**Herb Class:** Rare **Weight:** 0.15 kg **Uses:** *Novice:* This delicate plant can be used to create a shield potion *Initiate:* Can create a salve that when applied increases hearing *Apprentice:* A spell component to make summoned Water creatures stronger

There was an entire patch of the lanterns. They looked like small orange tomatoes at the top of green stalks. What made them interesting though was that surrounding each "tomato" was a sphere of fronds. The wire-thin fronds were crocheted together into a loose cage, leaving large holes that made visualizing the inner orange globe easy. He reached out and grasped a stalk.

The green stem the lantern was attached to was surprisingly tough and well-anchored to the lake floor. Richter had no doubt that he could have uprooted the thing easily if he had been standing on land. Underwater though, with his chest already becoming almost painfully tight from his rapidly diminishing air supply, was another matter. He knew he didn't have much time left, but just yanking the plant free would most likely have destroyed it. Forcing himself to remain calm, he closed his eyes and connected with the energy of the plant. His Herb Lore skill told him in seconds that the head of the plant was the only viable part, so he took his +3 moonstone dagger out of its sheath and started sawing. The strong blade cut through the stalk easily. When he moved onto the second frond however, his skin brushed against the wicker frond.

A painless but clearly felt pulse emanated from the orange fruit. It radiated outward in all directions, a quickly moving distortion in the water. It had no immediate effect that Richter could see, but that meant little as his visibility in any direction but up was limited to only a few feet. Whatever it meant, he was pretty sure it would suck for him. He braced his legs against the lake floor and pushed off, the stalk of one of the lanterns clutched in his hand.

The discomfort in his chest started to become actual pain, and he knew that soon his stamina would begin to fall. If the green bar reached zero, his red health bar would plummet as he actually drowned. This brought an uncomfortable sense of déjà vu, reminding him of his frantic underwater swim while he was unlocking his Life magic. Richter wasn't overly worried though. His stats were much higher than they had been at that time and he had mentally worked out that he should easily be able to make the surface before he was in any real danger.

A distant part of his mind replayed what Charlie Murphy had said about Rick James. Wrong. WRONG!

Before he was halfway back up to the top, he started seeing large numbers of fish. A second later, he was drowning in them. The shock of being swarmed by hundreds of small pescados was almost enough for him to ignore the fact that even when faced with situations both odd and dangerous, he was still friggin hilarious. Drowning in fish indeed!

Silly as it may have sounded, Richter began to realize he was in actual danger. The pulse, which was obviously the stillwater lantern's defense mechanism, appeared to summon every aquatic animal within the vicinity and made them extremely aggressive. Each of the fish began to bite and nibble at his naked body. This would have been cute in certain circumstances, but with his pecker dangling like the world's most tantalizing bait, Richter suddenly lost his sense of humor. It didn't help that some of the little fuckers had teeth.

Even the bites would not have been a real problem if not for the sheer volume of fish that were around him. They were so plentiful that he couldn't effectively swim and his ascent had slowed to a crawl. As the pain in his lungs magnified and his stamina bar dropped below the halfway point, he started feeling the first pangs of panic. On land, he could have cast any number of spells, but underwater, his inability to perform the vocal part of his magic made him essentially mute. So he did the only thing he could. He unleashed the power of his ring.

Happy that he had never forgotten the lessons from his boy scout days, Richter used his prepared spell, *Weak Sonic Wail*. The duration of the spell was only three seconds, but that was enough to instantly stun and kill many of the fish around him. He whipped his hand around him in all directions, taking care not to point the ring at his own face. The fish scattered.

Richter's stamina had fallen beneath the one quarter mark and he was still only halfway to the surface. He wasted no more time. Doing a frog crawl upwards for all he was worth, Richter swam with a frantic need to live. With his stamina nearing zero and his arms feeling leaden he finally broke the surface with a gasp. He looked up and saw Futen floating above him and Alma flying towards him across the water.

"You called, my lord?" Futen asked in his deadpan voice.

My love! You're bleeding! Alma thought to him with concern. A golden glow surrounded her and his small wounds healed.

Richter put his head back in the water and squeezed his eyes shut while he treaded water. When he opened them, he had a furious look on his face, "What the fuck. Does *everything* on this planet have to try and kill me? Those were fish. Little, cute fish!" As he spoke, the bodies of said swimmers started floating to the surface. The fact that he had become a mini-ecological disaster didn't improve his mood. Maybe it really was the nature of Earthers to destroy whatever they touched. Then he thought, fuck those fish. A couple had taken bites of his balls!

"I believe you should be concerned about what is happening on your left, my lord." Futen said.

What, Richter thought. He looked to the left and saw a bubbling and broiling on the water's surface, a couple hundred yards away. He had no idea what that was, but he sure as shit wanted no part of it. A fish leapt out of the water in the middle of the disturbance and Richter realized that what he was seeing a conglomeration of maybe thousands of fish. Then it started moving towards him. Quickly.

"Blast it, Alma! Blast it! Wide beam!" he shouted.

Richter started swimming as quickly as he could towards the bank. Alma flew past him towards the disturbed water. She shrieked in defiance at the numerous fish coming to mob her master. Richter just kept swimming. He channeled his internal Sam Jack, using the anger to propel him on while he went through a mental mantra, "I've had it with these muthafuckin fish, in this muthafuckin lake! I've had it-" He would have moved faster if he let go of the lantern plant, but he'd be damned if he had almost become fish food for nothing.

Alma crossed the distance to fish and let loose with her *Psi Blast* on it broadest setting from the highest altitude that would still make it effective. Every fish in the aggressive school was stunned or killed. A few minutes later, Richter was safely back on land. He lay on his back, the lantern clutched in his hand, breathing quickly to catch his breath. His stamina was already refilling quickly thanks to his high Constitution. After a bit he looked out over the lake. A few fish floated dead at the top, but Alma's psychic attack had apparently only stunned most of the rest because now they were nowhere to be seen. His familiar had already grabbed one of the dead fish and was consuming it on the grass next to him.

Thank you, love. Enjoy that fish. You deserve it, he thought to her fondly.

I know, she thought back smugly.

Smiling, Richter stood up and started walking back to where he had left his bag. As he walked he reflected on how crazy it would have been to be killed by a couple hundred salmon. It would have been the curveball of all time. Weird or not though, there was no denying that those fish had been all over him. In fact, they'd been practically swarmy!

CHAPTER 25 -- DAY 112 -- KUBORN 2, 15368 EBG

Richter made it back to his bag and pulled out a fresh set of pants. He put nothing else on, allowing his body to dry in the air. He also put his Ring of Health back on, putting the Fish Ring in his bag. Futen was instructed to get the weavers to fashion a bag that Alma could carry. He also told the remnant to gather the scribes to wait for him near his office. The glowing orb floated off.

Richter looked at the plant in his hand. The lattice-like cage around the central orange bulb had been torn and misshapen, but the bulb itself was unharmed. The entire thing went into his bag. Richter thought about the field of these things that was at the bottom of the lake and resolved to get more later. He thought he might be able to avoid its defense if he just didn't touch the lattice. That was a concern for another day, though.

The day was getting late, and he had several more stops to make before the feast that night. When he had come to the lake, his primary goal had not been to go swimming or to search for plants. It had been to check on the skath eggs. So he jogged over to where the eggs were kept, leaving Alma to her meal.

Richter heard voices before he saw anyone. The clutch of skath eggs was partially hidden from view by the bank of the lake, so he didn't see anyone at first. Several feet down from that lip, the eggs were nestled in the mud. Once Richter was closer, he saw two naked figures, covered in muck, laughing with each other while they slowly turned the eggs.

"Derin. Deera," Richter greeted them.

"Hello, Lord Richter. That seemed," Deera began with a smile.

"like quite an exciting event," Derin finished with a jaunty smile of his own.

"You were watching?" Richter asked surprised.

"From the beginning," Derin said with a laugh. "I am glad that you finally went swimming. You have seemed,"

"so tense," Deera said as she stood up. Mud spackled her body but did nothing to cover up her lady bits. She smiled when she saw his admiring gaze. "Will you join us in caring for the eggs, my lord? And,"

"perhaps for some more relaxation?" Derin finished, standing up as well.

Richter looked at the twins. Their abnormally high Charisma had given them the kind of bodies and faces that would get them on a magazine cover, or at least to the front of the line at New York clubs. They moved even closer and held hands while they looked at him. He sighed while his hand reached for the fastening on his pants. Being the lord of these lands was a responsibility. He supposed it really was his duty, to please that booty. Richter took some star zenia from his bag and popped it into his mouth. His pants and bag dropped to the ground, and he clapped his hands together, "Who wants a mustache ride?"

An hour or so later, the three of them swam in the lake to rinse off. Richter had been cautious to get back in the water at first, but thankfully no more fish came to attack him. It would have been completely irritating if his relationship with all the fish in the lake had dropped to Hatred for the rest of his life. As he cooled off, it did make him wonder, though.

His Herb Lore skill had shown him some very impressive uses for the stillwater lantern, but the description hadn't included that defense mechanism. Specifically, for the lantern plant, it would be amazing if he could call on the very beings of the deep to fight for him. It was a good reminder that his skill only showed him up to three possible uses for plants. There was always more knowledge to unlock and discover.

Richter swam back to the shore, leaving the twins to splash and frolic in the water. He wanted to check on the eggs. He walked to the clutch, feeling the cool mud squish between his toes. Kneeling down, he touched each egg in turn. The last time he had seen the eggs, a prompt had told him they would hatch "in a matter of days." After gaining his new Animal Husbandry skill, though, the prompt changed to say specifically "seven days, fourteen hours and thirty-eight minutes." Because of that, he now knew where he would be a week hence.

It also meant that Krom had a few days to build a cage. Richter envisioned an iron grate with holes large enough for water to pass through easily, but small enough that the baby skaths could not enter the rest of the lake. It would extend far enough out into the lake that the skaths could swim, and would also circle around onto the land. It would be a perfect pen.

Richter held each egg and, in turn, connected with the almost-formed creatures. Through his inspection, he was able to see that they continued to be perfectly healthy. The hunger he had felt coming from each egg before was a touch stronger. Satisfied that his infant amphibious cavalry was well cared for, he washed the rest of the mud off of his legs and feet and climbed back up onto the bank. The chaos seed swiftly put on his clothes. He considered forgoing his armor, but the fact that he had already been attacked multiple times today, the last of which involved hundreds of cod, made him a bit cautious. His green sprite armor went back on and his body flooded with increased strength as the armor's enchantments affected him. Both swords settled onto his back. Still hearing the twins playing in the lake, he jogged back towards the village.

Richter stopped at the garden, "Isabella, I have a surprise for you."

The chestnut haired beauty turned toward him with a smile. Her skin was the golden brown of toasted honey. "What have you found, Lord Richter?"

He pulled the stillwater lantern out of his bag. She clapped her hands in delight. "Well done, my lord!"

> Quest Update: **If It Grows From The Ground, It's Probably Okay II.** You have found your first rare herb and brought it back to Isabella. To finish this quest, bring four more rare plants back to the Dragon's Cauldron.

Isabella examined the herb in her hands. "Truly this is amazing, my lord, but it is an aquatic plant. I do not think we will have a place to plant it. I would hate for it to die when we could cultivate it. Can you help with this?"

You have been offered a Settlement Quest: **If It Grows From The Ground, It's Probably Okay III**.
You have brought Isabella a *rare* plant. Despite the incredible Core building you have provided for herbs, it lacks a facility for growing aquatic herbs. Isabella has asked you to help with this.
Success Conditions: Provide a space to grow aquatic herbs
Reward: Increased village Loyalty
Penalty for failure or refusal of Quest: None
Do you accept? Yes or No

Richter selected 'Yes'. He thought about it for a moment and then beckoned for Isabella to follow him. He went into the greenhouse attached to the Dragon's Cauldron and pulled open the trap door set into the floor. Summoning a mist light, he walked down the steps that had been revealed. The stairs crossed back and forth three times and ended at a stout door. He pushed his way inside and saw the wall sconces and rows of tables that were supplied to cultivate plants that were better suited to growing in the dark. Wasting no time, he walked to the back of the room and placed his hand on the back wall.

Greetings, Master of the ***Dragon's Cauldron****. It appears you wish to add a room with a pool of water to the structure of the Cauldron? This will cost 112 Alteration Points. Currently, there are 83/100 Alteration Points available in your Core building at level one. Would you be interested in a different option? Yes or No?*

Richter chose 'Yes' and a list of options appeared.

A small room with a pool will cost 91 Alteration Points. A large alcove with a pool will cost 60 Alteration points. A small alcove with a pool will cost 38 Alteration Points. Do any of these options interest you?

Richter selected 'a large alcove'. The wall started ballooning outward away from his hand. The surface bubbled out like a sheet of glass exposed to high heat. It slowly stretched back for several minutes and then stopped. Corners appeared and the surface of the widening sphere began to solidified and harden. The final space was shaped like a cube, fifteen yards to a side, all made of glass. The floor was the only surface that wasn't flat, instead sloping down another fifteen feet, leaving space for a deep pond. The bottom was pockmarked with divots that resembled the scalloped spaces on the walls. Each would be perfect for soil. The only problem was, there was still no water. Even as he was thinking that, a clear glass column rose up from the floor. Inside were two hollow tubes. One filled with water that spilled out of the bottom, filling the pond. It took several minutes, but the pond filled. Richter started being concerned about the water overflowing, but when it was a foot shy of the level of the floor, the other tube filled with water. This one flowed up towards the ceiling, though. Richter smiled. It was a filtration system!

"Will this do?" Richter asked smugly.

"You are amazing, Richter!" Isabella exclaimed. She immediately caught herself, "I mean, my lord."

"Just call me Richter, Issy. Terrod is my Companion, which almost makes you two family."

Her answering smile was as bright as the sun, and she wrapped her arms around him in a warm hug. He chuckled and hugged her back before letting go. He really had meant what he'd said. Isabella was a beautiful woman, but the affection he felt for her was the same as he would feel towards a sister. When he let go, she said, "This is perfect. I will just need to bring dirt to line the bottom of the pond."

"I think I can help with that too," he said.

Richter summoned three mist workers and left them with Isabella. Before they had even reached the surface again, she was giving them instructions. Don't tempt a woman with a sale, a knick-knack or someone she could put to work on home improvements. Just like the women who raised him, he thought with a chuckle. Richter said his goodbyes and started walking back down to the village. On his way down the hill, he was passed by several mist workers and villagers carrying items up to the meadow for the night's feast. Richter checked his new prompts.

You have completed the Quest: **If It Grows From The Ground, It's Probably Okay III**
You have provided a location for growing underwater herbs. You have gone above and beyond the call of this quest by

> supplying a **Core**-level building! All rewards **doubled**! As this was a Settlement Quest, it will aid in the progression of your Administration skill.
> **Rewards:**
> 2,500 (base 2,000 x 1.25 x 2.0 x 0.5) experience points.
> +10 (base +5) village-wide Loyalty.

Congratulations! You have reached skill level 7 in ***Administration.*** *+7% to Morale, Loyalty, and Production for your village.*

Richter greeted his people as they walked by. Everyone had caught on that something special was going to happen tonight. Seeing as how it involved being near the Quickening, they had guessed that the birth of the pixies might be imminent. The village was practically buzzing with anticipation. The chaos seed smiled as he quickly made his way to the catacombs.

Richter jogged up the hill leading to the entrance and returned the salute of the guards stationed there. He walked down the several hundred yards of the corridor and entered the room of the Great Seal. The spirals representing his Life and Air magic pulsed with light and color. The other two dormant spirals, Water and Dark magic, seemed almost to reproach him for not having claimed mastery of them yet. A part of Richter itched to do just that and improve his personal magic, but he couldn't take the risk. Each Power he awakened increased the amount and the level of the monsters around his village. The monsters were already more than most of his guards could handle. Unlocking his powers had to wait.

He moved past the seal and walked back to Randolphus's office. As usual, the chamberlain was doing his Sisyphus act, trying to overcome his mountain of papers. He looked up when Richter walked in, "My lord. It is great that you are here. There is a long list of things we need to discuss. First, there is a report of a female guard beating her husb-"

"Ah! Randy. Stop. Stop! How did you even manage to say that much? I was planning to cut you off as soon as I got in here. It's like you cast a spell on me!" Randolphus just stared at him sourly, not appreciating his lord's wit. Richter still smiled, "It's time to have a talk with the scribes, and I want you there with me. So grab your clipboard and come on."

Richter turned around quickly, not giving his chamberlain a chance to retort. He was happy the two of them had had a heart to heart. Despite that, speaking with Randolphus was still like getting cheese out of a mouse trap. If you didn't move quickly, you would be caught up in a soul-crushing vice of conversation for what seemed like the rest of your life. So he extricated himself from Randy's office and walked over to the room the Scholars occupied. The two men worked closely with the chamberlain, so they had been situated just down the hallway.

He approached the door and was about to knock but decided to wait for Randolphus. The tall chamberlain caught up a few ticks later, though, so he rapped on the door and let himself in. Two rudimentary wooden tables were pressed together and were serving as desks for the scribes. The men were currently writing upon sheaves of parchment. Several books were open in front of each of them, and they seemed to be compiling information. Both stood when they saw who was standing in the doorway, though. He used *Analyze* to remind himself of their names.

"Greetings, Lord Richter," Bartle said.

"Greetings, Lord Richter," Bea said.

The two scribes were both six feet tall and athletic. Richter had been surprised when he had first met them. He had expected the Scholars to have gangly frames, with The Land's equivalent of pocket protectors, but that wasn't the case with these two. They did not have the large muscles of warriors, but it was clear that the training the men had gone through was not limited to taking notes. Both were human, but there the similarities ended. Bartle's face was pockmarked, and he had shoulder length hair that always seemed oily and perhaps the slightest bit greasy. Bea's face, on the other hand, was smooth and slightly rounded in a way that seemed incongruous with his lean frame. His long red hair was woven into a single braid that hung down his back.

"Hey guys," Richter greeted. "Sit down, sit down. We need to talk."

CHAPTER 26 -- DAY 112 -- KUBORN 2, 15368 EBG

"We are at your service," Bartle said, taking his seat. Richter and Randolphus pulled two other chairs over and joined them.

"The first thing I need to know is, what can you do?" Richter asked. "Basil told me about some of your Talents: Association, Still Image, Copying, and…"

Richter looked to Randolphus for help. "Confidential, Perfect Scribing, and Knowledge Tablet, my lord," the chamberlain supplied.

The chaos seed snapped his fingers, "That's right!" He pulled out the knowledge tablet. The two by two-foot wooden item came alive when he pressed the white stone in the corner. A picture of one of the villagers appeared, along with her name, level, and skills. He felt a bit bad that he hadn't gone through the tablet in depth yet, but it always seemed like there were other things to do. "I want to know, can you make this thing bigger?"

Bartle and Bea exchanged a look, "Bigger, Lord Richter?"

"Yes," he responded. "bigger. Ideally the size of a large table. I also want to know if you can put other information on this kind of device. Off the top of my head, I would want to be able to examine an interactive map."

Bartle nodded in understanding, "What you are describing is a cartographer's table. The Traveler's guild utilizes these to combine the information from the maps of their many members. The creation of such an object is well beyond our abilities, unfortunately. Only the Traveler's Guild knows the secret of making their interactive maps. Even then, a high level crafter and enchanter would be required. I know that the guild sells such devices, but the costs are… prohibitive."

"How much gold are we talking?" Richter asked.

Bea gave a soft snort, "Suffice it to say that only nobles and guild masters normally have them."

Richter nodded. Bartle seemed like a good guy, but Bea's superior attitude was already somewhat grating. It wasn't worth making a big deal out of, though. At least not yet. He focused on the information he had been given. The versatility of such an object would pay for itself. The reportedly high cost was not a surprise. His own small Traveler's Map had cost him more than five thousand gold. He had even paid over a hundred gold for the mapping ring that he had given Sion, and that thing only worked if you already had a map.

No, it seemed that the cartographer's table was beyond his economic reach. Perhaps he could use other, more covert, means to get one… The Scholar had said that nobles had them. From what Richter had seen, most nobles were total asshats. It might be time to make a little trip back into Yves. A faint smile played across his face. It would be great to get a few more rugs and paintings to hang next to Count Stonuk's.

The chaos seed shook his head. He needed to focus. "What about just making a large version of the knowledge tablet?"

"That will cost much less," Bea replied. "I would still need access to powdered crystal and a specially treated wood, but the task is within my capability. Specifically, I would require wood from a tree with a rarity of *scarce* or higher. There are several options, though lumina pine would most likely work best. The Knowledge Table would not auto-update as a Cartographer's Table would, but map information could be added manually and the picture could be manipulated to be made larger or smaller."

"So you could add information from my Traveler's Map, and we could periodically update it?" Richter asked.

Bea thought about it, stroking his chin, "If you affixed a specific image onto your map then I could add the information. You would only be able to access that particular map, however, Lord Richter. We could add various images from your Traveler's Map, but it would be a time-consuming process." The Scholar did not seem excited about the prospect. "A Knowledge Table is still a powerful and versatile tool, however. Many other types of information could be uploaded to aid your chamberlain in the administration of the village's daily affairs. Simple functions such as basic math and acting as a recording tablet are well within its capabilities." Bea's face adopted a smug look, "Creating such a large item is outside of the scope of the contract we signed with your trader, however."

"How much?" Richter asked flatly. Everyone was always trying to nickel-and-dime him.

When Bea spoke, his voice had the practiced cadence of a sales pitch, "For a simple knowledge tablet like the one you are holding, the cost is normally forty to fifty gold. Updating the information costs several gold each time. For a project such as you are describing, a knowledge table one could say, I believe a fair amount would be," he paused and looked at Bartle before continuing, "two hundred and eighty gold."

"Oh, is that it?" Richter asked. A bit of irritation had worked itself into his voice. "From what I understand, Basil paid off your debt to your guild, and you agreed to provide your services for six silvers a week. 50% more, by the way, than I am paying others in this village. I have fed you, given you shelter, and now you're trying to shake me down?" He raised up from his chair as he spoke, stabbing one finger down on the table to punctuate his words. Alma rose up on all fours and the ridges running down her back stood up a bit. She glared at the Scholar.

Bea looked a bit off put by Richter's tone and more than a bit bothered by the dragonling's aggressive posture. He also looked confused, "I am not going to attack you, Lord Richter."

Richter glared at the man, confused himself. An amused voice spoke in his head.

You have used another idiom, my love. Alma continued to look aggressively at the Scholar, but the entertained tone of her mental message made it clear it was just an act. He ran the words he had used through his head and realized that 'shake me down' did indeed translate as 'wrestle me to the ground.' Somewhat amused that his familiar was basically conning the man, he had to struggle to keep any mirth off of his face.

"Well… your insulting offer *feels* like an attack," Richter covered lamely. Fucking idioms. "I do not believe for a moment that, if you were tasked to create a Knowledge Table while you were still under contract in Yves, you would personally be pocketing nearly three hundred gold." Richter examined Bea's face, and, sure enough, he saw just the slightest flicker of doubt. Bartle wouldn't make eye contact, and Randolphus nodded to show that his lord was right. He turned back to Bea. The man looked genuinely scared, so Richter decided it was time for a little good cop bad cop, "Now I'm not going to take the fact that you tried to cheat me personally, despite the fact that I pay you a good wage. Nothing wrong with a man getting his beak wet, right?" As soon as he said it, Richter almost rolled his eyes in irritation. IDIOMS! He pressed on, though, not wanting to lose momentum.

"Alma, on the other hand, seems to be getting all riled up." The dragonling's wings flared. A slight hiss came from her mouth, and she took a threatening step forward. Bea leaned as far back in his seat as he could. He looked at Bartle for help, but the other Scholar wisely decided not to try and intercede with whatever the lord of the village planned to do. As far as Bartle was concerned, if his cocky friend had foolishly decided to fleece the sword-carrying, magic-wielding Master of a Place of Power, then he could deal with the consequences. Blood drained from Bea's face when Alma's body started glowing yellow.

Aren't you laying it on a bit thick, love? You're not actually going to fire a lightning bolt, are you? Richter kept glaring at Bea while he silently communicated with Alma.

Haha. How can you even ask? This is only a bit of motivation. He will offer to build it for free soon. This sweaty man must be a fool to try and cheat you, master! She really was a loyal and loving creature; he thought fondly. Even though she said she was bluffing, though, her last comment was also just a touch savage. His familiar really didn't like the fact that Bea had tried to cheat him. Richter was actually concerned that if the Scholar said the wrong thing, she might zap him. Lucky for all concerned, Randolphus diffused the situation.

"I believe this is all a misunderstanding, Lord Richter," the chamberlain said. "The price to build such a table would indeed cost several hundred gold if it were commissioned in Yves. You are also right, however, that the price would normally involve a guild charging a premium for the construction and also charging for the materials. I am sure that Scholar Bea was going to inform you that the actual cost to you, my lord, would be much lower." He looked pointedly at the pale Scholar, "Is that not right?"

Bea nodded so quickly he looked like a bobble head. The whole time Randolphus had spoken, he had not taken his eyes off of Alma. Anyone that heard this story might find it strange that a fully grown man would be afraid of something the size of a cat. That would only be because that person had never been hissed at by a dragon cat that could shoot lightning, though. Randolphus continued.

"Normally, whichever Scholar that would be involved in making such an item would be given a small stipend in addition to their salary for their work. Constructing a knowledge tablet requires some skill in crafting as well, Lord Richter."

"Is that right?" Richter asked stroking Alma's back. He locked eyes with Bea, "How much of a stipend do you think would be fair?"

"Ahhhh, normally a Scholar would receive seven gold when paid for a larger project like this, but I would be happy to do it for six gold and two silver. To show respect for your lordship."

Richter adopted a speculative look, continuing to keep his hand on Alma. To the Scholar it might appear that the only thing holding the dragonling back was Richter's good will. After a few moments, he nodded. It was a small extra cost to pay in light of the potential functionality of having a table that doubled as an interface. Not that he was fooled for a second by the 'respect' he was being shown. His Trade skill was at level fifteen which entitled him to 7.5% discount whenever he was buying something. Bea had no more choice about reducing the price than a rock had a choice to fall when dropped. The laws of The Land forced the man to offer that discount. As Richter did the math, though, he realized that fear of Alma might have dropped the price a bit lower, though.

"I accept your offer," Richter said magnanimously. Alma stopped her aggressive posturing and the light surrounding her went out. She jumped up onto her master's shoulders. Bea let out a sigh of relief. Richter looked at Bartle, "Do you have anything to add?"

"No, my lord. I am quite happy to be here!" The Scholar was laying it on a bit thick, but Richter didn't mind. "I will help however I can, Lord Richter, though I will not be much help in the formation of this table. I do not have the Knowledge Tablet talent."

"What can you do?" Richter asked.

"I have obtained the second level of Association, allowing me to organize and understand large amounts of data. I have been helping your chamberlain organize his notes."

"Quite well, I would add, my lord," Randolphus interjected.

Bartle nodded his head in appreciation at the commendation, "I also possess the talents of Perfect Scribing and Confidential. Finally, I have raised my Copying Talent to level two."

Richter rechecked the man's level. It was only thirteen. "How have you been able to purchase so many talents without leveling higher?" he asked. If a normal human only received ten talent points per character level and a max of five points for having a high affinity in an associated skill, at most Bartle should have gotten forty-five TPs. Unless the Scholar talents were much cheaper than his Enchanter talents, Bartle should not have been able to purchase as many as he had.

"Ahhhh… You do have a Profession, do you not, my lord?" Bartle asked. Bea was deciding to be quiet for the moment.

"I do," Richter replied. "I think that you're about to explain something that you think should be common knowledge. Let me say that I will never object to you asking questions or offering information that you think I should know. So speak freely."

Bartle nodded, and his face relaxed somewhat. Richter felt better about that. He didn't want his negative experience with Bea to give the Scholars the wrong impression of him in general. "Very well, my lord. Are you aware that Professions can spawn quests that give talent points as a reward?"

When Richter nodded, the Scholar continued, "One of the benefits of being raised in a guild is that you are given many tasks to complete. Both Bea and I have scribed thousands of documents. When we successfully completed our trials, we were offered strings of quests that we had already completed. As such we received a large amount of talent points all at once. Every Scholar's guild requires their Professionals to purchase the Confidential talent. Our guild, The White Quill, also required us to purchase the Perfect Scribing talent. After that, the decision of how to allocate our TPs was left to us."

Richter nodded, things were becoming much clearer. He looked at Bea and said, "So you have the Still Image and Knowledge

Tablet talents?" If that was all the Scholar brought to the table then he was a bit of a one trick pony.

"I possess the talents: Perfect Scribing II, Copying, and Confidential, as well, my lord."

"Hmmm," Richter said speculatively. There were other things to discuss, but first, there was a formality to dispense with.

"Neither of you have sworn fealty to me, but from what I understand, you have no power to share any confidential information once you have given your word, is that right?"

The Scholars both answered, 'Yes.' Richter continued, "I still have to assume that you're telling the truth about having purchased that talent, though, don't I?"

Randolphus spoke up, "Every guild Scholar in Yves must obtain the Confidential Talent first, my lord. There have been stories about fake Scholars, but I read the Writ of Authenticity that both brought from their guild. I will also say that the Guild of the White Quill is one of the most respected organizations in Yves."

"How do you know this 'writ' they brought was real?" Richter asked.

"A writ is not a simple document, my lord. It is a magical note that cannot be altered. The king issues such writs to licensed guilds which officially recognizes their charter in Yves. The same magic is given to the nobles recognizing the validity of their land claims. Any writ which a guild issues is bound by the same magic. There is no way to fake the magical signature that is specific to each writ. There is also no way to create a magical writ if the creator knows, or even seriously suspects, that what they are vouching as true is, in fact, a falsehood. The signature at the bottom of their writs was that of the Guild of the White Quill. Not all guilds that have been given writs in the recent past are respectable, my lord, but the Guild of the White Quill has existed for centuries and has an impeccable name. If the guild states that these two have the Confidential Talent, it can be trusted."

Richter listened carefully. He absolutely trusted and respected what Randolphus was saying, but he didn't believe that any system had ever been created that couldn't be exploited or circumvented. What Randolphus was describing sounded relatively airtight. Still, better to be safe than sorry, "I am going to have you two swear to something in a moment. Just so that I am clear, however, after we finish speaking today, you will both go with Randolphus to find Sumiko. She will test you both to ensure the authenticity of this writ and that you both have the Confidential Talent. If you are lying about either one of these things, you will be killed before the sun rises." Richter's face was a cold and unyielding as stone.

Both of the Scholars looked at him in shock. Randolphus, hesitantly spoke up, "Uhh, my lord, perhaps-"

Richter held up a hand sharply, and the chamberlain stopped speaking. He stood up and looked at both Scholars, though his gaze settled on Bea, "Maybe you thought there was no harm in trying to squeeze gold out of me. Maybe you would have lowered the price later. Maybe you're just a dick. I don't care. The people of this village are my responsibility, and we have real enemies that have already claimed lives. I will not have a potential threat in our midst. I will not allow another infiltrator to live. If you lie to me, I will take your head myself." He clipped his final words, "Do not tempt my anger. Do you understand?"

"Yes, Lord Richter," Bea said with fear in his voice. All previous arrogance was gone. Richter looked at Bartle who nodded his head and said solemnly, "Yes, Lord Richter."

The lord of the Mist Village stood over the Scholars for another few seconds; then he sat down. "Repeat after me…"

Richter had them promise to never divulge any information about the village or what happened within it to anyone outside of his domain. He further instructed them to never discuss with any other villagers what they were made privy to by himself and Randolphus. The Scholars were also never to keep secrets from Richter or Randolphus. He ordered them to do their best to provide any information that he might find useful or interesting. Lastly, they were to do their best to adhere to the spirit of these oaths as long as they did not betray the letter of them. He didn't need an I-robot situation. The Scholars agreed to each point. They ended the agreement by saying 'We so swear.' A prompt appeared in Richter's vision.

Scholar Bartle and Scholar Bea have agreed to your terms and are bound to them by their Talent: ***Confidential****.*

Richter blinked it away. He felt better now and almost changed his mind about them seeing Sumiko, but he decided to stay the course and be thorough. "Well, that's all behind us. I agree to your terms regarding the formation of the Knowledge Table, Scholar Bea. What I need to know is, how else can you help me? With my journeyman rank in Enchanting, I can make magic books and skill books. What do you know about that?"

Bea straightened in his chair, perhaps seeing a way to redeem himself, "I have helped other magi and enchanters create spell books before. I can help greatly with that, my lord. I have mastered the penmanship of my journeyman rank which should help greatly."

"What does that mean? Penmanship?" Richter asked.

It was Bartle who responded, "Let me show you, my lord." He took out a piece of paper. He did not pick up the quill that was on the table. Instead, he removed a lacquered wooden box from a bag at his side. He opened it to reveal a wooden pen with a sharp metal tip.

"Why did you change pens?" Richter asked.

"Many people think that scribing is simply a matter of writing things down. In truth, it is much more complicated. The writing tool one uses can alter and affect the end result, just as the type of ink being used can come into play. For instance, the petals of the red ginja flower can create an ink that is ideal for writing scrolls for higher level fire magic. Different types of paper and even the leather used to bind books makes a difference. What I will show you now is the importance of various writing styles." He dipped it into the open inkwell on the table. "This is what is called *scrawl*." He wrote a short phrase. It looked like any other information he had seen written in Yves.

"'Perfection is our virtue'," Richter read.

"Yes, my lord," Bartle said. "This next writing style is called *print*." Bartle wrote the same thing, but this time, each letter was perfectly formed. If Richter hadn't seen it happen, he would have sworn that a typewriter had produced the string of letters. "I am sure you see the difference, Lord Richter. Writing in *print*, as opposed to *scrawl*, will give a bonus to a spell being successfully learned when a magic book is read. The same applies to skill books."

"That makes sense," Richter said. "It's easier to read."

"Many think the same, Lord Richter," Bartle said. "You should know that the measured way that each letter is written comes not only from practice but is also a bonus granted upon achieving the rank of initiate in the Scribing skill. *Print* writing still must be practiced upon reaching level ten in scribing, but it is nearly impossible to perfect this type of penmanship without reaching the initiate rank. The next writing style bonus comes at the rank of apprentice and is called *cursive*." Bartle wrote the same phrase again. It was not the flowing cursive script that Richter had learned in grade school. This had dots and swirls that he would not have added, and it even looked like extra characters were added. Side by side, *cursive* and *print* seemed like two different languages. Upon seeing it, however, Richter immediately saw the inherent pattern to those extra touches.

Bea spoke up, "Do not feel troubled if you cannot read this script, Lord Richter. It takes special training or the scribing skill to read this."

Richter furrowed his brow at the Scholar, "What are you talking about? That clearly says 'Perfection is our virtue and our weapon.'"

Both Scholars looked startled. Even Randolphus raised his eyebrows in surprise. He took the pen from Bartle and wrote another phrase in cursive. Bartle complimented the chamberlain as he wrote. His writing did not have the effortless perfection of the Scholars', but it was still well-written. "Can you read this, my lord?"

"The seven moons mirror the magic. The sun guides the Light," Richter read without difficulty.

"You have had no other training in reading formal script, my lord?" Bartle asked. Richter shook his head but thought that he already had the answer to their mystery. His Gift of Tongues ability let him understand almost any sentient language. The ability was not confined to simple auditory understanding, however. He could also read most languages. In a dungeon, he had even come across words written in ancient high elvish, a language which had not even been spoken for nearly one hundred thousand years. If he could read that, a simple cursive style of writing in Common would be no difficulty. The real question was, did his ability extend to writing?

Richter took the pen and dipped it in the ink again. He waited for a drop of black liquid to fall from the sharp end, then put pen to paper. He first wrote Randolphus's phrase in scrawl, then in print. The characters did not have the perfection of the Scribes, but it was a close facsimile. More than that, three prompts appeared.

Congratulations! You have learned the skill: ***Scribing.*** *"True Glory consists of doing what deserves to be written, and writing what deserves to be read." The foundation of any civilized society is the written word. You have now started the path towards enlightenment.*

Congratulations! You have learned a new writing style: ***Scrawl.***

Congratulations! You have learned a new writing style: ***Print****. +10% success in creating magical books and items reliant on writing when you use this writing style. +10% writing speed.*

"How did you-," Bartle started to ask, but stopped when Richter continued to write the phrase in cursive. The chaos seed didn't stop to question how he could write letters that he had never known, but instead just let his ability guide him. In no time at all, the phrase was written, and another prompt appeared.

Congratulations! You have learned a new writing style: ***Cursive****. +20% success in creating magical books and items reliant on writing when you use this writing style. +20% writing speed.*

"Are you toying with us?" Bea asked with indignation. "You have the Scribing skill!" Alma raised her head from Richter's shoulders. The Scholar remembered that he was already on thin ice, and relaxed his posture, but still kept a defiant look on his face. Richter raised an arm and stroked his familiar soothingly before she could threaten the Scholar again.

"No," Richter said evenly, "but I have abilities and skills that you do not need to know about." He looked at the page and considered his new skill. It was with a bit of a shock that he realized, except for simple notes, these were the first words he had written in the few months that he had been in The Land. That, as much as anything else, showed in stark relief just how different his life was now compared to when he had been a simple medical student.

He looked at Bartle and asked, "What is the next writing style?" His Gift of Tongues ability apparently let him skip the weeks, or maybe even the years, of practice that mastering these writing styles normally required.

Bartle looked at Richter with a bit of wonder in his eyes, "This is astounding, Lord Richter. The next writing style is called, *calligraphy*. I have not mastered the technique, however. Bea would be the one to show you."

Despite Bartle's statement, Bea's expression conveyed, 'I prefer not to.' While one Scholar seemed delighted at Richter's natural ability, the other was clearly resentful that what he had worked so hard at came without effort to the chaos seed. Whatever his reservations, though, Bea was not so foolish to show Richter further disrespect or defiance. "This is *calligraphy*, Lord Richter."

Bea dipped Bartle's pen in the inkpot again and started writing. His hand movements were much more pronounced than his fellow Scholar's had been. They had to be as the characters he was making were an entire level of complexity more involved than cursive. Long flourishes extended above and below each line as his hand moved from left to right across the page. When Bea ran out of room on the paper, he moved his hand down immediately and began writing right to left, in opposition to his previous progression. Richter's eyes widened when he saw that the flourishes on the lower line intersected and connected with the lines of the letters above. Before long, he could see that a third line of letters had been created by the union of the first two lines. Bea was not done. When he ran out of room again, he moved his pen downward on the page and began writing left to right again. The flourishes on this new line intersected not only with the line above but also with the first line. The top and bottom lines now formed even larger letters. He marveled at the complexity and efficiency of this writing style. Not only would someone need to know how to write with it, but they would also have to have planned out exactly where each word would fall so that the lines could interact to create the resulting script. *Calligraphy* was a marvel of talent and planning. Despite the complexity, Richter could still clearly make out what Bea was writing.

Now understanding the patterns, the chaos seed thought for a moment about what he would write and then settled upon the perfect topic, the first original poem he would add to The Land.

Already seeing exactly where each word would go in his mind, Richter's hand moved with a smooth and steady stroke. After a few seconds, he laid the pen down with a smug smile. Randolphus read it aloud.

There once was a man named Tag
Whose girl was a horrible nag
But he pushed as hard as he could
And she still swallowed his wood
And all he could do was brag!

The chamberlain looked at Richter, "Very… creative, my lord."

"I thought so," Richter said with a chuckle. Bartle chuckled as well. Bea didn't laugh, but his expression had become one of respect. Respect tinged with jealousy, but respect nonetheless. Richter was pretty sure that change was because of his writing skills, not his poetry. The Land confirmed a moment later.

Congratulations! You have learned a new writing style: ***Caligraphy****. +30% success in creating magical books and items reliant on writing when you use this writing style. +30% writing speed.*

You mad scribing skills have impressed ***Bea*** *and have led to an increase in relationship!*

Congratulations! You have gained ***+301 Relationship Points*** *with* ***Bea****!*

Your relationship with Bea has improved from ***Irritable (-250)*** *to* ***Neutral****.*

"… meh…"

Total Relationship Points with the Bea: ***+5****.*

So you were irritable with me, were ya, ya little cunt rag, Richter thought. He glared at the Scholar again, who had no idea what he had done to pique the chaos seed's ire once again. Richter took a deep breath and let his frustration go. Whether Bea was a punk or not was less important than the fact that their relationship was moving in the right direction. "Are there other writing styles?" Richter asked.

"There are, Lord Richter," Bea said. "They are called olde writ and runic and are granted for reaching the adept and master ranks of Scribing, respectively. Neither of us know the styles well enough to even give you a proper example, however, Lord Richter. Adept and master scribes don't let lower ranked scribes see examples of these higher writing styles unless you are training beneath them. Even within our guild, you must climb to the position of officer to be allowed access to those books. If you get a sufficiently advanced book, however, I might be able to identify the script. It would actually be greatly appreciated if you would teach us how to write in a more advanced script." Bartle nodded vigorously in agreement.

You have been offered a Quest: **The Right Words.** Scholar Bea has offered to identify advanced writing styles in any books that you might have. If you were to share information about these advanced writing styles, he and his fellow Scholars would be extremely grateful. **Success Conditions**: Find an example of an advanced writing style **Optional Success Condition:** Teach the Scholars a more advanced writing style. **Reward**: A more advanced writing style **Penalty for failure or refusal of Quest**: None **Do you accept?** Yes or No

Richter selected 'Yes.' The only question was where would he find a book that had been written in an advanced writing style? One corner of his mouth pulled up. Perhaps in a high level magic book? Richter pulled out the highest level Death magic book that Beyan had given him.

You have found: **Book of Potent Waking Nightmare**	**Durability:** 64/71 **Item Class:** Scarce **Quality:** Superb **Weight:** 1.8 kg **Spell Type:** Death **Spell Level:** 62 **Spell Tier:** 5th (Potent) **Traits:** Casting this spell upon a target will summon a Death creature in the form of their own worst nightmare. This creature will be three times the level of the target. Death of the target will trigger the banishment of the summoned creature. Only the target will be attacked by the Waking Nightmare unless it is attacked by others.

	In this case, the Nightmare will continue to attack these fools until the spell elapses or until each attacker is severed from the mortal coil. **Unmet Requirements:** Skill level 62 in Death Magic

Richter hadn't really scrutinized the book once he had seen that it was far beyond his current skill level. He could now see why it was a journeyman-ranked spell. According to his Lore book, spell strength generally followed a pattern: *weak, minor, inferior, average, strong, potent, superior, powerful* and *grand.* All of his spells fell into the *weak* category so far. Even those had been enough for him to win most of the fights he had been in. A spell that could summon a creature three times your own level and was custom made to strike fear into your heart, though… that was some next level shit!

He examined the object. The book was bound in a grey skin of some type. The binding was also well made, and it was a heavier book than any of the others that Richter had handled in the past. Richter placed it on the table, and both Scholars got up from their seats so they could get a better look. He opened the book. He immediately got another prompt saying that he could not learn this spell at his current Death magic skill level. Seeing as how that actually worked in his favor, in this case, he dismissed the notification and started reading the book. Before he had even been able to turn the page, Bea broke his concentration.

"Can you read this, Lord Richter?" The anticipation and hunger for knowledge was evident in the Scholar's voice.

"Yes," Richter replied. "You can't?" He had never said he wasn't a dick.

Bea ground his teeth, "No."

"Man, that must be frustrating," Richter said with a smile. He went back to reading. Actually taking the time to see how a spell was described was an interesting experience. As Richter continued to turn the pages, he found that a spell was actually a mixture of being in the right mindset, channeling energy through certain parts of your body in a specific way, keeping a certain spell form in mind and many other details. Even proximity to certain ley lines came into play. Richter was amazed at all the information that he was able to access intuitively upon absorbing a spell book. He knew that lower level spells were probably not as intricate, but even if they were a tenth as involved, the rapid absorption of knowledge from a magic book was centuries beyond available technology on Earth. This was like that Matrix movie President Reeves had been in.

After he had read several pages, Richter felt like he had a good grasp on the style this was written in. He turned the page of scrap paper over and started writing. This style not only incorporated the flourishes and extra strokes that calligraphy demanded, but also used expressions of language rather than concise words. It was almost poetic.

Unfortunately, he had no idea how he could teach it to the Scholars. His intuitive comprehension of how to use the penmanship style didn't mean he understood the basic principles of it. He supposed it was the same as a native English speaker being unable to explain what the pluperfect tense was. Bea was going to be disappointed. That might actually be a plus as far as Richter was concerned, though, so it really wasn't a problem. Besides, Richter had just gotten some good news.

Congratulations! You have learned a new writing style: ***Olde Writ.*** *+40% success in creating magical books and items reliant on writing when you use this writing style. +40% writing speed.*

"May I see that book, my lord?" Bea asked quickly. Though he was speaking to Richter, his eyes didn't leave the book. Bartle had the same avaricious expression, but he was more reserved.

Richter slowly closed the book. He hated to waste quest experience, but these books were Beyan's, and he was just holding them. Also, he didn't trust Bea completely, so he wouldn't be handing them over. With his decision, he received a prompt.

You have completed a Quest: **The Right Words**
The Book of a Potent Waking Nightmare is scribed in *Olde Writ*. Examination of this text has granted you an understanding of the writing style. You have decided to not share this information unless Beyan has given his approval. You have **failed** the optional portion of this quest.
Rewards:
Olde Writ writing style.
625 (base 1,000 x 1.25 x 0.5) experience points.

Not a lot of experience, but he would take it. Richter looked at the Scholars, "These books are not mine to give or lend out. You will have to speak with Beyan about that, and he just went for his Trial. If you and he come to an agreement, then I will help you. Do well on building my table, and I will speak to him on your behalf."

Bea didn't look happy, but he nodded, "As far as the table is concerned, my lord. I will need certain materials. I will need several measures of powdered crystal, the help of someone with the Wood Working skill and, most importantly, the magically conductive wood I mentioned, the rarer, the better. Can you arrange to have these things brought to me?"

You have received a Quest: **Raw Materials**
Bea the Scholar has agreed to make a larger version of the Knowledge Table, but you must supply the raw material.
Success Conditions: Obtain wood from a type of tree with a rarity of s*carce* or higher t
Rewards: A Knowledge Table
Penalty for failure or refusal of Quest: None
Do you accept? Yes or No

Richter perfunctorily selected 'Yes' again. Bea might be a bit of a dick, but the guy also seemed to be a quest factory. He wanted to get back on track, though. It was always good learning about various things, but there was going to be a birth tonight. There was still one more thing he had to go over with the Scholars.

"We keep getting off track. Like I said before, since I have reached the rank of journeyman in Enchanting, I can create spell books. I need a blank book to try and make this happen."

Bea looked hesitant, but still said, "I can sell a blank book to you, Lord Richter." Richter started to glare at him, but the man raised his hands to calm the chaos seed, "This is standard procedure, my lord. I promise. I am sorry for our earlier interaction, but making books is a laborious process. Bartle was right in that we had to make many books as part of our training, but even our guild would pay us for our work at this point. I will offer an extremely fair price. I promise you that I have learned my lesson regarding any… tricks, my lord."

Richter nodded. He would believe in Bea's dedication to fair play when he saw a pattern of it, but the man at least seemed genuine in this case. The Scholar had already shit the bed in regards to Richter having faith in him. The chaos seed decided to focus on the task at hand, "I respect your work and will pay a fair price for it. How much per book?"

"It depends on the quality, Lord Richter," Bea said. "There are eleven ranks for book quality: *trash, poor, average, above average, well crafted, exceptional, superb, exquisite and masterwork*. Starting at *above average*, those books can be used to make magic books. One of the reasons that all scribes are required to make books in service to the guild is that Book Binding is a subskill of Scribing and must be leveled. I, for instance, am an initiate in Book Binding. Most of the books I make are *above average* in quality."

"What about you?" Richter asked Bartle.

"I am an apprentice in Book Binding, almost progressed to journeyman rank. I have equal chances at this point to make *well crafted* or *exceptional* books. I will also be able to make them faster than Bea, but it will by no means be a quick process." the Scholar replied. "The baseline time to make a blank book is one week, Lord Richter. The required time decreases by one day for each subskill rank. In Yves, I can sell my *well crafted* blank books for one silver each. I sell *exceptional* books for one silver and four coppers."

"I will sell my above average books for seven coppers each," Bea added.

"I can handle that," Richter said. He bought all of the empty books they had with them and ended up with four *above average*, six *well crafted* and seven *exceptional* books. He also bought four vials of *well crafted* black ink. It was enough for him to start working, but it was also all that the Scholars had. The bigger problem, they informed him, was that they were running out of combed flax, which was the base component they used to make paper. "How do you go about making more?" he asked.

Bartle shrugged, "We actually are not involved in most of the process. There are dedicated alchemists in Law who have made their own guild, the Guild of Woven Trees, who take raw wood to make untreated flax and treat it to produce this." Bartle took a small amount of rope of what looked like straw-colored hair from his pouch. "This is combed flax. You can tell the quality of the material by the softness. It may not look like much, but this one kilogram of combed flax required over twenty-five kilos of raw flax to create. It needed to be treated with various acids and purification techniques. Once we have this combed flax, we can turn it into paper. This one kilo is enough for me to make one small book. We only have six more of these, Lord Richter."

God, Richter thought. What he wouldn't give for a CVS. He could see now why even a blank book would cost as much as an average laborer made in a fortnight. Actually, now that he was thinking about it, something else occurred to him, "Randy. Do I even want to know how much we are paying Abbas and his brothers for paper?"

"I do not believe so, my lord," Randolphus responded.

Richter grunted. At least the man was honest. There had to be an easier way to do this, though. He asked that exact question.

"There is a Talent called Writing Tools," Bartle admitted. "The first level of the Talent allows me to make books using raw wood at the same quality as if I did it the hard way. I would also be able to make a passable stylus and ink from raw materials. The Talent costs ten talent points, though, my lord. That is an entire level's worth of TPs. I am saving for a more advanced talent dealing with long range communication. I am sure you understand that as a noncombat Profession, it is extremely difficult for Scholars to level and I cannot countenance wasting my talent points in such a way. I have to think about my future."

Richter listened intently without interrupting. Hearing the man bemoan the loss of ten talent points really did underscore how fortunate he was to have the extra TPs from his high affinity and chaotic nature. When Bartle finished speaking though, Richter still felt like he might have something to convince the Scholars to do as he wished, but he decided not to push the point yet. Instead, he bought one other item from Bartle. It was the most expensive item yet, but Richter agreed it was well worth it. The man had pulled out another small wooden box. Inside was a pen.

You have found: **Steel-tipped pen**	**Durability:** 17/17 **Item Class:** Common **Quality:** Well Crafted **Weight:** 0.3 kg

The Scholars explained that precision was the hallmark of success in their Profession. Even the best quills, they said, were at best broad-based and often caused ink to bleed across the page. The pen allowed Richter to write clearly and concisely. Bea stated that there were enchanted pens that gave all sorts of bonuses, but to learn how to scribe, a basic pen was apparently a must. It cost him another five silver and four coppers, but now he had what he needed.

"How do I make my magic book?" Richter asked.

The Scholars guided him through the process, and it wasn't exactly cheap. He had to use two measures of powdered crystal. One was mixed into an inkwell, and the other was sprinkled through the pages of one of his new books. Richter received two prompts.

You have created: **Basic Black Ink (enchanted)**	**Durability:** 5/5 **Item Class:** Uncommon **Quality:** Smooth **Weight:** 0.1 kg **Traits:** Can be used to make enchanted and magical documents.
You have created: **Blank Book (enchanted)**	**Durability:** 11/11 **Item Class:** Uncommon **Quality:** Above Average **Weight:** 0.5 kg **Traits:** Can be used to make a magical book

"Okay, what do I do now?" Richter asked.

Bea shrugged.

Richter's eye twitched, and he thought to himself, did this dick just shrug at me?

CHAPTER 27 -- DAY 112 -- KUBORN 2, 15368 EBG

Seeing Richter's irritated expression, Bea decided to try and be a bit more helpful, "This is as much as I have ever helped a mage or enchanter to start a spell book. Magicians always just seem to know what to write, and very few would willingly share their knowledge. Once you have written the spell, though, I can use my Perfect Scribing Talent to potentially improve the quality of the book."

Richter sighed, "Why is this so complicated? And how does Perfect Scribing help to improve anything? Honestly, when I first heard about it, I thought it was kind of useless."

Bartle chuckled in understanding, "You are not the only one who has thought this, Lord Richter. Part of our training in the guild is actually explaining why this is one of the more useful talents. As the name implies, at its first level, Perfect Scribing lets us write perfectly. That allows us to make documents look pretty, but I agree, it seems a waste of talent points. At the second level, however, Perfect Scribing lets a Scholar correct a document or book that someone else has written. For a small amount of mana, I could alter anything you wrote to reflect what you *intended* to write. It lets a Scholar remove any errors in spelling, stray inkblots, poor spacing and other inconsistencies. All of these things can greatly affect the final effectiveness of a spell or skill book. Whatever ability you have that is allowing you to learn advanced writing styles is amazing, Lord Richter, but everyone makes mistakes when writing. This is especially true if you are using more advanced penmanship styles."

If Richter was understanding correctly, level two of the Talent was like what a book editor was supposed to do, spell and content checking. Considering that he would be having to write everything by hand, he could see the value of the second level of Perfect Scribing. Abbas the trader had taught him that using a spell book was no guarantee to actually learning the spell. It wouldn't make too much of a difference with low-level spells, but with a more complex spell, a lower quality product might mean failure when trying to learn new magic. The spell book would still be destroyed, and that could mean that you had basically just pissed away anywhere from dozens to thousands of gold. Richter saw the benefit in making his literary creations as perfect as possible. He might as well start and give it a shot.

He opened a blank book to the first page, hoping for inspiration. After a few moments, he still felt fuckall. Hoping for some type of prompt to appear and guide him, Richter dipped a pen into enchanted ink. Tapping it against the inside of the bottle twice, he removed any excess and then moved his hand to put the metal tip to the page. He focused on the spell he wanted to write down, but before the pen touched paper two things appeared. A notification appeared in Richter's vision, and a faint smirk appeared on his face.

It appears you wish to create the spellbook: ***Book of Summon Weak Bile Rats****. This level one spell will require twenty-one hours and forty-nine minutes of scribing time to complete. You will have twenty-four hours to complete this task. Do you wish to start? Yes or No?*

His smirk disappeared. What the hell was this? It took a whole day to write this one spell? Did that include bathroom breaks? There had to be something he was missing. Richter put the pen back into the inkwell and asked the Scholars about it. It was Bea who answered.

"Now you see one of the reasons that Scholars and scribes are so valued, Lord Richter. I believe I can explain. First, until your Scribing skill is leveled, writing anything more than short notes will be very time-consuming. One of the perks to leveling Scribing is that each level increases writing speed by 2%. I also know that the other factors that determine spellbook creation are the level of the spell and your personal skill level in that branch of magic. Mages may not have wanted to share information, but every one of them enjoyed complaining about what slowed them down. I learned that, at baseline, the level of the spell determines how many days are required to create the spellbook at a one to one ratio. A level one spell would take one day, and a level ten spell would take ten days.

The maximum amount of time you have to create the spellbook is determined by your skill level, also at a one to one ratio. If you were level fifteen in Water magic, then you would have fifteen days to finish a spell book. Failure to finish in the allotted time will destroy the book and any work that you have done."

"Okay, that makes sense," Richter said. "I'm hoping you have more to tell me. I can't even devote one full day to making a spell book, let alone more for higher level spells. Also, waiting for my scribe skill to level is going to be a pain."

Bea nodded, "There is a third factor to consider, Lord Richter. Your skill level in a given spell school will reduce the total time required. Simply divide your skill level into the total number of hours required. If you were skill level twelve in Fire magic and attempted to create a level one Fire spellbook, it would only take two hours instead of the original twenty-four."

"Using more advanced writing styles will also increase your writing speed, Lord Richter," Bartle added.

Hmmm, Richter thought. He hadn't consciously chosen to use one of the forms of penmanship he had just learned. He picked up the pen again and focused making the Death magic spellbook, but this time, Richter envisioned writing in *olde writ.* A prompt appeared.

It appears you wish to create the spellbook: ***Book of Summon Weak Bile Rats****. This level one spell will require twelve hours of scribing time to complete. You will have twenty-four hours to complete this task. Do you wish to start? Yes or No?*

Richter selected 'No' again and reached for the scratch paper they had been writing on. Now that he knew how expensive paper was in The Land, it kind of made his stomach hurt to waste even this page. The damage was already done, though, so he didn't stop. He didn't quite understand how the hours required had changed. After a few quick calculations, he felt that he had a handle on it.

With a level one skill level in Death magic, his base writing speed could be called one hour, or one point one hours, if his 10% increase in speed from his talent, Faster Creation Time I, was taken into account. That was why at baseline it would take twenty-one hours and forty-nine minutes to finish the level one Death spell. The shorter time frame on the latest prompt came from his ability to write using *olde writ*, making the process 40% faster. So his base speed of one hour speed had become one point five hours. Richter paused his calculations with a self-satisfied smile. His Gift of Tongues ability had always been something that just made things easier for him in The Land. By giving him mastery of an advanced writing style, though, it had effectively increased his speed to be the same as a scribe of skill level twenty. Watch out enemies of the free press! Lord Richter of the MV is coming at cha! He turned his attention back to the scrap paper.

Even though the time required had dropped a good deal, Richter decided to hold off on trying to make the summon rats spell until he had leveled his Death magic skill. He pulled up his status page quickly and checked his magic skill levels. Air and Fire magic were his most advanced skills. He could share any Air spells directly in light of his Mastery of the Power so making a spellbook was kind of a waste of time. Richter decided to try his hand at creating a spellbook of one of his go-to magics, *Weak Flame*.

Before he started, he remembered that there was another opportunity that creating his own spellbooks would allow him. Richter looked at his chamberlain, "It's time that I learned the spells that my new aeromancers received when I awakened their magic. Who is the villager that learned *Glitterdust*?"

"May I borrow the knowledge tablet, my lord?" Randolphus asked.

Richter handed it over but kept staring at the man. Randolphus noticed his attention and returned his lord's gaze. Richter looked pointedly at the chamberlain's clipboard then back to the knowledge tablet while arching an eyebrow. Analog had always been good enough for the stolid man before. Randy took his meaning and said defensively, "It is faster this way." Richter raised both hands with his palms out and just chuckled. Randy kept going through this villagers' info with a slight grimace.

After a minute, Randolphus had the answer, "Her name is Telena, my lord. She is an arcane gnome and serves with the guard." The chamberlain started flipping through his clipboard, eliciting a cough from Richter. The chamberlain closed his eyes momentarily as if asking for strength, then flipped through until he found the appropriate page. "She is currently on duty at the wall. Would you like me to send for her?"

Richter nodded, and Randolphus called out into the hall. A guard jogged up and was given instructions to find Telena and take over her shift on the wall. That done, Richter decided to focus on starting his first spell book. He held the pen over the book again and waited for the prompt, focusing on the spell *Weak Flame*.

It appears you wish to create the spellbook: ***Book of Weak Flame****. This level one spell will require one hour and thirty-six minutes of scribing time to complete. You will have ten days to complete this task. Do you wish to start? Yes or No?*

That's more like it! Richter selected 'Yes,' and the most amazing thing happened. The page in front of him took on the appearance of a watermark. His hand also adopted a red glow. He realized that he was summoning his magic without actually forming it into a spell. It was similar to the technique his ship builder, Shiovana, used to make the ships she built stronger.

Richter also noticed that the end of his mana bar was flickering. The blue bar wasn't falling, but something was clearly happening, so he checked his action log. Reading for a moment, he discovered that his mana was falling at a rate of zero point one per second. It looked like the spell level was subtracted by his skill level and was then divided by ten to determine the mana drain. Since his skill level was higher than the spell level, the drain defaulted to the lowest number, point one.

He finally understood why only casters normally made spellbooks. Mana needed to be infused into the pages. Even enchanters needed to be in the presence of a caster who knew a spell if they wanted to make a book. Richter wondered if he would be able to split the mana cost if he was working with someone else. It could definitely come in handy. Right now, his mana regen was higher than the mana drain, so there was no issue, but if the drain ever rose above forty mana a minute, then his pool would begin to drain. He would have to stop periodically because of mana loss. Suddenly, he felt a lot more understanding of the inflated prices Abbas had been charging for the spellbooks he had bought.

After learning of the small leak in his mana pool, he was reminded to channel the rest of his mana regen to unlocking the second level of his sonic enchantment. Dismissing the action log, he got to work. Almost without effort, his hand started moving, supplying ink where the watermark indicated. Mathematical and mystical calculations began to fill the page. Without even noticing, he turned to the next page and continued writing. His hand wavered from time to time. Small mistakes were made, and he quickly came to appreciate the fact that he had the pen to work with rather than a quill. Despite his intermittent errors, Richter quickly began filling the pages of the spell book. Occasionally, he dipped his pen into the ink again, but it was done absently. The task filled him with contentment, the simple act of creation reassuring and comforting in an unexpected way. A hand shook his shoulder.

"What?" Richter asked absentmindedly. He looked up to see Randolphus smiling bemusedly at him. A black smear was on Richter's cheek where he had scratched an itch after using his thumb to blot an ink drop.

"I said that guard Telena is here now, my lord."

Richter looked beyond the chamberlain to the slight guard behind him. The woman was wearing light leather armor, marking her as both a guard and a caster. The chainmail worn by the other guards would have raised the possibility of a spell miscast to an unacceptable level. Ideally, as a mage, she would be wearing cloth armor or a robe, but Terrod had decided that his guards would have at least minimal protection. Telena clapped a fist over her heart in salute and bowed her head, "Reporting as ordered, my lord."

Richter smiled and waved her over, telling her to bring a chair. While she brought one over, he looked down at the book he had been working on and saw two small sets of numbers hovering in the right-hand corner. They had the same translucent appearance as his prompts, and he knew they were a small application of his interface, visible only to him. The top number showed the time remaining to complete the book and the second set showed the amount of time required to finish the project and the percentage done. Happy with his progress, he blew on the latest words he had written and then closed the book. The partially completed work went into his bag. Telena pulled her chair up and sat next to him.

"I would like to make a spell book based on your spell *Glitterdust*. Are you alright with that?" he asked.

"Of course, Lord Richter. I am not sure how to help you accomplish that goal, however. I do not know how I cast the spell exactly, my lord. I simply will it to happen."

Richter laughed, "Then we are in the same boat. Let's just give it a shot."

The chaos seed opened another one of the *above average* quality books. After sprinkling another measure of powdered crystal through the pages, he received a prompt saying the book was enchanted. Richter dipped his pen in the inkwell, but before he could even hold it over the blank book, Telena asked a question.

"Would it be helpful if I were closer, Lord Richter? Should we be touching?"

Richter looked at the woman. For a gnome, her face was thinner than normal, but she had the same short stature and large bosom typical of her people. The days training with the guards had given her a firm and narrow waist. Soft brown eyes looked at him from beneath raven black hair. He was still watching her full lips when she spoke again.

"My lord?"

Randolphus coughed, and one of the scribes snickered.

Richter shook his head slightly to jostle free the impure thoughts, "We can just try it without touching first." Then with a smile, he added, "Stay close, though." She smiled back. Oh, Richter, you're going to hell, he thought. Then another part of him thought, what a way to go!

Tapping away the excess ink, Richter held the pen above the enchanted book. A moment later, a prompt appeared.

Do you wish to create the spellbook: ***Book of Glitterdust****. You have been given permission to create this book by the mage who knows this spell. This will be a collective effort with another, and so all scribing values will be averaged. Mana regen rates will also be combined to offset mana drain. Average skill level in Air Magic: 10. This level one spell will require one hour and thirty-six minutes of scribing time to complete. You will have ten days to complete this task. Do you wish to start? Yes or No?*

Richter asked Telena what her skill level in Air magic was. She proudly told him that she had reached level seven. He had suspected that would be her answer seeing as how he was level thirteen in Air magic but wanted to confirm. It meant that it would take more time to scribe spells with the pretty guard than if he knew the spell himself. On the other hand, it meant that making spellbooks with Quasea or Zarr might go faster because of their high level. Richter chose 'Yes' on his prompt and started writing.

A yellow glow surrounded his hand and one of Telena's. Again, his mana bar flickered, but the overall amount in his mana pool remained constant. Looking at the book, a watermark appeared, and he started scribing in olde writ. Richter went back into the zone. His hand moved smoothly, filling in the marks that only he could see and he did his best to follow the outline. Again and again, his pen dipped into the ink, and the pages turned. He absently heard Randolphus and the scribes speaking around him, but he remained focused on his task. *Glitterdust* was one of the spells that he had coveted when he unlocked Air magic in his villagers. The ability to not only blind enemies but also to reveal hidden opponents was something he needed in his magical toolbox. Richter only stopped when a prompt appeared.

The mage you are working with has left the effective area for you to be able to scribe her spell.

Richter blinked and realized he could no longer see the watermark. Looking around, he saw that Telena was at the door to the chamber. A slightly strained expression was on her face, and she was shuffling from foot to foot. He had to stop himself from laughing at seeing the Air mage doing the pee pee dance. He shooed her out the door, asking her to come back as soon as she could. It looked like she could be about ten yards away from him while he worked, but no further. Richter made small talk until she came back. Once she reentered the room, the watermark reappeared in the book, and he got back to work with single-minded intensity. Before he knew it, he finished his spell. Several blank pages were left, but the watermark had disappeared. The book smacked shut of its own accord and rose a foot into the air. A soft yellow glow surrounded the book, reassuring and tranquil. He smelled a clean scent, like a fresh wind coming through new pines.

You have found: **Book of Glitterdust**	**Durability:** 13/13 **Item Class:** Common **Quality:** Well Crafted **Weight:** 0.4 kg **Spell Type:** Air **Spell Level:** 1 **Spell Tier:** 1st (Weak) **Traits:** Creates a 5x5 area filled with shimmering dust. Anyone in the AoE will be covered by the particles, revealing invisible or stealthed enemies.

Know This! Your use of **Olde Writ** *has increased the quality of your Book of Glitterdust from Above Average to Well Crafted.*

Congratulations! You have reached skill levels 2 and 3 in **Scribing**. *+6% to scribing speed. +6% more likely to successfully scribe a document.*

Richter dismissed the prompts, pleased with both his skill progression and the increase in book quality. He reached up and grabbed the hovering book. When his hand came in contact with it, the yellow light winked out.

"Congratulations, Lord Richter," Bea said respectfully. "If you do not mind, I would love to examine that book. It might give me insight into Olde Writ, and there should be no conflict of interest this time." The same avarice as before was in the man's eyes.

Quest Update: **The Right Words**. You have been given a second chance to share an example of Olde Writ wth Scholar Bea. Do you wish to lend him the Book of Glitterdust? **Yes** or **No**?

Hmmm. Richter had never been given a second shot to fulfill a failed quest before. Of course, he didn't make a habit of failing quests either. He could definitely wait a day or two to learn the spell, but before he agreed, he needed to know a thing or two.

"Can you copy this?" Richter asked holding his new spellbook.

Both Scholars shook their heads. "I have leveled my Copy Talent to level two," Bartle said, "but spell books are beyond me. I can copy any scrolls you might have, however, Lord Richter."

"And, unfortunately, my Copy Talent is only level one, Lord Richter," Bea said. "I can only copy non-magical documents."

Richter took his new scroll case out of his bag. "Show me how it works," he said, handing it over to Bartle.

The Scholar took the Scroll Case of Monster Attraction and examined it with great curiosity, "This is old." He turned it around and examined it further, "Very old. These cases are specially made with a preservation enchantment to maintain scrolls. If the *case* is suffering, though, there may only be dust inside," he warned.

"I won't hold anything against you if there is," Richter said.

"Very well, my lord. I will need to blow out the lantern, however. I don't want to risk even a shuttered flame near such a potentially fragile document. Can you create a magical light? I also need loose sheets of enchanted paper. One measure of powdered crystal should be enough to enchant twenty scrolls. Simply sprinkle the crystal on top of a stack of the chamberlain's blank paper. You may also want to create more enchanted ink. I believe you used most of the first bottle in making the spellbook."

Richter nodded. Seeing no reason to skimp, he summoned nine mist lights. After poking his sleeping familiar, she begrudgingly summoned another eleven, nearly emptying her mana pool. Then she blew a small gust of wind into his ear as punishment for waking her and then settled back into sleep on his shoulders. He shook his head at his sassy dragonling. The fact that such a small creature could have a mana pool of over six hundred was astounding to him. Richter looked at Randolphus and said, "Distribute these around the catacombs as you see fit. I plan on having enough mist lights to cover the entire village soon."

With twenty mist lights, it was almost too bright in the room, but the soft grey light didn't hurt anyone's eyes. Richter used another two measures of crystal to make the blank scrolls and more enchanted ink. Bea extinguished the lantern. Now ready, Bartle opened the case and gingerly took the scroll out. The paper was yellowed, and the edges were cracked. Richter examined it and saw that the scroll itself only had two points of durability left out of an original total of fifteen. Bartle examined the scroll, obviously fascinated by such an old document until Randolphus gave one of his characteristic throat clears. The scribe came back to himself.

"I must again state that I can make no promises, Lord Richter. My Copy skill has an almost 100% success rate with items in good repair, but this... Suffice it to say that having powerful magic constrained by such a moldy and weak scroll might cause a reaction with my magic."

"What type of reaction?" Randolphus asked with concern.

The Scholar started to reply, but Richter forestalled the answer. He needed to see if this could work and saw no reason to delay trying. After all, he possessed another scroll that the Scholar could try to copy if the first attempt was unsuccessful. "I'm sure it will be fine, Randy."

"But, my lord!" the chamberlain protested.

"I'm sure Bartle is up to this task, aren't you?" Richter asked, looking at the Scholar. Randolphus turned his gaze to the man as well.

The scribe quailed slightly under such scrutiny, but then said with false confidence, "Of course, Lord Richter." Bartle placed the steepled fingers of his left hand on the scroll and his other hand on the stack of blank paper. A glow surrounded his hand and then the scroll began to pulse with the same brown light. When sparks started flying out to the sides of the magical document, Richter started to feel a bit of concern. The feeling worsened when Bartle snatched his hand back, but it was when the scroll exploded that he was completely sure that something was wrong.

Papers flew through the air, and the loud bang echoed in the enclosed room, deafening Telena and the four men. Richter fell to the ground, stunned. When he sat up a few seconds later, he blinked randomly, dazed. Looking over, he saw Randolphus glaring at him and moving his mouth in a furious pantomime. Richter's addled mind just couldn't figure out why the chamberlain would go to the trouble of pretending to be furious, but not actually yell out loud. Mystery or not, the chaos seed watched Randolphus really commit to the act. The chamberlain's face even turned red as he pointed first at the scorch mark on the table where the scroll had been, then at the mess, then at his own ears. Richter *really* began to enjoy the show when Randolphus stopped looking at him and instead started stomping around in a circle while throwing his arms in the air, silently screaming his anger to the gods.

CHAPTER 28 -- DAY 112 -- KUBORN 2, 15368 EBG

Luckily, the damage done was actually minimal. It was more of a very expensive light and sound show than a true explosion. Once Richter got his senses back, he and Alma cast *Weak Slow Heal* on everyone, and their deafness debuff disappeared. The dragonling also bit the shit out of his finger. She had never done that before, but apparently being blown up while sleeping and finding out that it was his fault was her trigger. She flew out of the room as soon as the spells had been cast. Randolphus kept opening and closing his jaw while glaring at his lord, but once Richter apologized for not heeding his warnings, the chamberlain seemed mostly mollified.

Bartle took a bit more cajoling to calm down. Richter found this to be completely understandable seeing as how the tips of the man's fingers had been blackened by the exploding scroll. After being healed and given a few minutes, the scribe had been able to collect himself.

When Richter pulled out the second monster scroll case, though, the Scholar got all riled up again. All told, it took about thirty minutes before Bartle would try his Copy Talent for a second time. He only agreed in the end because the second scroll had survived the ravages of time to a greater extent and had a significantly higher durability once removed from the case. Richter also had to agree to stand next to the Scholar while he attempted to use his Talent again. The unspoken understanding was that whatever happened to Bartle would also happen to Richter. Randolphus and Bea wisely waited by the door. Telena looked panicked so Richter told her she could wait down the hall. She beat a speedy retreat.

Bartle once again placed one hand on the unfurled scroll and another on a stack of paper. Closing his eyes and crinkling his face in anticipation of calamity, the Scholar's hand began to glow again. This time, the scroll and the stack of papers adopted the glow, and no sparks flew. A second later, Bartle let out a relieved sigh and opened his eyes. "Done."

"That's it?" Richter asked.

"That is it," Bartle said brightly. He gingerly rolled the original parchment back up and placed it in the case. He handed it back to Richter. Then he peeled back the top four sheets of parchment from the stack and handed them over as well. Randolphus and Bea rejoined them.

You have found: **Scroll of Monster Attraction (Luminous)** x 4	**Durability:** 12/12 **Item Class:** Uncommon **Quality:** Well Crafted **Weight:** 0.7 kg **Traits:** This is a Scroll of Monster Attraction. Activating this scroll will attract the strongest monster within a one-mile radius. This scroll will only affect creatures with a luminous soul level or lower.

Richter smiled. Woot! He owed Basil a fruit basket. The trader-turned-diplomat had been right; the Scholars were worth every copper. He looked at the rest of the stack, "Why only four?"

Bartle pointed to the rest of the stack. The remaining pages were still blank. "Each level of my Copy Talent allows for two copies to be made. Before you ask, copies cannot be made of copies and a document that has been copied can never be copied again. This includes blank books. For instance, if you asked me to make copies of some the books you had just bought, and then you created a spellbook with one, I could not make more copies of it afterward."

Richter's face wrinkled. The Copy Talent was awesome, but it seemed like The Land itself conspired to compartmentalize information. "What happens if one of you just open the book and write down what you see? Using that Perfect Scribe Talent. It would take longer, but you could still make a copy."

"We could do exactly that, Lord Richter," Bea said. "and the result would indeed look perfect, but it would not be a magical document. Only the Copy Talent can accomplish that. It not only replicates the writing, but it also replicates the magic inherent in the book. Simply trying to write down what is seen in another book will make an imitation that is magically moribund." Bea was still casting furtive glances at Richter's new Book of Glitterdust.

Richter had already assumed that would be the answer. The chaos seed looked at his new book and thought how it was strange that he hadn't absorbed the spell information just by writing it down. Every pen stroke and whorl that would sink into his mind if he triggered the spellbook had been put there by him. When he searched his mind, though, he still didn't know how to cast *Glitterdust.* Apparently, there were no shortcuts.

The lord of the Mist Village held the book up, "I am willing to let you two examine this book, but I want something in return. I need you," he said to Bea, "to get whatever that bookmaking Talent is. I have a feeling that I am going to need a great deal more blank books than we have." He looked at Bartle, "What I need from you, is for you to purchase the third level of the Copy Talent."

"I have already told you that I am saving my talent points for a more expensive Talent, Lord Richter," Bartle protested. The man's expression grew guarded. Richter could almost read his mind. He could see the Scholar's fear that he might be just another noble who would force his own agenda.

Bea spoke up as well, "The Writing Tools Talent, while useful, is a waste for me. I must choose talents that will increase my attractiveness to one day obtain a position in a noble household. Unlike fighters, experience is very difficult for us to obtain."

Richter smiled like the cat that had gotten the cream. He had already known that would be their protest and had a response prepared, "I might have a solution for that. Have you ever heard of the War Leader skill? More specifically, the Power Level badge?"

Both of the scribes' faces had lit up at hearing how they could gain experience on a daily basis. Bea already had ten talent points in reserve, and he agreed to purchase the book making Talent as soon as Richter ran out of spell books. The chaos seed also handed over his new spellbook as a sweetener. Since Bea was only interested in examining Olde Writ, and not the spell itself, Richter gave him one day to copy the book. The copy might not be a true magical book, but it would still serve the Scholar's purposes. In return, the scribe agreed to provide Richter, free of charge, all of the books he would need.

Convincing Bartle was more difficult. Apparently the third rank of Copy cost sixty TPs. When Bartle explained what he was saving his points for, Richter actually agreed that it might be more useful. The Talent was called Transmission. At level one, it allowed two Scholars with the Talent to pass written messages to each other, even if they were separated by hundreds of miles. Level two allowed the Scholars to transmit voices in real time. The third level apparently allowed each Scholar to create a virtual room. When that was done, people on opposite sides of the world could interact with each other will full visual, auditory and tactile sensation intact. The Talent was prohibitively expensive, though, with the first level costing a whopping one hundred talent points. Even though Richter desperately wanted to be able to copy spellbooks, he ultimately agreed to help level each Scholar intermittently and told them that there was a permanent place in the Mist Village for talented people of character. The thoughtful look on Bartle's face showed that Richter's words had taken root.

With everything done, Richter stood up. He told Bartle to meet him at the village gate after lunch the following day and to see Krom to be outfitted in armor first. Richter had decided to take one noncombatant out each day. He would also assign a five-man squad whose sole duty was to protect that person. The squad wouldn't be added to the war party, of course, making the division of experience less. Bartle said he would be ready and waiting.

It was about eight at night, and it was time for the feast. The Scholars started to follow him, but he held up a hand and reminded them that they had an appointment with Sumiko. Bea protested, asking if testing their loyalty was really necessary. Richter just smiled and told Telena to escort them to find Sumiko. He also told the guard what she was to do with her sword if either of the men proved false. The blood drained slightly from their faces as they saw the seriousness in his gaze. Richter didn't start chuckling until he was well out of sight. He thought it was a pretty good joke. Well, it was *mostly* a joke.

As he walked out of the catacombs, he saw another minimized prompt blinking in the corner of his vision.

Congratulations! You have reached skill level 16 in ***Trade****. 0.5% bonus to buying and selling per level.*

Quest Update: You have lent the Scholar Bea your Book of Glitterdust. You have fulfilled the optional requirement of the Quest: **The Right Words**.
Rewards:
313 experience (base 500 x 1.25 x 0.5)
+562 Relationship Points with Bea

Your relationship with Bea has improved from ***Neutral (0)*** *to* ***Kind (+500).***
"Please know that I am happy to help!"

Total Relationship Points with the Bea: ***+567***

Every little bit helps, Richter thought. The fact that his Trade skill went up was particularly gratifying. He was sure that Abbas had taken him for a ride when they had last traded, and he needed to start leveling the playing field. Richter dismissed the notifications and kept walking. Not many villagers were walking around, but he was sure he would find them in the northern meadow. Alma flew ahead at his request to start creating more mist lights to hang around the Quickening. Richter wasn't sure what this birth would look like, but he didn't want to miss a thing.

The chaos seed enjoyed his walk through the village. It seemed like every time he looked there was some new change: a path worn through the grass or flowers planted in a sunny spot. The few villagers still around smiled and bowed their heads as he passed. Richter greeted each of them in kind. When he was almost to the hill, he paused because he had the strangest feeling that someone was approaching behind him. Richter turned but didn't see anything. A moment later, however, Futen phased into view twenty feet away.

"Greetings, Lord Richter," came the deadpan greeting.

"Hello, sexy face," Richter said jokingly. "Did you make any noise before you spoke? I could swear that I felt you coming before you made yourself visible."

"I made no sounds, my lord. It is possible that your bond to your Place of Power has deepened. That could, in turn, strengthen your bond to me."

"Maybe," Richter said, thinking. He started walking again, and Futen floated quietly beside him. The feeling he had had was similar to his knowledge about the location of his war party members. He cocked his head to one side and wondered if that meant his Traveler's Map was involved.

Richter opened a translucent version of his map that superimposed against his field of vision. His war band hadn't been disbanded so he could still see exactly where Terrod and Sion were. Of Beyan, there was no sign, unsurprisingly as the gnome was in another dimension for his trial. Thinking about Nexus made Richter's face crinkle in irritation, but he pushed the ebony giant out of his mind. Richter zoomed in on his map until it was only ten feet around him. He didn't see Futen, but that could have just been because he already knew the remnant was there. The chaos seed stopped walking and performed a little experiment. He closed his eyes and ordered Futen to move to another location nearby. After counting to five, he examined his map with his eyes still closed. The picture remained the same, but off to the side, there was a slight distortion on the map. Focusing on it, a prompt appeared.

Do you wish to add the location of those you are powerfully bonded with to your Traveler's Map? Yes or No?

Richter chose 'Yes' and suddenly the distortion formed into a small grey orb. He could see the remnant on his map! Zooming out, he was also able to see exactly where Alma was. Even more importantly, his ability to see through her eyes was reflected on the map. He could now see what she saw in real time! Sion and Terrod were also on the map, though he couldn't see through their eyes. Strangely, Elora didn't show up on the map. Testing a theory, he dissolved the war party, and Terrod disappeared from his interface. So my Companions won't automatically show up on my map, he thought. Sion was still there because he had the mapping ring, but he couldn't count on tracking Terrod or Elora. Still, Richter was happy about his increased capabilities.

Richter further expanded his view, searching for the shale adder, but to no avail. He hoped it would show up when it was completely tamed. Either way, the ability to know what Alma saw as a real-time feed was awesome. It meant that she could update his domain from an aerial view. Whether this was only possible because of their increased Psi Bond or whether it had always been an option and he had just been too much of a dumbass to try, he didn't know, but he would take it!

The chaos seed quickly climbed the hill to the northern meadow and took in the sight before him. Mist lights hung in mid-air, forming a lighted path between where he stood and the Quickening. More grey-white lights hung around the celestial tree. His people had brought up the long tables from the feast area, and he was happy to see that they had not bothered with his own "high table." Tonight was a night to be with his people and celebrate life, not sit above them. Those with musical abilities were already playing, and the communal table was heavily laden with food. He was especially happy to see that the mist workers he had tasked to cut the grass had already done a great deal of work. He could make out one of them continuing to work a bit to the west.

When Richter got closer to the impromptu feast area, one of the villagers raised a mug of whatever he was drinking and shouted, "Cheers to Lord Richter! Lord Richter and the Mist Village!"

Other shouts of, "Here here," and "I need another drink," rang out. There was, of course, also the obligatory call of, "Gnomes Rule!"

He waved to all of them as he walked into the dining area. Everyone got quiet while he approached the table. Richter grabbed a mug and poured himself a large ale. Then he hopped up onto one of the tables in one smooth jump. The chaos seed's Strength and Agility were high enough that he was able to do this even in full armor. The casual display of power and prowess was not lost on his people, who cheered him. The abilities of his body made the move easy enough that he didn't even spill a drop of his drink. Richter looked out at his people, and said, "Greetings, my people!"

More cheers rang out, and people shouted back greetings. "Tonight," Richter continued in a loud voice, "we will see the rebirth of a lost people. A light that was once lost in the dark will blaze back to life. Because of you and your efforts, these pixies have a home to welcome them. A home of love, strength, and laughter!" Much louder cheers rang out. Richter paused before continuing. Then he lifted his tankard, "But until they get here… Let's! Get! PISSED!" He tilted his head back and drained his mug in one long quaff. The shouts and applause were deafening as others followed their lord's example. Richter wiped a bit of foam from his lips and tossed the mug to one of his villagers who went to fill it again. He waved to everyone one last time and then hopped down. It was time to bond with his people.

The night was clear, and he kept summoning mist lights as the hours passed. He handed them to his villagers who started a game of throwing them back and forth. He was confident that his people would take them back down to the village later and spread them around. Alma played her favorite game of dive-bombing unsuspecting feasters and snatching food out of their hands. Each successful raid was followed by curses from her victim and cheers from everyone around her vanquished foe.

Lorala walked by him, trailing a sweet fragrance. She didn't say anything, but her smile made it clear he should have some Star Zenia ready for later. When he saw her walk over to the twins and start drinking and laughing together, his mouth started to water while, somehow, his throat went dry. Sion kicked his foot to bring him back to the conversation they had been having. Richter stuttered and made excuses, but his friend just gave him a smug look and kept talking.

The chaos seed walked around, meeting with everyone he could. Sumiko walked up at some point and gave him the good news that he could trust the Scholars' words. He was not as happy to get an earful about how she was not a slave slash lie detector there to quiz people at his whim. It was only by throwing Sion under the bus that he was able to escape a major tongue lashing. After he had asked if his friend's 'bad cough' had resolved itself, Sumiko started examining her fellow sprite. The exam seemed to mostly involve her poking Sion with a bony finger, but it still let Richter retreat to the sound of his Companion squawking in protest.

After people had eaten and drank their fill, they started filing under the canopy of the Quickening. In ones, twos, and larger groups, his people found spots on the grass to relax. Some had planned ahead and had blankets with them. He walked over to Terrod and Isabella, who greeted him warmly. The captain had apparently made peace with their earlier disagreement. He returned their salutations and told Terrod to make sure the war party was ready to go after lunch on the morrow. Richter told the captain they would be trying for the shiverleaf frond again. Terrod also nodded when Richter told him to also arrange for a backup strike team to protect Bartle. After that, he left the loving couple and continued to make his rounds.

His people talked and laughed together for hours. Richter spent time with many of them, but he also took a solitary moment to observe what he had created. Gnomes, humans, elves, sprites and dwarves broke bread together and shared a joyous camaraderie. The grey luminance of the mist lights reflected off of the silver undersides of the Quickening's leaves, giving the feel that they were all standing in a castle's great hall rather than in the middle of a forest. Moments like this reminded him of what his battles and sacrifices were all about. He was making something to be proud of, something that was worth fighting for and something that deserved his all.

Richter did one other thing while he was walking around. He tried to keep it quiet, but soon there was a bit of an uproar when people caught on. After that, there was a lot of pushing and shoving, but it was all good-natured, and before long, everyone of his villagers had drunk a Potion of Clarity. The potential lost revenue was astronomical, between fifteen hundred and two thousand gold, but Richter decided it was worth it. With the birth of the pixies, he would fulfill at least two quests, both of which involved the Quickening. The last time he had finished a quest involving the celestial tree, everyone in the village had received five thousand experience points. That was enough to get most of them two levels!

He knew that there was a possibility that he was just wasting an extremely valuable resource, but his people were worth it. There was also another benefit. More than once, he received a prompt that his relationship with a specific villager had increased because of his largess. The chaos seed smiled happily. No matter what happened, he could rest easy knowing his people were happy.

More hours passed and some of the villagers fell asleep on the grass. Everyone woke, however, when a large creaking noise echoed through the meadow. Richter looked quickly towards the trunk of the Quickening and saw that some of the smaller trunks that comprised the octuple helix of the whole trunk were moving apart. It had always been possible to see through gaps in the helix and visualize the hollow interior of the tree, but now one of those hand-sized holes was stretching larger and larger. The gap widened, and the creaking noise grew louder as the tendrils of the silver tree drew further apart. It didn't stop until the hole was several feet across. The noise stopped, and the air was pregnant with anticipation.

Everyone watched the tree in breathless excitement. No one spoke, and the tree remained still. Then, almost gracefully, a slender branch bent down from the celestial tree's canopy. The tip of the branch reached inside of the hollow trunk and then withdrew smoothly. Hanging from the end of the silver tendril was the cocoon that held every pixie in The Land.

The cocoon shone silver in the mist lights, made of the same material as the Quickening's trunk. Light seeped through the threads of Elora's nest in many places. The cocoon rotated slightly at the end of the branch that had hooked it. Blue, yellow, black and gold lights shined in all directions, making it look a multicolored disco ball. Slowly, the rotation stopped. All was quiet again. Then came the sound.

It sounded like a crystal bell the size of a mountain had been lightly struck seven times.

TING! TING! TING! TING! TING! TING! TING!

With each pure note, an invisible and insubstantial distortion emanated from the cocoon and spread out in all directions. The sound was almost deafening, but the clarity and purity of the chimes made it impossible to be upset or even to consider that the tones heralded danger. Everyone present knew that what they were hearing and seeing was one of the purest expressions of good they might ever experience. They waited, breathless, as the lights coming from the cocoon faded away.

The top of the cocoon began to unravel. Several inches of silver thread fell away, and a sphere was revealed. It was white as cream and reflected the light of the mist lights around it. The ball rose slightly in the air and moved free of the silky nest that had covered it. As it slowly floated free of the silver womb, different colors played across its surface. First the light blue of glacial ice, then the darkness of predawn followed by the gold of the setting sun. The last color Richter could see was the rich yellow of marigolds in spring.

The cocoon continued to unravel, and more spheres floated free. These had only one color each, however, either black, gold, blue or yellow and were smaller than the first. The globes continued to float free of the cocoon one after the other until one hundred and one spheres floated in the air in front of the Quickening. The silver threads of the silky nest piled on the ground beneath the branch that had held it. The tendril withdrew back into the canopy, and the loud creaking began again as the helical trunk of the celestial tree moved back into its original position. Silence reigned once again.

The first and largest sphere began to vibrate. Then with a barely audible *pop*, the top of the ball disappeared. All that was left was the bottom of the globe and the figure that knelt upon it. The pixie was clad in a silver dress that contoured to her small body. It was neither demure nor provocative. It was simply perfect.

The pixie stood and faced the villagers, and Richter realized with shock that he was looking at Elora. He easily recognized her face, but she had changed. When she had initially been released from the chrysalis, she had the softer features of a girl on the cusp of womanhood. She had also been six inches tall, and her skin was the color of ripe blueberries. That did not describe the creature that now stood before him.

Elora now had the refined features of a woman. She stood a foot tall, and her skin was a smooth silver. Smooth white hair fell straight and full down her back until it reached her knees. It was not the white of age, but rather of freshly fallen snow. Her four wings extended behind her and all present could see that each wing was the color of one of the lights that had come from the cocoon. Her eyes opened, and the blue sclera he remembered were replaced by the creamy white of the Quickening's leaves. The irises remained violet, but were now a purer purple than Richter could ever recall seeing before.

Each villager instinctively knew what they were seeing. They had witnessed the rebirth of a queen. Richter continued to look at his Companion, unsure as to what would happen now. When they had first met, Elora had been a frightened girl, but this woman floating in the air above him was something else entirely. This was a ruler. A cynical part of him began to wonder if he had actually done the right thing by allowing her to bind to his celestial tree. Had he just given up ownership of his own Place of Power? Richter hated that his pragmatism and insecurity was marring such a wonderful and pure moment, but this was who he was. Doubt and suspicion started to worm their way even deeper into his heart, but then she locked eyes with him and smiled.

Her smile was not that of a conqueror or a usurper. It was the smile of a friend who had missed his face. Richter chided himself silently for his weakness and fear. Her simple expression of affection halted his downward emotional spiral. Then she began to sing, and he knew in his heart that he would never doubt her again.

Elora's wings beat, and she rose into the air, leaving the remains of the sphere behind. It faded away, and she hovered in the air as her song enspelled everyone present. It began as a haunting melody. As before, her song had no words, but they were not needed. When she had first spoken to Richter after being released from her chrysalis, her voice was like the piping notes of a piccolo. Now, however, her singing was the smooth tones of a soulful flute. She sang of her mother, of forlorn loss and of a daughter's love that stretched through the centuries. Her voice grew deeper, and it spoke of loneliness. She had awoken, alone in a world that had turned strange, bereft of family or comfort.

There was another soft pop, and a second sphere opened. A pixie knelt on the remains of the sphere and unfurled her wings. Her skin was silver like Elora's, but her wings and hair were pitch black. Unlike her queen, she was only six or seven inches tall. Her face and body were that of a young girl, and she was wearing a simple silver slip. Her eyes opened, and he saw that they were a pale lavender. The pixie's wings beat, and she rose into the air, the remains of her sphere fading away, the same as Elora's had. She flew to hover behind her queen, and her soprano voice rose to match her queen's cool alto.

The two pixies did not sing alone for long. More spheres faded away, and each gave birth to pixies who joined the song. All were silver-skinned and clothed in either silver slips or pants. They all looked like young teens, and as more were birthed it became clear that there were four basic groups. Some had raven hair like the first of Elora's brood that had been born, but others had shining golden hair with wings like translucent gold foil. Another type had curly blue hair with white tips, giving the appearance of waves breaking on a shore and their wings were made of a thin, blue gel material. The last type were blondes, and their pale yellow wings softly diffused the light that passed through the delicate membranes. The males were one or two inches taller than the females, but of the hundred new pixies born, only twenty were men.

Each pixie born raised their voice to sing with their queen. Beneath the silver-white boughs of the Quickening, the mist villagers watched and listened in awe as the pixies created a miracle of music. More emotionally charged than any music Richter had ever heard before, his emotions reflected the song. The leaves of the Quickening began to vibrate, adding a subtle hum to the pixies' chorus. Elora led her people to sing of the history of her people, of endless miles of carefully tended forest and of a race selflessly devoted to life. Her voice rose in jubilation as she sang wordlessly of a people reborn and of a future bright with promise.

Tears rolled down Richter's face as his heart was filled with the beauty of hope. Though neither he nor any of the villagers were aware of it, the song changed them all. Everyone present relaxed and their faces smoothed as some of the worries of the years fell away. Richter smiled and shared joyous looks with his people as they watched the pixies sing of the past, present, and future. Everyone present made a silent vow to do whatever was necessary to safeguard this new and fragile race.

The pixies' voices crescendoed and one at a time they ceased their song. First Elora, then the rest grew silent one at a time. The harmony they created still hung in the air like the lingering peals of a church bell and the leaves of the Quickening continued to vibrate ever so slightly in counterpoint. Elora and the rest smiled down at the villagers. Prompts began to obscure Richter's vision.

HARK AND REJOICE!

A new race has been born to The Land! The union of Elora the Royal Pixie Queen and the Quickening has created: ***Celestial Pixies!*** *A celestial race has once again made its home on this plane. Enemies of Good will shake in fear this day while Avatars of Purity will rejoice!*

Congratulations! You have won +7,000 Fame points! Your actions have directly led to the creation of the ***Celestial Pixies****!*

CHIME!

Congratulations! You have advanced to Reputation Level 4! "You are a man worthy of respect." New quests and opportunities will now become available to you!

Know This! Your presence at the birth of the first Celestial Pixies and hearing their ***Song of Joy and Remembrance*** *has changed you, and all others who witnessed this blessed event! The Song will hang in the air for one month and will affect all who hear it in the following ways:*

-5% lifetime ability to deal damage for all present with a negative Alignment

+5 to Charisma for all present with at least a 0 Alignment

+5 to Luck for those present with at least +1 Alignment

-5% mana cost for those present with at least a +2 Alignment

+5 to Intelligence for those present with at least a +3 Alignment

Quest Update: **Tree of Power III**.
To increase the level of a celestial tree requires more than sun and rain. Goodness and virtue are also necessary to increase the vigor of the Quickening. Involving it in the birth of a new celestial race has greatly increased its progress towards Level 3! Continue to involve it in such births to reach its next iteration. Being in the presence of celestial beings will also increase this growth.

Know This! Pixies are born of the union of pixie females and trees. The close bond of the Quickening with your Place of Power has told in its progeny. Each pixie born will be linked to at least one of the Basic Elements. The celestial nature of these pixies also increases the chance of birthing a new royal pixie.

You have completed the Quest: **Resurgence of Life III!**
Your diligence and hard work have resulted in the birth of a new race! You have protected Elora and her progeny while they have grown and they have been transformed into Celestial

Pixies! Your generosity in allowing Elora to bind to the Quickening has paid dividends for The Land and also for you!
Rewards:
All Celestial Pixies have a high regard for you. Baseline relationship: *Trusted.*
12,500 (base 20,000 x 1.25 x 0.5) experience.
+150,000 Relationship Points with Elora, the Celestial Pixie Queen.
Bonus Rewards:
Your people have once again been present at the emergence of a celestial event! All villagers present receive **2,000** experience! Your relationship with everyone present at the birth of the Celestial Pixies is improved by one level!

Your relationship with Elora has improved from ***Loyal (+55,000)*** *to* ***Kind (+100,000).*** ***"You enemies have become my enemies. They shall fall before us!"***

Total Relationship Points with the Elora: ***+218,552***

Know This! Your efforts have drastically aided the development of your people!

Change in Morale is doubled in light of your generosity with the Potions of Clarity. Morale increased by ***+500*** *(base +250).*

DING!

The Morale of your village has increased from ***+174*** *(base 151 + 5% Health + 7% Richter Administrative skill) to* ***+755****. Morale rank increased from* ***Neutral (0)*** *to* ***Happy (+250)****. Your guidance has made the general mood of your village increase!* ***+10% to Population Growth. +10% to Productivity. +10% to Fighting Spirit.***

Change in Loyalty is doubled in light of your generosity with the Potions of Clarity. Loyalty increased by ***+500*** *(base +250).*

DING!

The Loyalty of your village has increased from ***+215*** *(base +192 + 5% Health + 7% Richter Administrative skill) to* ***+801. Neutral (0)*** *to* ***Dependable (+250).*** *You have shown yourself to be a capable leader and exemplify ideals they believe in. Your people are not just a collection of individuals anymore, they have a common goal.* ***+20% to Productivity.***

Know This! The Song of Joy and Remembrance has caused many of your people to now be dedicated to the Celestial Pixies. Any betrayal or serious damage to their ranks could negatively impact the Loyalty of your people.

Know This! More than 90% of your people had increased their Charisma by ***+5. +5%*** *bonus to population growth.*

Richter was stunned by the massive amount of prompts. He shuffled through them quickly. Each was important, and he couldn't wait to get to the next. A quick check of his status page showed that his Charisma had indeed increased by five points. Even more importantly though, there was a new race. He had hoped that the pixies might gain some sort of power from being linked to the Quickening, but he hadn't expected that they would evolve.

Richter used *Analyze* on one of the black pixies.

Name: ???	**Race:** Celestial Pixie	**Disposition:** Trusted
Level: 1, 0%		**Age:** 0
	STATS	
Health: 30	**Mana:** 110	**Stamina:** 50
	ATTRIBUTES	
Strength: 2	**Agility:** 12	**Dexterity:** 13
Constitution: 3	**Endurance:** 5	**Intelligence:** 11
Wisdom: 10	**Charisma:** 12	**Luck:** 10
	DESCRIPTION	
Pixies have always been a force of good in The Land. Peaceful by nature, but deadly when necessary, the forest and plants of		

> this world flourished under their care. The union of Queen Elora and the Quickening has created the race of Celestial Pixies! Celestial Pixies are bound to at least one of the Powers that comprise the Mist Village's Place of Power. This pixie is bound to **Dark** magic. The customary magical attack of the pixie is now augmented by this magic and can cause momentary blindness. Magical attacks will increase in power with character leveling, and extra effects may be added. The evolved state of these pixies results in extra points to distribute per level. Celestial Pixies receive two points to distribute per level, and each level gives **+3 to Dexterity**, **+1 to Agility** and **+1 to Intelligence**, unlike their predecessors which received one point to distribute per level and +2 to Dexterity and +1 to Agility. Celestial Pixies, like their predecessors, receive a racial boost to movement speed.

Richter's eyes bulged. The celestial pixies got seven points per level! Just like the angel Hisako had summoned once, he could see that beings of higher planes were in a different league than those who lived on his plane. The small flyer's Dexterity and Agility were high for only being level one. On the other hand, her Strength, Constitution, and Endurance were abnormally low. It confused Richter for a second until he remembered the conversation he had had with Sion about characteristic modifiers based on size. It then made perfect sense that such a tiny creature would have lower hit points and Strength and a have higher Agility. It meant that as the pixies leveled, their speed would be truly amazing. On the other hand, even if they added every free point to Constitution, their health might not break one hundred. He also realized that the characteristics were probably lower because he was analyzing a child. Her stats might be higher when she was fully grown.

What was the magical attack that was referenced, though? Richter used *Analyze* on the other types of pixies. Their stats were basically the same, though the Strength and Constitution of the males were usually a point higher. The pixies with the blue wings had an attack that slowed enemies, and the pixies associated with Air magic had a chance to stun opponents. The gold pixies were associated with Life magic. Their attack had no extra effect, but apparently, they had a second ability to heal. The more he learned, the more one particular question started spinning through Richter's head. Where could he get more celestial pixies?

The pixies had just been hovering after their song ended, as caught up in the emotions of the song as the villagers had been. They seemed to come out of their reverie all at once, however, and they let loose peals of joy. One hundred small voices seemed to speak at once as the pixies greeted their brothers and sisters and paid respect to their queen. Richter couldn't follow the conversation of all of the small creatures at once, but he could at least understand pixie-speak, unlike most everyone else present. He smiled bemusedly as he was able to zero in on individual conversations. He discovered that though the pixies might look like teens, their babble was that of ten-year-old children.

The pixie children kept asking each other if one had seen this person or another had smelled that scent. It struck Richter that he was watching a race experience the world for the first time. Everyone else just gazed at them in amazement. As they flew about, trails of sparkles were left behind like an afterimage that faded a moment later.

Richter's gaze was brought back to his Companion. Elora began flying towards him, and he accessed her status page.

Name: Elora	**Race:** Celestial Pixie	**Disposition:** Ally
Level: 16, 72%	**Age:** 17	**Languages:** Pixie, Common, High Nature
Alignment: +3	**Reputation:** Lvl 1 "Who are you again?"	
STATS		
Health: 70	**Mana:** 270	**Stamina:** 80
ATTRIBUTES		
Strength: 4	**Agility:** 32	**Dexterity:** 73
Constitution: 7	**Endurance:** 9	**Intelligence:** 27
Wisdom: 10	**Charisma:** 11	**Luck:** 11

SKILLS (Name: Skill level, Progression, Affinity)		
Air Magic: 1, 0%, 100%	**Herb Lore:** 58, 91%, 96%	**Life Magic:** 1, 0%, 100%
Dark Magic: 1, 0%, 100%	**Water Magic:** 1, 0%, 100%	
RESISTANCES		
Air Magic: 16%	**Water Magic:** 16%	**Dark Magic:** 16%
	Life Magic: 16%	
ABILITIES		
Celestial Pixie Song – Evoke strong emotions, summon images and grant status changes. Stronger songs will be triggered by specific events **Tree Communion –** Female pixies can bond to a specific tree and bear young. Being separated from her bonded tree will weaken a pixie over time. **Fate's Companion –** Form a meidon with their destined sprite **Force Blast –** Focus mana into a concentrated magical beam		
DESCRIPTION		
Celestial Pixies receive two points to distribute per level, and each level gives **+3 to Dexterity, +1 to Agility** and **+1 to Intelligence**. Celestial Pixies receive a racial boost to movement speed.		

Looking at her page raised far more questions than answers. The first thing that piqued his curiosity was her advanced level. If he remembered correctly, she had only been level seven when she entered the cocoon. Now Elora was level sixteen. Had she really been able to gain nine levels just from being his Companion as he completed quests? Richter thought about it and realized that she must have gained over one hundred and twenty-thousand experience since she had emerged from the chrysalis. He shook his head slightly in bemusement at his own industriousness. She stopped to hover before him. Before Richter could speak, one more prompt appeared.

> Know This! Your Companion Elora has completed a Quest: **Revival I.**
> Your Companion had been given the impossible task of reviving her species. She has succeeded beyond the expectations of any god or goddess that might still observe The Land and she was rewarded appropriately. As her Companion, you will receive the same experience reward.
> **Reward:** 93,750 (base 150,000 x 1.25 x 0.5) experience.

Richter's mouth dropped open. Judging by Elora's startled expression, the massive amount of experience was a surprise to her as well. It was the first time that he regretted using his talent point conversion. Once she got over her shock, he watched her face firm with a decision made.

"My Lord Richter," she began with her musical voice. "You have kept me and my people safe. You are a man of honor and strength. In this new world, my people and I will need the strength of a ruler such as you. Will you accept us into your tribe? Will you accept our oaths of fealty?"

Richter hadn't known what his Companion would say, but it wasn't that! He looked at the celestial being in surprise, "You are welcome to reside in my village forever, Elora. You do not need to swear fealty to me to make this true."

Elora raised her voice and spoke clearly in pixie-speak. All of her chattering children ceased what they were doing and flew down to hover behind her. Elora descended until she was only an inch above the ground, and then to his surprise, she landed. The graceful creature then knelt and bowed her head. All of her progeny landed as well, and they formed a triangle, fanning out behind their queen. Richter went down on one knee to help her up, but before he could, she started speaking again in Common, "I, Elora, Queen of the celestial pixies, formally swear allegiance and loyalty to you, my Lord Richter. From now, unto my very death, I will protect you and your interests, to the best of my ability and without deceit. Furthermore, I swear my line to you, my Lord Richter. Until another queen is born to make choices of her own, I ask that you protect my people and, in my absence, guide them. We will live and fight under your command."

***Elora, the Celestial Pixie Queen**, formally swears fealty to you. More than that, however, she has sworn her entire clan and bloodline to your service until another queen is born, who will make decisions of her own with her progeny.*

The entire meadow was silent. The people of the Mist Village held their breath as they watched a queen kneel before their lord. Richter felt the weight of their attention, but he also felt something else. The air was heavy with possibility. It felt like he could feel the fulcrum of the universe balancing in that moment of time. This was a moment. It might even be a Moment. What he did and said next might change the fate of worlds. He could refuse her pledge. Part of him felt that he ought to do just that. Elora was only seventeen years old, after all. She felt bereft and alone in the world. Maybe he shouldn't trust the impulsive decision of a lonely child, queen or not…

Richter searched his heart. There were a thousand reasons why he shouldn't accept and a thousand why he should. All of these arguments spun through his head in that frozen moment in time. Ultimately, he just stayed true to who he was. He was a man who would rather live his life by what he hoped to be true, rather than what he feared to be true. Words rose from something inside of him and spilled out into The Land, "I accept your oath of fealty, and swear to honor your pledge with the same gravity in which it was given. I swear to do my utmost to preserve your line and clan. If any raise a hand against you, I will strike that hand from their body. If any raise arms against you, my blade shall take their life. If any set their will against you, I will break their mind and soul."

As had happened before, Richter felt that he was merely the conduit for these words. These were not merely words. They were the spoken component to a spell older and more powerful than any he had ever cast. He had bound the fate of a fledgling race to his will and power. Only time would tell if he had furthered the cause of good or evil. As that thought crossed his mind, a small voice inside asked, was there not a third option?

The pixies rose back into the air and started chatting again, but this time, they were joined by the villagers who *oohed*, *aahed* and fawned over the tiny celestial beings. Richter and his flying Companion just looked at one another and shared a moment of camaraderie, a calm island in the sea of noise around them. Richter was about to start peppering the queen with questions, but then something fascinating occurred.

Sion walked past everyone, moving towards the trunk of the Quickening. Above him floated a pixie male. His wings were yellow with Air magic, and he looked down at the sprite as he flew. The distance between them decreased as the pixie lost elevation until the two were eye to eye. Richter watched his friend, curious as to what was happening. Without ceremony, Sion went down on one knee. The sprite cupped his hands in front of his face, and the pixie landed in them. The yellow-winged man reached out and placed his hands on Sion's temples before he leaned forward until their foreheads touched. Sion spoke a phrase in sprite-speak that had the cadence of ritual. The pixie responded in his own language and a silver egg sprung into existence around the two of them. The bottom of the oval spheroid was buried in the ground giving the shell that marked where Richter's best friend had stood the solidity of an obelisk. All the chaos seed could do was stare into the reflective surface and wonder at his friend's last words, "I accept my fate."

CHAPTER 29 -- DAY 112 -- KUBORN 2, 15368 EBG

Richter was alarmed and was starting to run over until Elora's small hand touched his face. He looked at her, and she told him not to worry. "It is the *meidon*," she said. Richter had to actively engage his Gift of Tongues ability to understand the concept she spoke of, but after a moment he knew she was speaking of the 'fate bond.' She went on to explain that one of the pixies' racial abilities was Fate's Companion. It apparently created a lifelong and irrevocable bond between the pixie and their meitu'meidon, the sprite that held the other part of their destiny. The bond was intense and eternal, apparently stronger than the Companion bond he already had with his friend.

He remembered when Hisako had first spoken of the pixie race several months ago. She had said that every sprite was born with half of a destiny and that a pixie possessed the other half. The chaos seed had thought the Hearth Mother had been speaking in hyperbole, but apparently not. Inside the sphere, Sion and the pixie were creating a bond forged of their very souls. Elora assured him that his friend would emerge stronger than before.

"When will he come out?" Richter asked. He walked towards the silvery shell but stopped short of touching it. Other villagers had noticed the shining egg and were coming over to inspect it as well. Elora floated up beside him and gently placed a hand on the shell with a smile on her face.

"The meidon will end when they are both ready. You do not need to fear, my lord. Shetu'meidon (Fate bond shell, Richter translated silently) are normally very strong. With the essence of the Quickening involved, I imagine they will be quite safe until the bonding is complete."

Richter still didn't like the idea of his best friend being sealed away from the world, but excited exclamations caught his attention and made him look to the right. One of the pixie guards had gone down on one knee, and a gold pixie was flying down into his hands. Richter could see that it was the same guard that said he had heard voices. As soon as the pixie alighted, she placed her forehead against his and another silver shell sprung into existence. The remaining sprite guard looked around in disappointment, but no other pixies came down to join with him. There was one more meidon to be created, though.

Sumiko came running up to the Quickening, faster than Richter would have thought possible. She didn't even seem to see any of the villagers around her. Before anyone could say anything, she knelt, said the words and bonded with a Life pixie. Another silver shell popped into existence.

WTF, Richter thought with irritation and alarm. How could she just bind to a pixie like that without talking to him first? What if there were more undead to fight? What if someone got seriously hurt? What if… Richter suddenly stopped his mental recriminations of the woman when he realized how he sounded. He just finished his last thought with, what if he just put his big boy pants on and made do until she finished her transformation? He shook his head at his own panic. When had he come to be so dependent on the sprite? He supposed that was how it worked in any world, though. One moment a woman is yelling at you, the next, you can't live without her.

Several dozen pixies did start to crowd around Elora. They spoke in pixie-speak, faster than even Richter could understand and they looked agitated. For some reason, the existence of the silver shells had triggered something in some of the pixie children. One of the life pixies started flying away from the tree, but a sharp word from Elora brought the child back into the throng surrounding her. Her offspring continued to speak in excited and stressed tones, which was strange because dozens of others seemed not at all concerned and continued to play with the villagers. Three were even chasing Alma around, though they weren't fast enough to catch her yet.

Elora listened for a few more moments, then with the special irritation ability all mothers are born with, she spoke sharply. One pixie had started to fly away. Her children quieted as she continued to speak, and they started hanging their heads, cowed. Richter smirked a bit. The loose translation was, "You WILL do as I say. You will NOT leave this village without permission. You WILL regret it if you try." The last thing she said was somewhat confusing, though, "I will ask him. Yes, now!" Then she shooed them away with her hand. It was quite comical to see seven-inch tall creatures hanging their heads as they slowly floated away. If they didn't have wings, he was sure they would be shuffling their feet.

The chastised pixie children flew back several yards and, for some reason, they all started staring at him. The other pixies continued to play with the villagers, much to his people's delight. Elora came forward, and her expression was intent. Richter was still smiling, but his grin slipped a bit. "What is it?" he asked.

"My lord, I am sorry to ask a boon of you so soon after swearing my loyalty, but there is a problem." She began to explain. When she was done, a quest prompt appeared.

You have unlocked the Quest: **Fate's Companion I**
Some of the celestial pixies can feel their meitu'meidon through their ability Fate's Companion. They wanted to leave the safety of the Quickening immediately and search for the sprites they would bond with, but Elora wisely has forbidden that. The queen cannot ignore the needs of her people, however, nor can she refuse to honor one of the core facets of pixie nature. She has told you that the birth of the celestial pixies from the cocoon sent a signal through the land. Sprites that have a pixie meitu'meidon waiting for them will be drawn to this location.
Success Conditions: Escort the sprite meitu'meidons to the village
Rewards: You will be rewarded for each meidon that is successfully created. Exact Reward unknown.
Penalty for failure or refusal of Quest:
Decreased relationship with Elora.
Decreased bonding of pixies and sprites
Do you accept? Yes or No

Richter accepted the quest. No matter what Elora had asked, he would have said yes, but inside he was gnashing his teeth. Sprites were natural woodsmen, so he didn't really have too much fear about them making their way safely through the forest. The problem would happen when the sprites got to the mists. Richter couldn't rely on the sprite's "sense" of their pixie meitu'meidon to bring them safely to the village. *Confusing Mists* was a spell created to do exactly what it said. Even if you thought you were putting one foot in front of the other, the mists would lead you astray.

"Is there anything you can do to help me find these sprites?" he asked his Companion. "I will do what I can, but the mists around us cover more than three hundred square miles."

"My children will be able to sense the general direction of their meitu'meidon when they are close, my Lord Richter. The ones that were speaking to me can feel their counterparts, so they must be relatively close. The one that tried to fly off told me that her meitu'meidon was very close and in that direction," she gestured to the south. "My other children say that their meitu'meidon are approaching."

Richter's eyes followed the direction of her pointed arm, leading into the forest. The pitch black forest. The one full of monsters. The one where a lone sprite might be lost in at that very moment. After a deep sigh and a mental query of why things could never just be easy, Richter shook his sleepy, ale-addled head, and said, "Let's do this."

CHAPTER 30 -- DAY 112 -- KUBORN 2, 15368 EBG

At his command, Terrod and Caulder started to get together their best fighters. Richter told them to choose people that had both speed and endurance. This was going to be a surgical operation. They would find the sprite, add him to the war party and haul ass back to the safety of the village. He specified that everyone needed to be clearheaded. Richter himself had had an ale or seven, but his high Constitution had already filtered out most of the effects.

For the first time, Quasea stepped forward and volunteered to help. The Dark magic adept said that there was no better time for her to offer aid. Richter wasn't about to argue. Besides, he thought, she was right. Only two distant moons were present in the sky, and neither were full. He simply thanked her and sent her to stand with Terrod. Zarr also stepped forward and told Richter he had a spell that could increase the speed of a group going through the forest.

"My child can guide you with better accuracy as she gets closer," Elora said. "We will both go with you."

Richter shook his head, "I wish I could refuse the help of both of you, but I will need your child to have any chance of finding the sprite. You, however, cannot come, Elora."

"Lord Richter," the queen said in a stern but high voice, "I will not allow my newly born offspring to go into danger without me. Pixie young are born with some inherent memories and so are not as helpless as most newborns, but they are still children. They are without guile. I can't let my daughter go into such danger without me."

Richter looked at Elora, forcing himself to listen, and not just speak without considering her viewpoint. She made a valid argument. He knew next to nothing about pixies in general, let alone pixie children. The fact remained, the queen was ignoring the more important issues.

"Elora. I understand what you are saying. This is your child, and you take her safety seriously." She nodded earnestly. Richter pointed up, "Then what about them? All of your other children need you as well. They need you now." He sighed but didn't shy from what he said next, "The other point, though, is that you cannot risk yourself. Your children are precious, but you, and you alone, are the key to the survival of your entire race. If you die, then pixies vanish from the face of The Land. You must stay here." Elora opened her mouth to argue again, but Richter beat her to the punch, "If you die, the Quickening dies as well."

The queen's mouth snapped shut, and tears welled in the corner of her luminous eyes. For the first time since emerging from the cocoon, Richter saw the young girl that the queen still was. "I have to protect my daughter. That is what a queen does. My mother gave her life for me!"

He wished he had time to comfort her, but the forest was full of danger, and a lone sprite was lost in it. "Protect all of your children, Queen Elora," Richter said formally. "As your liege, I order you to safeguard them while I search with your daughter for her meitu'meidon. This is my command." He felt like an absolute shit speaking to the vulnerable woman like this, but maybe the best thing he could do for her was to give her an escape hatch from her guilt.

The pixie queen's face firmed and despite the tears rolling down her cheeks, she replied just as formally, "As you command, my lord." Elora called to the Life pixie girl that had tried to fly off on her own. The child came and hovered in front of her mother. "You will obey Lord Richter immediately and without fail. Find your meitu'meidon and return immediately to the Quickening. I name you Yura." Richter's ability translated the name as 'Seeker.'

"I will take care of her," Richter said. Elora nodded and corralled the rest of her children towards the silver trunk of the Quickening. A few seconds later, they had all disappeared into the leafy canopy. The chaos seed walked over to the captain of his guard, and Yura floated along behind him. Before he spoke to the captain, he looked at Alma. "Your main job is to keep her safe," he told his familiar, indicating Yura.

I will see her back safely to Quickening, master.

I know you will, my love, he thought back.

"Yura, you will stay with Alma the entire time. If things become dangerous, you will ride her back to the village even if we have not found your meitu'meidon."

The pixie girl bowed her head and in a small voice spoke in pixie-speak, "Yes, Unca Wichter."

His heart twinged at hearing her small voice. What was he doing? Was he really taking a newly born child out into the wild at night? He shook his head. Elora would not have asked him to do this if it wasn't necessary. Richter supposed he could understand if these two were truly bound by fate. What would it mean if one of them died? Would either of their lives have meaning afterward?

Richter focused on the task at hand. He gave a command before addressing his war party, and it was for Roswan. Richter told him to build defensible walls at the top and bottom of the hill leading up to the meadow. It had been in the back of his mind to do that for some time in light of the many valuable areas that were in the glade: the skath eggs, the Dragon's Cauldron, the crystal garden, the Quickening, and now, the pixies. If Richter could have put the Forge of Heavens in the meadow as well, he would have. The builder answered with his customary nonplussed, 'Grrrmmm.' Richter took that as assent.

The chaos seed turned his attention to the group his captain had assembled. Terrod, Caulder, Ulinde, Quasea and Zarr stood next to two hunters with bows and two other guards in leather armor with maces at their waists and shields slung on their backs. He already saw one problem, "Caulder, there is no way you will be able to keep up with the pace I'm going to set with the medium armor you wear, let alone that vault door you call a shield. I don't have time to argue. Besides, I need you to stay here and organize strike parties for tomorrow. I have a feeling we are going to be getting a great deal of company over the upcoming days, and we will need teams to do double time to escort pixies and then bring sprites back safely."

Hearing the firm tone in his liege's voice, Caulder merely saluted and walked off to bark orders at his fellow guards. Richter quickly analyzed the others and saw that one of the guards with maces was still level five. He told her to stay as well. Then he checked both swords in their scabbards. Looking around at everyone else, he brought them into his war party; then he took off at a fast jog. Behind him, Randolphus carefully gathered up the silver threads of the cocoon.

Richter sent out a mental call before he got to the village gate. He jogged through, the war party running past the sentries who stood at attention with fists covering their hearts. They whispered to each other afterwards, and one said he felt sorry for whoever and whatever had stirred their lord's ire in the middle of the night.

The war party stopped at the inside of the second trench. They clustered together and Quasea cast a concealment and a high level darkvision spell on them while Zarr cast *Strong Forest Travel.* The very darkness of the night cloaked them from view and their movement speed increased by 50% as long as they stayed within the AoE of both spells. Richter gave both adepts three mana potions each and then they took off. His adder and familiar kept pace beside him as he led the party.

Miles flew by. The adepts periodically updated their buffs. One of the benefits to working with higher level magic users was that each knew enough spells that they could cast another similar spell while they waited for their stronger spells' cooldowns to elapse. Yura took up position in Richter's fallen hood, and she whispered directions to him. Alma scouted ahead. Twice the dragonling had them alter course slightly. The first time, to avoid a pack of grey scorpions that were the size of cats. The second time, to skirt a shambling humanoid with long arms and overly developed muscles. Richter knew he would have to go out again tomorrow and attempt to hunt these things down, but tonight was about finding the sprite.

While they traveled, Richter dealt with a series prompts that he had yet to address.

Your village has grown by leaps and bounds! Another one hundred and one sentients have been added to your population, increasing it to six hundred and sixty-seven. Never forget, there are consequences to your actions. The following adjustments have been made to your village values.

Average Morale has decreased from ***+755*** *to* ***+641***

Average Loyalty has decreased from ***+801*** *to* ***+679***

No change in Morale or Loyalty ranks.

After eight miles, Yura grew excited and said she could feel that they were close. The war party ran down a hill and saw the sprite. It was immediately apparent to Richter that she was different from the sprites he had seen before. The people of the Hearth Tree celebrated nature and lived in the forest, but they were civilized and structured. This woman looked almost like a wild creature. Her hair was gnarled, and she wore animal skins of various colors. She had a bow in her hand, and an arrow nocked. The weapon was pointed in the direction of the war party. It was clear that she could not see them, either due to the natural darkness, Quasea's spell or the mists, but she had heard them. A blue nimbus surrounded the arrow as she charged it with her magic.

Richter motioned for everyone to stop. He took cover behind a tree, and the other party members did the same. "We are friends," he called out in sprite-speak. "I have brought your meitu'meidon."

At his words, a visible relief crossed her face, but she was still not wholly convinced. "I cannot see you."

"Put down your weapon and I will come out to meet you. My name is Richter, and I am the lord of these lands. I have brought a war party to bring you to safety, but we cannot linger, the woods are not safe at night."

She hesitated for a moment longer but then discharged her arrow at a nearby boulder. A large boom sounded, and a few stone chips flew, but otherwise there was no harm done. Though the sprite skill *Imbue Arrow* was impressive, once the mana was committed, the arrow had to be shot. That meant that any bad beasties out there now knew their position.

Richter had Quasea dismiss their concealment, and he selected the sprite female and gave her immunity to the mists. *Analyze* showed that her name was Moesa. What was interesting was that her race was 'forest sprite' not 'wood sprite.'

Name: Moesa	**Age:** 23	**Disposition:** Neutral
Level: 7, 39%	**Race:** Forest Sprite	
STATS		

Health: 150	**Mana:** 78/100	**Stamina:** 140
ATTRIBUTES		
Strength: 12	**Agility:** 15	**Dexterity:** 29
Constitution: 15	**Endurance:** 14	**Intelligence:** 10
Wisdom: 11	**Charisma:** 9	**Luck: 9**
DESCRIPTION		
Forest Sprites have the same reverence for nature as their cousins the wood sprites but to a greater degree. They cherish unbroken wilderness and strive to live within the natural order of life. More solitary than other sprites, forest sprites can often forge bonds with animals. Forest Sprites get three points to distribute per level, and each level gives **+2 to Dexterity**.		

"Moesa," Richter greeted her when she was able to see him. "I have someone who wants to meet you. This is Yura."

The golden pixie flew from out of his hood and towards the forest sprite. Moesa's face took on an expression of wonder, and she started to go down on one knee. Richter strode forward and quickly grabbed her arm. The sprite looked at him in hostility, and one hand reached toward a hilt at her belt.

"We don't have time for this," Richter said in sprite-speak. "There is plenty of time for the meidon once we are safe. I cannot risk Yura being out in the wilds any longer."

The sprite's face calmed, and she nodded, "This is wisdom. I am certain something has been stalking me."

Richter's eyes widened, and he looked around, "Then let's not waste any more time. I am going to bring you into my war party. Do you assent?"

She nodded, and he brought her into the last position in the war party. Quasea reestablished their Dark magic concealment, and they took off. Yura wanted to fly next to her meitu'meidon, but a firm word from Richter was all it took for the pixling to go back into his hood again. With Alma leading, they were able to avoid any attacks and safely made it back to the village. The journey had taken several hours, but they had been successful.

Richter left the adder outside of the walls again, telling it to hunt and keep guard, and led the forest sprite up to the Quickening. He was somewhat unsure about leading a stranger to the celestial tree, but he decided to put faith in the pixies' cosmic bond. "Allow me to bond with Yura," Moesa demanded.

Richter was exhausted after battling for almost an entire day, not to mention a forced run through the woods at night. He just waved away Moesa's bad manners and arrogant request, "You'll come meet the queen. She will decide who is bonding to whom. Now come on!"

Richter walked to the Quickening, Moesa continuing to speak in agitated tones behind him. Yura stayed in his hood as he ordered. As soon as the forest sprite saw the celestial tree, her mouth snapped shut. When she was under the actual leaves, a look of wonder crossed her face as the Song of Joy and Remembrance took effect. Richter wasn't sure what her alignment was, but having between five and fifteen characteristic points added to your stats all at once must have been astounding to the forest sprite either way. One odd thing was that the remaining sprite guard seemed to be glaring daggers at the forest sprite, but Moesa barely spared him a glance. She looked with interest at the silver shells around Sion and the sprite guard, but she fell to her knees in adoration when Elora and the other pixies flew down from the silver canopy above.

Yura flew over to Elora. Mother and daughter held hands and placed their foreheads together while hovering in the air. Sparkling dust fell from their bodies to evaporate a moment later. They let go, and Elora flew to look at Richter, "Thank you for bringing my daughter and her meitu'meidon back safely, my lord." Elora nodded to her daughter. The Life pixie flew down to nestle inside of Mosea's hands. They touched foreheads, and a shell appeared around them. A prompt appeared in Richter's vision.

Quest Update: **Fate's Companion I**
You have successfully brought two meitu'meidon together and enabled the formation of a meidon. Continue to bring celestial pixies and sprites together! Each meidon created gives the following rewards.
Rewards:
You gain 100 XP per meidon created.

The leader of the group that brings a sprite safely to the Quickening to form the meidon gains 250 XP for each instance. The supporting group members that bring a sprite safely to the Quickening to form the meidon gain 100 XP for each instance.

Richter checked and saw that he had indeed just gained two hundred and nineteen XP. It wasn't a lot, but by his guess, there were about seventy more pixies that were still waiting to bond. He didn't know why some of the other pixies weren't clamoring for their meitu'meidon. Maybe the sprite hadn't been born yet, or maybe they were just too far away, but there were still dozens of pixies waiting. This repeatable quest could be exactly what was needed to level his strike teams.

He wanted to speak with Elora more and ask questions about her abilities and her people, but the long day of battles and stress had done him in. It was probably his imagination, but he thought he saw a blinking battery in the corner of his vision that didn't have any bars in it. Richter walked up to the trunk of the Quickening and sat down with his back against it. Alma flew down to rest in his lap. In a few moments, the lord of the Mist Village was sound asleep, while glowing pixies pranced above his head.

CHAPTER 31 – DAY 113 -- KUBORN 3, 15368 EBG

The next few days fell into a routine. Periodically, one of the pixie children would get agitated and say that they felt their meitu'meidon were close by. Then either Richter would form his war party, or another strike team would venture out to find the sprite. There were occasionally monster attacks, and minor to moderate injuries, but nothing that the village healers couldn't handle. Without Sumiko, several guards were forced to rest in bed for days, but thankfully no one died. More and more meidons appeared around the Quickening until the area looked like a tiny silver egg forest. For some reason, no one else that Richter shared that observation with thought it was as clever as he did.

That wasn't to say that his people weren't friendly. He actually noticed that since the birth of the pixies, and the resultant relationship boost with everyone there, his people smiled at him even more than usual. The men were quicker to salute and the women were more free with their smiles. In a few cases, it was clear that they would have been free with a good deal more if Richter were interested. In general, his people just seemed happy and productive. It gave Richter a warm feeling as he patrolled every day and led more sprites to their pixie counterparts.

Many of the sprites that arrived were of the forest subtype. One added perk was that many of them brought saplings or plants with them as gifts for their pixies. Many of the trees and herbs were rare. As such, they would hand over the trees before entering the union. Richter had each planted somewhere along the empty eastern edge of the village. The chaos seed wasn't sure how the trees were going to help yet, but he was sure they would.

Outside of retrieving the pixies as they entered the mists, Richter started following a pattern. His Sustenance Belt let him make do with only two to three hours of sleep a night. When he woke each morning, he would immediately start performing mental exercises with Alma for two to three hours. The advanced Psi Bond let him progress quickly and after four days he increased his rank in Self Awareness from novice to initiate.

Congratulations! You have advanced from Novice to Initiate in ***Self-Awareness.*** *Control within will be mirrored by control without. 20% less likely to betray nonverbal cues to others. This is cumulative with further ranks.*

You have received 1,250 (base 2,000) bonus experience for reaching level 10 in the skill: ***Self-Awareness****.*

They also worked on his mental barriers, which was, unfortunately, a slower process, but still beneficial. After meditating with her, Richter would go to the forge and start creating daggers. Again and again, he forged iron daggers, melted them down, created ingots and then forged the daggers anew. His skill level increased to level six over the next few days. The time spent in the forge was more meaningful in that he was able to gain a new enchantment.

Congratulations! You have reached skill level 6 in ***Smithing****. +6% Damage or Defense. +6% Durability.*

Congratulations! You have learned the enchantment: ***Life Damage****. Life magic damage will be done to the enemy struck. A secondary enchantment makes healing spells and potions more effective on the wielder of the weapon.*

After that, Richter immediately began forging Life daggers for all of his guards. All of his efforts only increased his movement to the next level of Enchanting by 2%, but this was not a surprise. While his 100% affinity let him ghost through skill levels one through ten, he had found that his skill progression slowed substantially as he progressed to level twenty in some of his skills. He assumed that advancement would continue to be exponentially more difficult as he got into the higher levels. With his Enchantment skill at level forty-eight, it was basically at a crawl. He complained about it to Krom and the smith said he didn't know about enchanting, but for his own Smithing skill, he had to try new and harder projects to see a real boost to his progression.

Richter nodded. The dwarf's reasoning made sense. It wasn't helpful seeing as how he only knew a few enchantments, but it was always better to know. It also did not bother him overly much and he just focused on practicing his Profession. Just like with *Freeze,* the cost of the Life enchantment was 1.5n. Luckily, there was no shortage of soul stones. The hunters continued to bring the stones in, but the main source was his own little predator. The village weavers had made a sack that was specially created for Alma to carry. It had a metal hook that allowed her to hang it securely from the branches of a high tree.

Every night, Richter would fill the sack with empty soul stones. After the two of them were done with their mental training and he went to the forge, Alma would take the bag and go hunting. Though she only captured *common* souls or below, it made a difference. Also, not only did she often come back with five to ten soul stones by lunch, but she was also making good use of her special attack, *Brain Drain.* Because of her efforts, the experience he had spent on talent points was slowly, but steadily, being replenished.

After leaving the forge, he would head up to the meadow and do a quick lap. He would first stop at the Cauldron and get some facetime with Tabia and the other alchemists. Richter considered starting to train his Alchemy skill, but he figured it wasn't the best use of his time. Next, he would make his way over to the skath clutch. After ensuring the eggs were healthy, he would finish his time in the meadow checking on the pixies.

After he had left the meadow, he would go the feast area. The tables had been brought back down from the Quickening following the pixies birth. Richter hadn't even needed to ask, Randolphus had simply organized a group of mist workers to carry the tables back down to the village. Some of the villagers had protested that they could no longer go into the meadow regularly, but Randolphus had squashed their complaints. He stated that entrance to the meadow was a special privilege and only those who had sworn fealty would even be considered. This was further emphasized by the thick walls of marbled quartz that Roswan had started building at the top and bottom of the hill leading up to the meadow. Rather than angering the villagers though, several bent the knee over the next few days.

Each day after lunch, Richter would go hunting with his war party. One noncombatant was taken out with the hunting party each day and 20% of the earned experience went their way. Richter always made sure to have a completely separate strike squad of five guards there to trail the main war party and keep the noncombatant safe. The daily fighting not only let him train his War Leader skill, but it also let him get to know his guards better. The war party was truly large now that Terrod could command his own troops.

It wasn't only the increased size of the party that made it more formidable than before. The scout, tank and healer ability were just as amazing as he had thought they would be. A hunter normally took the position of scout, one of the guards served as tank and Richter was sure to include at least two Life magi in each party, one of them serving in the official position of healer. The hunter and Richter led the war party and made use of their ability to highlight enemies in red. The job was amazingly easy as Alma helped to guide them. She normally had found a potential threat from her earlier hunts and pointed them in the right direction. With Richter's tracking skill, finding dangerous beasts or packs of monsters was almost too easy.

Once Richter and the scout found their quarry, they would both let loose one arrow and then draw their prey back to the tank. After that whatever they were hunting came to a swift end, and Alma normally delivered the coup de grace.

The flow of dead animals and monsters ensured that his people had more than enough food and the stack of tradeable skins grew larger every day. Tabia also benefited from the continual flow of potion components. As often as not, curses could be heard coming from the Dragon's Cauldron, usually accompanied by smoke of various colors. Not all of her attempts at new potions worked out well, but since the building was still standing, Richter didn't interfere.

The forays of the war party served one more purpose. Richter was also able to explore notable locations on his map and explore his realm. The next two *interesting* locations were thankfully not nearly as dangerous as the decaemur knight's dungeon, but they still let him finish his third village-spawned quest.

The second location was a cave. It reached deep into a hill and on the far back wall was a pictographic history. Many of the images were faded, but Richter was able to make out that it told the story of an old god or a devil. He wasn't able to be sure, but what was clear was that this had been a place of sacrifice. The walls showed humans, elves, goblins and what he assumed were orcs having their hearts removed and then thrown down a hole. At the back of the cave was the pit that the pictures had shown. It was only a rough hewn opening in the floor, but had been greeted with a prompt.

You have found: ***Ancient dungeon***

After he had seen that the pit was an entrance to a dungeon more than ten thousand years old, Richter had immediately started backing away. Almost as if to speed him on his journey, a gust of wind rose out of the hole and washed over the war party. It stank of fetid rot and decomposing flesh. Everyone in the cave had run out of it and breathed sighs of relief when they once again could feel the sun on their faces. Richter still shuddered when he thought about it. There hadn't been any overt physical danger, but he knew in his heart that there was something sinister down that hole.

He had almost been reluctant to finish the quest after that, but he still powered through. Thankfully, the third *interesting* location was relatively benign. His map had led him to the foothills to the north of the village. After climbing a narrow and winding trail, he had found himself in a small clearing. What he found was a miniature Stonehenge. Each of the upright rocks had a symbol carved into them, though weather had worn almost all details away. Luckily one of the wood elves in his party knew of the importance of such sites. She said that it was thought stone circles like this could lead to the world of the fey. The elf had scoffed right after she had said it, stating it was a tale grandmothers told children and nothing more. Richter wasn't so sure though. Right after the elf guard had finished speaking, he had received a prompt letting him know his quest had been completed…

Congratulations! You have completed a Quest: **Know Your Backyard I**.
You have examined and discovered the importance of three locations of **Interesting** rank or higher! You are one step closer to becoming a true master of your domain!

Rewards:
4,688 experience (base 7,500 x 1.25 x 0.5).
+0.04% chance of locations within your domain of **Interesting** rank or higher becoming a Dungeon!

The experience wasn't that much, but that wasn't really the point. He had finished three out of four of the quests needed to level his village! Richter had been worried that he would need to unlock all of his Powers for the settlement to reach level two. He wasn't sure what level of monsters would appear, but he knew his people weren't ready to deal with it. The fact that other quests would be spawned by the village was a game changer.

Even more exciting was the second reward. Richter initially had no idea why "Dungeon" was capitalized, but once he spoke to Terrod, he knew that he wanted one. According to the captain, notable locations often attracted monsters and beasts. That was how lairs were created. In very rare instances, the energy of the monsters could infuse the locations with their magic and souls. From that point on, the lairs were known as a Dungeon, and the monsters would continually be reborn. Terrod said that while this might sound horrible, Dungeon monsters sometimes dropped coins and items when slain so Dungeons were coveted locations. Richter's face almost split in half by the time his Companion had finished speaking. He did have one question, though, "Is there usually a really difficult monster to beat at the end of the Dungeon?"

Terrod nodded, "So you have heard of these special dungeons before, my lord?"

Richter nodded with extreme satisfaction. All that was going through his mind was, "Ohhh Baby!"

Even though the chance to obtain such a dungeon was slim, it was still exciting. In the meantime, though, he focused on what he could do. Another benefit from his daily excursions was that he was able to discover various plants that were *scarce* or even more rare. The first day, for instance, Richter was finally able to retrieve the shiverleaf frond that was on the edge of his domain. It had been difficult because it was at the bottom of a submerged cave. He had had to use his fish ring to get to the bottom of the subterranean lake, and it was populated by a type of large eel. The creatures were weak, though and after he killed one with a dagger strike, its fellows occupied themselves with eating the corpse.

Richter had to search for a while, but he finally found fronds hidden under a rocky overhang thirty feet underwater. Once Richter saw them, it became clear how the rare plants had earned their name. The green fronds vibrated slightly, creating small bubbly disturbances. He harvested more than twenty of the plants along with handfuls of the muck they had been growing in, leaving eight behind. The plan was to plant some of them in the Dragon's Cauldron, but in case they did not grow there, Richter wanted to allow this patch of plants to regrow.

The daily raid let him finish a quest and get another.

Congratulations! You have finished a Quest: **If It Grows From the Ground, It's Probably Okay II**
You have brought five rare herb to Isabella: Stillwater Lantern, Shiverleaf Frond, Hellfire Shrub, Tulaberry, and Target Lilly.
As this was a villager supplied quest, it will aid in the progression of your Administration skill.
Rewards:
1,563 experience (base 2,500 x 1.25 x 0.5).
+5 Village wide Loyalty. +10 Loyalty for anyone with the Herb Lore or Alchemy skills.

The war party was normally out for two to three hours, though the first day required the entire afternoon. He ended each hunting trip by reestablishing his control over his tamed adder. He made sure his entire war party was present for two reasons. One, to kill the snake in case it broke free of his control, and two, to restrain him if the Blood magic made him a danger again. Luckily, his improvement in Self Awareness paid huge dividends in his use of Blood magic. Richter actively linked to Alma each time that he cast *Tame*, and though he felt the bestial side of himself rise up, he was able to keep it under control. Richter felt a swell of pride at his new magical proficiency. It was true that he was only casting the weakest of Deep Magic spells, but it was a start.

After his war party was safely back behind the walls, Richter finally tried his hand at working with the builders. Roswan had spoken to him with his customary "real men have calluses" attitude when Richter had first walked up, but the builder still welcomed another able body to work beside him. The chaos seed quickly gained the Construction skill. He also gained a subskill in Masonry when he worked with stone and a subskill in Carpentry from helping to lay a wooden floor. After four days, he had leveled all three several times.

Congratulations! You have reached skill level 4 in ***Construction****. +8% to Building Speed. +4% Durability of the finished building.*

Congratulations! You have reached subskill level 3 in ***Masonry****. +6% to Durability when building with stone. +6% Longevity of finished buildings.*

Congratulations! You have reached subskill level 4 in ***Carpentry.*** *+4% Durability when building with wood. +4% weather protection for finished buildings.*

Even Roswan seemed impressed at the quickness that Richter was picking up the good building practices. When the elf heard about Richter's Masonry and Carpentry subskills, he let loose his most expressive "Grrrmmm" yet. Richter almost blushed.

Once Richter gained his Construction skill, he was able to add more unskilled workers under him which made the building pace increase. The increase in the mist workers he could summon was also good for productivity. For instance, ten to twenty were dedicated to pulverizing simple stone into gravel each day and making rudimentary roads between the buildings and up to the village gate. Even that simple change made it a good deal easier to move around.

Three other factors made a bigger difference, however. The increase in village Loyalty increased productivity by 20%; the increased Morale upped production speed by 10% and his own modest skill in Administration further increased productivity. The boost in productivity coupled with the mist workers nearly doubled the work that could be done every day. Piles of wood and harvested stone grew, waiting to be used. With the excess resources came renewed complaints about needing a storage shed, but it was a good problem to have.

Richter also received another subskill while working with his people.

Congratulations! You have reached subskill level 5 in ***Lead from the Front.*** *+5% Productivity for projects you ordered that you help with yourself. This is a subskill of Administration.*

Each day he worked with the builders until it was time for dinner. The number of mist lights multiplied as Richter, Alma and Futen made them whenever they could. The mile of cleared land around the village wall was soon festooned with the glowing grey orbs. His people could now see easily, day or night. Key areas within the walls also had lights hung regularly at about fifteen feet above the ground. Richter planned to have the rest of the village lit as soon as possible.

After sharing a small meal with his people, Richter went to the eastern edge of the village alone. Alma normally perched somewhere nearby. Some of the villagers started coming to watch what their lord did each night, enjoying the show from a safe distance. Richter had decided to do something he had put off for too long. It was time to grind.

The chaos seed faced off against a small boulder each night and started casting. He would go through his spells one by one, chaining them together without pause. *Weak Flame, Weak Ice Dagger, Weak Acid Sphere, Weak Lightning Bolt, Weak Life Bolt* and *Weak Dark Bolt.* Richter pushed himself to go as fast as possible until his mana ran out. He intentionally pushed until the blue bar in the corner of his vision almost completely depleted. Then he would wait until it refilled completely, before starting again. He didn't gain any bonus characteristic points, but his ability to deal with the pain of mana depletion improved.

For at least an hour each night, he focused solely upon his Fire magic. His Book of Weak Fireball was calling his name, but he couldn't learn the spell until he reached skill level twelve. Richter kept at it each night, and his magic skills slowly improved. It was frustrating how much slower his skills progressed outside of combat, but there was no denying that fighting a boulder was infinitely safer than battling monsters.

After two to three hours, Richter would call it a night. His villagers would clap and then retreat to bed once the show was over. The chaos seed then walked into the catacombs with one of the novice mages in tow. With their help, he would then spend a few hours transcribing a new spell. Over the first few days, he was able to make several books.

You have created: **Book of Virol's Blessing**	**Durability:** 11/11 **Item Class:** Common **Quality:** Well Crafted **Weight:** 0.4 kg **Spell Type:** Life **Spell Level:** 1 **Spell Tier:** 1st (Weak) **Traits:** Casting this spell will increase the yield and potency of a 20x20 yard area of plants by 5%. Successive casts of this spell create a cumulative effect for a max of 100%. This spell can be cast once per day. This is a spell of Life, level 1.
You have created: **Book of Weak Air Push**	**Durability:** 13/13 **Item Class:** Common **Quality:** Well Crafted **Weight:** 0.4 kg **Spell Type:** Air **Spell Level:** 1 **Spell Tier:** 1st (Weak) **Traits:** This spell creates a column of air ten feet in front of you, one foot in diameter. Does no real damage, but will knock enemies back and possibly prone.
You have created: **Book of Weak Life Beacon**	**Durability:** 11/11 **Item Class:** Common **Quality:** Well Crafted **Weight:** 0.4 kg **Spell Type:** Life **Spell Level:** 1 **Spell Tier:** 1st (Weak)

	Traits: This spell shoots a golden flare high into the air. Any creatures with a relationship to you, friendly and above, within one mile, will be compelled to come to your aid.

Richter learned each of the spells, as well as *Glitterdust.* Soon all of his magi who had sworn fealty, and had the required affinity, learned the spells from him as well. After scribing each night, he would retire to his bed chamber. His final task of the day was spending some, ahem, quality time with one of the twins or Lorala, and on one special night, all three. Admittedly, that was Richter's favorite part of the day.

After the first day, Elora and the other pixies started making their way into the village. Every last man, woman and child fell in love with the beautiful fliers. The celestial children definitely had a mischievous streak, but they played tricks on each other as much as on the villagers. As far as Richter could see, no one really minded. For his own part, he quickly came to love them all as well. Many called him "Unca Wichter" and happily buzzed around him as much as they could. One of their favorite games was chasing Alma and Futen, the only other two fliers in the village. The dragonling took the attention in stride, but the remnant seemed to pulse in irritation when he was mobbed with children. At least that was the way it appeared to Richter.

Richter and Elora also spent time alone, discussing various things. The conversations, unfortunately, stopped after one day, but one of the topics they covered was about the pixie queen's status page. First, they spoke of the adjustments to her characteristics. It turned out that there was indeed a significant alteration in her numbers in light of her size. At thirteen inches, she was considered 'tiny.' Tiny creatures normally had a 50-60% reduction to Strength, a 20-30% increase to Dexterity and Agility, a 20-40% reduction in Constitution and a 10-20% reduction in Endurance. Racial differences could make even more profound impacts on character stats, but it explained why her numbers were so skewed. She told him that was one of the reasons that she was having such a hard time distributing her characteristic points.

Through their talks, she also explained her abilities. Celestial Pixie Song was the racial ability pixies had to evoke strong emotions and summon images with their music. The ability could be evoked at any time, but special songs could only occur at certain times. The Song of Joy and Remembrance, for instance, could only happen at royal pixie births. Elora admitted to never having known the song to give such powerful and lifelong buffs. She could only think that it must have been the combination of her race evolving to be celestial and also most likely because it was the first birth seen in the land for centuries. Elora said she doubted that any future Songs of Joy and Remembrance would have such an effect.

She also described the ability Tree Communion. It was fairly self-explanatory, but there were facets that Richter hadn't been aware of. Each female pixie could bond to a tree, and that allowed the pixie race to continue its lifecycle. Female pixies could bond to a tree once per year, and two children would result from that union. Royal pixie queens were different in that they could produce offspring twice per year and one hundred young would be produced. Richter also learned that bonding to the tree meant that a pixie could not travel beyond a certain distance from the tree they were linked to. Doing so would cause the pixie to weaken and risked damage to the tree as well. This distance increased as the bond deepened and the pixie leveled, but apparently never completely disappeared. Elora didn't seem distressed by this, however, and in fact told Richter that there were boons to the Communion such as increased mana regeneration.

The ability Fate's Companion dealt with the creation of a meidon. As Richter had already seen, some pixies and sprites were predestined to bond. Elora said she had never witnessed a bonding before, but she had been taught about them by her mother. The stories she had been told said that both the pixie meitu'meidon and the sprite meitu'meidon were changed by the union. It made Richter wonder if his friend would be different when he emerged from the silver shell.

The last ability, Force Blast, was used for offense in battle. The pixies could apparently focus their mana and fire it in a concentrated blast. That was what he had read about when he analyzed the various types of sprites. Something that was shocking was that Elora could access the extra effects of all four of her offspring. Her Force Blast ability let her use Dark, Air, Life or Water effects. She told Richter that all pixies had always had the capability to weaponize their mana, but that the extra effects had only existed since she had bonded to the Quickening.

Richter found it very interesting that Elora's Blast ability seemed more evolved than that of her children. Her Dark blast not only blinded, but also disoriented enemies. The Water attack slowed, but could also freeze. The Air strike could stun and also be used continuously, not allowing enemies to recover. Elora finally said that after comparing her healing ability to some of her children's, hers appeared stronger. The change might have been because she was royal, but he hoped it was just because she was of a higher level and that her children could have stronger offensive abilities as well.

The next thing she explained was her skills. Elora revealed that only royal pixies could cast spells. Despite her royal blood, though, Elora said she had never had a high enough affinity to cast spells before. Being level one in four of the Basic Elements had been a surprise to her. She told Richter that her Herb Lore skill had been earned through dedication, however. For years, she had followed her mother while they struggled to stay ahead of the plague that had ravaged her people, and everyday had still been spent in service of nature. Her resistances, she could only assume were part of her new celestial nature as she had had no resistances prior to bonding to the Quickening.

Richter had a crisis of conscience when he finished getting all of this information. She was a journeyman in Herb Lore and was also above level ten. That meant one vitally important thing: she could go for a trial. The decision of convincing her to test for a Profession was made even more attractive by the fact that she still hadn't allocated her characteristic points. If the same rules applied as when he had gone for his own Trial, then she would get nine levels worth of talent points. On the other hand, Elora was a new mother. Wouldn't it be wrong to send her to get her Profession, especially as Nexus seemed to grab people as soon as they so much as thought about going for their trial? Ultimately, he just couldn't help himself, "Do you plan to go for your Profession soon?"

"It is interesting you would ask, my lord," Elora said. "I have been considering that very thing."

Richter looked around quickly, but no giant hand appeared. He whipped his head back and forth like a crazy person until Elora asked if something was wrong. Befuddled, Richter said no. Then a sound like a trumpet rung out. A small black disc appeared in the air near Elora. Rather than grabbing her, however, a black plank extended out from the portal towards her. Right after that, a bundle of red carpet unrolled, stopping at her feet. A moment later, out walked Nexus, dressed in a formal black doublet with gold buttons. It was strange seeing the giant shrunk down to only a foot in height, but it was definitely him. He stopped at the end of the platform, only inches away from Elora who was looking at him in alarm and surprise.

"Oh, fairest queen. I, a humble Auditor, do offer your august presence the opportunity of Trial. You have progressed in your skills and level and deserve the opportunity to reach your potential. Though you will need to be apart from your loved ones for a short time, afterwards you will be better able to provide for them in perpetuity and also care for your celestial tree. The choice, of course, is yours my lady, but I offer my humble services in this endeavor." The cosmic figure dipped into an elaborate bow.

Nexus's polite speech accomplished two things. Elora was put at ease and began to smile. Richter grew suspicious and began to scowl.

"Can I go speak to my children first?" the pixie asked Nexus.

"Of course. This is your right and responsibility, your ladyship. If I may suggest, have them check in with Lord Richter regularly. He, I am sure, will safeguard their continued health while you are apart."

"Would you watch them, my lord?" Elora asked. She clearly wanted to gain her Profession but was concerned for her children. Her soulful eyes pulled at his heartstrings. That was how Richter became the nursemaid for nearly one hundred children all at once. Elora flew up into the limbs of the tree once he said yes.

"What are you up to, asshole?" Richter asked the ebon-skinned man.

"Whatever do you mean, Lord Richter?" Nexus asked benevolently.

"You know what I mean!"

Nexus smiled evilly, "What I know is that I am only here because of events you set in motion, fuckface. Let's stop talking about it, though. It's babysitting time for you."

Elora flew back with all of her children in tow. Hearing almost a hundred flying children shout "Unca Wichter, Unca Wichter" all at once as they vied for his attention was suddenly less cute than when he had heard it before. Elora thanked him again and, without further ado, flew through the black portal. Nexus walked after her, but turned back at the end and looked at Richter. The chaos seed was already getting stressed at trying to wrangle flying children that had super speed. They made eye contact and Nexus smirked.

"Bye, douchebag," was the last thing the man said before going through the portal himself. The disc popped out of existence. Richter ground his teeth and thought about how much he hated that guy!

CHAPTER 32 -- DAY 117 -- KUBORN 7, 15368 EBG

Several other important events happened over the days after he had escorted Mosea to the village. The first of which was Tabia completing the quest, Prove Your Worth.

Your Quest, **Prove Your Worth**, has been completed. Tabia has created a noteworthy potion for you. Beyan has forfeited the contest as he has not created a potion. Tabia has won the right to be placed in charge of the Dragon's Cauldron, second only to yourself and Sion. Will you keep your word and give her this honor? Yes or No?

Richter didn't hesitate to select 'Yes.' Not only had he intended to honor the terms of his agreement anyway, but when he made the quest, the prompt had been clear of dire consequences if he didn't. Also, the fact of the matter was, he needed someone to run the Cauldron, and Beyan would be focusing more and more on his magic. Richter placed his hand on the central cauldron and gave her access secondary only to Sion and himself. She beamed and looked around at her new domain while he examined the kickass potion she had made.

You have found: **Potion of Gaseous Form** x 37	**Alchemy Class:** Unusual **Alchemy Level:** Elixir **Alchemy Strength:** Processed **Durability:** 5/5 **Weight:** 0.1 kg. **Traits:** Swallowing this potion will change your body into a semi-gaseous form for one hour. 35% less damage received from physical attacks. The

	imbiber will be seen to flow across the ground. While this does not cause true flying or levitation, the rate of falling will be decreased by 35%

She had outdone herself. Richter's comment that he hoped the potion didn't make him gassy was met with a flat stare from the alchemist, but he let her inability to recognize great comedy go. These things would come in handy! She had also used the Cauldron's special ability to make more copies of the original potion. Tabia apologized that she had run out of ingredients before she could get the max of forty potions, but he waved her apology away. Richter had been happy with what Sion could do with the mana and health potions, but the chaos seed saw the true power of the Cauldron now. It had taken a week of painstaking work to make the four doses of the gaseous potion that her journeyman rank in Alchemy allowed. The fact that she could make dozens more in the blink of an eye, with a 100% success rate no less, was astounding.

As happy as Tabia was to have won, the dark skinned elf was silently gnashing her teeth at hearing how Beyan hadn't even tried to win, especially since she had been busting her hump for the last week. Richter had a feeling that the gnome's little prank might backfire when he had to work under her. The brown-skinned elf kept her composure in front of her new lord, though. Both she and her wife had bent the knee several days prior to Sumiko forming the meidon, and the sprite had said they were both operating in the village with true intentions.

The elf's eyes lit up when she saw the shiverleaf fronds. She made a big deal about the size of the plants and said she could make six or seven potions out of each. This was good because the only recipe they knew for the luck potions was at an elixir level, meaning there was a high risk of failure. From what Richter had been told, a journeyman in Alchemy had only a 50% chance to successfully make an elixir. The Cauldron increased that by 10%, but it still meant that she might go through two or even three measures of the plant before the potion was created. It also meant though that if it was successfully made, one plant would be enough to make all four doses that were allowed at her skill rank. Unfortunately, she told him that the recipe would take at least five days of work to finish. She asked if she could bring other villagers with the Alchemy skill to help. He just smiled and told her that she was in charge now. The elf smiled back as she realized the truth of what he had just said: she was running her own lab! Richter left her with a massive smile on her face.

Isabella greeted him with her customary hug and warm smile. The happy elf exclaimed in delight when he showed her the shiverleaf fronds. The fledgling Life mage hustled him down the stairs of the herb shed and into the basement. Isabella grabbed a mist light that was hovering outside of the door to light their way. Richter was happy to see his people making good use of the mobile glowing globes. The gardener wasted no time walking to the back of the room, stopping in front of the pool. She told him that she had already had mist workers line the bottom of the pond with dirt. Warning him to stay clear of the back of the pool, because that was where she had planted seeds for the stillwater lantern, she took each of the fronds that Richter had collected and harvested seed pods from their bases. He was pleased that the entire plant wasn't required to grow more, but was less pleased by what she said next.

"I believe the deeper you plant these, the better, Lord Richter."

"Me plant them?" Richter asked.

"If you would rather I do it, that is fine," Isabella responded, slowly reaching up to unfasten the clasp on her shirt.

"Bah, bah, bah! I'll do it," Richter grumbled. "I brought muck from the cave I found it in, should I add that to the dirt at the bottom?"

"That is a wonderful idea," Isabella said brightly. Richter removed his armor again and placed it in his bag, grumbling under his breath. He cast a suspicious eye at Isabella, fairly certain he had just been manipulated into getting wet. Thinking back to the earlier years of his life, he figured it was just karma.

Richter removed all of the muck from his bag, mixing it with the dirt Isabella had put at the bottom of the pond and buried the seedpods. Swimming back up, he saw Isabella holding the rest of the fronds.

"I will take these to Tabia, my lord. I assume that she is now running the Cauldron?"

Richter nodded and laughed, "So you knew that Beyan would have to forfeit because of his trial?"

Isabella sniffed, "No. I just assumed that a woman of Tabia's quality would naturally triumph over any man." Then she gave him a bright smile and swept out of the room.

Looking after her in bemusement, he called after her, "Can I at least get a towel?"

There was no response.

CHAPTER 33 -- DAY 119 -- KUBORN 9, 15368 EBG

Richter continued his daily schedule. His power continued to grow, and he was able to first write and then learn two more spells.

You have created: **Book of Gentle Rain**	**Durability:** 11/11 **Item Class:** Common **Quality:** Above Average **Weight:** 0.3 kg **Spell Type:** Air **Spell Level:** 1 **Spell Tier:** 1st (Weak) **Traits:** This spell summons a small rainstorm. Can only be cast outside.
You have created: **Book of Weak Cure Disease**	**Durability:** 11/11 **Item Class:** Common **Quality:** Well Crafted **Weight:** 0.3 kg **Spell Type:** Life **Spell Level:** 1 **Spell Tier:** 1st (Weak) **Traits:** This spell will cure most common diseases.

A wonderful surprise came when Richter realized that creating the spell books not only leveled his Scribing skill, which had reached level five already, but it also leveled the spell skill he was writing about.

Congratulations! You have reached skill level 9 in ***Life Magic****. New spells are now available.*

Richter made sure to teach the new spells to any of his people that could learn them. The capitalist side of him wanted to start charging for the magic, but the pragmatic side of him knew that having more people who could water the crops or having more people who could prevent disease was a positive thing. He received sporadic updates that his relationship with certain villagers had increased, but his decision was further justified after he had taught the cure disease spell to all thirty-two of his Life magi.

Know This! ***5%*** *of your population has the ability to halt common diseases before they spread!* ***+1*** *to Village Health.*

It wasn't a huge boost, but Richter would take it. Small things could make a big difference. After all, there were all those sayings like, 'Mighty oaks from little acorns do grow,' and that other one about the motion of the ocean.

The chaos seed also stole extra time here and there to go see the skath eggs. Each day, the sense of life he felt from them increased. The twins told him that spending time with the eggs would increase his Animal Husbandry skill and the Exotic Beasts subskill. He didn't know if he simply didn't allocate enough time, but the skills stayed at level one. One day at lunch, though, Deera came running up and excitedly said, "It is time."

Richter dropped the piece of meat he had been gnawing on and started running towards the meadow. When he saw that the sexy, but low Agility woman couldn't keep up, he picked her up in a cradle and kept running. Even his battle-hardened body had a hard time sprinting for miles while carrying someone else, but he kept at it. His green stamina bar was close to empty when he got to the lake on the western side of the north meadow, but what was important was that he got there in time!

The chaos seed put Deera down and looked at the steel enclosure that now encircled the baby skath nest. He thought back to a few days ago when he had stood here with Roswan. It hadn't taken Krom long to make the simple steel fence, but the builder was needed to properly install it. When Richter had shone the taciturn elf the skath nest, though, the man had made his customary noise, but somehow had also added a 'Yum!'

"Grrrryuuum," Roswan had said while staring at the nest. "Big eggs." The elf's eyes had widened slightly, and his fuzzy caterpillar mustache was crinkling with a faint, half-hidden smile.

"Back AWAY from the eggs!" Richter had shouted. He was convinced that if a pig had wandered by at that moment, Roswan would have pulled a skillet from his back pocket and started to make a fire. As it was, the twins had picked up on the vibe and physically positioned themselves between the eggs and Roswan, until he and his fellow builders had buried the fence into the ground. Afterwards, Richter gave discreet instructions to the guards to stay close to the nest and not to let Roswan near it under any circumstances.

Despite his weirdo builder's egg fetish, both he and Krom had done good work. The enclosure was round and twenty yards in diameter. Half of the fence extended out into the water and was much longer in height than the land half so that it could sink at least five feet into the lake bottom while still being five feet above the surface of the water. The land side of the fence was also sunk five feet into the earth and similarly extended up five feet above the ground. Richter figured it should be more than enough to keep the squat babies inside of their pen.

A latched gate hung open on the ground side. Richter and Deera ran through to see Derin hovering nearby the largest egg. He had wiped away the mud that was usually there to incubate the eggs. Several of them were vibrating, but none as much as the first. Derin looked up and said, "Quickly, my lord. There isn't much time."

Not sure why he had to be down in the mud, Richter did as he was instructed anyway. The muck got all over his clothes, but he was soon caught up in the excitement. Deera picked up the bull skath egg and handed it to Richter. She passed it over gingerly like she was holding a child which, Richter realized, she was. The three of them knelt there, Deera to Richter's left and Derin to his right, while the lord of the Mist Village cradled the large egg.

The shaking increased and cracks spread across the surface of the football-sized grey egg. A black claw broke through the shell, withdrew and then struck the interior of the shell again. A piece fell away. Another claw broke the surface of the shell and pushed outward. In an increasing cascade, pieces fell away until the face of the baby bull skath was revealed. It mewled with its eyes still closed, crying out at the injustice of being born. Without thinking, Richter spoke to it softly, "It's okay. It's okay. I'm here."

The small creature opened its eyes and looked at Richter. White sparkles formed in the air around Richter's kneeling form. Something changed.

Know This! Dragonkin Richter, you have been present at the birth of a bull skath. Your strong relationship with reptiles and your Psi Bond ability has moved this moment beyond a simple birth. The bull skath has Imprinted! This creature will have increased loyalty to you. For the duration of its life, it will perform better, take to training easier and be more likely to follow commands. This is a wild animal, but Imprinting greatly increases the chance of domestication!

Congratulations! You have reached skill level 2 in **Animal Husbandry***. +4% effectiveness in training. +2% stats for trained animal.*

Congratulations! You have reached skill level 2 in **Exotic Beasts***. +4% more likely to domesticate wild beasts. +2% stats for trained animal.*

Congratulations! You have completed the Quest: **Beast Tamer I**
You have successfully protected the skath clutch until it has hatched! More than that, you have Imprinted upon the bull skath! For making such a connection, you shall receive a bonus reward!
Rewards:
625 experience (base 1,000 x 1.25 x 0.5)
Baby skaths!
+50% increase chance to domesticate this clutch in addition to other modifiers.
Bonus Reward:
Progeny of any imprinted skaths from this clutch have a +10% chance of hatching a monster of increased strength!

Richter's eyes opened in shock. He could *feel* the connection with the small reptile he was holding in his arms. It had ceased bawling and was now looking at him in rapt fascination. For his own part, he felt a strong paternal instinct to protect this small creature.

It was nothing compared to the soulful bond between himself and Alma and was very different to the dominance he had over the shale adder. Perhaps only someone who had owned a dog since picking it from a litter or had raised a foal since it was still wet from birth would understand. This was a covenant.

The bonus reward also opened fascinating possibilities. Did that mean he could breed not only monsters but some sort of enhanced monster? Could he do it with the young of other types of dangerous animals? The carnasid piglets were down in a pen near the village pastures. The twins had said they could not raise the animals to follow commands, but that the piglets could easily be raised for meat. It didn't mean that there weren't other animals he couldn't domesticate, though.

He needed to know more. How long until the skaths matured enough to breed? Would they be considered a resource and benefit from the Quickening's level two 25% bonus? He didn't think the animals could benefit from the population bonus that stemmed from the village's increased Morale and Health, but then again who knew? Maybe one of the rank perks of leveling Animal Husbandry would let them mature faster. Richter was excited by the possibilities!

He was also excited about the level perks from his two skills. A part of him had wondered what the point of raising animals was when he could simply dominate them with his Blood magic. It was clear now though that raising the animals could make them much more powerful than if he simply found them in nature. His Beast Bonding skill increased his tamed animals' attack and defense by 1% for each skill level he achieved, but if the perks from both Animal Husbandry and Exotic Beasts were cumulative, by the time he reached level ten in each, his trained creatures would be 40% stronger than any found in the wild!

"You did it, my lord," Deera exclaimed. "You are,"

"Simply amazing," Derin continued in fascination. "I never expected you to imprint onto the baby. Truly, you,"

"Are something to behold!" Deera finished with a smile.

Derin handed Richter a fish, saying he needed to feed the baby to finalize the bond. Richter held it before the skath's mouth, and the reptile grabbed it and began to feast. The baby started to squirm as it tried to get more of the fish into its mouth, so Richter gently laid it down on the grass of the bank. As the bull skath continued to eat, Richter removed the shell pieces from its back. He poured water over it, gently cleaning away the bloody membrane that was clinging to its hide.

The bull skath had soft skin that already showed the pattern of the hard scales that it would one day grow. Its body had the same squat, bulldog appearance as the older versions of its kind. It finished eating the small fish and then to Richter's surprise started eating the remnants of its shell. Richter reached down into the mud and put the rest of the shells within the easy reach of his newly imprinted skath.

Five more skaths were born that day, leaving nine more unhatched. Richter held each egg as they hatched and they all imprinted upon him. The bull skath quickly established dominance over the other baby skaths, but after that, they played nice. Richter was worried about them getting mired in the mud or not knowing how to swim, but soon all of the reptiles were exploring the edges of their enclosure, both land and sea. The creatures appeared to be natural swimmers.

One interesting thing was that Alma dropped onto the ground in the middle of the six skaths. She was longer than the baby skaths, but her body was far more sleek, making it look like she might be out of her weight class. The bull skath obviously thought so as well. With a mewling roar, it charged at Alma. She merely watched it approach, then, at the last second, flapped her wings while jumping. The dragonling let the skath pass beneath her, and then easily reached down and plucked it from the ground. Another beat of her wings was enough to lift the green creature into the air. She flew forward a few meters while it whined and pissed, before dropping it unceremoniously. The fall was only two feet, but the baby was stunned.

Alma landed atop it, flipped it over and placed a taloned hand to its throat. The other skaths had been approaching, but she extended her neck and hissed. All five backed down. She looked down at the squirming bull skath and pressed her claws down ever so slightly. It stopped moving and laid still, limp and submissive. The message was clear. The bull might be the baddest dude on the block, but Lady Alma was the head bitch in charge.

The sound of dozens of tiny hands clapping filled the air. Richter looked up and saw that the skaths' birth had attracted the attention of the pixie children. They looked at the baby skaths in fascination. Richter warned them to stay away from the reptiles, to which they agreed, but he still saw them looking at the hatchlings with mischief in their young eyes. The chaos seed sighed. The last thing he needed was for Elora to come back from her Trial only to find out several of her children had been eaten.

After spending a few more minutes with the baby skaths, Richter rinsed his clothes off and put on a fresh set along with his armor and weapons. He summoned a mist worker to take his dirty clothes for cleaning and then left the skaths in the twins' care while he started walking towards the village gate. In his haste to make it to the birth, he hadn't cancelled the war party he had planned for the afternoon. His group was waiting for him, and not one of them questioned his tardiness. Richter appreciated the deference, but also found it somewhat boring. His thoughts turned wistfully to Sion and he hoped his best friend would be back soon.

As it turned out, he wouldn't have to wait much longer.

CHAPTER 34 -- DAY 119 -- KUBORN 9, 15368 EBG

The war party was able to take down a cave of breath stealers. The snakes were two to three feet long and possessed a venom that gave them their name. It was only a small nest and Richter's party dispatched it with no real difficulty, but he received some unpleasant news during the fight. He stunned the last remaining snake with *Weak Lightning Bolt*. Then he grabbed it right behind its head and began to cast *Tame*, but he received a prompt first.

At your current rank, you may only Tame one animal at a time. Once an animal is completely under your control, you may start to tame another. Do you wish to break your control of the ***Shale Adder*** *to begin taming the* ***Breath Stealer****? Yes or No?*

Richter quickly broke off his incantation and selected 'No' on the notification window. It was a bit irritating that he was limited to gaining control over only one animal at a time, but it just drove him to have a better understanding of his Blood magic. The snake started spitting and trying to reach him to bite. Almost absent-mindedly, he grabbed the snake's tail in his other hand and stretched it out. Alma latched onto its body and drained it to death. All of the snake's bodies were gathered, and they started back to the village.

That afternoon, Richter was helping to put the finishing touches on the village's new workshop when a guard started running towards him.

"Lord Richter," the guard wheezed.

"Catch your breath," Richter replied. Still need to work on those calisthenics, he thought.

"Thank you, my lord." The guard took several deep breaths and wiped his brow, then he said, "Something is happening by the Quickening. One of the silver things is… acting strange."

Richter almost asked him what "strange" meant, but then realized that if the man had a better word, he probably would have used it. So instead of pursuing a useless line of questioning, something that he hated doing, he just told Roswan he would be back soon. Then the chaos seed took off running to the meadow to see what had the guard so worked up. When he was finally beneath the Quickening, he said, "Huh. That *is* strange."

There were over thirty meidons present now, and one of them was phasing in and out of existence. The shell would fade to transparency, then disappear completely, before snapping back to full solidity. When the meidon was gone, Richter saw what looked like a pillar of yellow stone. The surface was irregular like a stick of rock candy, with faint sparkles in its granular surface.

The disappearances started happening faster and the periods of disappearance lasted longer until, finally, the shell did not come back. A stiff breeze began to blow. Richter squinted while his short hair was tossed about. The wind grew stronger, but also more focused until it was only swirling around the yellow pillar. Particles began to fall off of the column, scoured from the surface by the miniature tornado and were swept away. Soon the pillar was gone, and in its place was a kneeling figure with his palms cupped before him. A small humanoid stood in his hands.

"Sion!" Richter called out excitedly. He started running forward.

The pixie flew up from his perch in the sprite's hands and shouted his rebirth to The Land, arms extended out. Sion stood as well and mirrored his meitu'meidon, extending to full height. The sprite threw his head back and took a deep breath in… or at least that was what it looked like he tried to do. What actually happened was that Sion fell over with a strangled cry.

"Sion!" Richter shouted again, this time in panic.

The sprite's face started turning red and he rolled around on the ground, tearing at his armor. Richter's heart started beating wildly in concern. Had this union turned his best friend into some sort of insane monster? Was Sion having some sort of horrible reaction to the meidon? Did something awful happen because the union was with a celestial being?

Richter was stopped from any other concerned thoughts by his Companion making eye contact and in a strangled voice saying,

"Why are you just standing there? Help me get this fucking armor off. It's too TIGHT!"

Richter started laughing as hard as he could. Sion was still Sion! The sprite stared at him with widened eyes and nostrils flared, promising violent retribution for Richter's inaction. The chaos seed walked over, still chuckling, while Sion tried to dig his fingers into the knots that held his armor in place. Richter tried to help as well, but between the tension on the straps and the sprite's antics, it was an impossible task. Richter made a command decision and tackled his friend. Once Sion was relatively immobilized, he drew his +3 dagger and cut through the side straps holding his Companion's chest plate in place.

The blade cut through the ties easily, so easily in fact that the white dagger cut through Sion's skin as well. The wound was superficial, but Sion still squawked in protest. He was finally able to take a deep breath, though, and his complaints morphed into a bout of coughing.

"Don't complain, ya big baby," Richter said. He didn't know how Sion's armor had become a shrinky dink, but he didn't really care. The band was back together! Richter hadn't realized how much he relied on his Companion until the sprite was gone for a week. He was about to cast *Weak Slow Heal* when he was struck in the back of the head by a blast of electrical energy.

"Gahhh!" Richter exclaimed. The damage done to him was minimal, but even a weak sucker punch was still a sucker punch. Before he could recover, what felt like a giant moth with sharp wings started attacking his face. He was about to swat at it as hard as he could when Sion called out, "Sapir! Stop!"

The attack ceased, and Richter stood there confused as to what had just happened. He wiped dripping blood from his forehead, clearing the bit that had fallen into his eyes. In his peripheral vision, he saw a golden glow and then his wound healed. Alma settled onto his shoulders. He turned his head to look at her.

A lot of help you were, he thought in irritation. **Did that fucking pixie attack me?**

The dragonling blew a short gust of air into his face, **You're fine, master. No one likes a complainer, and yes, the pixie attacked after* you *cut his meitu'meidon.** It was clear from her tone that his familiar thought the attack was all his fault.

Richter rolled his eyes, but breathed out slowly, letting his irritation go. She was probably right. He looked over at Sion. His friend was still sitting on the ground and was talking quietly to his pixie. The flyer's head was hanging, and he looked ashamed. Richter walked over and offered the knife that was still in his hand. Sion started cutting the rest of his armor free. When the greaves came off, he let loose an intense sigh of relief that only a man would understand. Sion started speaking to him once the armor was off.

"I am sorry about that, Richter. Sapir was just trying to protect me. He did not understand that you were only trying to help. I have spoken with him, and he promises…"

Whatever else Sion was going to say was lost as the two Companions looked at each other in shock. Richter had helped his friend to his feet, and they realized something at the same time. Sion had always been a solid three and a half feet tall, and his head was only a bit higher than Richter's waist. Now, however, the sprite's eyes were even with his chest. If Richter had to guess, he would say his friend was closer to four and a half feet tall now. They both started talking at once.

"Are you bigger?"

"Did you shrink?"

"What happened?"

"You tell me."

"How long have I been gone?"

"Three months?"

"You cannot be serious!"

"I'm not," Richter said with a smile, "It's only been a week."

"… … … fuck you."

"Welcome back."

The two friends realized they were babbling at the same time and stopped speaking. They stared at each other for a moment, then just started laughing. Richter examined his Companion, while Sion examined himself. The mystery of the shrinking armor was solved. The armor was the same size; it was just that his friend had gotten bigger.

"Well, you were overdue for a growth spurt I guess," Richter said with a cocky smile.

"That is so funny," Sion responded. "Your girlfriend was just telling me you were overdue for some growth too."

Richter's mouth wrinkled into a smirk. Being able to mock his best friend and be mocked in turn really tugged at his heart, "I missed you, bud."

Sion smiled broadly, "Love you too, man."

"Alright! Enough mushy shit. Let's figure out what happened." Richter accessed Sion's status page. At the same time, Sion looked up at the limbs of the tree and said, "I can still hear the song…"

Before Richter's eyes, his Companion changed again. It was not nearly as dramatic as growing an entire foot, but the bonuses from the Song of Joy and Remembrance still caused a noticeable effect. The sprite's facial features grew more refined and pleasing to look at. His gaze also sharpened somewhat as he looked at Richter. There were no other outward changes from the +5 to Luck or the +5 to Intelligence, but it was still fascinating to behold. He checked his friend's status page to see exactly how far the sprite had progressed.

Name: Sion	**Level:** 18, 58% to next level	**Alignment:** +3
Race: Meidon Sprite	**Languages:** Sprite, Common, Pixie	**Age:** 34
	STATS	
Health: 243	**Mana:** 340	**Stamina:** 192
	ATTRIBUTES	
Strength: 20	**Agility:** 18	**Dexterity:** 66
Constitution: 20	**Endurance:** 16	**Intelligence:** 34
Wisdom: 23	**Charisma:** 15	**Luck:** 17
	RESISTANCES	
	TYPES OF MAGIC	
Life 10%	**Earth** 10%	**Light** 10%
	SCHOOLS OF MAGIC	
	Enchantment 50%	

SKILLS (Name: Skill level, Progression, Affinity)		
MARTIAL SKILLS		
Archery: 43, 64%, 72% *Double Shot*: 8, 82%, 87% *Enhanced Imbue Arrow:* 31, 32%, 87% *Drill Shot*: 6, 61%, 90% *Focus*: 26, 78%, 81% *Stun Shot: 5*, 51%, 95%	**Small Blades:** 19, 82%, 72% **Tracking**:14, 34%, 76%	**Light Armor:** 26, 48%, 81% **Swordsmanship:** 8, 68%, 92%
MAGIC SKILLS		
Air Magic: 13, 12%, 100%		
CRAFTING SKILLS		
Alchemy: 8, 7%, 77%		
MISCELLANEOUS SKILLS		
Tracking: 14, 34%, 76%	**Herb Lore**: 12, 8%, 63%	**Animal Husbandry**: 1, 15%, 83% *Exotic Beasts*: 1, 9%, 71%

ABILITIES
Wood Craft – Natural bond to the forest **Forest Concealment –** Great increase in Stealth while in a Forest **Know Thyself –** +50% resistance to the Enchantment School of Magic, i.e. Charm, Daze, Compulsion **Meidon –** Bonded with a pixie
MARKS

Adventurer

The first thing that Richter noticed was that his friend was close to level twenty. Soon he would be going for his own Trial, as long as the sprite could level his archery skill to forty-five. The next was Sion's new ability, 'Meidon,' and that his race had been modified with the word as well. Looking down a bit further, Richter saw that his friend's Alignment had increased by one. That sent Richter's eyes back up to his Companion's stats. He confirmed that the the sprite had indeed received the extra +5 to Charisma, Intelligence, and Luck from having a +3 alignment. The chaos seed smiled when he realized that also meant that his friend's spells would cost 5% less mana in the future!

Looking at Sion's overall build, it was clear that it was starting to be weighted toward mana utilization. When they had first met, the sprite hadn't been able to cast spells though he had always wanted to be a caster. Sion had always been able to use the racial sprite skill of Imbue Arrow but had never been able to cast spells until Richter had awakened Air magic in him. It appeared that ever since that moment, all of his free characteristic points had gone into Intelligence.

There still remained two large questions that Richter needed answered. What exactly did the Meidon Ability entail and why was Sion's Imbue Arrow suddenly 'Enhanced?'

The answer to the first, was a resounding, "I don't know." His friend was unable to access any more information. Apparently, examining the Meidon ability just gave the prompt, "The manifestation of the realization of destiny." Richter couldn't think of a more useless tagline.

Sion said that his mother might know more, but also said it might remain a mystery. He reminded Richter that pixies had not been present for countless years in The Land. Furthermore, celestial pixies had never before graced The Land, at all, so discovering what it meant to have undergone meidon would most likely be a matter of trial and error. The only thing that Sion had discovered so far was that the Air magic his pixie was attuned to had increased his own affinity back up to 100%.

The second question, what 'Enhanced Imbue Arrow' meant, Sion did not have an answer to either. The sprite smiled so broadly, though that Richter smiled in response. "I have a plan to figure out exactly what 'Enhanced' means," the sprite said.

"What is the plan?" Richter asked. Sion looked so happy that he was sure this would be an awesome idea.

Sion picked up his bow and set an arrow to the string, "Well depending on your perspective… this is the easiest part."

Richter's smile slipped.

CHAPTER 35 -- DAY 119 -- KUBORN 9, 15368 EBG

Sion's experiment involved a half-drawn bow, a minimally-imbued arrow and a shot center mass to Richter's chest plate. Initially, of course, Richter told his friend to fuck off, but Sion used a two part counter-argument of how it was Richter's turn to do the stupid part of a plan and that the chaos seed was being a *youn'da.* Richter was completely confused at first because the word translated into goat hoof. Sion gave him a smarmy look and then deliberately looked at Richter's crotch. He finally got what the sprite was saying. The son of a bitch had just called him a camel toe.

With typical guy logic, that guilted him into agreeing. Even though it was as weak as his Companion could make it, Richter still fell backwards, and the *boom* of the arrow exploding set his ears ringing. Before he had even gotten up, he was healed by his familiar who mentally called him a *gyoti.*

The reason he took a bit longer to get up wasn't just because the arrow had rung his bell. He also discovered what 'enhanced' meant. Binding to the celestial Air pixie had given Sion's imbued arrow the capability to stun his target. Richter was able to shrug off almost all of the secondary effect with his 50% resistance to Air magic and because of the weakness of Sion's imbuement, but he realized it could still be a game changer.

Sion helped him up, congratulating Richter for 'taking it like a man' in the asshole way only best friends can pull off. Richter told him real men wear pants and looked at the tattered remains of clothes that the sprite was wearing. Before Sion could retort, his pixie, Sapir, flew up to Richter's face and gently said, "I sawry, Lord Wichter."

Richter almost told the flyer to cut off the baby talk, until he realized that the pixie was a baby. Instead, the chaos seed just tapped Sapir lightly on the head with one finger and said, "It's okay, little buddy." Richter kept looking at the pixie, though and was confused by something. The flyer looked just like his brothers and sisters. He had no sharp claws, and all the pixie was wearing was the same silver pants he had been born with. How had Sapir cut him?

"How did you cut me when you attacked, Sapir?"

"I so sooo sawry!" the pixie boy looked entirely remorseful.

Richter smiled to put the small youth at ease, "I'm not mad, but I want to know how you were able to cut me. Can you show me without actually hurting me?"

Sapir just shook his head, "I do not know how." The pixie was almost wailing in distress, thinking he was going to be punished. It was clear that the kid either wouldn't tell him anything else or couldn't tell him anything else. He used *Analyze* again.

The pixie was still level one, and his stats seemed the same as all of the other pixies he had seen. Sapir's outside appearance seemed relatively the same as the other pixies as well. There was only really one difference that Richter could see on the stat page. There was a new ability called, Battle Form.

Looking at the ability didn't give Richter any more information. Asking Sion about it proved similarly pointless, and Sapir was too distressed to give him a clear answer. Richter was sure that the ability was the answer to his question, though. He thought about it for a moment and remembered that Sapir had looked normal when emerging from the meidon. Whatever had happened had only occurred when the pixie had thought Sion was in trouble. Maybe there was an unconscious trigger…

Richter clapped both hands suddenly near Sapir's hovering form and shouted, "Shark!"

Sapir shot back several feet. While he darted back, he changed! The celestial pixies normally had fine features and slightly pointed ears. Despite their silver skin, though, they looked like a simple mix of elf and human, albeit on a much smaller scale. Cute and pretty were the words that came to Richter's mind when he was looking at them. Now, however, the first word he thought of was "fierce."

The celestial pixies face had grown gaunt and sharp teeth could be seen behind his half-snarl. Sapir's ears were more pointed, and his silver fingers now ended in sharp talons. Perhaps the biggest change were his wings. Pixie wings always seemed delicate to

Richter. It was easy to see the tracings of vessels flowing through the thin membranes. Now, however, the wings looked like metal. They were moving too fast for Richter to be sure, but he thought they had a sharp edge!

Sion rushed up and let the agitated pixie land on his hand, "My meitu'meidon is not a toy, Richter!"

"Says the man who just shot an arrow into my chest," Richter said.

Sion didn't have an answer for that, but he still wasn't pleased. Richter sighed and said, "I'm sorry, Sapir. I was just trying to help you change. Let me say that you did a great job. Your battle form is amazing!"

Richter thought he was laying it on a bit thick, but Sapir did calm down. Speaking softly now, Richter kept speaking simple platitudes as he plucked a piece of grass from the ground. He moved closer to the pixie that started quivering at his proximity, but Sapir stayed still. The chaos seed brushed the grass clipping against Sapir's wing and smiled as even that light contact caused the grass to shear in half. The pixie's wings were razor sharp. Richter suddenly felt a great deal better about the race's chances for surviving in The Land. After that, he and Sion simply spoke comfortingly to Sapir. What fully calmed the pixie down was Alma landing on Richter's arm and then licking the pixie's face.

The boy predictably said "Yuck!" as he wiped off dragonling drool. Alma playfully blew a light gust of air at the pixie who giggled and transformed back into a simple pixie child. Alma took off through the air with Sapir in pursuit. Soon the air above Richter and Sion was alive with blurs of color and the shrieks of small children as they played with the beautiful ignorance of youth.

CHAPTER 36 -- DAY 119 - KUBORN 9, 15368 EBG

A few minutes later, another meidon dissolved. As opposed to revealing a pillar of yellow stone this time, Richter saw what looked like a statue covered with a shining gold cloth. A moment later the cloth lifted into the air, disappearing as it did so. Underneath were the sprite guard and his bonded Life pixie.

The sprite guard went through the same antics that Sion had had to deal with. The two Companions were able to get his armor off in short order, though. Luckily, Sapir helped this time, and neither of the Companions were attacked by a Life pixie in battle form. The two friends looked at each other and had the same thought, 'Remove your armor BEFORE you bond. Important safety tip.'

Not much later, a third meidon disappeared, and Sumiko was brought back to the village. The Life mage didn't have to go through what the warriors had, seeing as how she was only wearing a simple robe of gold and white. When she stood, Richter could see that she had gained the same height as Sion and the other sprite meitu'meidon, but that wasn't the only change. Sumiko had always had long white hair, and while her face still had the childlike smoothness of all sprites, her crotchety nature had made him think of her as a grandmother.

That wasn't what Richter thought when he saw her stand now. She threw out her hands to shout her rebirth in conjunction with her pixie. Then, Richter was never sure if he had imagined this or not, but she did the slow, head shake thing hot girls with long hair did when they were walking out of the ocean. Her hair had changed to blonde-white, and no longer looked aged, but instead appeared slightly exotic. She reminded him of someone that he couldn't place, but either way, she was looking… good!

Sumiko turned toward him and picked up the cane that had been trapped in the meidon with her. She walked towards Richter with an ease in her step that she hadn't had before, and her white linen shirt stretched out in two very key places that he didn't remember being so interesting before. She walked without support, but when she got close to Richter, she put the cane to good use. Gently placing it under the chaos seed's chin, she pushed up slightly and said, "My eyes are up here, Lord Richter."

Then she walked, almost sashayed past him, and very deliberately threw her cane away. Sion coughed as Richter continued to stare at the youthful transformation the Life mage had undergone, but the chaos seed paid it no mind. He just absently scanned his vision to see if another prompt would appear promising an increase in population growth.

CHAPTER 37 -- DAY 119 -- KUBORN 9, 15368 EBG

After Sumiko had walked away, trailed by her pixie, he walked back down to the village. The only thing that held him up was that the meidon sprite wanted to speak with him. Richter finally learned his name and that of his pixie.

"Lord Richter," Disote said. "I know that Curia, and all of her people, have sworn fealty to you. I am bound to my pixie for life. If you will have me, I will pledge my bow to your service. I only ask that you allow me to continue to man my post protecting the Quickening until I am relieved by the Hearth Mother."

To say that Richter had been shocked would have been an understatement. It wasn't like he would turn up his nose to the service of an experienced sprite archer, but he didn't want any problems with Hisako. The wood sprites were his strongest, and only, ally. The Hearth Mother was generous, but she might feel a certain kind of way if she thought he was poaching her fighters. He answered somewhat carefully.

"I am honored, Disote. I would be lucky to have your strength on my side. I am worried, however, that I would offend Hisako by taking one of her strongest warriors."

Disote looked confused, and answered as if what he was saying was common knowledge, "Every sprite has the right to choose his own path and follow his own destiny, Lord Richter. My path has led here, and my destiny will forever be tied to Curia. If you do not wish me in your service, I will accept that, but I then beseech you to allow me to stay near the village so I can be close to my meitu'meidon."

Richter looked to Sion for help. The sprite seemed to understand and simply said, "We all follow the will of the forest."

Richter rolled his eyes, thinking, thanks Yoda. He thought he understood what his friend was trying to say, though. The chaos seed was distracted for a moment by the sound of a tinkling bell heard up in the canopy followed by laughter, but when he looked up, he saw nothing. Turning back to Disote, he formally said, "Speak the words."

Disote went down on one knee and intoned the words of fealty, "I formally swear allegiance and loyalty to you, my Lord Richter. From now, unto my very death, I will protect you and your interests, to the best of my ability and without deceit."

Richter rested his hand on Disote's shoulder, "I accept your oath of fealty, and swear to honor your pledge with the same gravity in which it was given."

After that was done, Richter suggested that the two sprites go to the forge and see about being outfitted with armor that fit or at the very least trying to fix the straps on their old gear. Sion just smiled and said that it wouldn't be an issue. His Companion walked off to the Dragon's Cauldron to brew some potions. Disote affirmed that their armor wouldn't be a problem and then followed Richter's next set of instructions to go and put himself under Terrod's command. When the chaos seed asked why neither of the sprites were concerned by the fact that their armor didn't fit anymore, Disote just shrugged and said, "The Hearth Mother will be here soon."

Richter decided that if they weren't worried, then he wouldn't be either. Besides, something exciting was happening in the village. The construction crew was finishing the workshop! Richter rushed back down to the village and reformed his small construction crew under Roswan's direction. The increase in village Productivity had let the crew power the construction through and get a great deal of work done over the last ten days. Richter was also able to learn more about construction. In a rare occurrence of communication, Roswan strung an entire sentence together, remarking they could have finished the project earlier if they had simply used wood as opposed to stone. Richter had asked him why they had gone with stone then. Surprisingly, the elf's answer was clear and concise.

"Grmm, already been attacked once and had the longhouse burned down. Don't want the same thing to happen here. Also wanted to build a proper workshop. If we had built using only wood, then the best we could have made would have been a workman's shed. This here is a true level one workshop."

Richter had decided to push his luck and asked, "What is a level two workshop?"

Roswan had fixed him with a glare and said, "Grrrrmmmmm. The next level."

Richter had then decided to quit while he was still ahead and had gotten back to work.

That hard work was about to pay off. After getting back to the build site, he asked Roswan where he could be useful and went where he was instructed. Several hours later, the last stone was set.

The workshop was built like a capital T. The primary building material was marbled quartz, but well polished wood could be seen through the construction as well. The white stone gleamed dully in the mist light. Windows had been installed at regular intervals in the walls, ensuring that air could freely circulate. Each window also had stout wooden shutters that could be battened shut against the storms Sion had promised him would come in winter. A small fireplace was situated in the back wall, and a chimney peaked up over the wooden roof. The building had a beautiful simplicity. As Richter gazed at it in appreciation, prompts appeared.

Know This! You have built a fully functional **Workshop (Level 1)**. *Your settlement will now enjoy the Building Bonus of increased Production and Durability from having such a building.*

Know This! Up-to-date information is now available for your village buildings.

1) ***Longhouse*** *(wooden). Durability: 1272/1272. Houses 30/60/90 people (luxuriously/ comfortably/overcrowded) Quality: Well built.* ***x 5.***
2) ***Livestock Pen*** *(wooden). Durability: 170/170. 60x20 yards. Quality: Above Average.* ***x 4.***
3) ***Skath Pen*** *(steel net). Durability: 613/614. Circular pen, 20 yards in diameter. Quality: Well Crafted.*
4) ***Walls*** *(mix of earthwork and marbled quartz). 5 feet tall.*
    a. *Types*
        i. ***Hard packed Earthworks*** *(53%) – Durability: Variable due to variation in Building Quality. Building Quality: Slum to*

Well Crafted

ii. ***Marbled Quartz*** *(47%) – Durability: 15,225/15,225. Building Quality: Well Built*

b. *+10% defense for defenders (2% per foot)*

c. *+15% Line of Sight (3% per foot)*

5) ***Ship Cradle.*** *(wooden) Durability: 156/163. Building Quality: Poorly Made*

a. *Building Bonus: +0% Shipbuilding speed bonus. 0% bonus to ship stats.*

6) ***Inner Trench*** *– 20 feet deep x 30 feet wide. Lined with wooden stakes.*

7) ***Outer Trench*** *– 10 feet deep x 10 feet wide. Lined with wooden stakes.*

8) ***Earthwork Towers*** *– Durability: 276/276. Building Quality: Slum. +60% Line of Sight (3% per foot)*

9) ***Rudimentary Gravel Roads*** *– +6% travel speed while on gravel roads*

10) ***Forge of Heavens.*** *(Elementum). Durability: 5,500,000/5,500,000* Building Quality: CORE.*

a. *Access title for more information*

b. ** indicates this is a self-healing building*

11) ***Dragon's Cauldron.*** *(Aged Glass). Durability: 8,000,000/8,000,000* Building Quality: CORE.*

a. *Access title for more information*

b. ** indicates this is a self-healing building*

12) ***Workshop (Level 1).*** *Durability: 15,988/15,988. Building Quality: Well-built*

a. *Building Bonus:*

i. *+1.2% chance of a building being spontaneously increased one quality level on completion.*

ii. *12% increase to Production when erecting buildings.*

iii. *12% increase to village building Durability*

Congratulations! You have completed the Quest: **Every Tool has its Place**.
You have created a Level 1 Workshop! As this was a villager-supplied quest, it will aid in the progression of your Administration skill.

Rewards:
1,250 experience (base 2,000 x 1.25 x 0.5) points.
+5 Village-Wide Loyalty.

Congratulations! You have reached skill level 8 in ***Administration****. +8% to Morale, Loyalty, and Production for your village.*

Congratulations! You have reached subskill level 6 in ***Lead from the Front.*** *+6% Productivity for projects that you help construct yourself.*

Richter was blown away. Another 12% productivity for creating more buildings? That was awesome. He did some quick math. His Admin skill was giving +8% to Production. His Lead from the Front subskill gave another 6%. The fact that the village Loyalty had increased to 'Dependable' gave a 20% production boost and the new Morale level of 'Happy' gave another 10%. When you added the 12% from the workshop and the 6% from having given Roswan the village Job of Builder, it meant his people could now build 62% faster than they could at baseline. With the hundreds of mist workers, he could summon every day, that meant beaucoup buildings!

Richter dismissed all of the prompts, excited and motivated to start on the next project. He looked at Roswan and asked, "So what do we do now? What's next?"

Roswan gave back his customary almost-glare and said, "Ale." Then the elf just started walking way. Everyone dispersed after the construction chief.

Richter shrugged. When the man had a good idea, the man had a good idea, "It's Miller time!"

CHAPTER 38 -- DAY 119 -- KUBORN 9, 15368 EBG

Richter rode the high from finishing the workshop for a while and even got Roswan to talk a bit more. The elf agreed to start building the healer's hut in the morning. Richter asked the builder if they would use stone, but Roswan just grunted and said there wasn't a point. Once again, the one topic the builder seemed willing to converse about was construction.

"Grrmm. I do not know the plans, or have the blueprint, to build a level one house of healing. There would not be any extra bonus. Almost any type of building can be built as a shed without blueprints, though, and the village will still get the minimum building bonus. So wood will be good enough, and it will go up faster. If we keep the same pace, we might be able to raise it in four to five days."

Richter was more than pleased that they could build Sumiko's clinic quickly. For a moment he got lost in thought about exactly how much he would like to please the revitalized sprite and exactly how she might express her appreciation. Once his musings reached completion, he gave a faintly pleased sigh and then focused back on the mustached elf. Roswan was staring at him in concern and confusion over what had just happened, but Richter didn't let that slow him down, "I'm happy that we can get it done so quickly, but how do we get the plans for a level one building?"

Roswan took a large bite of the eggs that were part of his contract as the village Builder. The elf slowly chewed, his mouth moving in a left to right circle as he made eye contact with the chaos seed. Richter was momentarily mesmerized by the motion of the elf's thick caterpillar mustache that looked like it was doing that old eighties dance, the worm.

After a moment or two, Richter realized that he had been staring intently at the man's mouth and looked around to see if anyone else had noticed. It didn't appear that the awkward moment had been observed, but Roswan seemed determined to pay the chaos seed back for his earlier lapse in concentration. The builder kept eye contact as he chewed. Richter started to get uncomfortable, and the feeling wasn't helped by his realization that the only thing that would make the moment more icky and uncomfortable would have been if the builder was eating a banana. Not even Roswan would break that cardinal rule, Richter told himself. You *never* make eye contact when you're eating a banana.

After an eternity, Roswan swallowed the trough of eggs he had put in his mouth and answered, "You could always buy the blueprints. My skill level in Construction should be high enough to raise almost any level one building. Normally only builder guilds will sell these plans, however, and your relationship with the guild must be 'Friendly' or better most of the time. Even then, the cost is high, grrrrmmmm. Or-" The conversation ground to a halt again as Roswan slowly shoved two whole pieces of bacon into his mouth and started chewing.

At least he's not making eye contact, this time, Richter thought.

Once the elf stopped gnawing on the pork strips, he started talking again, "Or we could build the scholar's hut. Those Scholars you have writing stuff down would probably be able to get some research done, and they might be able to figure out the plans of some level one buildings."

Richter sat back and let the elf eat. Unfortunately, what he was feeling now was a familiar emotion from his childhood. Even though he had loved playing strategy and RTS games as much as VRRPGs, there had always been an agonizing tension. That stemmed from the age-old quandary of allocation of resources. In almost any strategy sim, you had to make choices about what direction you wanted your settlement to develop in.

On the one hand, you could spread your resources out and develop a village or civilization that equally balanced all facets of its society. Invest in military, then economics, then infrastructure then circle back to the military. The plus side of that strategy was that you didn't have a glaring hole in your development. It was a conservative way to play, though and had never really been Richter's style.

The other side of the coin was to develop heavily in one area until you could get a bonus, or an edge, that you could use against your opponents. Instead of investing in science to get better weapons you could just make a hundred low-level warriors and swarm a neighboring settlement. The downside was that if that attack failed and your opponent *had* invested in science, suddenly your club-wielding fighters were getting totally owned by guys in steel armor.

Right now, Richter had to make a decision about the building order for his construction crew. He had thought before about building the healer's hut first because having a Life mage as the village's official Healer was a real boon. Richter harbored a real desire to get whatever building bonus could come from having a healer's hut to augment Sumiko's already powerful abilities. Every day that he didn't have a place for research to be done, though, was a day that his village wasn't moving forward technologically.

The same argument could be made for getting a barracks built ASAP. Who knew how much more effective his strike teams could be with a formal training area? The barracks could also serve as a secondary housing structure. From his new understanding of the longhouses, they each had a max occupancy of ninety people, and that meant if everyone had to live in the five structures, they would be 'overcrowded' and still be insufficient for his needs. Richter knew that since it was near midsummer, many people slept outside to enjoy the temperate weather, so it wasn't an issue yet. He could foresee housing being a problem when it got colder, though. Somehow he had a feeling that if his people were 'overcrowded' for months on end, there would be consequences. It would most likely start with a drop in Morale, but could also possibly allow for the spread of disease, and those two eventualities were just off the top of his head.

So while his people ate and drank around him, Richter rethought the building order. Walls for defense, a tavern for morale, a market for economy, a research building for science; there was so much to be done. He spoke with Randolphus, Sumiko, Sion and several other people about the village's needs and priorities. He finally made his decision after he got support from an unexpected source.

Richter had just finished lamenting to Randolphus that anything they built would only be a shed when Bartle spoke up. The scribe said that he had spent most of his life living inside his guild house. Apparently, it was not uncommon for guilds to accept young children with promise and raise them, getting years of service in exchange. As part of his training, Bartle had worked with a guild deputy who had a focus in architecture. The Scholar didn't remember everything but seemed fairly certain that he could recreate the blueprint for at least a level one research facility if he worked with Roswan.

The taciturn elf just chewed eggs while he looked at Bartle, but finally stood up and said, "Grmm. Come with me." The two walked off to an empty table and started sketching. With the question of what to build next decided, Richter threw himself into having a good time.

Hours later, Lorala was sitting on his lap, laughing at a particularly bad joke, when Richter stood up suddenly. The shapely elf nearly fell to the ground. She groused her displeasure and swatted him on the behind, but Richter barely noticed. With a Constitution of fifty-six, he had to work hard to get a good buzz going and now that he had one, he wasn't about to let it go to waste. Besides, he had someone to greet.

"Beyan! Welcome back!" Richter laughed raucously and threw an arm around the gnome's shoulders, before pulling back, "Why the hell are you so dirty?"

The Death mage shrugged his lord's arm off and started speaking in an irritated voice, "I am 'dirty' because I just got back from my Trial and for some reason, I was released in midair, ten feet above the outer trench! I am now a Professed Alchemist, by the way, thank you so much for asking," he said sarcastically. "As soon as Nexus told me of my success, a portal opened, and I was sucked through. I fell the ten feet to the lip of the trench, and then the other ten to the bottom of the ditch. That was almost the least of my worries because I nearly got a sharpened stake up my butt!"

Richter was openly laughing now which clearly irritated Beyan, but the gnome still wasn't done with his story, "I was finally able to climb out of the trench, not the easiest thing to do when the walls are steep, and it's night, by the way, and I started walking towards the village. The next thing I know, one of your moron guards is running at me with her sword raised, shouting "Monster!" If it wasn't for the fact that I ran into the light of one of those grey globes and that her squad leader stopped her, the damn fool might have cut my head off!"

Tears were coming down Richter's face.

"I finally got inside the gate and decided to come here and eat because I am starving. THAT is why I am so dirty, my *lord*." Beyan clearly did not appreciate Richter's lack of empathy.

After a few moments, Richter got himself under control and said, "I'm happy you're back, Beyan, and I'm sorry I laughed. If it makes you feel any better, I know exactly how much of an asshole Nexus can be."

Beyan's face wrinkled in confusion, "I do not know what you mean, my lord. Admittedly, the location of my portal home was unfortunate, but I am sure that was simply bad luck. Auditor Nexus was a wonderful host."

"What the hell are you talking about? What do you mean 'Auditor'?" That had been what Nexus had called himself when he had taken Elora to her Trial.

"Auditor, my lord." Beyan's slow cadence made it clear that what he was saying should have been obvious. When he saw that Richter was still looking at him with a confused and ale-addled expression, he explained further, "Auditors are beings tied to The Land. In any given location, a person undergoing a Trial will have it administered by the Auditor for that area. The Auditor for the Mist Village is Nexus. I personally found him to be wonderful company."

Richter shook his head. He had to be mishearing the man. "Are you talking about a black-skinned giant? Gold eyes?"

"Yes," Beyan said. "A truly wonderful man."

"What aaa... What did you guys do during your Trial?" Richter asked.

"My lord, I am sure you know that the magical nature of the Trial prevents me from discussing details." Richter nodded. He had actually been wondering about that. A few times he had tried to speak with Randolphus or Sion about his torture at the hands of Nexus, but he had never quite seemed to be able to. From what Beyan was now saying, the trial must impose a geas upon anyone who underwent it that prevented them from sharing details. Beyan looked thoughtful for a moment, then he smiled, "I believe that I can share one thing, however."

At seeing Richter's raised eyebrows, Beyan started talking again, though he chuckled a few times first. Even though Richter wasn't sure why the gnome had had such a seemingly easy time during his trial, he was looking forward to whatever this story was. It seemed hilarious.

"This is actually a story that Nexus told me," Beyan started. "It was after I said the ritual words, 'I am Alchemist,' then he-"

"Wait, what?" Richter interjected. "Ritual words?"

"Yes, my lord," Beyan's voice had that tone again that implied what he was saying was obvious, "the words to guide your trial." Richter just nodded, not wanting to further interrupt the story. "As I was saying, I told Nexus 'I am Alchemist' to begin my Trial, but before he began testing my knowledge and skill, he smiled and said he would share a story." Beyan laughed aloud again as he recalled the memory. "You will not believe this, my lord, but some idiot not only didn't say the ritual words, but he actually challenged the Auditor to a fight." Richter's face started to go red. "I think I can only share this because Nexus specifically said that I could tell this story. Obviously, I did not believe him at first; I mean who would be dumb enough to actually challenge… an Auditor? It was just like that children's story, the Professional Moron." Beyan laughed again, holding his sides this time. Richter started to hear a high pitched ringing in his ears, that along with his drunken state, drowned out his self-control. Beyan went right on speaking, oblivious to the maelstrom he was summoning, "I mean what kind of dumb asshole would challenge such a powerful being in the heart of its own realm? Can you believe that, my lord? That person would have to be the stupidest, ugliest, fug-"

Whatever else Beyan was going to say was lost to history when Richter tackled him. The Death mage went down, and Richter fell right on top of him, continuing the attack. Sion body checked his friend a few moments later, but not before all the villagers got a show of their lord shaking Beyan and shouting, "You think you're better than me? You think you're better than ME?!"

CHAPTER 39 -- DAY 120 -- KUBORN 10, 15368 EBG

Richter awoke the next day with a headache. Memories of the night before started filtering back into his consciousness, and he groaned, both from the hangover and from remembering that he now owed Beyan an apology. He stumbled out of bed, leaving a sleeping Lorala twisted in the sheets. Thankfully, there was no giant snake to lick him this time. Futen was waiting by the door and started giving him various reports. Richter jogged outside, barely listening and made use of the latrine. Once he was done, Alma flew up to land on his shoulders.

Luckily, Futen knew where Beyan was and so, following the remnant's instructions, Richter headed for the the Dragon's Cauldron. When he got to the top of the hill, however, he saw a host of his villagers gathered in the distance around the Quickening. Curious, he jogged to the northern end of the meadow and discovered what was so interesting. All of the pixies were singing. Wings of blue, yellow, black and gold flew in circles around a central figure. The song spoke of love, welcome, and homecoming. The central figure, was, of course, Elora.

Richter smiled up at his Companion who basked in the love of her children. The song went on for long minutes and brought a sense of peace and joy. A thought occurred to him, and he checked his personal interface. Sure enough, he had received a buff.

Song of Homecoming – *Queen Elora is welcomed back by her children after she has undergone her Trial. The joy of the celestial pixies soothes all hurts and acts as a balm for troubled souls. Those who hear this song will have a positive outlook for the rest of the day.*

Looking around, all of his people had smiles on their face. A prompt appeared when the song ended that showed that Morale had increased for everyone present by +50 for the next twenty-four hours. The buff was temporary unlike the sprites' Song of Joy and Remembrance, but it was still more than welcome. In that moment, Richter knew that despite what the future might bring, he had made the right choice in allowing Elora to bond with the Quickening. It had also helped banish his hangover; he noted happily. The pixie queen flew down to greet him. He used *Analyze,* and his smile grew even wider.

"I see you have you returned, my lady," Richter said with a smile.

"I have," she said with joy in her voice. "I have found my Profession."

Richter nodded happily. He already knew though because that had been what made him smile initially when he analyzed her. Her status page was the same as before, but with an important addition, "Profession: Herbalist."

"It was wonderful," Elora said. "Auditor Nexus took me to a realm filled with plants. He adopted the form of a beautiful black butterfly, and we flew through a garden the size of an entire world. For weeks, we just floated through the flowering paradise. At the end of my trial, he even told me that because I had not allocated my characteristics points from the levels that I gained while in the cocoon, I would get all of the talent points for each of them. You are truly blessed to have such a benevolent being as the Auditor for your domain, my lord."

Richter kept a fake smile on his face, but had to struggle against the urge to scream at her. 'How can you fall for that? Are you a moron? That's just a game! He's playing you!' He didn't though, just making small talk for a few more minutes. He was happy that she had so many TPs to play with. Something occurred to him, though, and he urged her to allocate her points quickly before her time ran out and they were randomly allotted. She smiled and just told him not to worry. Apparently, Nexus shared that he could completely control the flow of time in his dimension and he had altered it so that she still had days to decide where to put her points. Richter's eye began to twitch.

Ultimately, she broke off the conversation and went in search of Isabella, eager to use her new Profession to help in the garden. Richter left the Quickening, shaking in silent rage about

Nexus, and went off to find Beyan and apologize for getting upset about Nexus. The irony was not lost on him.

He found the gnome in the Dragon's Cauldron and from what he could hear, Tabia was already asserting dominance. Richter took a sadistic satisfaction from the knowledge that he wasn't the only one having a shitty morning. As he listened, a faint smile crossed his face as he realized that in one move, he might be able to make up for last night and avoid having to eat too much crow.

Richter walked into the Cauldron and simply observed Tabia dressing Beyan down for a few seconds. When they both looked over, Tabia with a questioning expression and Beyan with a beseeching one, he simply nodded magnanimously and gestured for them to continue. A look of brutal glee crossed the elf maid's face, and she unleashed the full force of her sharp tongue on the gnome's bald head.

Richter let the beating go on for a few more minutes, then he made his move, "Tabia, I want to congratulate you again on winning the quest."

"Thank you, my lord," she replied with a bow of her head.

As Richter spoke, he swung his hands in large arcs indicating various portions of the Cauldron, "I think what you have accomplished is amazing. The gaseous potions, not to mention the luck potions that will be coming soon… I just have to say that you are wonderful. I think it is great that you don't mind sacrificing your own Alchemy progression to serve the village."

"Ahhhh, yes. Of course not, Lord Richter," Tabia agreed. She went from basking in his warm praise to feeling a bit off kilter by his last comment.

Richter nodded vigorously, "I also want to congratulate you on organizing other villagers with the Alchemy skill to help out. Though I would never want to disrupt the flow of your operations here, I will of course need to take Beyan with me when the war party goes out daily. He is, after all, our only Professed Alchemist. What he can add to the village's potions is unique and must be endorsed. I am sure you understand, Tabia." Even to himself, Richter's tone sounded quite reasonable.

"Errr, that makes perfect sense, my lord."

Richter shook his head regretfully, "I only wish that you and Mimi could find the time to finally go for your own Trials. This really would be the perfect time… but I understand your dedication to the Cauldron. I am sure that Beyan won't mind taking more responsibility here as his Profession advances." Tabia opened her mouth again, but Richter just smiled and clapped her on the shoulder before walking out.

Later that night, both she and her wife met him at dinner and announced that they would like to go for their Trials. A large black disc appeared and Nexus exited dressed like a punk rocker. His golden hair had been shaved on the sides, and the middle strip was a pointy Mohawk that stuck a foot up into the air. He wore blue jeans, red allstars and jean jacket with safety pins in it that had the phrase, "Salt Lake City Rules!" inked on the back with a black sharpie.

Everyone in the feast area stared at the irascible being in shock and surprise. Nexus just sniffed disdainfully, "If it's too loud, then you're too old." He looked at Tabia and Mimi and said, "Come on babes, let's rock." Then he walked back through the black portal, disappearing.

It was obvious that neither of the statuesque elven women like being called 'babes,' but it was also clear that they were smarter than Richter and decided not to antagonize their Auditor. Tabia handed Richter a small wooden box that made tinkling sounds when it moved. Then the two elves walked into the black portal holding hands. It disappeared soon after. Conversation resumed in the feast area, the sight of individuals going for their Trials was now so commonplace that it didn't cause a great stir.

Beyan walked over to Richter. One of the gnome's eyes was blackened from their scuffle the night before, and he had a slight bruise on his cheek. For a few moments, the two men just stood there looking at each other. Then a broad grin appeared on the Death mage's face, and he stuck his hand out, "Apology accepted, my lord."

Richter grinned right back and said, "I'm glad you got that I did it for you, buddy. Us Death magi need to stick together, right?" He clasped wrists with Beyan, but then tightened his grip and pulled the gnome in close. The smile stayed on his face for the benefit of anyone that was watching, but his tone was deadly serious, "But if you tell *anyone* that fucking story again, I'll kill you." Beyan pulled back with a shocked look. The chaos seed let go of the mage's wrist and with a manic grin and said, "Huzaah!" before walking off.

As Richter went to pour himself another mug of ale, he reflected that it had been a good day. He'd apologized to Beyan, gotten more training done, started construction on the level one house of scholarship and, with any luck, in a week he would have two more lesbian Professionals. A solid win in anyone's book!

CHAPTER 40 -- DAY 121 -- KUBORN 11, 15368 EBG

All was right in the Mist Village. In turned out that the box Tabia had handed over had been filled with his long-awaited luck potions.

You have found: **Potion of Selak's Luck** x 40	**Potion Class:** Scarce. **Potion Level:** Elixir. **Potion Strength:** Refined **Durability:** 5/5 **Weight:** 0.1 kg **Traits:** Swallowing this potion will give you the luck of its creator. The alchemist Selak was a middling alchemist, but on an ill-fated trip, he was attacked by ogres, survived by fleeing on a ship that suddenly and mysteriously sank, and then was trapped in a town that was decimated by the weeping plague. He survived it all and is reported to have discovered the formulation for this potion while waiting to be released from quarantine! Increases the imbiber's Luck by **+32** for **three hours and forty-nine minutes!**

Richter fingers immediately began tingling as he thought of all of the things he could accomplish now. He dove back into his training with renewed gusto and was able to scribe the last of the level one spells from his Air and Life magi.

Congratulations! You have learned the spell: **Summon Weak Luminous Butterflies**. Summons a small number of glowing butterflies. Any creature of positive alignment who catches one of these butterflies will have a boost to their stamina for one day. Total boost equal to 1% per number of alignment. Only one butterfly may affect each individual. This is a spell of Life, level 1. Cost: 17 mana. Duration: 10 minutes. Range: 1 foot. Cast Time: 1 second. Cooldown: 1 minute.

Congratulations! You have learned the spell: **Call Weak Small Creature**. If there is a non-sentient creature of 'Small' size, two to four feet long, in the immediate area, it will be called to the caster, and it will follow simple commands. This is a spell of Life, level 1. Cost: 12 mana. Duration: 10 minutes. Range: 50 feet. Cast Time: 2 seconds. Cooldown: 14 minutes.

His inner free market American rose up for a moment again, but another part of him knew this was short-sighted. The potential benefit to the village was massive. Also, all of his magi had sworn fealty and so he knew they wouldn't be leaving at the end of the year. Each and every one of his twenty-three adult Air magi had the spells, *Glitterdust, Weak Air Push, Gentle Rain, Weak Haste* and *Weak Errant Wind.* He made sure that the eleven children with Air magic knew everything except the first two. He also taught his thirty-two grown Life casters: *Weak Charm, Weak Slow Heal, Weak Cure Poison, Weak Cure Disease, Soul Trap, Weak Life Armor, Weak Life Aura, Weak Courage, Summon Weak Life Wisp, Weak Banish Undead, Weak Stabilize, Summon Weak Luminous Butterfly, Call Weak Small Creature, Weak Detect Hostile Intent* and *Weak Life Bolts.* Richter was stunned by the number of Life spells he had been able to amass, even if they were all low level. He supposed that was what happened when you made allies with a Life Master, though. The children with Life magic were given all of the spells except for the offensive spells, *Weak Life Bolts* and *Weak Charm.* The one other person he taught his spells to was Elora.

Richter passed along the knowledge for all of his level one Life, Dark, Water and Air spells. She beamed when she received his gifts and promised to practice her magic every day. Checking his action log, he saw that he had gained interpersonal points with the pixie queen again, though not enough to increase their relationship rank.

As the days passed, more sprites showed up and created more meidons. The first silver shells continued to dissolve and release tall sprites and pixies that could use the ability, Battle Form. Those bonded to Water pixies were encased in a pillar of fluid that slowly drained away revealing the meitu'meidons, and those bonded to Dark pixies appeared as a silhouette that drew in all light. The blackness would then slowly be supplanted by light, like a darkened mountain being revealed by sunrise. To the last, every sprite birthed from the silver eggs swore fealty to Richter. The effectiveness of the mist village's fighting force swelled.

In addition to increasing the settlement's martial strength, Richter made an amazing discovery when he was speaking with one of the meidon sprites. The forest sprite revealed that she knew a simple Earth spell, *Weak Thorns Underfoot.* It was a level one earth spell that would create a thirty by thirty-yard area on the ground that was irregularly studded with thorns for a few minutes. It wouldn't bother anyone with stout boots, but it would make movement painful for animals or anyone with soft shoes.

Upon hearing that she had magical ability, Richter asked if she knew any spells. The sprite shook her head and said that she had had to struggle to learn that one Earth spell and hadn't had any affinity with the other Basic Elements. Richter nodded and was going to walk away, but then on impulse, leaned in placed one hand on her head and the other on her chest. The sprite was startled, but she did not resist her new lord.

Richter spoke the words, "By the Right of My Power, I Awaken Your Power." Warmth kindled in his chest and spread down his arms. The feeling passed from him, into her, and magic was kindled in her soul. She looked at up at him with wonder on her face.

Awakening Cettiona's Power has greatly improved your relationship!

Congratulations! You have gained ***+1,018 Relationship Points*** *with* ***Cettiona!***

Your relationship with Cettiona has improved from ***Pleased (+250)*** *to* ***Friendly (+1,000). "It has been too long since we've seen each other…"***

Total Relationship Points with the Cettiona: ***+1,357.***

Cettiona told him that she had gained the skill Air magic. Not only that, she had an affinity of 100%. Richter had no idea how strong her skill would ultimately be, but he excitedly sent Futen and two nearby guards to gather all of the meidon sprites. Most resided under the canopy of the Quickening, so he did not have to wait long for them to return. In the meantime, Cettiona told him that she had learned an interesting spell, called *Weak Aided Flight*. The spell would only be useful to ranged fighters, but it was potentially powerful. The spell took three seconds to cast, a long time for a level one spell, but it lasted for thirty minutes. For the duration of the spells, it made any projectile shot by the spell recipient fly forward 10% faster than it would otherwise. The gears in Richter's mind started turning. If force still equaled mass times acceleration in The Land, then the spell would not only make it harder for enemies to avoid arrows, it would also increase the kinetic payload when the blow landed!

Richter tried to awaken Life magic in Cettiona as well, but nothing happened. He had a theory to test but needed to wait for the other meitu'meidon. Nine others had emerged from the silver shells, three Air, two Life, one Dark and three Water. Once they were all assembled, he was ecstatic that he was able to awaken the corresponding magic in the sprites that had bonded to Air and Life pixies. Even better, each sprite had a 100% affinity. It was true that Sion had enjoyed an increase in his Air magic affinity, but now it seemed that the celestial pixies gave any sprite they bonded to a starting affinity of one hundred!

He taught the five of them the level one spells he knew. Unfortunately, the rest hadn't obtained any magic that he didn't know when he awakened their Powers. In retrospect, he realized that luck might play a role in this. He didn't have enough luck potions to give each meidon sprite a vial before awakening their magic, but he decided that *he* would imbibe one the next time he awakened anyone's magic.

The Dark sprite he sent to Quasea, hoping she could teach him to use his presumed Dark magic skill. The Water mage he couldn't help, but he resolved to scribe a Book of Slow at his earliest opportunity. Richter immediately took Cettiona to the scribes' office and began scribing her Air spell. Over the past several days, his Air magic level had increased to level fourteen and his Scribing ability had reached level eight. With that, his Olde Writ writing technique and his Faster Creation Time Talent, it made the time required to create the spellbooks almost ridiculously short.

It appears you wish to create the spellbook: ***Book of Weak Aided Flight****. This level one spell will require one hour and two minutes of scribing time to complete. You will have fourteen days to complete this task. Do you wish to start? Yes or No?*

Uhhh, yeah, Richter thought with a smile. He selected 'Yes' and got to work.

Once the required time had passed, he got started on her Earth spell. His Earth magic was only level nine, but it still took almost no time for him to write the spellbook and then learn the spell himself.

More days passed.

Richter kept to his schedule of smithing, enchanting, patrolling, building, scribing and skill grinding. The Belt of Sustenance proved to be one of his most powerful items. With the reduced amount of sleep required, he was able to work for almost twenty solid hours each day. Minus the necessary functions of life, of course, and minus a few unnecessary functions when one of his paramours gave him, 'The Look.'

His spell skill levels kept advancing every few days. He was finally able to get his Fire magic up to level twelve after burning a large lizard that attacked his war party. It had required fighting almost exclusively with his *Weak Flame* spell for several days, but it finally happened. With a look of pure glee, he withdrew The Book of Weak Fireball from his bag. Richter started reading and, as always, the pages began to turn on their own as the knowledge streamed into his mind. The book slammed shut fell to dust, and he *knew*!

Congratulations! You have reached skill levels 11 and 12 in ***Fire Magic****. New spells are now available.*

You have received 1,250 (base 2,000 x 1.25 x 0.5) bonus experience for reaching level 10 in the skill: ***Fire Magic****.*

Congratulations! You have advanced from Novice to Initiate in: ***Fire Magic****. +5% Resistance to Fire Magic. +5% Spell Strength when casting Fire Magic.*

Congratulations! You have learned the spell: **Weak Fireball.** Fires a ball of flame that detonates upon impact. Flames are spread out from this area dousing anyone in a ten-meter radius in fire. This is a spell of Fire, level 12. Cost: 79 mana. Duration: 1 second after impact. Range: 100 feet. Cast Time: 3 seconds. Cooldown: 10 minutes.

"Woot!" Richter said throwing his fist into the air.

Sion looked over from a rock he was sitting on and arched one eyebrow in question.

"I finally learned my fireball spell! Back where I come from, people talk about a lot of different kinds of magic and types of spells. There is one mac daddy spell that lets people know how big your nuts are, though, and that's if you can throw a fireball." Richter was grinning from ear to ear.

Sion smiled back, "Congratulations, my friend. I am happy for you."

"Thanks," he replied. He looked around for a safe place to cast the spell, but they were in a heavily wooded area.

"Just so that I understand, is this a spell that shoots a ball of fire that explodes on contact?" Sion asked innocently.

"Yeah," Richter said, still looking around.

"And then, the flames spread and have a high chance of burning and lighting things on fire, right?"

"Yeah," Richter said, not liking where this was going.

"Like all the trees around us?" Sion asked. "Or all the trees that will *always* be around you, because you live in a forest?" The sprite's smile was practically glued to his face.

"Yeah," Richter said in a slightly disappointed and defeated voice.

"And you have just realized that you won't be casting that spell very often because you would risk burning down the forest?" Sion asked gently.

"Yeah," Richter said, sounding like he had just heard his puppy was sick.

"Yeaahhh," Sion said slowly, then he hopped up from his seat and walked away.

Richter looked after his friend, "You're a real dick! Do you know that?"

Sion just started whistling and threw up two fingers into a peace sign as he continued to walk away. The chaos seed glared at him, regretting having taught the sprite about pop culture references.

CHAPTER 41 -- DAY 127 -- KUBORN 17, 15368 EBG

The next days followed the same pattern. Whenever a sprite that had felt the pixie call got close, a team was sent out to guide him through the mists, day or night. Richter was not able to be there each time, and some mornings he was surprised to see a new meidon under the limbs of the Quickening despite not even knowing another sprite had made it safely back to the village.

His daily hunting trips also unlocked two new subskills of War Leader. The first happened after he and Alma were finishing a solo hunt. When Richter read the prompt he felt an immediate vindication.

Congratulations! You have learned the subskill: ***Army of One.*** *Not all battles can be fought with an army around you. Too often in The Land, you will find yourself alone. If you cannot put your back to the wall and fight your way out of the dark, the only thing shorter than your life will be the memory you leave behind! You have fought seven battles without any support personnel and have unlocked this new subskill! You now have access to all promotions that you have earned as a War Leader when hunting alone. Available promotions:*

Promotion	Description
Vigilant I	+5% to perception of future hidden enemies. +5% to response time to future surprise attacks.
Sapper I	+5% to attack against an entrenched enemy.
Subterranean I	+5% to defense when fighting underground.

Overwhelming Odds I and II	I: +10 to Fighting Spirit II: +20 to Fighting Spirit

Know This! At the rank of Novice in the subskill ***Army of One****, you will earn only 10% of the War Points you would earn if you were leading troops.*

All of the hen pecking he had received for fighting alone seemed suddenly justified. Part of him wanted to run to Randolphus immediately and say, 'See! See! Fighting alone has its perks!' As good as that might feel, Richter realized that he was just being childish. The feedback he had received from both Terrod and Randolphus had been warranted. Even the tirade Jean's wife had gone into had been a good reminder of his responsibilities. He couldn't take unnecessary risks. His new subskill did also show that there was merit to his argument of growing stronger and being self-reliant as well though. He looked forward to advancing it.

The next subskill appeared after a bloody fight with a pack of nindani. The beasts were reptilian and had two thickly muscled and clawed arms. The lower half of their body was a powerful tail. What made the fight so difficult was that their scales gave them a partial resistance to most magic. The entire fight had come down to physical combat. There had been six of the creatures, and most were level twelve or thirteen. The pack leader was level twenty-five, though!

His war party was hard-pressed during the battle and there had been a few serious injuries. At the end though, all of the monsters lay dead and one of Richter's short swords was sticking out of the nindani leader's chest. After the battle, a prompt had appeared.

Congratulations! You have learned the subskill: ***Beacon****. You are not only a leader, you are also a fighter! For the past seven battles, you have slain the most powerful opponent that your war party faced. This has allowed you to unlock this new subskill. Your actions will now be a focal point of any battle. Your status as Champion now gives an increased boost to the Fighting Spirit of your war party (+10 per skill level). Slaying enemy Champions will now give a greatly increased boost to the Fighting Spirit of your war party for the duration of the battle. Conversely, your death in battle will cause massive damage to the Fighting Spirit of your forces.*

Richter still didn't understand the importance of Champions in battle, except that they were tied to the Fighting Spirit of those around him. When he received his War Leader skill, the prompt had told him that he was now considered a Champion. He also remembered that when Yoshi had killed the bugbear raider Lif'alt, the other bugbears suffered a -100 to their Fighting Spirit while his own forces got a +50 bump. His new subskill seemed to make those kind of swings more pronounced. It was easy to see how killing a few Champions might turn the tide of a battle. It meant putting himself in danger in battles, but if there was one thing he had learned, it was that safety was an illusion in The Land. Like his grandpappy had always said, "Big risks mean big rewards."

His own progression wasn't the only thing of note to happen. It was an exciting time for everyone in the village and a big event seemed to happen every day. Richter had some excitement himself as he made use of the luck potions. The first thing he did was to finally sacrifice the Glass Boots of Shockwave to the Forge of Heavens. He watched, with extreme gratification, as the boots turned to dust and another green light took its place in the heart of the massive green anvil. He was also able to successfully disenchant his Arrow of Multishot and the Cobalt Mace of Mana Stealing.

He wasn't able to learn those two enchantments, but he was able to glean others. Two lights, one black and one red came to occupy the corner of Richter's mind that held his enchantments.

Congratulations! You have learned the enchantment: **Goblin Slaying**. *Weapons instilled with this enchantment will do extra damage to goblins.*

Congratulations! You have learned the enchantment: **Confusion**. *Enemies struck with weapons instilled with this enchantment risk being confused to various degrees.*

Richter also finally sacrificed the Poison of Nil Abilities to the Dragon's Cauldron. He held his breath while he poured the rare and valuable potion into the central glass cauldron. There was only one measure of the blue liquid left, and if he didn't learn the recipe this time, he wouldn't get a second chance. A moment after he poured it into the Cauldron's heart though, the blue potion was absorbed by the vessels and it drained into the floor. Tabia had successfully returned from her Trial as a Professed Alchemist and was standing nearby. She excitedly placed her hands on the central cauldron to access the recipe, but then her face fell. The formula called for six ingredients, all *scarce* or even more rare. The Dragon's Cauldron showed Richter where five of them were on his Traveler's Map, but the sixth was nowhere to be found. Either there wasn't a local equivalent or Richter hadn't explored the area where it could be found. No matter the reason, the fact was he wouldn't be making any of the poison until he could find some umbral root.

His people were making strides as well. Over the next two weeks, the villagers were able to finish two more buildings and make large strides in converting the village wall to marbled quartz. According to Roswan, structures built with marbled quartz were at least 50% stronger than those built with regular stone. Richter had also enacted a plan to expand the wall once the conversion was complete.

After Richter had seen the defensive benefits of having a wall of increased height, he had instructed Roswan to start building it up to fifteen feet once the bottom layer was done. The taciturn elf had nodded his head and said, "Grmm, my lord." He also told Richter that the defensive bonus capped at some point, but that walls could also give a bonus to dodging projectiles once they reached a certain height.

An added bonus of working with Roswan everyday was that the builder had started to treat him with greater respect. Just like on countless worlds through time, playing with blocks was enough to bring two males together. In no time at all, Richter was awarded with a prompt.

Know This! You have built a fully functional ***House of Scholarship (Level 1)****. Your settlement will now enjoy the Building Bonus of increased Research, Scribing and other Scholarly pursuits from having such a building.*

Richter appreciated the workshop even more than before now that he could know exactly what the buildings did just by examining the village interface.

House of Scholarship (Level 1). *Durability: 15,914/15,914. Building Quality: Well-built. Building Bonus: +12% Increase in village* *research speed. +12% to upper limit of research points that researchers can add per day. +12% to Scribing speed and success while inside of the building. +12% to village education (knowledge retention, conceptual understanding, etc.) +1.2% chance to have a scientific breakthrough.*

With the research building done, new options opened up on Richter's village interface. A screen appeared that showed the village in the center. It looked like a real-time rendering of the town, accurate to the last detail. Around the model village were a multitude of spheres, arranged three-dimensionally to maximize the distance between them. All of the globes were a drab white except for one, which glowed slightly. More spheres were visible, extending out from that one lit sphere. Each had lettering on them that Richter could easily read. Glowing lines connected all of the spheres out from the globes extending outward in all directions. The entire scene looked very much like Richter's Talent page.

The main difference was that while his Talent interface was two-dimensional and was set against the backdrop of a star-filled and colorful nebula, the caricature of his town and the land it was built upon seemed to sit in a bubble of grey fog. The spheres around it were easily seen, and they pushed back the thick mist. Panning out only showed more fog. Luckily, he never completely lost sight of the town no matter how far he zoomed out. The sphere of available techs glowed like a lantern through a storm. He could see faint outlines of other spheres in the fog, but couldn't make any other details. To make it even more difficult, the globes seemed to gradually shift in and out of sight, like they were being moved by a slow moving current.

Richter looked over the tech window. As he panned out further, he finally got a feel for the scope of what he was looking at. There had to be thousands, if not hundreds of thousands, of spheres. He wished he could see what was hidden under the fog. If each science sphere could be researched multiple times, which seemed to be the case, it would take eons to learn all of this tech.

He kept zooming out and saw only grey, but then something caught his eye. In the bottom right corner, well away from the sphere that surrounded the model of his village, there was another well-lit break in the mist. He focused his attention in this new area and saw that several spheres were revealed, but again only one was glowing. The reason why this other patch of fog had been revealed became clear when Richter zoomed in on it.

The globe read, "Portal Construction III," and had several other spheres branching off of it. There was also another a filament leading off into the surrounding fog, but he couldn't see what it attached to. This was the knowledge he had obtained from the Tefonim queen. It was an actual tech! Richter's mind started flooding with possibilities. He didn't know what to research first.

After a moment, Richter decided to look at the other prompts that had come up with the first one to see if they added any clarity to how to proceed.

Know This! As Master of this Place of Power and the Mist Village, you are bound to your settlement. As with all rulers, your character, abilities, and soul will affect your land and your people. Your Limitless ability now applies to the techs that your settlement can research. You are not limited by race, alignment or any other specifics in the techs which you can pursue. Purchase and procure technical manuals to jumpstart your science. Steal, bribe and co-opt technology and knowledgeable people to increase the capabilities of your people! Be warned, something once known can never be fully unknown. "The difference between stupidity and genius is that genius has its limits."

Well that's awesome news, Richter thought. He wasn't sure why certain techs would be limited to certain races, but it was still good to know that his people could advance in any direction.

Congratulations! You have unlocked the ability to do research! The following areas of tech are available to you.

1) ***Farming I.*** *Cost: 89 Research Points. Successful research will increase yield from cultivated crops by 5% total.*
2) ***Animal Husbandry I.*** *Cost: 102 Research Points. Successful research will increase the health of your animals by 5%. Usable products from domesticated animals are also increased by 5%. <u>*Requires your settlement to have domesticated animals.</u>*
3) ***Soldiery I.*** *Cost: 98 Research Points. Successful research will increase the learning curve of your soldiers by 10%. Also increases attack and defense of trained soldiers by 5%. <u>*Requires a barracks.</u>* ***UNAVAILABLE!***
4) ***Construction I.*** *Cost: 132 Research Points. Successful research*

increases building speed and building durability by 5%. *<u>*Requires a workshop.</u>*

- *This Tech provides new blueprints!*
    - ***Mason's Shop (level 1):*** *When built, will decrease waste and increases efficiency when quarrying stone. Increases usable yield of local quarries by 10%. Increases productivity when quarrying stone by 10%.*
    - ***Logging Camp (level 1):*** *When built, will decrease waste and increase efficiency when logging. Increases usable yield of local wooded areas by 10%. Increases productivity when harvesting forests by 10%.*

5) ***Enchantments I.*** *Cost: 61 Research Points. Successful research opens the possibility of learning, altering and creating basic enchantments.*
6) ***Astronomy I.*** *Cost: 52 Research Points. Successful research will give a basic idea of the movement of the stars, planets, and other cosmic bodies.*
7) ***Basic Spell Theory I.*** *Cost: 56 Research Points. Successful research will provide a basic understanding of the magic of the Basic Elements and ley lines.*
8) ***Metallurgy II.*** *Cost: 214 Research Points. Successful research will decrease the amount of metal needed to make arms and armor by 5%. (Tech advanced by one level due to inherent knowledge of villager in the Job: Smith)* *<u>*Requires access to smithy</u>.*

The Metallurgy sphere was the only one of the eight that was glowing. Apparently, the techs lit up when they had been 'researched.' It seemed that Krom, in addition to having the practical skills of a blacksmith, also understood the science of Metallurgy to a certain extent. Since the dwarf's designation as having a village Job was mentioned, it seemed that assigning people to various positions had more importance than Richter had originally thought.

Richter examined techs that branched off of Metallurgy:

1) ***Alloy I.*** *Cost: 202 Research Points. Experiment with new combinations of metals to increase their capabilities. Successful*

*research will increase the likelihood of forming new alloys. This tech also increases the durability and either attack or defense of new alloys by 10%. *Requires: Access to smithy + whichever metals need to be experimented with. **Metals used in this research will be slowly consumed.*

2) **Smelter I.** *Cost: 254 Research Points. Increased heat in the smelter allows for greater malleability of worked metals. Successful research will increase production speed of forged items by 10%.*
3) **Smithing Tools I.** *Cost: 207 Research Points. Better tools increase the chance of a higher quality product. Successful research will increase the chance of your smiths to create arms and armor of higher qualities.*

All of the techs could be useful and beneficial to Krom. Best not to tell the dwarf about these research options, Richter thought with a smile. His smith wouldn't stop hounding him, especially for the Smithing Tools I tech. The chaos seed wasn't rejecting the idea of pursuing this research branch, but he wanted to explore his options before he committed. Richter examined the portal tech and the research that branched off of it.

1) **Portals IV.** *Cost: 2,302,583 Research Points. At level three, you are able to build a portal that can be linked to the same number of portals as ley lines in the immediate vicinity. The receiving portals must be built upon ley lines that mirror those which the home portal is built upon. Successful research of Portals IV allows receiving portals to be built upon any type of ley line.*
2) **Local Portals I.** *Cost: 67,956 Research Points. This tech unlocks the blueprint for local Portals. Local portals are linked to a home portal and only allow travel between these two points. This ignores the limitation of portals being built a minimum of 50 miles apart. Local portals do not count against the maximum number of portals that can be linked to your home portal. At level one of this tech:*
    a. *Local portals can be built within a ten-mile radius of the home portal.*
    b. *One local portal can be created per ley line present.*
    c. *A traveler can enter the home portal and arrive at the local platform. Travel is not possible from the local portal*

back to the home portal.

3) ***Pedestal Activation I****. Cost: 32,743 Research Points. The process of placing and removing an activation key to control the workings of a portal can be laborious and time-consuming. The creation of a pedestal key will greatly streamline this process. The creator of the pedestal can assign varying access rights to individuals or allow unrestricted access.*
4) ***Microportal I****. Cost: 58,311 Research Points. Learning this tech unlocks the blueprint for microportals. Microportals are devices that will give instant transport back to the home portal the device is linked with. At level one of this tech:*
    a. *The maximum distance this device can be used is five hundred miles.*
    b. *You must be in close proximity to a ley line of the same type that the portal is built upon.*
    c. *Individuals and objects within five feet of the microportal user can be transported as well.*
    d.

Richter's eyes bulged slightly as he read about each tech that was available to him through his knowledge of the Portals. Building a portal had always been high on his agenda, but now it was skyrocketing. He had actually started to lay the groundwork for building one, but there were factors that were stopping him.

Prompts had appeared that told that building a portal required a level of technical expertise. Both a Construction skill of forty-seven and a Crafting skill of eleven were required. The prompt had indicated that he could work under a builder of the appropriate skill, so Roswan could handle the Construction half of the requirement. Richter himself would have to assemble the various items that formed the portal, though. Because of this, he had been devoting at least an hour each night to working with Gloran and learning the skill, Crafting.

The elf only knew how to construct a few rings and bracelets, and sadly, was too low in both the Crafting and Enchanting skills to teach Richter how to make magic items, but still Richter had learned to make simple rings. He had started carrying coils of high steel wire around with him to make braided rings and bracelets in his spare time. It was monotonous, but it had allowed him to slowly increase his Crafting skill.

*Congratulations! You have reached skill level 3 in **Crafting**. +3% Enchantment Potential. +3% Success in combining components.*

Even if he had the requisite skills, Richter wasn't sure that he could afford to make a portal yet. From talking with Randolphus about the materials, it was going to cost him roughly four thousand gold to build a single portal. If the chamberlain's records were correct, which they always were, he had about forty-four hundred gold in hard coins. The chamberlain said that the jewels he possessed should be worth another twenty to thirty thousand gold and the Tefonim jewelry would hopefully sell for another several thousand gold, but Randolphus stressed the word "should." The last easily tradeable good Richter had were the kobold coins. The common ones were worth another five thousand or so, and there were also dozens of Dark Khan coins that Randolphus said should sell from anywhere between one hundred and one thousand gold each.

The problem was that the village was in a forest, weeks away from civilization. If they had to rely on Abbas, Randolphus warned that they would take heavy losses both in buying and selling. The best idea would be to make a trading expedition personally, but they would need Shiovana's ship to do that. The elvish woman said it was still weeks away from completion. The conclusion was simple. If Richter wanted to build the portal, they would have to leave the safety of the forest. With the threat of the bugbears, goblins, and worsening monster attacks, this was not a decision to be made lightly.

After the conversation, Richter shook his head, frustrated. Barely a month before, he had delighted in the fact that that he was rich, and by the standards of Earth or The Land, he had been right. Now that he was looking at his wealth through the lens of needing to build up his settlement, though, and not simply one man's finances, the truth was that he didn't have that much. One thing became abundantly clear: he needed to work on his village's economy.

Richter looked regretfully at the advanced portal techs a final time and realized that between the high research costs and the practical difficulties of even building a portal, he couldn't justify researching them yet. He closed that prompt and read the last waiting notification.

Know This! As Master of a Place of Power, you are granted one base research point per day for each magic that comprises your node of ley lines.

Richter closed the prompt. The math was pretty easy. It meant that at baseline, his village would earn four research points a day. The question was, how many research points had he earned by this point? Richter opened the town interface and quickly found the science tab.

Available Research Points (RP): 436
Daily Earned Research: 4.48 RP/day

1) **1 Point per Ley Lines:** 4 Total
2) **0.1 Points per level of Research Skill*:** 0.00
   Normal research restrictions apply

Research Rate Modifiers: +12% rate for House of Scholarship (level 1)

Richter examined the information in the prompt. He was happy that he had been earning research points, or RPs, since he had claimed the village, though it was a bit of a shock that he had been the Master of his Place of Power for more than a hundred days. The time had flown by. He got lost in reviewing everything that had happened to him for a moment, but then focused back on the task at hand. With four hundred and thirty-six RPs, he should be able to power through at least one or two of the low-level techs. How he would ever earn enough to research one of the portal techs, he had no idea, but at least this was a start.

Richter didn't understand how the Research skill came into play. He also didn't want to start researching something when, if he made another choice, an even better tech might be revealed down the line. Fortunately, both of the Scholars had immediately entered their new building. He walked over to where they were already arguing good-naturedly about who got the 'good' room.

"Bartle, Bea, I need a moment," Richter said.

"My lord?" Bea asked.

"Of course, Lord Richter," Bartle said promptly.

"I am trying to choose the first tech for the village to research now that we have this new building. Most of the tech tree that I can see is greyed out, though. I thought you two could tell me what is available after I research these initial techs." Richter ran through the sciences that were available for research.

Bartle didn't interrupt, but when Richter stopped his recitation, the Scholar shook his head, "I am afraid we will not be able to be of much help, my lord. The question of what lies in the Fog of Knowledge has plagued wise men and kings for millennia."

Richter could hear the special emphasis Bartle placed on "Fog of Knowledge." Bea was nodding his head and spoke up as well, "Yes, Lord Richter. The problem is that the tech tree changes for each settlement and race that is pursuing research."

The chaos seed furrowed his brow and sighed. Everything just *had* to be difficult. He motioned for the Scholars to continue.

"Neither I, nor Bea, are experts in the field of research, despite being Scholars," Bartle started. "We both focused on the scribing arts, though I do have a skill level of twenty-three in Research. Bea has…,"

"A skill level of seventeen," the other Scholar supplied.

Bartle picked up where he had left off, "The reason no one can know what is hidden in the Fog of Knowledge is that it varies based on multiple factors. The location of your village, the presence of ley lines, the buildings which have been constructed, the resources in the general area, and many other considerations affect what technologies can be discovered. Sometimes even the time of year that research is being done will change what techs are available. Many branches of research can only be studied by a specific race. For instance, I have heard of a tech called Ambient Particles that can only be learned by star elves. It opens a path of unique magic for their people."

"Okay, I think I follow you," Richter said, though it still didn't make sense to him why one type of person could research something that another group could not. That was the entire point of science. It was immutable and indiscriminate. Of course, that was based upon his view of Earth science. The same science that would say waving his hand and speaking an incantation shouldn't make fire shoot from his fingers, but Richter had definitely been lighting bitches up.

Ultimately, he decided not to pull too hard on the logic thread. Scientists back home couldn't even explain how a bumblebee could fly. Besides, he now thought that he understood about how his Limitless ability was coming into play with the village's research. His people had the chance to learn techs that had previously only been available to specific races. It might give his village a real edge in the future. There was one more question he needed to ask, "I still don't understand how the Research skill translates into research points."

"That is actually easy to explain," Bea answered. "Anyone with the Research skill can contribute to the research points for a settlement. Each skill level equals one tenth of a research point."

Richter nodded. It seemed straight forward enough. It didn't explain the asterisk, though; that had spoken about 'restrictions.' "Is there anything else to it?"

"As with all things, my lord," Bea answered, "there are many factors that can affect the final amount of research generated, but there is one other thing that I believe you should know now. The rank of a researcher determines how much total research can be generated in a given span. Novices, for instance, no matter how many are working on a given tech, can only generate ten research points per day in a level one settlement like this. You cannot decipher the secrets of the universe with one billion level one researchers. Certain buildings or techs can alter that limit somewhat, but a good rule of thumb is that each rank has an upper limit that is ten times as large as the rank below it. Both Bartle and I are initiates in the Research skill, so our maximum contribution would be one hundred RPs per day, though we are obviously well shy of that goal. It advances from there until you reach the rank of master. With enough master researchers, you could theoretically generate a million research points each day towards a specific tech. As far as I know, however, there are no master researchers on the entire River Peninsula."

"The other point I would add," Bartle said, "is that the RPs generated by researchers are only a potential daily yield. Having someone who has the research skill, but is spending their days as guardsmen will not aid in discovering new techs. It takes several hours of work each day for a person to generate their maximal research points, and that amount of time varies depending on the many factors, such as the researchers familiarity with a given topic of study." His lips twisted in mild distaste, "That is why both Bea and I focused on scribing instead." Bea nodded vigorously. The fact that neither Scholar liked doing research was obvious.

Richter heaved a big sigh when he saw that, "Sooooo, here's what I'm going to need you to do..." The Scholars listened to him attentively, but as he spoke, both their faces and their spirits fell.

CHAPTER 42 -- DAY 127 -- KUBORN 17, 15368 EBG

There was a great deal of wailing and gnashing of teeth, but ultimately the scribes bent to Richter's will. They both agreed to make research their primary responsibility each day. A quick check of tech window showed that the number of daily research points had increased.

Total Research Points (RP): 436
Daily Earned Research: 8.96 RP/day
1) **1 Point per Ley Lines:** 4 Total
2) **0.1 Points per level of Research Skill*:** 4.0
*Normal research restrictions apply
Research Modifiers: +12% for House of Scholarship

Randolphus was present, helping to coordinate the last minute needs of the scholars. After a quick check of the Knowledge Tablet, the chamberlain said that there were twelve other villagers, most of them arcane gnomes, that were listed as having the Research skill. Richter grimaced at hearing how few of his people could advance the village's pursuit of technology. Randolphus told him that the small number was not surprising. He further explained that it would be rare for anyone to even be tested for the skill, so more villagers might have it and simply did not know.

As soon as Richter heard that, he made a proclamation. Every villager, including the children, was to be tested for an affinity in Research. Randolphus then asked a question that gave him pause, though. "Should people be forced into research if they want to do a different job, my lord?"

Richter waffled on that for a moment, but only for a moment. He wouldn't be running a forced labor camp, but he also wasn't offering a free lunch. "Anyone already pursuing a specific position can remain in it, but make it clear that incentives will be offered if they would like to switch. Any of the dozens of unskilled villagers that are getting a wage, though, will be assigned under the Scholars." He didn't think it would be a hard sell seeing as how the unskilled villagers were normally used for the dirtiest, and smelliest, duties.

Richter gave the Scholars one more responsibility, the education of the village's children. Every child from the age of six to the age of maturity, fourteen, was to attend classes for three hours every morning until the noonday meal. Any adults that were not otherwise occupied were also welcome to attend the classes, regardless of age. Richter said he would leave the specific topics to be covered in the hands of the scribes. He also said that they were welcome to have other villagers lead the classes as guest lecturers. The Scholars were given permission to say that Richter 'strongly recommended' that other villagers cooperate. Surprisingly, both Bea and Bartle seemed intrigued by this latest duty, though they were still not happy about having to do research every day.

Before he left, Richter decided to sweeten the pot. He took a folded piece of paper out of his Bag of Holding. They watched him while he slowly unfolded it, and then their eyes widened when they saw that it was a copy of the rubbing he had gotten from the runes near the Dark magic portal. Both Scholars immediately forgot about their reservations and started pouring over the two sheets of paper. They both knew that they would have to advance in various techs before they could formally research Runes, but having a tangible reminder of the knowledge that could one day be at their fingertips lit a fire in them. Richter left the two men with a smug smile, feeling confident that they would do what was needed to drive research in the village.

All that remained was to decide what branch of research to pursue. For Richter, it was pretty much a no-brainer. He chose to play to the village's strengths, namely, his Core buildings and his own ability to enchant. The chaos seed made his choice. A bright light appeared in the sky and a white beam descended onto the house of scholarship.

Know This! Anyone relevant who belongs to your settlement will now be able to access this information!

Congratulations! You have researched: ***Smithing Tools I.*** *Smiths in your settlement will now have an increased chance to make higher quality weapons and armor.*

You now have ***229 Free Research Points*** *available.*

You have unlocked new research!

Smithing Tools II. *Cost: 396 Research Points. Refine the tools used to create the weapons of your people. Successful research will increase the chance of your smiths to create arms and armor of higher qualities.*

Two more techs were revealed branching off of Smithing Tools II, and the fog rolled back.

Keen Edge I. *Cost: 362 Research Points. Edged weapons created by your smith will have 5% better armor penetration.*

Improved Balance I. *Cost: 426 Research Points. Your smiths will learn to make weapons with better balance. Attack speed on anyone using these weapons will be improved by 5%.*

More filaments stemmed from these two sphere and the Smithing Tools globe lit up. Part of Richter wanted to stop there, but he decided to take a chance on a tech that might show great dividends.

Congratulations! You have researched: ***Astronomy I.*** *Your people now have a rudimentary understanding of the movement of the stars, planets, and other cosmic bodies.*

You now have ***177 Free Research Points*** *available.*

You have unlocked new research!

Astronomy II. *Cost: 105 Research Points. Successful research will give your people a basic idea of how to predict the movement of the stars, planets, and other cosmic bodies.*

You have completed a Settlement Quest: **My God! It's Full of Stars I!**
You have obtained a rudimentary understanding of planetary bodies. As this was a Settlement Quest, your Administration skill increases.
Rewards:
625 experience (base 1,000 x 1.25 x 0.5) points.
+5 village-wide Loyalty.
Additional +5 Loyalty from Krom.

Congratulations! You have reached skill level 9 in ***Administration****. +9% to Morale, Loyalty, and Production for your village.*

Richter had hoped that the tech would resolve the quest. He looked at the prompt and saw that two more spheres were revealed as the Fog of Knowledge was pushed back. The first didn't interest him too much, but the next one made Richter want to do a happy dance. The Scholars stared at him because he decided to take a minute and actually dance!

Astrology I: *Cost: 117 Research Points. Obtaining this tech will give a rudimentary understanding of how the movements of the cosmos can predict events in The Land.*

Forge of Heavens: *Cost: 138 Research Points. This technology will unlock a branch of research that is specific to your Core building, the Forge of Heavens. (Unique)*

Congratulations! Through your pursuit of knowledge, you have discovered a ***Unique Tech****! Dedication to this line of research will give benefits that are exclusive to your Settlement!*

Richter couldn't buy the second tech fast enough.

You now have ***39 Free Research Points*** *available.*

You have unlocked new research!

Learn Enchantments I (Forge of Heavens): *Cost: 294 Research Points. This tech will increase the chance of the Forge learning new enchantments by 5%*

Predict Auspicious Times I (Forge of Heavens): *Cost: 320 Research Points. The tech will provide knowledge of specific dates and times to forge weapons and armor to obtain extra effects.*

Elementum Bonus to Spell barriers I (Forge of Heavens): *Cost: 438 Research Points. This tech will increase the spell barrier penetration of Forge of Heaven Weapons by 20%.*

Elementum Bonus to Spell Resistance I (Forge of Heavens): *Cost: 437 Research Points. This tech will increase the spell resistance given to each piece of armor by 20%.*

More filaments branched off all of the new research spheres. It was a bit frustrating to not be able to afford any of these new techs, but it was also exciting to see the new possibilities. He chose Predict Auspicious Times I and a prompt appeared.

You have 39 free research points available. Once they are assigned to a specific tech, they cannot be redistributed. Do you wish to assign these points to ***Predict Auspicious Times I (Forge of Heavens)****? Yes or No?*

Richter reaffirmed his choice.

The Mist Village has begun research on ***Predict Auspicious Times I (Forge of Heavens).*** *Progression 39/320 RPs. Predicted time to completion: 31 days, 8 hours, 38 minutes and 24 seconds.*

Know This! Any future research must be invested directly into a specific tech. Further free Research Points may be earned in various ways.

Now he was cooking! Richter did a fist pump. Then in response to the Scholars' confused looks he described what a fist pump was. One thing was now clear to the chaos seed, research had to be a priority. A smile crossed his face as a cherished childhood memory rose in his mind. Knowledge is Power!

CHAPTER 43 -- DAY 133 -- KUBORN 23, 15368 EBG

The healer's hut was built only a few days after the house of scholarship. Roswan had been right that building with wood was much faster than building with stone. Despite the building's "hut" rank, it was still helpful.

Know This! You have built a fully functional ***Healer's Hut****. Your settlement will now enjoy the Building Bonus of increased village Health and other healing bonuses from having such a building.*

Healer's Hut. *Durability: 1,060/1,060. Building Quality: Well-built. Building Bonus: +6% village Health. +6% disease prevention. +6% recuperation speed after injury.*

You have been completed a Quest: **House of Healing I**.
You have provided a Healer's Hut for your people and for Sumiko. The Life master's "request" has been for the good of the village and definitely for your good. The fail condition for this quest was "haranguing" on a daily basis from the healer. Though you would not admit it, you are happy to avoid her sharp tongue and bony poking fingers.
Rewards:
1,250 (base 1,000 x 1.25) experience.
Village-wide Loyalty +5 (+10 for healers).
+100 Relationship Points with village healers.

The healer's hut and the house of scholarship weren't the only change to the village infrastructure. Roswan started moonlighting on his own recognizance. As the village Builder, he had access to the workshop's interface and had apparently taken the *poorly made* quality of the ship cradle as an affront. On the same night that the workshop had been finished, he rounded up several of the villagers who had the Construction skill along with more than one hundred mist workers.

Shiovana had apparently been sleeping on the half-finished boat when some of the mist workers lifted it up and carried it to the side while the rest demolished the wooden cradle. A few of the guards had heard her screaming in rage and had run forward to help but stopped once they saw the comedic scene of the short elf maid shouting down at Roswan and the other builders. The mustached elf had just ignored her and went about constructing a *well-built* ship's cradle to replace the 'bundle of sticks assembled by a blind shit eater' as Roswan called the original ship berth.

Shiovana had let go of her initial irritation and had become ecstatic when she saw the quality of the building that was being made for her. That goodwill apparently disappeared again after Roswan had commented so harshly on her earlier efforts. Richter decided to stay out of all of it and was just happy with the results.

Ship Cradle*. (wooden) Durability: 1039/1039. Building Quality: Well Built. Building Bonus: +6% Shipbuilding speed bonus. 0.6% bonus to ship stats.*

It wasn't a level one building, so the bonus was meager, but it was still an improvement. When Terrod heard about Roswan's willingness to take on smaller projects, the captain asked for a favor. After the ship's cradle had been completed, Roswan started a new pet project creating simple wooden towers that were twenty feet high. They each stood on four legs that were buried at least a yard into the ground and had a small platform. Four reinforced wooden walls topped the platform, and a simple roof sat atop it. The towers greatly increased the line of sight of anyone in the crow's nest, and it also gave a shielded location for archers to fire down on enemies. With the abundance of raw materials, Roswan was able to create one or two per night.

Richter was more than pleased. The village was operating with a well-oiled efficiency and his own skill progression advanced daily. Nothing really disrupted the flow of events until one overcast morning. He was eating a handful of berries when a mass of pixies flew towards him sounding extremely agitated and speaking all at once. The high pitched sounds hurt his ears, and it took Elora to calm them down.

"They all say that their meitu'meidons are close."

"All of them?" Richter asked, surprised. Usually, the sprites only approached in groups of two to three.

Elora nodded, "They also agree that they are approaching from the south."

Richter turned his head to look in that direction despite knowing that he wouldn't be able to see anything. After a moment, he grinned. He had a feeling that he knew what was going on. He walked over to give an order to Randolphus.

Terrod and Sion had been eating with him when the pixies arrived and had heard everything he had. With a nod of his head, the two moved off. Terrod to gather the guards and Sion to gather the meidon sprites. His Companion had become the impromptu leader of the bonded sprites, which Richter thought of as a good thing.

One thing that had become obvious since more forest sprites had emerged from their meidons was that there was a bit of friction between the forest and the wood sprites. Both Sumiko and the other sprite guard Hisako had left behind had been seen arguing with their more woodsy cousins. From what Richter could gather, the wood sprites thought the forest sprites were uncultured and uncivilized, and the forest sprites called the wood sprites, *heoltea*. It loosely translated to 'city boy,' but they said it with a dismissive twang that, back on Earth, only someone who had gone cow tipping could pull off. Sion was able to bridge the gap, being a woodsprite, a meitu'meidon and the son of the Hearth Mother. Needless to say, Richter was glad his Companion was there to smooth ruffled feathers. HR had never been his strong suit.

Ten minutes after Elora spoke to Richter, a war party was formed and waiting at the gate. Richter had a strong hunch on what they were about to find, so he handed out Potions of Clarity to all the members of the war party. After that, they headed out of the gate.

Richter took only one of the pixie children with him as a guide. That had caused the expected tantrum in the other fifty or so pixie children, but the fact that so many sprites were coming at once meant they were probably in a group, so only one pixie was needed to find them. Richter didn't want to risk having dozens of the flying children in the wild at once. The small celestials weren't without power, but all it would take would be a swooping hawk to end one of their lives.

The war party had to travel the entire way to the edge of the mists before they found the sprites. Richter crossed out of the hazy enchantment and walked to the top of a hill. What he saw brought a broad smile to his face. Just as he had thought and hoped, Richter saw Hisako's war band. Approaching from less than a mile away, there was a host of sprite warriors at least three hundred strong. Several sprites at the front rode what looked like abnormally muscled stags. At their head was Hisako and Yoshi.

"Greetings, Hearth Mother!" Richter shouted, waving.

Hisako smiled back and rode closer, "Greetings, Lord Richter." He walked down to meet her. When he got close, the deer she was riding grew unsettled, but she calmed it with a touch. His *Analyze* skill identified it as a 'strike stag.' The Hearth Mother reached out a hand, and he gently took it and kissed the back. Her smile broadened, "I ask permission to bring my warriors into your domain."

Richter raised his voice so that everyone could hear him, "The people of the Hearth Tree are always welcome in the Mist Village." Scattered cheers met his pronouncement. The sprite warriors stood erect, but they had clearly had a hard time. More than one wore severely battered armor. "I invite you all to join us for respite and relaxation." He turned to Hisako, "I will give your fighters immunity to the mists, but while I do, I would like to introduce you to someone."

Sion walked up behind Richter and smiled at his mother. She looked at his face, and her mouth dropped open in shock. "Sion? Is it you? Were the legends really true?"

Richter's Companion helped his mother down off of her steed. She reached up to touch his face in wonder before embracing him. Richter smiled and started selecting each of the sprites to give them immunity to the village's protective enchantment. Soon, all three hundred moved back towards the village. For once, Richter had almost no fear moving through the forest. Animals and monsters made way in front of the large force. The one exception was an attack by an undead creature called a barrow beast. It lunged up from a fold in the ground as the host approached. On reflex, Richter used *Analyze*.

Name: Barrow Beast	**Level:** 4	**Disposition:** Enmity
STATS		
Health: 140	**Mana:** 20	**Stamina:** 140
ATTRIBUTES		
Strength: 9	**Agility:** 7	**Dexterity:** 9
Constitution: 14	**Endurance:** 14	**Intelligence:** 2
Wisdom: 3	**Charisma:** 1	**Luck:** 10
DESCRIPTION		
Barrow Beasts are zombies created from the bodies of predators. They are often formed by simply being in the presence of other undead or are created accidentally by exposure to ambient Death magic.		

Richter barely had time to read the prompt before the creature was destroyed. There was a reason the other monsters were smart to avoid the armed party. Five imbued arrows impacted against the barrow monster as soon as it appeared and destroyed it utterly. All that was left were gobbets of decaying flesh and a filthy rib cage. The pace of the group didn't even slow. Despite the very minor threat of the attack, Richter was bothered by the presence of the undead creature. Hisako met his eyes, and he could see that she was discomforted as well.

"Have you seen more of these foul creatures?" she asked him.

"As you warned, monsters and dangerous beasts are becoming more common around the village. Over the past two weeks, though, there have been several sightings of undead creatures. I have had to deal with several of the spirits myself as conventional weapons don't seem to work, but outside of an initial encounter, there haven't been any major threats."

"Have the undead been appearing during the day like this?" she queried further.

"Most of the encounters are at night, but a few have been during the day," he answered

Hisako's face adopted a grave expression, "We will need to discuss this further. Seeing a creature like this during the day may bode ill for the future. It is possible there is a further threat we are not aware of."

Richter immediately thought of the Death portal and the eldritch magician. Part of him didn't want to believe that there was now yet another danger to deal with, but the timing was too coincidental. Still, he hoped he was wrong, "Maybe we just startled it awake from where it had been hiding during the day?"

Hisako nodded slowly, but from her expression, she remained doubtful. Then she looked at Sion, though, and an expression of love and affection crossed her face. She let the matter drop for the moment. The rest of the trip was uneventful, and soon they crossed into the village.

It had been several hours since they had left and night had fallen. Thankfully, the order Richter had given to Randolphus had been carried out. Suspecting that they would have a great deal of company, the chaos seed had ordered a feast to be prepared. More impromptu tables were set up, and they had been laden with meats, fruits, and nuts from the village stores. Many of the sprites started grinning at seeing the banquet that had been prepared, but a good many still strode inexorably towards the hill leading to the northern meadow. Richter knew he could not stop the meitu'meidon from going to find their pixie counterparts. He also thought he knew an even better way to revitalize the sprites than food and drink.

"My sprite allies," Richter said, raising his voice. "You are welcome to all of the hospitality the Mist Village has to offer. Before breaking your fast, however, please come with me. I promise you will not be disappointed." He started walking, and all of the sprites filed after him. Richter heard some of the fighters complaining in spritespeak, mostly centering around what kind of dick would show hungry men food and then not let them eat. The chaos seed just smirked and kept walking. He knew the naysayers would be quiet soon enough.

They reached the top of the hill, and many of the sprites got their first view of the Quickening. Just as Richter had predicted, they all forgot their grumblings, and many started to run forward until they remembered themselves and stayed behind the Hearth Mother. Yoshi and Hisako kept their decorum and remained with Richter. The statuesque sprite didn't look back at her riled up troops, but from the wry twist to her mouth, Richter wouldn't have been surprised if she was taking a perverse pleasure in having her fighters chomping at the bit.

As they approached the Quickening, something magical happened. Dozens of pixies flew out from the white leaves of the celestial tree. Their colorful wings stood in stark contrast to the cream-colored canopy and in front of all her children flew the queen herself. Beneath the flurry of pixies stood the other fifteen meidon sprites that had emerged from the silver shells so far. Those changed by the Quickening under the wondrous tree, a small promise of a wondrous future to come.

The sprites with Hisako all went down on one knee as they observed what, until very recently, would only have been considered an impossible miracle. Pixies had returned to The Land, and not only that, they had become celestial. A Quickening existed on their plane and most important, meitu'meidon were in the world again. Alma flew down to rest on Richter's shoulders as the sprites looked on in wonder.

It was Elora who broke the spell. She flew down to hover in front of Hisako. The Hearth Mother looked at the pixie queen and said, "You have changed much, since last we spoke. Our bows and magic are yours, my queen." Then the sprite leader bowed deeply.

Elora curtsied in midair and said, "The love of the sprites is a treasure beyond measure. Please come and hear our song." And with that, the Hearth Mother and the pixie queen crossed under the white bows of the Quickening to hear a song of rebirth and wonder.

CHAPTER 44 -- DAY 139 – KUBORN 29, 15,368 EBG

Another fifty-three sprites formed connections, leaving Elora and six other sprites the only ones who had not formed the bond. When Richter asked her about it, she said that if her meitu'meidon had been born, then they would find each other in due time. Then she looked up at the silvered undersides of the Quickening's leaves and smiled in contentment. Once the last meidon was created, A prompt appeared.

Congratulations! You have completed a Quest: **Fate's Companion**
Greater than **90%** of the **101** celestial pixies have bonded to the sprites that carried the other half of their destiny. The forces of good in The Land rejoice! As you have seen, your role in bringing this wonder back to The Land has paid dividends. You are the Master of this Place of Power, the planter of the Quickening, and the Companion of the pixie queen. The fate of the celestial pixies is intertwined with your own. You will be rewarded with the experience promised, but you are further gifted with the True Reward of your chosen path! Stay true to yourself to continue the benefits!
True Reward: Fealty of the meidon sprites!
Further Reward: 17,156 experience. (base 9,700 XP for 100 meidons created + 17,750 XP for personally leading 71 meitu'meidon to their pixie counterparts).

Know This! You have received ***3,625 experience*** *(base 5,800) from your* ***Companion Sion*** *being a support member for the party that brought 58 meitu'meidon to their pixie counterparts.*

*Know This! You have received **3,625 experience** (base 5,800) from your **Companion Terrod** being a support member for the party that brought 58 meitu'meidon to their pixie counterparts.*

Richter smiled broadly. He hadn't really understood why the changed sprites had bent the knee when they emerged from the silver shells. It was now clear that they were driven to it by the magic of the meidon. For a moment, the chaos seed wondered if this was wrong somehow. Were the sprites and pixies being brainwashed into serving him? He didn't let such a potentially malicious thought take root, though. Hisako and the other sprites believed that the pixies led them to their destinies. Who was he to question that?

Richter looked around at the rest of the war party who had all received the seven thousand two hundred and fifty XP. Checking with Analyze, he found that every single member of the war party was at least over level ten now. His people were high fiving and laughing as they celebrated their rapid ascent. Richter received more than one prompt with a relationship increase as he dissolved the war party and told his people to celebrate.

The villagers weren't the only ones in great spirits. All of the sprites received the bonuses from the Song of Joy and Remembrance. Richter was pleased, if not surprised, that the bonus raised his personal relationship with every sprite by one or two levels. The chaos seed still didn't fully understand the importance of relationships, but it seemed to be a good thing to increase either way, so he wasn't complaining. Thinking about the importance of relationships made him broach a potentially sensitive topic with Hisako, namely the meidon sprites swearing fealty to him. The Hearth Mother being upset was the one potential downside he had foreseen stemming from the 'true reward' from his quest. He had to interrupt a joyous reunion between both her and Sumiko, but the two sprite women took it in stride and, thankfully, she waived his concerns away. Then, to his surprise, she embraced him.

"We all serve the forest," she said. "If my people feel the best way to do this is to swear fealty to you, then that is for the best. You should know, Lord Richter, that I would forgive you any slight, however. You have begun to heal my people."

Richter was relieved at hearing the Hearth Mother had such a magnanimous attitude but was confused by the healing she was referring to. When he asked, she looked at him consideringly for a moment, but then spoke. "I would not tell you this except that I view you as an ally, Lord Richter. I ask that you keep what I am about to tell you in the strictest confidence, for it is a secret of the sprite people." Richter assured her that he would, and she continued, "You may or may not have noticed, but wood sprites and forest sprites do not exactly get along. This was not always the case. Once, we were one people. We were neither *sorat'mota* nor s*orat'sur;* we were simply *sorat'shin.*"

Richter's Gift of Tongues ability easily translated the sprite-speak into 'wood sprites,' 'forest sprites,' and the last phrase as 'true sprites.' He nodded again and asked, "So you split into two peoples?"

Hisako shook her head sadly, "I wish that was the end of the tale. The sorat'shin have broken into more races than even I can say. Wave sprites, dune sprites, swamp sprites…" she sighed unhappily. "I do not believe there is anyone in The Land that truly knows how many races into which we have fractured. With the loss of the pixies so long ago, sprites across The Land were bereft. Where once only harmony existed, small disagreements between sprite enclaves grew into petty rivalries. These divisions worsened until we split into different groups with different ideologies. Over the millennia we have become different races. Each of us are less than what we could be together." There was a tone of loss and regret in her voice, but then she smiled. She embraced him again and said, "This is the first step in bringing the various sprite peoples into harmony again, and it is because of you."

A prompt filled Richter's vision.

You have been made aware of and completed a Secret Quest:
Unity of the Sorat'Shin I!
Your strong bond with Hisako, the leader of the wood sprites of the Hearth Tree, has convinced her to share a secret knowledge with you. The loss of pixies in The Land was a tragedy for all forces of good, but especially for the sprites. Without the race that helped guide their destiny, the sprites had fractured into disparate peoples. By bringing pixies back to The Land, you have completed the first step in bringing back the Sorat'Shin!

Rewards:
A boon from Hisako!
+10 skill levels to Imbue Arrow!
31,250 experience (base 50,000 x 1.25 x 0.5)
+ 1,000 Relationship Points with all sprite races that have been linked with their meitu'meidon. Current bonus in relationship, applies to Wood sprites and Forest Sprites.

Know This! A dramatic increase in your subskill, ***Imbue Arrow****, has caused an increase in the main skill!* ***+6 skill levels to Archery!***

Congratulations! You have reached skill level 12, 13, …, and 17 in ***Archery****. +34% bonus to aim. +34% bonus to damage.*

Congratulations! You have reached subskill levels 8, 9, …, and 17 in ***Imbue Arrow****. +85% magical damage. +85% speed of mana flow.*

Congratulations! You have advanced from Novice to Initiate in ***Imbue Arrow.*** *Energy transfer 20% more stable allowing for more energy to be imbued before improper arrow detonation. This is cumulative with successive ranks.*

You have received ***625*** *bonus experience (base 1,000 x 1.25 x 0.5) for reaching level 10 in the subskill:* ***Imbue Arrow****.*

You have unlocked a Secret Quest: **Unity of the Sorat'Shin II**
Continue to unite pixie and sprite meitu'meidon to help bring about the reemergence of the sorat'shin!
Success Conditions: Help five different races of sprites create meidons to fulfill this quest
Current count: 2 of 5
Fail Condition: Sharing this information with anyone other than a sprite
Rewards: Unknown
Penalty for failure or refusal of Quest: Decreased Relationship with all sprites
Do you accept? Yes or No

Richter hugged Hisako back even harder and accepted the quest. The sprite leader squawked slightly, but she soon chuckled, appreciating the bear hug in the joyous manner with which it was given. It looked like his good relationship with the wood sprites was continuing to pay dividends. Without such a strong connection Hisako probably would never have shared this part of the sprite's secret history, which had led to him finding a secret quest! It was kind of like helping an old lady across the street and *poof,* she turns into a sexy genie… and she likes Firefly!

He shook his head as he kept reading the prompts. Not only did the quest give a very respectable chunk of experience, but it also increased his relationship with *all* forest and wood sprites. One thousand relationship points was nothing to sneeze at. Richter and Hisako had the relationship rank of *Ally*, which meant they already had at least twenty-five thousand relationship points, so it didn't alter their interplay too much. The thousand was enough to push his relationship with any new wood or forest sprites from *Neutral* to *Interested* though, three full ranks up.

The boost in *Imbue Arrow* was amazing too. At skill level one, every ten mana Richter had invested in a strike increased the final damage by one, and he was able to store ten mana in the arrow every second. Now that he was level seventeen it meant that every ten mana increased the damage by almost two points, and he could transfer eighteen and a half mana per second. On top of that, he could put more mana into his arrows without risking them blowing up in his face. The real prize, though, as far as he was concerned, was the 'boon.'

Richter let go of Hisako and was preparing to ask about it, but she beat him to the punch, "If there is anything that I can do for you or your people. You only need to ask."

Richter put a thoughtful expression on his face, "I actually have something in mind…"

She motioned for him to walk with her. The two of them conversed as they moved back through the village. Yoshi walked behind them, not comfortable leaving Hisako unguarded and in the open, even behind the village's walls. He outlined exactly what he wanted and how it could benefit them both. At the end of his pitch, she told him that the resources of her people were not unlimited, but that if he handled his side of the proposal, then she would handle hers. She laughed a bit at seeing the relief on his face, but then her face firmed. The leader of the sprites started to fill him in on what had been happening in the war.

"We have had several battles with the bugbears," she reported in a serious voice. "We have had losses, but we have held the line. They dare not push too far into our territory because of our ability to hide in the forest and then strike quickly. More than one of their patrols has not returned because of sneak attacks with our imbued arrows. Still, their own abilities with concealment are not inconsiderable. My people are excellent at ranged combat, but have difficulty if they are drawn into a melee battle with the bugbears."

Richter nodded. He understood that she was making a profound understatement. As fierce as the sprites could be, they were still only three to four feet tall on average, built more for speed than strength. The bugbears that had attacked the village had all been at least six feet tall. Richter shuddered to think about what would happen to any sprite that got within weapons reach of the goblinoid creatures.

Hisako paused for a moment, and a look of sorrow crossed her face. When she spoke again, there was steel her voice, "Despite our losses, we will prevail. I can tell you now that we have discovered where their base resides. They are building a fortification in the wooded foothills of the Firetip Mountains."

"I am sorry for your fallen, my lady, but at least we now know where our enemy is located."

She nodded wearily, "The information came at a high cost. Of the four sprites sent to find the base, only one returned." Hisako shook herself, and spoke with steel again, "These matters are serious, but are still secondary to the more grave threat of the eaters. There are still mysteries about their unexpected appearance that I have not unraveled. I do not know why they have come decades before they should. I do not know why they are not currently overrunning the forest. I have learned one thing, however. Through a powerful divination, I was able to determine that their nest is deep underground. Through… less elegant methods, we have discovered that the kobolds have been fighting them."

"Less elegant?" Richter asked. Yoshi cleared his throat and then grinned wolfishly when he had the chaos seed's attention. "Enough said," Richter answered his own question.

"Yes," Hisako said, not squeamish at all about torture. "The information, unfortunately, has not availed us."

"Why not?"

"As loathsome as kobolds can be, there is no doubting their cunning. While a few of my warriors might cross unseen into their underground warrens, the preponderance of traps and twisting tunnels make a large assault almost impossible. Every entrance that we know of is so heavily defended that we cannot enter in force. According to the kobolds that we have captured, they are taking the swarm seriously, which is the only good news. The clans have even stopped their perpetual warfare to battle the eaters. The lizards we interrogated revealed that there have been heavy losses on both sides. This might be why we have not seen the eaters on the surface, which would be a boon." Hisako's resolve broke, and a bitter frustration made its way into her voice, "None of this information means anything if we cannot make our way down into the Depths. We have to destroy the queen."

As they had walked, Richter had led them to the catacombs and now they stood over the Great Seal. He looked pointedly at the stairway leading downward. With a broad grin on his face, he exclaimed, "You know, itt's funny you should say that."

CHAPTER 45 -- DAY 139 – KUBORN 29, 15,368 EBG

Yoshi, Hisako, and Richter went into one of the side rooms that had served as the Scholars old workspace. Both of the scribes had now moved into the house of scholarship. The room wasn't completely empty, however. It had taken weeks, but now Richter was the proud owner of a Knowledge Table.

One of the forest sprites coming to the village had told Richter about a stand of Yodan wood he had come across. It was fifteen miles from the village, but when Bea had heard about the *rare* trees, he had immediately insisted that they be harvested. Richter had taken a large group to retrieve several trees and took care to harvest a few of the saplings that were present as well. They had had to carry the trees themselves until they reached the mists, but then Richter had been able to summon mist workers to take over the burden. The trip had taken most of the day, but Richter had fulfilled his quest.

Congratulations! You have completed a quest: **Raw Materials**. You have found a wood capable of holding a large amount of sustained magical charge.
Rewards:
A Knowledge Table.
625 experience (base 1,000 x 1.25 x 0.5)

The experience Richter had gained was not much, but Bea had started working with carpenters the very next day. The green wood emitted a faint heat even when cut, and it required at least a Carpenter of apprentice rank or higher to work the wood effectively. Luckily, there was one wood elf with a skill level of thirty-four in Carpentry. Bea and the carpenter worked together for more than a week, but it was finally done. Richter now had a Knowledge Table, and all of the documents, maps and other data that could be uploaded, had been. He also negotiated to have Bea create another Knowledge Tablet at a substantial discount. The Scholar agreed for the sake of 'future positive relations.'

Richter placed his hand on the activation crystal to bring the green wood table to life. What had been a well sanded wooden top became a glowing white panel. He placed his hand on the side of the tile and willed his map to appear. As the Scholars had said, it was not a fully linked version of his Traveler's Map and the information was only as up-to-date as the last time it had been uploaded by Bea. It was still an incredible tool, though.

The first thing Richter did was to bring up a map of the forest. Then he zoomed out to be able to see the wood in its entirety. He needed to know where the bugbear encampment was. For a moment, Richter bemoaned the fact that the mapping ring he had given to Sion did not work as effectively for anyone that wasn't his Companion.

When his friend had placed the ring on, it had not only shown whatever the sprite was currently looking at; it also showed everywhere the sprite had been in his entire life. As was always the case with Traveler's Map, areas Sion had been to more recently were brighter, and locations the sprite hadn't been to in quite a while were only in grey scale. Nonetheless, it had greatly increased the cartography info on Richter's mental map.

He had tried to get other people to wear the ring since, but it had only added what that person was currently seeing to the map. The one other person that it had worked for in the same way was Terrod. Sections of black on the map were replaced to reflect the captain's travels. Specifically, Terrod had increased Richter's knowledge of the terrain in the Kingdom of Yves and in the capital city of Law to a great extent. That did not, unfortunately, help much with the topography of the forest. Asking Elora to wear the ring was out of the question because of her small size.

Still, Hisako was quickly able to point out where the main encampment was. Richter mentally annotated his own map with as many details as she could provide. He would have Bea update the table later that night. After that was done, he zoomed back to the village and showed Hisako and Yoshi the next level of the catacombs. The two sprites started intently pouring over the map, moving it themselves as they examined this tunnel and that. Yoshi even complimented Richter on the level of detail.

After some time had passed, Richter grew bored with watching them. Hisako and Yoshi seemed to have mostly forgotten his presence and were speaking quickly to each other in what seemed to be a sprite-speak shorthand. Yoshi had also pulled a large number of maps from his bag that looked to be sketches of other sections of Depths leading down from other entrances. It was no surprise to Richter that he had them. He knew from his own experience that *Weak Charm* could get enemies to spill their guts. He didn't even want to think about how strong of a charm spell Hisako could wield. His own spell would break if he attacked his target. The Hearth Mother could probably make a man eat his own flesh. He shuddered slightly when he thought about the horrible possibilities and hoped he never met an evil Life master.

Richter left the sprites to their plotting. He had other things to do after all. Before he made it to the door, Yoshi called over his shoulder, "We will do some sparring after dinner tonight. I hope you have been practicing your sword forms. I have been collecting stout sticks over the past few weeks to aid in your training."

Richter grunted. The 'aid' Yoshi had offered in the past was using a hard stick to spar with him. While that might initially seem like a better choice than a sword, it allowed Yoshi to break the sticks on various parts of Richter's anatomy. Something the half-sprite took a sick pleasure in. Still, Richter was no punk, "I appreciate your training offer, Adept Yoshi. I will see you after dinner." Richter got back to his daily routine. It was time to help the builders.

The next building that was being erected was one that was near and dear to everyone's heart, a tavern. In line with that goal, Richter made one stop before he went to help the crews. He had been checking on the copper still daily, and he had so far been able to distill over twenty bottles of moonshine. When he had first examined them, several prompts had appeared.

Congratulations! You have learned the subskill: ***Distillation****. This is a subskill of Brewing. Various combinations of plants, herbs, and fruits can create spirits of various strengths and properties. As you have learned this subskill, you have also learned the skill Brewing.*

Congratulations! You have learned the skill: ***Brewing****. "Beer is living proof that God loves us and wants us to be happy." You can now take the mundane, such as boring barley, and make something truly wondrous… Beer!*

You have created: ***Harsh Moonshine****. Durability: 7/7. Strength: Blackout. Sensation: Rough. Weight: 1.5 kg. +1 to Constitution, -2 to Agility, -1 to Dexterity. +15% to lyrical composition*

When Richter had first tasted the drink, he was forced to agree with the description on the prompt. It went down hard and, he couldn't be sure, but he was fairly certain his eyes crossed for just a moment. For some reason that thought made him think of one of his exes in Texas, but he couldn't figure out why.

Over the past several days, though, Richter had come to appreciate his vicious brew. He uncapped one of the bottles and took a swig. The liquid burned his throat but then gave him a nice, warm feeling inside. Recapping the bottle, he put it in one of the Cauldron's storage cubbies. Aside from being a recipe for fun, the moonshine was also part of a project for the chaos seed.

When the first batch had been completed, Richter had numbered each bottle. His intention was to test the Cauldron's property of increasing the traits of potions that were left to age. So every day he took a swig to gauge the progress of his experiment. His hope was that one day it would taste better than ass. It wasn't clear if the potions actually had to be left in the glass building or not, or even if the moonshine would be considered a potion, but who didn't want to do experiments like Mr. Wizard?

CHAPTER 46 -- DAY 140 – KUBORN 30, 15,368 EBG

The following morning disrupted his routine. It would have been more accurate to say that it derailed it completely and that the dawn brought not only sunlight but also a sense of fear and wonder that swept through the village. During the night, people had disappeared. No children were taken, but mothers, fathers, and elders were absent from their beds. Concern and terror swept through the village quickly.

Richter had stayed up late and had finally fallen asleep under the Quickening, so he was one of the last to know. The training with Yoshi had been predictably painful and humiliating, so he had sought comfort afterwards under the celestial tree. He, Elora and Hisako had spoken for hours before sleep claimed him.

He was awoken by a guardswoman shouting his name. Alma flew up into the air from her perch on his lap, and Richter scrambled to his feet. She quickly informed him that villagers were missing and how panic was spreading through the settlement. Richter ran towards the hill leading down to the village, regretting that he hadn't slept in his armor. By the time he got to the slope, Sion was running up it to meet him. The expression on the sprite's face was inscrutable.

"What? What is it?" Richter asked with major stress in his voice. He looked out over the village, the top of the hill providing an excellent vantage point. The sun was up and was peaking over the trees, and Richter didn't see any immediate threat of attack. The guards still patrolled the village walls, and the *Confusing Mist* defensive spell was still in place. Sion still hadn't spoken yet, but the corner of his mouth was tilting up. "What the hell man? What's happening?"

Sion looked at him and raised a placating hand, "First, everything is okay. I have already had Terrod start calming people down. I know exactly what is happening. Before I tell you any more, though, I need to know something." He looked at the piece of paper in his hand before sounding out a word, "What is a *cockgobbler*?"

The word sounded strange in Sion's melodic voice, but the meaning was still clear enough. Richter snatched the piece of paper from his friend and started reading. As the villagers began to calm down, his blood pressure began to rise.

Dear Richter,

Now that your friends, the sprites, are here, I see no reason not to start the Trials for any of your people who are eligible. I'm sure you will be upset about this. After all, cockgobblers never like to share…

It was all Richter could do not to tear the paper into small pieces. The tone of the letter became increasingly insulting and patronizing as he read. It was signed at the bottom.

Besties 4 Life,
Nexus

What the fuck had he done to deserve a being like Nexus, Richter wailed silently. Sion just stood there with a smarmy look on his face. Richter glared at him, and then said, "Come on, shithead." Richter started walking down towards the village, but Sion cleared his throat and arched an eyebrow. Richter rolled his eyes, "Fine! If you must know, a cockgobbler, or CG for short, is…"

Once everyone still in the village had been accounted for, Richter found out that Nexus had apparently taken people at various times throughout the night. The fact that no one else had seen it happen meant that the asshole Auditor had taken people when they were alone or when anyone else nearby must have been sleeping. Richter was seriously irritated and railed to anyone who would listen that it was just like the douchey cosmic being to pull people into their Trials in a manner that would maximize chaos in the village.

It took an hour to finally calm everyone down, and the final count was that twenty-seven people were missing. It probably would not have caused such a stir in a village of a population greater than six hundred in other circumstances, but as everyone stayed together in large longhouses, the panic had spread quickly.

Despite his irritation with Nexus's methods, Richter secretly admitted to himself that he was excited to see exactly what Professions his people came back with. He had been wondering about the fact that no one had gone for a trial after the last infusion of experience from the pixie's birth. He was slightly less excited when he found out exactly who had been taken: Roswan, Krom, Quasea, Zarr, Sumiko, Ulinde, Shiovana, Gloran, the entire nonhuman elder council, and several others. Productivity in the village effectively ground to a halt. Unsurprisingly, people were even more upset when Richter halted construction on the tavern. He wouldn't risk its quality being lower than what Roswan could create, though. Thankfully, Randolphus still remained behind, and he quickly organized the villagers to compensate the loss of so many village leaders.

Richter actually started thinking that freeing up his afternoons might be a good thing for a week, but as he was preparing his war party to leave for the daily hunt, Elora flew up to him with a small, Dark pixie boy in tow. At this point, the chaos seed was well familiar with the expression on the pixie child's face. Either the boy's meidon was coming close to the village, or he was doing a midair peepee dance. Richter was fairly certain that there was a sprite somewhere out in the mists.

The young pixie took up position in Richter's hood, and the chaos seed took his customary place at the head of the war party. Surprisingly, the pixie's directions led the war party to the east. Every other sprite that had been brought through the mists had come from the south or west. This hadn't been a surprise, as the Mist Village sat on the northern boundary of the Forest of Nadria and sprites were forest creatures. To the north were the Serrated Mountains and to the east lay the Azergoth Swamp. Miles of forest still lay to the east of the village, but nowhere near as much as the unbroken leagues of trees to the south and west.

Despite the strangeness of a sprite approaching from the east, Richter still followed the pixie's directions. The war party traveled quickly. Weeks of hunting had generated hundreds of additional war points. Richter's next purchase was a no-brainer. He paid one hundred and fifty points and bought *Lead by Example I.* In battle, Sion would scout, Caulder would fill the role of tank, and if Sumiko did indeed come with them to raid through the Dark portal, she would obviously be the healer. Otherwise, Krom would fill the role. With his latest purchase, Richter could now double in any of those roles. He had been right. He *had* become more badass!

Richter also bought a second rank of the badge *Movement Speed.* War parties that he led now traveled 20% faster through forests.

The way was made even easier with Sion scouting ahead and Alma flying overwatch. The shale adder continued to slide along beside its master. Richter had cast the spell *Tame* about twice a day for the past several weeks. The Blood magic casting ensured loyalty of the subject creature for forty hours, but Richter still used the spell as soon as the twelve-hour cooldown expired. The long cooldown meant that he had only progressed to level two in Blood Magic, but still it was progress.

His frequent use of *Tame* proved wise as the spell periodically failed to take root in the adder. Each time he reestablished control over the large snake, there was a thrum in his blood that was unmistakable. Eight times over the past several weeks, though, he had felt nothing. If he had waited until the spell was about to elapse to cast *Tame* in any of those instances, Richter would have found himself in battle with an enraged twenty-foot long predator.

The war party continued to move forward. After an hour, they found their first prey. The pixie child wanted them to press forward, of course, but when Sion came back stating he had found a herd of gynor elk, Richter called a halt. The sprite moved quietly, silent and almost unseen in his green armor. Hisako had enjoyed a laugh at the story before she resized the sprite armor with her magic. Sion was less than amused as Richter recounted the experience.

Sion hadn't even needed to relate any details of what he had seen thanks to the mapping ring and the fact that he was the war party's official scout. Sion had already tagged the enemies, so they appeared as red dots on the chaos seed's internal map, and red markers showed their position in everyone else's vision when they were close enough. Richter quickly showed everyone on the physical Traveler's map where the herd was and then had them all wait. Caulder immediately started giving hushed orders to make a basic defensive perimeter while Richter and Sion did more scouting. As had become protocol, the physical map was left with one of the other party members so they could see the distribution of enemies while he and Sion tagged any monsters the sprite had missed on his first pass.

Richter shooed the pixie child out of his hood and left him with one of the Life magi in the party. He warned the tiny flyer to stay away from the fighting in the strictest terms. The boy pouted and kicked his foot in midair, but he obeyed his liege. It was an interesting trait he had noticed about the small celestial beings. The pixies could be as mischievous as a child in a candy store, but at the end of the day, they followed Richter and Elora's instructions to the letter.

The two Companions moved forward, circling around the spot where Sion had seen the creatures. Richter had pulled the hood on his Cloak of Concealment up and activated *Stealth*. Alma flew above, her dark body a natural camouflage against the thick canopy above. The shale adder slid along beside Richter, silent and unseen. Ten minutes later, Richter got his first sight of the animals. In his mind, when he had heard Sion say 'gynor elk' he had imagined something that looked like bambi's uncle. When he finally saw the beasts, he realized… not so much.

The creatures were structurally similar to normal elk. Meaning that they stood on four legs and their heads were shaped like a deer's. Their antlers, however, were three feet long and were multipronged. Each tip ended in a wickedly sharp point. The gynor elk were covered in short brown hair that was almost black. Light green stripes of fur crisscrossed their bodies. Each was six feet tall at the shoulder, and large muscles stood out under their skin. As Richter moved closer, he saw that their hooves were wedged. The tips were hard and sharp enough to leave gouges in the flesh of the bear the beasts were feeding upon.

Red blood covered their muzzles as they reached their heads down and tore pieces of flesh and fur off of the bear. They snapped at one another when one got too close to another's feeding spot. Richter could see that their mouths were filled with sharp teeth and each had two large fangs in place of incisors. These were not peaceful herbivores. He was looking at deadly pack hunters.

There were five in all, and from the well-masticated state of the bear's carcass, they were almost done with their meal. Richter knew he couldn't let these things escape. He had a quick mental conversation with Alma who then flew, quick as an arrow, back towards Caulder. Her ability to have limited communication with others made coordination in the war party much easier. Reaching into his bag, he withdrew his bow and waited.

A few minutes later, the dragonling quietly alighted on a nearby tree branch.

They are coming, master. I will be ready when the rest of the war party gets close.

Thank you, love, Richter thought back. A grim smile crossed his face. The elk were about to have a bad time. Since his familiar had been hunting on her own, she had leveled three times over the past weeks. She had then distributed her own points in a way that Richter completely supported.

The first thing she had done was purchase the first rank of *Psi Channeling*. Psi Channeling was the newest addition to her abilities and offered extremely interesting possibilities. One of the biggest problems with his spells was that he had to be almost within striking distance to use them. If Alma could swoop past an opponent while unleashing a spell, though, it drastically increased his range. The greatly increased mana cost made the skill prohibitive, though.

Your familiar has chosen to increase her ability: ***Psi Channeling*** *to level 2. At level 2, the range of Psi Channeling has increased from one hundred to two hundred yards. Using the ability now requires 250% greater mana usage rather than 300%. Any other spell requirements will remain unchanged. You and your familiar may now also share mana at a loss of 3:1.*

The increase in distance and decrease in mana usage was pretty much what he expected. The ability to share mana was a welcome bonus, though. When he had gotten the prompt, he had realized that he didn't even know how quickly her mana regenerated. Unfortunately, her status page didn't show her individual stats like his did. Richter had reviewed his Life and Air spells, he had decided to test her regen rate.

Richter had told her to cast *Summon Weak Life Wisp*. The sixty point mana cost had made the math easy. She had cast the spell, and he had watched her regen closely. It took one hundred and one seconds for it to refill. He stopped a moment to do a quick calculation and figured out that her mana was refilling at a rate of around six points every ten seconds. It was faster than his own regen rate.

She hadn't stopped there though. Her *Psi Blast* was finally level three. It had improved upon her mental attack, and a new feature had been added. Richter had been thrilled when he had read the prompt.

Your familiar has chosen to increase her ability: ***Psi Blast*** *to level 3. The mental disruption and health damage are now more powerful. The 5-7 second stun effect is increased to 8-10 seconds, and the health damage will be more severe. A third effect is now added. There is a possibility of disorientation for those affected that will last up to five minutes at the standard AoE of 10 feet. The AoE of this attack can now be widened to 20 feet at the expense of the blast's strength or narrowed to three feet with an increase in the blast's effectiveness. Effective range of Psi Blast is now doubled compared to baseline. Cooldown decreased to three and a half minutes.*

With the beasts clustered together, Alma should be able to focus her psychic beam to its strongest effect. She flew up into the trees and waited to strike. The other party members made their way through the forest as quietly as possible, save the support team whose sole purpose was to protect Bea. Richter had been able to earn each Scholar one level in the last two weeks by channeling the 20% of the war party's experience to the noncombatants.

Even though they were trying to be quiet, most of the war party lacked woodcraft or stealth skills. Before they got within thirty yards of the elk, the pack lifted their heads in the direction of the advancing fighters and Richter could see them tense. Whether they then planned to attack or retreat, he would never know, because that was what Alma had been waiting for. In that split second of the elks' indecision, the dragonling dove from above and unleashed her *Psi Blast.* The psychic beam caught all five elk broadside, the energy passing easily through the flesh of one to strike the others.

The beasts fell to the ground, legs kicking spasmodically. Blood leaked from their nostrils and one bit through its own tongue as its body locked in rictus. Richter would never know how effective Alma's level three *Psi Blast* might have been if he had upgraded it earlier, but with her being a level twenty-nine creature, it packed a serious punch.

Richter dropped his bow as none of the elk had escaped and drew both swords. Alma landed on her master's shoulders, and her body was enveloped by a golden glow. His familiar cast *Soul Trap* again and again as Richter's sword rose and fell. He wasn't trying for fatal blows. Instead, he targeted the animals' leg muscles, ensuring that the elk would not rise even if they could fight off the effects of the *Psi Blast.* Sion was right beside him doing the same. The sprite had been through this process daily and knew what was required. Alma hopped down from Richter's shoulders with a feral shriek and started draining them. Her level seven *Brain Drain* dropped their health, stamina, and mana at a prodigious rate, and Richter helped by delivering coups de grace.

The last three elk awoke before they could be put down and started squealing as they tried to escape the butchery Richter and his familiar were delivering, but they could do little more than thrash about on the ground. Even that ceased when Alma latched on, her special psychic attack overcoming their conscious will. In less than three minutes, it was done.

His familiar shot into the air with a cry of triumph drunk on the psychic energy she had absorbed from the predatory animals. Richter smiled at her, enjoying the savagery of his familiar while the last swirl of rainbow light disappeared into his bag. Five more souls were now his to use as fuel for his enchantments. Those were not the only prompts he received.

You have been awarded ***2,716*** *experience (base 62,072 x 0.07 x 1.25 x 0.5) from Brain Drain against Level 11 Gynor Elk.*

You have been awarded ***1,468*** *experience (base 33,559 x 0.07 x 1.25 x 0.5) from Brain Drain against Level 8 Gynor Elk.*

You have been awarded ***1,937*** *experience (base 44,283 x 0.07 x 1.25 x 0.5) from Brain Drain against Level 9 Gynor Elk.*

You have been awarded ***919*** *experience (base 21,008 x 0.07 x 1.25 x 0.5) from Brain Drain against Level 7 Gynor Elk.*

You have been awarded ***1,135*** *experience (base 25,931 x 0.07 x 1.25 x 0.5) from Brain Drain against Level 8 Gynor Elk.*

*For slaying five **Gynor Elk**, you have been awarded 20 War Points!*
Total War Points: ***112**.*

Richter had a very good idea about how to spend his new war points. He would attend to that later, though. Now, there was a sprite to save. He looked around and saw that the war party had done as instructed.

When Alma had flown to communicate with Caulder, she had transmitted a single word, "Support." The sergeant knew that meant Richter and Sion would handle the kills, and the role of the war party was to protect them with a loose perimeter while they worked. The war party, including the auxiliary team, had fanned out in a circle around his position.

The melee fighters held shields and each was paired with a meidon sprite archer. The noncombatant was also always placed inside of the perimeter. The purpose of the other fighters wasn't to aid Richter, but instead to ensure that other predators didn't attack, drawn by the sounds of death and combat. Three times over the past several weeks, monsters and dangerous beasts had been drawn by the death cries of Richter's kills.

This time, there was no issue, however. Richter cut a piece of the elk free and threw the bloody chunk to his adder. The snake snapped the morsel up. He had been making an effort to spend time with and feed the snake. Initially he had asked if the twins were crazy. What he actually said was, "Why the hell would I play with a twenty foot snake?" He decided to trust them, though.

Richter wasn't sure if the twins' advice actually held any merit, but he had been able to quickly raise his Beast Bonding skill to level five, so he kept at it. Then he and Alma summoned mist workers to carry the bodies of the gynor elk as well as the bear's remains. In this world, the practice was 'waste not.' Even if the meat were tainted, the skin might still be of some use.

The grey figures trotted off to the west carrying the kills. It was always a possibility that another monster or beast might attack the mist workers, but it hadn't happened yet. When the only other options were to leave the carcasses or to make the mist workers travel with the war party, sending them back unattended really was the best choice. The war party continued on.

More predators crossed their path, but none were worth chasing down, so the fighters continued, led by the Richter and the pixie child. After a few hours, they were only a mile from the edge of the mists and Richter was starting to wonder if the pixie child might have been wrong. Then red dots began to appear on his mini-map.

Richter called a halt. Five minutes later, Sion dropped down from a tree branch directly in front of Richter. A look of utter disgust and anger was on the sprite's face. He didn't so much speak as spit a single word, "Goblins."

CHAPTER 47 -- DAY 140 – KUBORN 30, 15,368 EBG

"They are in the mist, and they are hunting someone. I don't know how they can see in the mists, but they can. I heard one of them speak in the common tongue. They have wounded a sprite, and now they are hunting him. We do not have time for more scouting; we have to go now!" Sion said urgently.

Richter's eyes flicked upward as he looked at his minimap. Sion had already spotted over twenty-five enemies in the mists. Who knew how many more there might be? Most of the goblins were still in a knot and the others Sion had spotted had not ranged far from the main group. That meant he could be missing any number of enemy scouts or advanced teams. Even another group of five enemies could be enough to turn the tide of a battle. Taking out beasts was one thing, but taking on an armed band was another. It was true the mists should protect their approach, but if Sion was right, the goblins had already found a way to defeat the village's enchantment.

Richter regretted not bringing Futen along with the war party. The remnant could have gone ahead invisibly and confirmed what Sion saw. It wasn't standard practice for Richter to take the orb with him on hunts. Futen was just too useful in the village, seeing as how he was the only other being, besides Alma, that could summon the mist workers. Richter had also decided that his war party needed to know how to make do without the remnant in case they had to venture beyond the mists. It was that same reasoning that had motivated him to have Terrod lead his own war party rather than make Richter's own war band larger. It all meant that his force was comprised of himself, Sion, the ten members of his war party, the five members of the auxiliary group, Bea and the pixie child. Facing a force that was possibly twice as large was not something he looked forward to.

Looking at Sion's face, though, he knew there wasn't really a choice here. The one thing he was glad of was that he had put his foot down and demanded that the meidon pixies stay behind during raids. It had caused arguments with the meidon sprites, but seeing as how they had all sworn fealty, it hadn't been a long discussion. Thankful for small favors, he started giving orders. Now was the time for action.

He pointed to three of the guards in the auxiliary squad. His orders came out clipped, and there was no question of argument, "You three stay with the Scholar. Retreat half a mile back towards the village. Stay in hiding unless you hear from one of us." The other two guards from the squad were Life magi, and he told them to support Caulder's strike force. He summoned two mist workers. "If you are attacked or hear sounds of battle getting closer, sacrifice these workers and double time it back to the village. Take the pixie with you." He looked at the small creature, "You are to follow the commands of the guards to the letter. If they are attacked, you fly as fast as you can straight back to the Quickening and Queen Elora. I know you are worried for your meitu'meidon, and I will retrieve him, but *you* will do as I command."

Bea nodded, understanding the gravity of the situation. The pixie's face showed fear, and Richter felt bad about speaking so harshly to the child. It served its purpose, though. The boy flew off and hovered by the Scholar. The three guards clapped their fists to their hearts. One asked, "Call signs, my lord?"

Richter had started instituting basic call and refrains as verbal passcodes among the guards. The possibility of infiltration was extremely low in their location, but it was never too early to start instilling good practices. The words he chose were always in English, making it nearly impossible for anyone in The Land to be able to guess the response. He nodded and replied, "The call is *ghost*, the response is *busters*."

They repeated the words and moved off. Richter allowed himself a faint smile. No reason not to have a little fun before a battle. His shoulders actually relaxed a bit. He looked at Sion and the rest of his party, "We are going in. To be clear, our goal is to save the wounded sprite, not to destroy the enemy. I don't know how they have defeated the enchantment, but it makes them dangerous. The sprites and I will move forward to observe the enemy. We have a fair chance of going undetected. If anyone can make a silent kill of a single goblin, do it; otherwise, don't take the chance. Melee fighters, come behind us."

Richter addressed the sprites specifically, "We will begin the battle by firing a volley of unimbued arrows. Don't forget that the glow from the imbued arrows will draw attention. If the goblins run off, fire another volley to keep them moving, but do not pursue. If they rush us, fade back, let the melee fighters engage and start picking them off one by one. Now this is where the enemy is," Richter showed everyone on the Traveler's Map. "We can't be sure that they are still there, we only know that we need to save that sprite. Everyone stay still a moment so that we can prepare. Then we move."

Richter, Alma, and the other mages cast what buffs they could. The chaos seed also dual cast *Summon Weak Saproling*. A few seconds later, a green disc appeared in the air and a boar made of leaves and branches ran through it. It stamped and huffed while it waited for its master's commands. Richter checked its stats and was pleased that his Summoning Ring had let him call a level twelve creature.

The war leader made sure everyone had consumed a Potion of Clarity and had at least one health potion, then handed out one more item to everyone. The entire party chewed the tough meat he gave them.

You have ingested: ***Rock Giant Jerky****. +3 to Strength and +2 to Constitution for 53 minutes.*

Richter swallowed some water to choke down the salted meat. He still wasn't sure if he felt more bothered or vindicated as he eat his mortal enemy's flesh, but it was a mixture of the two. He knew that now was not the time to think about it though. With a firm hand chop, his party moved forward. Alma flew ahead to the spot where the goblins had been seen. Because of her ability to share images with him, he was able to update the map by what she observed. More red dots appeared. He gritted his teeth. It was going to be a bitch of a fight.

A few of the goblins that Alma could see were scouts, but many were larger and seemed to be outfitted as fighters. One, in the center of the pack, was clothed in robes and had bones piercing his face. Richter grunted. A caster. He gathered all of the sprites around him and in hushed tones told them to target the mage first. Soon he heard the cackling sounds of goblin-speak.

Richter moved silently through the trees and got his first actual view of the enemy band. There were about thirty in all. He used *Analyze*.

Name: Eoq	**Race:** Goblin	**Station:** Scout
Level: 5		**Disposition:** Distaste
STATS		
Health: 160	**Mana:** 80	**Stamina:** 130
ATTRIBUTES		
Strength: 7	**Agility:** 17	**Dexterity:** 16
Constitution: 16	**Endurance:** 13	**Intelligence:** 8
Wisdom: 8	**Charisma:** 8	**Luck:** 10
DESCRIPTION		
Goblins can have subclasses that determine their specific powers. Most are a common variant however that are broken into different stations reflective of their physical and magical characteristics. Prolific breeders and woefully aggressive, goblins are a plague on other races. The **Scout** station is reserved for the smallest of the goblin race. They are often used as battle fodder and advanced scouts. Not overly bright, they are still vicious and cunning. Only a foolish fighter underestimates them because of their small size. That very characteristic allows them to get close without being detected and swarm enemies with overwhelming numbers. Goblin scouts receive three points to distribute per level, and each level gives **+1 to Agility** and **+1 to Dexterity**.		

Name: Yo-grin	**Race:** Goblin	**Station:** Fighter
Level: 9		**Disposition:** Distaste
STATS		
Health: 220	**Mana:** 90	**Stamina:** 170
ATTRIBUTES		
Strength: 21	**Agility:** 14	**Dexterity:** 19
Constitution: 22	**Endurance:** 17	**Intelligence:** 9
Wisdom: 7	**Charisma:** 8	**Luck:** 10
DESCRIPTION		
The **Fighter** station serves as the foot soldiers for goblin armies. They often lead small bands of scouts. Cruel and capricious, many children have been cautioned by their mothers to behave, or goblin fighters will take them away. Goblin fighters receive three points to distribute per level, and each level gives **+1 to Strength** and **+1 to Dexterity**.		

Name: Ton-ik	**Race:** Goblin	**Station:** Grinder
Level: 22	**Profession:** Warrior	**Disposition:** Distaste
STATS		
Health: 510	**Mana:** 150	**Stamina:** 340
ATTRIBUTES		
Strength: 28	**Agility:** 21	**Dexterity:** 25
Constitution: 51	**Endurance:** 34	**Intelligence:** 15
Wisdom: 13	**Charisma:** 12	**Luck:** 12
DESCRIPTION		

The goblin **Grinder** receives better training than many other stations, and unlike most goblins have an innate intelligence equal to most humans. No less aggressive, these foes are not to be taken lightly. If they advance far enough, these goblins can obtain Professions.
Goblin grinders receive 4 points to distribute per level, and each level gives **+1 to Constitution**.

Name: Sin-ak	**Race:** Goblin	**Station:** Rikker
Level: 35	**Profession:** Mage	**Disposition:** Distaste
	Specialty: Witch Doctor	
STATS		
Health: 634	**Mana:** 378/827	**Stamina:** 226
ATTRIBUTES		
Strength: 18	**Agility:** 16	**Dexterity:** 15
Constitution: 48	**Endurance:** 21	**Intelligence:** 62
Wisdom: 64	**Charisma:** 15	**Luck:** 15
DESCRIPTION		
Goblins of the **Rikker** station are normally gifted in magical arts. Rikkers often serve as administrators and councilors for goblin leaders. Many offspring of various races have been sacrificed for their experiments. Goblin rikkers receive 3 points to distribute per level and each level, gives **+1 to Intelligence** and **+1 to Wisdom**.		

Richter's eyes widened as he began to fully appreciate the force arrayed against them. By his count, there were eighteen scouts, eleven fighters, two grinders who were also Professed Warriors and the rikker. And what the fuck was a Witch Doctor? More importantly, Sion was right. It was obvious that the goblins could see! Richter watched the group for a moment, trying to figure it out. Then he saw something.

Sion nudged him to start the attack, but Richter waved his Companion down. He knew time was of the essence, but he needed to know what was going on. The chaos seed watched intently but didn't see the blur again. Richter didn't give up. After another minute, his patience was rewarded. He still didn't understand, but he was sure he had seen a spirit circling the enemy party.

The goblins were all within fifty yards of the rikker and were arrayed in a loose circle around the mage. As the mage moved forward, the entire group moved forward with him, allowing the scouts and fighters to continue searching for their quarry. The grinders stood close to the rikker, and each held stout shields. Now that he had seen the spirit, Richter understood why the goblins stayed relatively close to the caster. Somehow the Witch Doctor was negating the effects of the mist. If the rikker's mana was any indication, doing so was a large magical drain, but it didn't change the fact that the Witch Doctor was still getting the job done.

Richter shook his head. This was a vastly more powerful force than he had been expecting. Even just the Mage and the Warriors might be enough to overcome his people. Why were they here in his domain? The goblins weren't dumb beasts. Even though the mage could negate the mists for a small time, the enemy party had to know they were performing a dangerous undertaking. Why would three Professionals risk coming into a hostile domain just to hunt one sprite? It didn't make any sense.

Richter was trying to decide what to do when he heard the excited babble of goblin-speak followed by a boom and a flash of blue. They had found the sprite. Richter had been planning to wait until the goblin mage's mana ran out, but time was up. The goblin band howled and began to move towards the tree the sprite had been hiding in. There was no more time to wait. Richter didn't know what was so important that would bring an enemy Specialist into his domain, but he planned to disappoint the asshole.

One positive thing came from the wounded sprite's discovery; it pulled the goblins' attention. The scouts and fighters surged north, leaving their southern flank unprotected, which just happened to be where Richter and the sprites were hiding. The chaos seed sent a mental order and then told the sprites to attack.

A second later, six bow strings snapped against green sprite bracers. The sprite arrows had been reinforced with the tips of the assengai spiders' legs, increasing the base damage of each by +2. The glowing blue missiles traveled hundreds of miles an hour and struck home. Faster than should have been possible, the goblin Professionals began to react. Both Warriors started to raise their shields, and a swirling energy sprung into existence around the Witch Doctor. One of the arrows struck heavily into a Warrior's shield doing no damage. The energy around the caster solidified in a split second into another spirit. The ghost imposed itself between the caster and the projectiles. Its insubstantial body caught flame and the two arrows burned to ash. Thankfully, the other three arrows struck home.

One arrow caught the goblin mage in the shoulder and a second struck him in the side. The rikker went down with a curse. Even as he fell, the caster's hand moved as he started to cast a spell. The third arrow caught one of the Warriors in the thigh, but if it bothered the goblin grinder, there was no outward sign. Both grinders turned towards the archers and held their rectangular shields up to protect both themselves and the Mage.

The opening salvo of this battle wasn't done, though. Richter had decided that desperate times called for desperate measures. As soon as he had ordered the attack, red light had begun to surround his hands as he dual cast a new spell. The arcane words grew thicker in his mouth, and he struggled to finish the incantation. The spell was of a higher level than he had ever cast before, let alone dual cast. Richter didn't stop. This had to happen.

The goblin Warriors had already positioned their shields, which would have stopped much of the destructive power of his spell, but they made a mistake common in a world without gods. They didn't look up.

Alma's small body descended almost straight down, and with a savage cry, she unleashed the most concentrated beam of her *Psi Blast*. The Warriors cried out and fell to their knees, and the rikker broke off his incantation. Richter forced the last syrupy words out of his mouth, "Igna Prati!" The spell shot forward.

A melon sized ball of orange and yellow flame shot from his hands and sailed unerringly towards the Witch Doctor. From the perspective of one of the goblin scouts, the human had thrown a ball of fire that grew bigger by the moment until it was two feet across. Then the human's spell struck, and fire rolled over its green skin.

CHAPTER 48 -- DAY 140 – KUBORN 30, 15,368 EBG

Sion was right. Casting *Weak Fireball* in a forest was absolutely irresponsible, but Richter knew that the force they were facing could very well wipe out his entire war party and he had to take the chance. When he had initially seen the size of the fire that he shot, Richter had been underwhelmed. When it expanded to the size of a beach ball right before impact, though, somehow, he felt a lot better.

The spell struck one second after Alma had unleashed her *Psi Blast*. The fireball flew between the slumped shields of the Warriors and impacted against the Witch Doctor. It immediately detonated and flames spread out from that point. The extra 10% spell strength that came from Richter's initiate rank in Fire Magic and his Dragonkin I mark told in the damage that was done. The fire washed over the grinders and ten other goblins that were unlucky enough to be within the spell's area of effect. Four more were knocked down by the force of the explosion.

Richter started rejoicing until the afterimage of the flames disappeared, and he saw a half-dome of energy covering the Witch Doctor. It dissolved into yet another spirit swirling around the goblin as he stood. The rikker extended a hand and shouted a word of Power. A black stream of energy shot forward and struck two of the meidon sprites, flinging them backward.

Richter looked behind him and saw two steaming marks on their armor. The scouts and unaffected goblins continued to run toward his position, now only thirty yards away. The chaos seed heard his people coming up from behind him and to the left, but his archers needed more time. "Kill the caster!" he shouted. Richter drew both short swords and, with his saproling at his side, ran forward to meet the horde.

His head ached from the large expenditure of magic. At level nine, his *Dual Casting* skill increased the cost of any spell by 182%. It meant that, in one go, he had expended two hundred and two mana, more than a third of his total mana pool. He didn't let it distract him, though. The saproling outpaced him and barreled into a knot of goblins. Several went down by its push and then its momentum slowed. It gored one scout, but others started hacking into its body.

Richter couldn't be concerned with the fate of his summoned creature, he had his own fighting to do. The chaos seed ran at a screaming green goblin. While he closed with the slavering enemy, time seemed to slow. He felt his mind descend into a place he had been avoiding, the uncontrolled id that came from his use of blood magic. This time he didn't fight it. Richter unshackled his base self and opened the gates of the emotional bulwarks he and Alma had been building up. A red haze came over his vision, and a bestial yell clawed itself from his throat as he swung his short sword with an overhand chop.

His left sword swung down at a scout who was lunging forward with a pitted iron dagger. The green elementum blade snapped the dagger with a loud *ping* and continued downward to cut through the three and a half foot tall man's sickly green body. Green blood sprayed over Richter's armored chest and his face. It tasted like iron and vomit. The chaos seed wasted no time on reflection. He was already stepping past the dead goblin.

His other hand snapped up, the blade parallel to the earth in a new sword form Yoshi had taught him called *Cliff of Stone*. Richter's sword intercepted the wooden haft of the steel axe that a goblin fighter had swung down at him. The sword pulsed, and the power of his Sonic Elementum Short Sword was unleashed. The axe flew out of the hands of the surprised goblin. Richter bared his teeth in what only a jackal might recognize as a grin, and he stabbed upward with his other blade. The sword entered the goblin's stomach and plunged upward. The tip of the weapon pierced the fighter's heart turning a traumatic blow into an instantly fatal strike. Richter's second victim still had a surprised look on his face as he fell to the ground, lifeless.

A constant barrage of imbued strikes peppered the Professionals, but the Warriors had gotten their high steel, banded shields up and were able to weather the shots. The sprites had spread out to strike from multiple angles, but whenever an arrow came close to hitting the Witch Doctor, another spirit materialized to destroy it.

In the meantime, the Mage finished a second casting. Black tendrils appeared around one of the sprites and wrapped around her body. From the woman's anguished screams, the pain was horrible. The Mage continued to hold one fist upright, and a black nimbus surrounded it. The goblin fed magic into the spell, draining away the sprite's life. Thankfully, two things happened. Alma fired a bolt of lightning in the caster's back, disrupting the spell, and the guardsmen arrived. Caulder and the other fighters attacked the mass of scouts and fighters in the side, and the three Life Magi Richter had brought from the village ran to heal the fallen sprites.

Caulder ran into the middle of the fray and bellowed. He swung his steel war door to hit one of the goblin scouts with a new shield subskill, *Bash*. The small being went flying backward like it had been kicked by a giant. The sergeant then swung his new weapon at a second goblin.

It had taken two days to forge and several valuable soul stones, but Krom and Richter had been able to create Caulder's Quicksilver Spiked Mace of Goblin Slaying. The weapon almost leaped into the goblin's face. The mighty blow somehow turned the goblin fighter's face into a meaty green ruin, but still left enough intact for it to scream as it fell down. The sound was somewhat bubbly, but there was no doubt as to the goblin's agony while he vainly searched for his own nose, eyes, and lips.

The sergeant fit his skilled position of Tank perfectly. He screamed defiance and every enemy within twenty yards felt an irrational need to attack him and ignore everyone else. It was not as powerful as a true Warrior's Taunt Talent, but it still gave everyone else some respite. The goblin fighter that Richter was facing learned that attention was vital in a battle when the chaos seed's elementum short sword swung through his neck and sent his green head flying.

The five guards crashed against more than twenty goblin scouts and fighters. They stood alone. Richter's saproling had already been torn apart. The forest creature had served a purpose in that it had gained Richter precious seconds of respite at the beginning of the battle, but it had been no match for the fury of dozens of goblins.

Despite being outnumbered, the battle was far from decided. Both sides had advantages. The guards had increased reach, higher quality weapons and the fact that they fought side by side in formation with shields. They were a far cry from a Roman legion, but they still fought together. The advantages of the goblins were their numbers, savagery, and fear of their leader. They knew that a fate worse than death awaited them if they did not fight as hard as they could for the Witch Doctor.

More than anything else, however, it was Richter's Profession that made a difference. Every weapon and shield that a member of his war party used was enchanted. *Freeze, Sonic Damage, Life Damage,* or *Goblin Slaying* were instilled into every mace and longsword. Every shield was enchanted with simple defensive bonuses, and most were at least +2 or +3.

Richter had wanted to give them stronger effects, but he had become much more familiar with the capacity of various metals to handle enchantments over the past few weeks. After a negative experience with an exploding high steel dagger, the chaos seed had started paying more attention to the feeling of pressure that appeared whenever he transferred the power of filled soul stones into arms and armor. Gloran had elaborated on what Krom had mentioned about different metals having varying capacities to handle soul power. Not only did metals have different capacities, but they also had different resistances to accepting soul power. The elf had said that most materials resisted being enchanted. The rising pressure that Richter felt was actually the soul power building in the air until it entered the item. If the will of the enchanter could not overcome the resistance of whatever he was working on, then the enchantment would fail, sometimes explosively.

Gloran had been amazed when he examined Richter's sword. The elf had cast a spell that allowed him to assess the properties of various materials, among them, enchantment potential. Elementum was apparently a substance that almost welcomed enchantments. The elf had cautioned Richter against trying to channel so much soul power through less 'friendly' mediums. The chaos seed had taken the warning to heart. As most of the guards' gear was made from leather or high steel, Richter could only manage enchantments that provided a +2 or +3 in most cases. Gloran said his control would most likely increase as he practiced the skill, but that was his limit for now.

Time had also worked against him. The truth was he just hadn't had enough hours in the day to enchant every weapon for every guardsman. Luckily, the solution for that was simple. The best weapons and armor were kept in the forge. It had become SOP for his war party to equip them before going out and to return them when they came back. Though the enchantments were nowhere near as strong as those on Richter's own equipment, the power of the magic weapons was immediately apparent. In the opening salvo of the battle, a goblin scout was disarmed by the sonic enchantment on a gnome guard's blade, allowing her comrade to easily dispatch the small creature.

As happened sometimes in battle, Richter oddly found himself in a moment of calm. He realized that he was in a moment of choice. On his left, his guardsmen were fighting the goblin scouts and fighters. On his right, the three standing sprite archers continued their attack, but with little success. The Warriors' shields and the Mage's spirits blocked ranged attacks too well. In that still moment, he had to decide: right or left. Before he could, Sin-ak gave a curt order in goblin-speak. Both Warriors nodded and unleashed their Taunts simultaneously.

The red haze over Richter's vision had subsided for a moment, but it came back with a vengeance, making the whole world appear ruby-tinted. Richter screamed in rage and ran towards the goblin grinders. His moment of choice was gone.

Sion and the other two meidon sprites turned their attention to the Warriors, ignoring the Mage. They fired indiscriminately, screaming in anger, but the arrows had no more effect than before. To make matters worse, since the start of the battle, the Professionals had moved closer to the sprites. With a roar, they finally stopped defending and attacked. One used a Talent, *Thrust*, and his body blurred forward, aiming for Richter's Companion.

Sion dropped his bow, and it was only with a massive contortion of his body that he avoided being gutted. He still didn't escape unscathed. The tip of the goblin's long sword stabbed through the sprite's armor, catching him in the right chest. Sion jumped backwards with a hiss. His hand wove in a particular configuration, and he muttered a word of Power. While the Warrior started swinging again, Sion released a lightning bolt that caught the Warrior in the neck. The goblin was able to resist being stunned, but it still gave the Air caster a moment of respite. Sion found two potions on his belt and downed them in one go. His wounds began to close.

The other Warrior used the talent, *Arc Strike*. He swung his sword crossways at the other two sprites, attacking both at once. The blade, powered by his Profession, swung left to right. Both meidon sprites were struck. Luckily, their armor was enough to keep them from being cut in half, but they still lost a good deal of life and were thrown to the ground. One of their bows fell to the ground in pieces. The Warrior moved in for the kill. The goblin leered as he prepared to end one of the sprite's lives, but he hadn't counted on one thing.

He hadn't counted on Richter.

The chaos seed moved with the superhuman speed afforded to him by his thirty-eight points of Dexterity. Warrior or not, the goblin was overcome. Perhaps if he had been of a higher level, or if his equipment were better, the green-skinned grinder could have prevailed. It was not to be.

Richter flowed through his sword forms; *Orc's Hammer* to put the Warrior off balance was followed by *Cat Swatting Mouse* to bleed him. Then Richter committed to the fast movements of *Willow in the Storm* to avoid the goblin's counterattacks, before arching his right arm overtop his enemy's shield in *Scorpion's Kiss.*

The clear green blade penetrated the goblin's arm. Not a deep wound, but his Elementum Short Sword of Freezing unleashed its power. The weapon flashed blue, and the goblin's entire body froze solid, becoming a statue of blue and white. It immediately began to thaw, but Richter wasn't going to give his foe that time. The Warrior had called him to battle, and so the goblin would reap the whirlwind.

His other sword swept up, striking a frozen sword arm and leaving cracks in the ice. Two more blows and the limb fell to the ground with a heavy thud. Melting blood fell from the stump like slush. Richter raised his sword again, but then he learned the folly of having allowed the Witch Doctor the time needed to finish a long casting.

The three spirits that served the Mage extended their hands. Beams of pure magic shot forward and mixed with the Dark power spilling from the caster's hand. They plaited into one larger ray of magic and struck the earth, sinking in and then disappearing. Everything was quiet for a moment, but the Mage stared at Richter with a triumphant expression. The chaos seed's stomach dropped. He didn't know what was coming, but he was sure it would be bad.

The ground started to shake. Large rents opened in the earth, and when Richter looked down, it seemed that they extended down for miles. At the bottom of the one near him was a roiling pool of black. A moment later, creatures of pure darkness began crawling up the sides of the shaft. Seconds later, his people were being overwhelmed.

Richter spared a glance back and saw Sion locked in melee combat with the other Warrior. The battle was almost one-sided as his injured Companion dodged blow after blow. It looked like the goblin was striking his friend, but apparently Sion was managing to stay just ahead of his deadly adversary. Richter desperately wanted to help his friend, but the Witch Doctor had just downed a blue potion and was already beginning to chant again. Praying his friend could just hold on, the lord of the Mist Village started running towards the mage. Before he had moved ten feet, though, a Dark creature in human form sprang out of a rent and attacked him!

Richter swung at the creature and his sword passed through its body. It shrieked as the magic in his blade harmed it, but the monster still struck and tackled him to the ground. Wherever it touched, even on his armor, a bone-chilling cold leeched strength from his body. Richter shouted as he tried to get up, but the monster managed to stay on top of him, raining blows down with claws formed of Dark magic. His head whipped back and forth, and even as he fought for his life, he took in the battle.

The bodies of both guardsmen and goblins lay unmoving on the ground. Flames had engulfed several trees from Richter's fireball, and the charred body of a goblin scout lay in the middle of the inferno. Three of his men, including Caulder still fought back to back. Only five scouts and fighters remained to stand against them, but all of the village fighters were bloodied. Now they were also battling the Dark monsters, who grew in number every few seconds.

Sion still fought the Warrior, and both bled from several places. Another creature of Darkness was approaching the sprite from behind, however. The Life magi had dragged the wounded sprites away from the battle and now stood guard over them. One fired a crossbow at a Dark creature shape like a giant fox, but the bolt passed through with no effect. Another cast *Weak Life Bolt.* The summoned Dark creature shied back from that, but the spell had a two-minute cool down, and the mage had no other offensive magic. Alma flew above the battle, her offensive spells and *Psi Blast* all in cooldown. She wanted to attack the caster directly, but whenever she got close, the Witch Doctor's spirits beat her back.

Richter took all of this in, but didn't truly quail until his gaze fell upon the goblin Mage. The green skinned caster's arms moved in conjunction and black energy was thick on his hands. A manic look was in his eyes as he spoke words of magic. The chaos seed struggled even harder against the Dark creature atop him and he managed to score a glancing blow, but he knew he would not get free before the Witch Doctor finished his next casting. Richter felt the end coming.

He was right, but it was not his end.

The very first order he had given in the battle finally bore fruit. Unseen by anyone, and forgotten even by Richter, the shale adder had slowly slithered its way closer and closer to the one target its master had identified for it. The twenty-foot long green snake melded perfectly with the trees and grass of the forest. Just as the Witch Doctor was preparing to cast his strongest spell, the adder struck. From only four feet away, the coiled reptile shot forward and buried its large fangs in the Mage's neck. Fast as the wind, the adder coiled itself around the goblin's body and began to squeeze.

The goblin's slave spirits immediately began to attack the snake, tearing at it with ethereal claws. Scales and red blood flew, but the snake squeezed and bit the magician even harder. Most importantly, Alma showed the bravery and ferocity that was at the core of her very being. Casting a quick spell that draped her body in golden light, she dove down and latched onto the Dark wizard's head and used *Brain Drain.*

The Mage would normally be too high level for her to incapacitate with her attack, but between the spell feedback and her level seven ability, the goblin swooned. The adder squeezed even tighter. Its body was like a vise and the goblin caster began to suffocate. The Witch Doctor's spirits attacked with even greater ferocity, but to their frustration, could not effectively penetrate the protection of Alma's *Weak Life Armor*.

Richter finally managed to bury his sword into the Dark humanoid above him and the creature faded out of existence. Its wails echoed strangely in the air even after it had disappeared. Wasting no time, he started to get to his feet and was surprised by a hand reaching down to help him. He tilted his head to see a weary smile on Sion's bruised face. His friend looked strange, though.

The sprite's face looked hazy somehow. The edges of his chin and nose were indistinct.. The rest of his body looked blurry as well. Richter looked at him in confusion, but then he realized that his Companion had drank a Potion of Gaseous Form. The blade Sion held was still sharp and in focus, as was the smear of green blood along the blade. The sprite nodded at him as they clasped wrists, "Tabia does good work. Let us finish this."

The two Companions moved as quickly as possible towards the Mage, but not quickly enough. The mental fortitude of the goblin was enough to finally overcome the stun effect of Alma's attack. With his one free hand, the furious goblin reached up and cruelly dug his nails into her little body. The familiar was helpless as she performed her special attack, but she did not stop as her blood began to flow over her delicate scales.

With a cry of rage, Richter reached the Witch Doctor and drove his blade down into the goblin's chest, while Sion skewered the goblin in the abdomen. The chaos seed and goblin leader locked eyes and their hate for one another was palpable. The caster released his grip on the dragonling and ripped the bone necklace from his throat. The goblin pointed a long nail at Richter and thought just one word. Into that word though, the Witch Doctor poured all of his malice, "Kill!"

The slave spirits, finally released from their primary duty of protecting the Witch Doctor by the destruction of his Necklace of Spirit Bondage, fulfilled their final geas and attacked Richter. The three freed souls struck his body with the force of a sledgehammer. He lost his grip on the short sword embedded in the Mage's body and was carried through the air. The spirits moved him back ten feet and then dropped him… into one of the bottomless rents in the earth. The three ghosts dissipated into the ether, joyous even as Richter fell into darkness. His last sight before being swallowed by the chasm was the light fading from the Witch Doctor's eyes and Sion reaching out to him as he wailed, "Nooo!"

CHAPTER 49 – DAY 140 – KUBORN 30, 15,368 EBG

Richter looked up at the opening in the earth sixty feet above him. As his muscles ached, Sion shouted down at him to hold on, and he heard another sprite voice shout in the distance, "Your lord! I must speak to your lord! He has to know!"

The chaos seed hung there, battered and bruised. A stack of prompts flashed in the corner of his vision, waiting to be read, including one that had the clear, pulsing border of an absorbed memory. None of this interested him at the moment, though.

Despite everything that had just happened, despite all of the things that were waiting to be done, and even despite the mystery of what he had 'to know,' there was only one thing on Richter's mind. He sighed heavily in frustration and pain, then shouted up to his people looking down at him, "Would you hurry the fuck up! I'm *literally* hanging off a cliff down here!"

~ The Story Continues ~

Thank you all for reading! This has been my most ambitious book and I hope that you found delight and joy in its pages! Creating this world is a labor of love, and as with all true love, it fills me with purpose… and sometimes I want to light it on fire! Lol
Being able to share it with you means the world! The story continues! As always, peace, love, and the perfect margarita!
Aleron

Good people of the Mist Village, **PLEASE** leave a review on Amazon.
You can just search "Aleron Kong".
I am an independent author, and you are my greatest strength
Even leaving some stars would be enough.
Thank you so much again!
I am honored to share my world with you.

~ Aleron

INDEX

Doing something new this time! Because I was threatened with bodily harm for having a long index in the past lol, I'm not putting one here. I HAVE made a page on my website that can only be accessed by this LINK!

Get all your status pages, list of Richter's Spells and other cool stuff!

Thanks ya'll!

If you want to stay connected and know when my next work comes out, the BEST way is by NEWSLETTER and my AUTHOR PAGE. The info is on the next page.

Unfortunately, Amazon doesn't update you when new works come out some of the time, but if sign up for the newsletter or like my author page, you'll know immediately.

You also get a secret FREE Comic for The Land when you sign up! Shhh, don't tell anyone!

How to contact Aleron!

1) AUTHOR PAGE:

Join me for almost weekly FB lives convos, giveaways and lots of laughs https://www.facebook.com/LitRPGbooks/

2) WEBSITE: www.LitRPG.com
It has a list of ALL the LitRPG out there, awesome t-shirts and signed books, my blog and just all around awesomeness!

3) PATREON: For sneak previews of upcoming books and seeing new artwork first, please join my patreon. You can even be written into one of my books! www.patreon.com/AleronKong

4) TWITTER and INSTAGRAM: @LitRPGBooks

5) NEWSLETTER: I do a weekly newsletter with updates, uplifting stories and funny vids. You can sign up here. If you sign up, you get a free copy of The Land Comic lol!
eepurl.com/cns1UH

6) YOUTUBE: Me and my friends make funny/stupid videos. I also do video testimonials with occasional spoilers! FREE on Youtube (yes I know youtube is always free but hey… its FREE lol) http://www.youtube.com/c/LitRPG

7) STREET TEAM: Perhaps most exciting! I've started a street team! If you're going to a Con, Book Fair, etc sometime soon, join the street team and let me know. I'll send you a free tshirt and some cards to hand out! Send me a pic of you wearing it and I'll put you on the site! Thanks! tinyurl.com/LitRPGStreetTeam

8) FACEBOOK GROUP: Join the largest LitRPG community on the PLANET! https://www.facebook.com/groups/LitRPGGroup/

9) FORUM: If you want to rave about The Land, or maybe just wail and gnash your teeth lol, join many other member of the Mist Village Mafia in my forum! Forum.litrpg.com

CPSIA information can be obtained
at www.ICGtesting.com
Printed in the USA
LVHW081247130220
646717LV00012BA/302/J